Hard Cas

(The Jo

MW01236206

by

Bernard Lee DeLeo

*****

PUBLISHED BY:

Bernard Lee DeLeo and RJ Parker Publishing Inc.

ISBN-13:978-1984915696

ISBN-10:198491569X

Hard Case X: No Mercy

*****

License Notes

*****

Nick McCarty's Unholy Trio and Dependents (Main Characters)

1. Nicholas McCarty – Delta Force – 6' – Nicknames: Terminator, Muerto, Dead-Boy, Delta Dawn, Gomez

2. Rachel Hunter McCarty

3. Jean Hunter McCarty – Nickname: Danger Girl, Daughter of Darkness, Viper

4. Deke the Dog - Dekester

5. Gus Nason – Nickname: Payaso

6. Tina Nason (Wife of Gus Nason) – Nickname: T-Rex

7. Ebi Zarin/Johnny Groves – Nicknames: Johnny Five, El Kabong

8. Cala Kadir Groves (Wife of Johnny Groves) – Nicknames: Cala the Cleaner, Reaper

9. Jian Chen – ex-terrorist – recruited to help Nick's crew – Nickname: Dark Dragon

10. Sonny Salvatore – Nickname: Cracker - Parents: Phil and Clarice Salvatore

11. Quinn McCarty – Nickname: Kong

12. Justin Rivers – Nickname: Jay, Predator – Parents: Dale and Beth

13. Neil Dickerson – Pacific Grove policeman – works with Nick's crew

14. Paul Gilbrech – Director of the CIA

15. Clyde Bacall – Assistant and driver for Paul Gilbrech -works with Nick's crew

16. Ben McCarty – Adopted son in future Nick and Jean bonus story – Nickname: Benny

17. Sammy – McCarty family's dog in future Nick and Jean bonus story – Nickname: Sammy the werewolf

John Harding's Monster Squad and Dependents (Main Characters)

1. John Harding – Force Recon Marine - 6'6", brown haired buzz cut, 250 pounds – Nicknames: Hard Case, Cheeseburger (Cheese for short), Recon, Dark Lord, DL

2. Lora Radcliff Harding – John's wife, 5'7", long auburn hair, 130 pounds

3. Alice Radcliff Harding – John's stepdaughter, long auburn hair, ten years old – Nicknames: Al, Beeper-Girl

4. Lucas Blake – Force Recon Marine - 5'8", Black, buzz cut, 155 pounds – Nicknames: Ahab, Pappy – Wife: Sarah, Children: Casey (named after Casey Lambert) and Linda

5. Casey Lambert – Delta Force - Nickname - Night-shot – Wife: Anna – Children: Lucas (named after Lucas Blake)

6. Tommy Sands – Nicknames - T, Snow White Sands – Wife: Rachel

7. Devon Constantine – Nickname – Dev – wife – Rosalie Maria Clairmont Constantine

8. Jesse Brown – Nickname – Jess – Wife: Rochelle

9. Florence Brown – Jesse Brown's mom

10. Jafar Kensington – Nicknames - Achmed the Dead Terrorist

11. Samira Karim Kensington – Jafar's Wife - Nickname – Sam - Children: Mia

12. Dennis Strobert – Marine - Nicknames - Denny, Spawn – Wife: Maria – Children: Brewster

13. Gus Denova – Cruella Deville minion – former Cartel enforcer

14. Silvio Ruelas – Cruella Deville minion – former Cartel enforcer

15. Quays Tannous – Cruella Deville minion – former Cartel enforcer

16. Clint Dostiene – Air Force SOCOM– Nickname: Man from Nowhere – Wife: Lynn Montoya

17. Lynn Montoya Dostiene – Nicknames: Cruella Deville, Crusader Crue, Dr. Deville – Children: Clint Jr.

18. Laredo Sawyer – Nickname: Laredo – Wife Sybil Moore

19. Danessa Moore - Nickname: Dannie – Lynn Dostiene's live in assistant

20. Amara Nejem – Lynn Dostiene's live in assistant

21. Earl Taylor – Oakland Policeman

22. Enrique Rodriguez – Nickname 'Rique – Oakland Policeman

23. Jeff Furlong – Oakland Policeman

24. Alexi Fiialkov – Former Russian Mob – Shipping Magnate – Handles UFC matches

25. Marla Tomlinson – Favorite Waitress at The Warehouse Bar – Fiialkov's Girlfriend

26. Claude Chardin – Former Terrorist and Assassin – works with John Harding's crew now.

27. Della Sparks – John Harding's neighbor – Children: Lebron, Jim, and Kara

28. Hollywood Bounty Hunters – Kensy (Buffster) Talon, Kevin Halliday (ex-felon), Les Tavor (ex-Hell's Angel), Jet Lemarkus (ex-gangbanger), Daniel Atkins, Jerry Sooner, Calvin Douglas, Sigfried Kandelus, Charlie Dubrinsky (Lawyer/Manager)

29. Tom Wilder – Commander of a Seal Team – works with John Harding's crew

30. Janie Labrie – FBI agent who works with John Harding's crew

31. Sam Reeves – Janie Labrie's partner – FBI agent who works with John Harding's crew

32. Chuck Buchholz – Force Recon Marine – Red Dragon Security – Lucas Blake's friend

33. Sal Sallaz – Force Recon Marine – Red Dragon Security – Lucas Blake's friend

34. Thom McGaffey – Force Recon Marine – Red Dragon Security, with his dog, Lando

As it will be with every novel I write from now until my own End of Days, I dedicate this novel to my deceased angel, wife, and best friend:

Joyce Lynn Whitney DeLeo

Chapter One

Blind Fury

I smashed a right knee into my opponent's rib cage, at least I think it was his rib cage. We fought in the street outside Alexi Fiialkov's new bar and restaurant. Forced by the city to sell the old place because of some historical technicality, Alexi bought another bar and restaurant nearby, renaming it 'The Warehouse'. The original great cop bar was being refurbished into 'The Seawolf Public House'. They opened for business after stripping away the memorabilia. My favorite waitress, Marla Tomlinson, from 'The Warehouse', Oakland's once great cop bar, now ran the new 'Warehouse', which we now frequented.

Alexi Fiialkov, a former Russian mafia chief, now a successful container ship line owner, and UFC fight magnate, married our Marla. He called me because a new gang of mixed race thugs calling themselves 'The Jack London Gang' decided 'The Warehouse' would be their bar and restaurant. We Monsters arrived in force to let the new gang know they would either be absorbed by the Oaktown Cartel, or annihilated. By the name they chose, I suspected they were a farce. Luckily, Tommy and I watched the streets outside the bar on the first watch. They came, strutting their stuff in force, a dozen thugs, ready for a Saturday night thug party.

I blocked their way inside. "Sorry, we have a no thug rule at the new 'Warehouse'. The Warehouse is under the protection of the Oaktown Cartel. My brother Tommy will explain the details."

They launched into a non-stop gang flashing, chortling, finger popping cacophony of amusement at my declaration. Tommy had already summoned the Monsters from inside. Their appearance, with Oaktown's Godfathers, Gus Denova, Silvio Ruelas, and Quays Tannous, all carrying MP5 submachine guns, stopped the entertainment quotient.

"Good," Tommy said, as Lynn Montoya Dostiene moved into a position next to him. "Now that I have your attention, we can negotiate, or your pack of turds can walk away and disband. Anything else you do will be met with death."

The giant hoodie, mixed in amongst them, stepped forward. He looked like a trailer/tractor rig, built for hauling big loads. "I say what goes with my crew. We disband nothin'. I heard Oaktown thinks they own the streets. We don't challenge nothin'. We come and go as we please."

"No, you won't, Betty," Lynn told him. "You and your gang of gangster wannabes will be absorbed, disband, or die. Damn, Tommy, I'd bet these two-bit punks don't have three bucks between the lot of them. They look like pussies, so ask them if they have a cutter. By the looks of them if you mention the knife, their dicks will retreat into their belly buttons."

"You got a big mouth, bitch!" One of the guys behind big hoodie decided to test the suicide waters. "I'll cut you a new pussy in your belly-button."

Lynn clapped her hands. "Oh…oh my, Tommy, we got us another poser."

"Step around to the side area of The Warehouse, young poser," Tommy told him. "The premier cutter in Oaktown will be glad to take your money and your life, punk. How much do you have? I have fifty grand at five to one odds, oh hell… make it fifty to one odds. You put up a thousand, and my associate will slice and dice you like a Thanksgiving Day turkey."

The offer stunned the gang, but we could tell they didn't have a thousand dollars, or even five hundred. All of us moved to the side alley except for my brothers, Jess and Dev, watching the bar entrance. It turned into a muttering affair. The gang seemed to be trying to gather money rather awkwardly to back their man.

Lynn tapped her foot with arms folded over chest. "Oh, for God's sake, how much do you pussies have?"

They had a collection that resulted in big hoodie holding up a bunch of ragged bills. "We got two hundred seventy-eight dollars."

Lynn sighed. "Well, that eliminates this bunch as some kind of secret threat. They barely have enough gas money to drive around town. We'll bankroll them, Tommy. Call it three hundred to our fifteen thousand. I don't have all night for cheap asses, Betty. Send the big mouth out here with a knife in hand."

The slim, wiry airhead, with more muscles than brains, slipped jauntily into view in true gangster style: head back, staring through half lidded eyes, flipping an eight-inch blade from hand to hand. "I goin' ta cut you bad, bitch."

"Best start this, Tommy, before I get an itch, and I scratch the nose off his face," Lynn said.

"Get it on!" Tommy stepped back, having lost some of his enthusiasm when Lynn would be giving lessons for a few bucks.

The big talker lunged at Lynn, stumbling through the area she no longer stood in, but instead, earned a slice down the side of his face, welling blood.

"First blood," Lynn said. "You're a waste of time. You're too slow for the knife, Dumbo. With those ears, you should be in a rock band. Can you play the tambourine?"

Dumbo tried what he thought as a lightning fast slash. His knife clattered to the ground, his hand no longer able to grip it. Our Cruella Deville slashed through nerve and tendon clusters from his wrist to his elbow. Dumbo screamed out in shocked agony, pitching to the ground holding his profusely bleeding appendage.

"Clamp your cut coat around it, Dumbo. Get those ears flapping so you can get off the ground. One of your magpies needs to take you to the ER," Lynn told him.

Dumbo sobbed his way to a standing position. Lynn gestured at his stunned companions. "Don't let Dumbo bleed to death. One of you other posers take him to the ER."

As one of the group moved to do as Lynn suggested, she moved next to Dumbo, doing butterfly knife tricks while he cringed away from her. She ended the demonstration by wiping Dumbo's blood on her knife blade off on his shirt. "I ever see your face again, Dumbo, I will cut those ears off and feed them to you. Nod if you understand. Otherwise, I'll cut the message into your forehead."

Dumbo nodded energetically. Lynn stepped away. Dumbo and companion hurried away. "That was mildly entertaining. Get on with this farce, Tommy. I promise not to arrange some gang stomp bet with Cheese."

"Thank you," Tommy replied with relief, knowing Lynn's penchant for making bets in these matches where I fight six guys armed with clubs. "Pay up the chump change first. Then, we get down to business. Hand it over, or Dr. Deville will cut off pieces of your gang until you do."

The big guy paid off the paltry amount, but he wasn't happy doing it. "We have no business. This a free country. We got the right to go in the bar."

"We explained the rules. Oaktown protects this area along with many others. You do the crime, we take away your time… on earth. If you have a champ to fight our champ, we find out who goes and who stays. Since you penniless punks don't have a dime to your names, if our champ loses, we pay you five grand. If your champ loses, your gang gets absorbed, or you disband. What'll it be? I'd give you five to one odds, but you don't have any money to make odds with."

"I know John Harding's your champ," big hoodie informed us. "He the UFC Heavyweight Champion. We saw the YouTube videos of him beatin' six guys with clubs. I tell you what. Blindfold him and I'll take a shot."

"Get serious or disband," Tommy told him.

"Let's get this done, brother. I'll put a blindfold on."

Even Lynn was surprised. "Cheese! Lora will never speak to me again if I let you do that."

"Stay out of this!" Big hoodie nearly became dead hoodie.

"Last warning for you, Betty," Lynn told him. "Open your mouth again and I open you another mouth at neck level, so shut your pie-hole!"

"I'll be okay, Sis. Hell… I can smell him from here. I doubt he can sneak up on me."

That remark earned some loud amused enjoyment. Big hoodie didn't think it was funny, although some of his gang did. I wasn't kidding though. The guy smelled like someone dumped a load of manure on his head. Either that or they invented a new cologne called 'Shitrus'.

"I don't mind you bunch picking out the blindfold and covering my eyes yourselves, but I don't want any article of clothing from this guy on my face. You have a couple of ladies with you. Any of you have a scarf or something?"

"Yeah…" one of the women dug in the bag she had with her and retrieved a black scarf from it.

I examined it and took a few tentative whiffs of smell testing. The scarf smelled like fresh laundry detergent. "That'll do. Thank you."

I handed it to big hoodie, after shedding my coat and giving it to Tommy, along with my Colt .45. I made sure to stay facing him while he came forward to take it in hand. I gauged the distances by the reek. He folded it into a band capable of covering my eyes. I turned, noticing how different the smell was with him at my back. I knew how stupid this was, but I kept training in the bay, and I was bored to tears. Eugene 'the Rattler' Cummings retired from the ring to work as Alexi Fiialkov's righthand man. We were to meet with Ian Wolf about a championship fight.

Mr. Big tied the blindfold tightly into place. I spun around slowly to face him again, checking on the intensity of stink. I heard the rustle of clothing and a mutter amongst my Monsters. I knew Big had thrown a punch to check my inability to see. I appreciated him letting me hear what a pre-punch clothing rustle sounded like. He did a couple more before being satisfied.

"There are no rules. Step back," Tommy ordered. He asked for and got our acknowledgement we were ready. "Get it on!"

Big moved in and tried to circle me. No such luck. I stayed with the smell. I heard the rustle of clothing. Keeping my fists and arms raised on the defensive, I shot a full power, behind the knee kick attempt, while blocking his overhand right. My boot smacked into his thigh instead like a thunder clap. I heard the grunt of pain, rushed toward it, and gripped him tightly to me. I left enough room to work alternating knees into his ribs until I heard him scream. I broke a couple of ribs for sure, but I don't stop for anyone but Tommy.

"Time!" Tommy called out.

I let Big drop to the ground. Surveying the scene after taking off the blindfold, I could see the thug posse decided today was not their day. Big rocked side to side, holding his arms and legs in tightly to his chest. Clint, Casey, and I carefully helped Big to his feet. We didn't want to puncture a lung with an actual broken rib.

"One of you show us where we can deposit Big. The rest of you stay where you are. The Oaktown Godfathers will explain the way we do business when your gang gets absorbed." One of the women, I figured came with Big, took us to his car. She unlocked it. We slipped him inside with only a few bloodcurdling screams.

"What can I do with him?"

"Take him to the ER," I answered. "He'll need x-rays. Remember to tell him we have the whole episode on video. If he gets any stupid ideas about trying to claim he was ambushed or something, we'll need to come see him, and settle things."

"I...I understand."

"Do yourself a favor and change your lifestyle," I advised. "Do Big a favor and talk him into a lifestyle change. He looked to be only in his early twenties. The Marines need a few good men, but they'll take Big, and make him into one. The service needs women too. At the very least, get him to take a bath, for God's sake."

I think she needed to bite her tongue not to shoot her mouth off. That in itself showed self-control.

"Damn, DL," Casey said, on the way back to our gang meeting, "blindfolded? Really?"

"Yeah, DL," Clint piled on. "You have another possible MGM Grand fight in the works. We had a blast when you kicked the crap out of Carl Logan. Quit thinking about yourself. Think Las Vegas blast, doing the Dark Lord and Dev bringing the Latin."

"I wouldn't have done it, except the guy smelled so bad, I knew at most I'd only need to take a few punches before I got him. He didn't lay a hand on me. I promise not to make it into a routine. I need the work. Only getting my head kicked in alongside the Sea Wolf works for quickness, delivery and stamina, but I need to fight. This was a short tune-up bout, but the blindfold gave me a little extra boost."

"You better tell Achmed not to put it on YouTube. Lora will get a glimpse of it and you'll be on the couch," Casey warned.

"You're right! I forgot to tell Achmed not to broadcast it." I jogged to where Jafar stood, watching his tablet with a big smile. I slowed. That was his 'I'm going to be bigger than cat videos today' look. "Please tell me you didn't upload the video already."

His startled look told me he had indeed uploaded it. "You know you're supposed to tell me yay or nay right after the fight, John. It has fifty thousand hits already from all over the world. I titled it 'The Dark Lord Schools Mr. Big, Blindfolded: Blind Fury.'. I can't take it down now. It would be useless. The video's being shared at the same rate as the original hits."

"It's my fault. Lora will understand eventually. I need to wash up before I have a couple of the brothers Bud and Beam. I got too close to Mr. Big when I cracked his ribs. I'm thinking of spraying myself with pepper spray. It would be preferable to Eau de Mr. Big."

"I noticed he got in the car with a woman. You should have pepper sprayed him before you let him get in her car."

"Good point, but I think she brought him." I thought about that for a moment while Jafar made disgusted faces. "I'm glad Tommy held my windbreaker. I'll strip out of my shirt and just put on the jacket. I have pine Febreze in my bag. I'll squirt a bit of it on my knees and coat. I'll smell like the 'Ghost of Christmas Past'."

"You can tie the shirt on the side mirror," Jafar suggested, comically getting into my smell situation. "The Uber ride guy will appreciate it."

Tommy joined us. He handed me my jacket and equipment bag. "That was insane, John. Meet me inside after you get rid of the stench."

He had my Febreze in his other hand. A couple of quick shots on my contaminated shirt and knees and I was singing 'Oh Christmas Tree… Oh Christmas Tree'.

Inside our new place, a happy Marla joked with my Monsters and Snow Whites. She readied my usual after I returned from the bathroom with fresh pine scent. I gulped both brothers down to get rid of the memory smell and taste of something foul. The new

'Warehouse' incorporated a long, curved, old-time bar, with everything done in a western and seafaring mode.

"Don't ever do that again, Champ," Marla ordered.

"Cheese had it covered, Mar," Lynn said. "The guy smelled so bad, he couldn't move under the Cheeseburger radar."

"I know, but he can't start doing the blindfold bit. He's a cement-head. Sooner or later, he'll believe he can do it without an accident."

"Marla's right," Tommy agreed. "The stunt was damn entertaining, but dangerous as hell. That guy was huge."

"The Bay and my monster poking tool, Rocky, has made you superfast, amigo," Silvio stated.

My face twisted in distaste at the mention of Rocky, the pole poking nemesis Lynn and Tommy use to condition me into a frenzy of quickness. "Stop right there… amigo. We do not talk of the tool, never to be named, in a bar with the brothers, Bud and Beam. Today, you can be forgiven, because I gave Cruella Deville a ride on the Rock into the Bay. How'd you like your swim, Sis?"

The Monsters, with the exception of Lucas, Tommy - and the Snow Whites, stifled amusement with great restraint. Tommy and Lucas enjoyed the always entertaining sight of Lynn propelling into the Bay. Tonight, even Lynn enjoyed my mention of an infrequent win on the training day next to the 'Wolf'.

"You got me good, Cheese," Lynn admitted. "When you bait me with the dolphin imitations, I go stark raving nuts."

"You carved that thug so fast, outside, I thought I was watching one of those old Ginsu knife commercials," Marla remarked.

"He was a poser, but it's always fun baiting the gangs into stupidity," Lynn replied.

"But your life is on the line."

The Monsters and Snow Whites kept silent. All of us knew Clint would never let Lynn bet her life. Lynn knew it too. "That's not really true, Mar. We don't do this stuff to die in a back alley. The man from nowhere has my back. I've asked him to spare anyone who can beat me in a knife fight, but whether he can... I don't know."

"Lynn won't be dying by some street thug's knife, Mar," Clint stated. "The closest I came to shooting Lynn's opponent was the Yakuza guy. He may have been near Lynn's speed and expertise. He thought he was in a kabuki theater, like our friend Nick kids about. He bowed before a knife fight - no take-backs at this level."

"Understood," Marla replied. "I feel a little better about watching the stuff. I don't think I could ever get used to watching John do a blindfold trick. My heart was in my throat during that one. Alexi felt the same way. The UFC championship match with Ian Wolf is very close to a deal, isn't it, Tommy?"

"Yep. Alexi and I are working it," Tommy answered. "The Wolf camp wants a meeting to discuss specifics. His supposedly fractured wrist, he ducked the Carl Logan fight with, healed completely now, according to his manager."

"Alexi told me you guys checked the hospital where the fractured wrist x-ray proof of Wolf's training injury was done, and they have no record of it."

"That's water under the bridge, Mar," I told her. "I cemented my being able to keep the heavyweight title by fighting Logan in Wolf's place, and I don't blame him for ducking Logan. I've been watching Wolf's fights. Wolf is nearly as big as 'Berserker', Rutger Northman. I'm not certain what his reasoning was for ducking Logan. If Wolf ever got Logan on the mat, his ground and pound would have overwhelmed Logan."

"I think Wolf wanted you to soften Logan up," Tommy said. "He knew no one in their right mind in the heavyweight division would have agreed to a fight with Logan as a replacement on a few days' notice, except you, blockhead."

Tommy's ace drew the hilarity expected when he decides to barbeque the Cheeseburger. "The Rattler could have beaten Logan. He could take a punch, and after fighting both, I would say Eugene Cummings had matching speed. What's that octagon name Wolf fights under, Tommy?"

"Death-Claw."

"Very cool." I sipped my Beam brother with relish. "Jess? You had the Logan watch. What's he doing now?"

"Still healin'," Jess answered. "I told you that hip pointer injury makes you think the arm on the injury side will need to be tied to your waist for life. I think you ruined him, brother. He shoots his mouth off about you being chicken to fight him under boxing rules, once in a while, but he even eased up on that. He was getting laughed at. I know one thing: he won't go into the octagon against you again."

"Wolf was smart," Devon Constantine added. "It was a win/win for him. If you lost, he knew you would still do damage, and if you won, he'd be fighting another UFC fighter for the championship. Wolf would figure if he beats you, it's like claiming a win over both you and Logan. I agree with Jess. Carl Logan wants nothing to do with the UFC. He may suck it up and go for the title in boxing again."

"Thank you all for confronting those thugs," Marla said. "They came in the night before last with over a dozen punks, spilling over tables and bothering our customers. We haven't been able to entice the old crowd of OPD officers yet. We bought all the memorabilia we could, and our gaming room is larger than the old 'Warehouse'. It will take time, but we're screwed if we have gangbangers intimidating our customers."

"We have them on our radar now, Marla," Quays Tannous told her. "We only give one warning. Silvio, Gus, and I talked with them. They're disbanding. They thought this was easy pickings. We explained in detail, with videos, what would happen if we catch them together again."

"It's a damn shame the local politicos throw the cops under the bus here like they do," Marla said. "They call Oaktown Cartel a vigilante group, but have no ideas about how to defend the city from these jackals."

It happened in a time warp, slicing through reality, and bringing with the assault a deadly silence, combat projects. Four men in black masks jogged in with body armor and automatic weapons. They fired bursts into the ceiling, ordering everyone to get on the floor with fingers locked. All four died in an instant, as the Monsters fired and pulped heads instead of wasting shots on body armor. Clint had beaten me by a split second on the leader. His shot hit dead center nose, while mine racked into his forehead in the split second he began to pitch backwards. We didn't fire many times. There was no need.

When Lucas, Casey, Clint, and I fire our weapons, nothing in sight lives beyond the first volley. Such was the case here. Clint dealt with a fiery mad Lynn, who didn't get a shot off before all four of the restaurant assault force lie dead on the floor. This was no coincidence. We would need to re-interview 'The Jack London Gang' in more detail, after we find out about the assault force. Clint and I were the closest to the rear exit, where we might surprise the driver. No one arrives in assault form at a busy restaurant without a driver.

The clichéd black GMC Denali awaited the returning thugs. Clint and I shot out all four tires before the driver knew anything other than things may not have happened as he expected. I broke the passenger side window with Colt .45 pointed at the driver's head. Clint went in the back with attitude but no joy.

"Clear."

"You, Sir, put your hands on top of your head until my associate collects you," I told the driver. "Do anything else and I fire a blast into your temple."

His shaking hands interlaced over his head. Clint retrieved him roughly from the van's driver's seat. I ran around to watch our backs as Clint patted him down with intimate expertise. Once he was clear of weapons and all other personal items, Clint jammed him against the Denali, restraining his hands behind his back with plastic restraints and gag. We had his cell-phone and tablet, which I was sure would be helpful.

"What'll it be, John?"

"We leave the van and put this punk in Jafar's trunk. Samira drove. They brought baby Mia. They were having a quiet dinner. We'll stuff this mutant in the trunk of their vehicle and take him to Pain Central for answers."

"I have his key fob. We look after each other's kids. We need to hurry. This one can disappear without a trace. The police will believe this gang attacked without a driver. Wipe down the steering wheel, while I deposit this cretin in Jafar's Camry trunk. Be right back. If we let the cops believe there was no driver, they'll have a mystery."

"Got it. Go on and do the deed. Do you need a syringe?"

"Nope. I have one of the new ones." Clint's fireman's crawl moved to Jafar's Toyota Camry. I ran around to wipe off the steering wheel.

Our actions meant Cruella Deville would meet with our prisoner. Soon, we would have a few answers concerning possible conspiracies or gangland thuggery. Clint met me by the entrance as Oakland PD rolled up. The officers were not known to Clint and me. We knelt and interlaced our fingers behind heads.

The OPD checked us out after we were restrained, inspecting our identification. A third policeman arrived, whom we recognized.

"Sorry, John," the policeman named Jerrod Boyle said. Yeah… we knew each other.

I gave him a synopsis of the incident, complete with what happened inside during the attack. The other officers confirmed our FBI credentials and returned them.

"Damn, you guys were lucky."

"Did you just insult me, Jer," I asked for Clint's amusement.

Officer Boyle enjoyed my inference. He waved his partner over, who had been keeping Clint and me under gunpoint negotiations, even though the first two officers cleared our identities. I like a careful police officer. I'm sure with all the illegal alien processing centers around, he had seen many superb fake credentials.

"I'm going inside with John and Clint," Jerrod said. "They don't have anything to do with this, other than bad luck, and being expert shots. I know they have FBI Agent status."

"The officers here will watch the Denali, John. Let's go inside and you can explain this to me or whoever else answered the call. I know there will be plenty of witnesses inside."

"Marla tended bar next to us, Jer," I told him. "She'll tell you about these guys. Their fully automatic weapons will be next to their bodies. This is a mess, my friend, and I don't know why it happened. They did fire the weapons into the ceiling to intimidate. That, in itself, was a death sentence with my crew. I need to ask a favor. We didn't bring extra weapons with us or in our vehicles. I don't know if the bad guys meant to get to us or rob the place yet."

"I'll talk with Lieutenant Gardner. I saw him entering the restaurant." Officer Boyle lowered his voice. "Gardner hates you guys. He backs the failed 'Controlled Crime Model', where we're forced to look the other way on petty crime. Gardner will paint your crew as vigilantes."

Clint smiled. "We are in a way, Jer."

Jerrod gripped Clint's shoulder. "Thank God you all are. You guys have saved us from being thrown under the bus by politicos many times. Like the 'Ghostbusters', when we get our hands tied by Oakland's liberal scum politicians, we know who to call."

Clint chuckled and then made shushing gestures at Officer Boyle. "Don't let our secret out, Jer. We back the Blue, and we will smash everything in our path until we reach your side."

"Believe my black ass when I tell you then to tread lightly with Gardner, Clint."

"Don't worry, my friend. John and I have lots of experience with treading lightly, right John?"

I tried and failed to think of something witty to say. I settled for a smiling, "no comment."

Two hours later, with all the customers' statements recorded, Lieutenant Gardner addressed my crew at the bar where we sipped coffee. Our mild celebration ended during the restaurant assault. Luckily, Clint texted Jafar, who had been with Samira and his daughter Mia, having dinner. Clint explained Jafar would need to take our prisoner to Pain Central, and get Mia an Uber to take her home. Lynn, because she wasn't involved in the shooting, happily accompanied Jafar. Her minions, Quays Tannous, Gus Denova, and Silvio Ruelas escaped being held for interrogation other than giving their statements. They joined the Pain Central party goers. Tommy, Jesse, and Devon all avoided closer scrutiny as well. Everyone at the bar knew every detail would be available to us once Lynn's minions tethered the van driver into our special interrogation room. The odd thing we noticed about the dead guys, after their masks were stripped off and they were rolled out, was all of them had dark features, but light blonde hair.

Gardner finally ambled over to us with a sour look on his face. My height, black, and carrying about thirty pounds too much, he had hands as big as catcher's mitts, with attitude to match. "Well...well... John Harding's squad of psychos and malcontents, protecting the poor unknowing innocents of Oakland."

"You forgot about our unappreciated protecting of fat-cat cheeseballs like you, Urkel," Lucas nailed him right to his toes.

The smirk fled. The thumbs in the bulging belt dropped with hands to his sides. His face reddened under a brown exterior slightly lighter than Lucas's drill sergeant's face. "You're lucky we're in a public place with witnesses, house ni-"

No one could grab Lucas in time, and I have reflexes honed in the Bay, being poked by my pole tool nemesis, Rocky: named after former UFC Heavyweight Champion of the world, Rock Costigan. Lucas slammed Gardner to the floor in a split second. At five feet, eight inches tall, Lucas is the deadliest package ever wrapped into a stocky frame of solid muscle and tendon, Marine Corps Recon to the marrow of his bones. We gestured the other Blue back in beseeching motions and pleas. They luckily didn't like Gardner any more than Officer Boyle did. He had a slight smile on his face as he sided with us in keeping the Blue away.

"You're lucky I stopped you before that BLM bullshit left the booty lips on your pie-face, Urkel! You ever call me that name, I will rip your lips off, and head-butt you into a faceless meat-pie with blood streaming out of your pores, piss-ant! Don't say anything! I can call in debts with people who can make you a meter-maid on Foothill Blvd. Stand your insolent, America hatin' ass up, straighten your clothes, and get the hell out of my sight, maggot!"

I could pretend all us guys Lucas trained didn't at least for a moment snap to attention as if we were back under his care in the CIA training center he graduated us out of... but I'd be lying. Casey had to nudge me out of my ramrod straight, eyes focused coma, I had launched into a moment before.

Casey chuckled. "It never ends, John. Ahab has our balls in a lockbox on the other side of the moon."

I sheepishly remembered where the hell I was, trading grins with my Lucas trained cohorts, Clint and Casey, hoping I could get to the bar cam recording before my brothers-in-arms. I knew beyond a shadow of a doubt, my at attention, tight-lipped coma reaction to Lucas's dress-down of Gardner would be on the first stream of video to our Lucas trained brother, Nick, in Pacific Grove. I shouldn't care though. Once Lucas sees the video, he'll make me wear my Muerto t-shirt for a week. If I could fit inside the El Muerto pajamas Nick sent to Lucas, he'd make me wear those for a month. The t-shirt reads 'Hard Case sleeps in El Muerto's pajamas' anyway. On the other side of the t-shirt is a formidable Nick, dressed as El Muerto with knife in hand and caption reading 'Live up to the Legend'.

Clint smiled back at us while clasping a gentle hand on Lucas's shoulder. "C'mon, Lucas. Lynn's working the case with the minions. We can have us a toast, right Marla?"

"Open bar to you boys," Marla stated. "I stay until you all want to go home."

Lucas pinched Gardner's chin. "Don't dwell and don't stray from what I told you to do, boy. Don't test me. Show you got a brain and take the lesson like a man. Do anything else, and I call in favors. I'm goin' to let you up. Grab your shirt at the chest. Let those hands stray anywhere else and you won't be goin' home under your own power, meat."

Lucas released him. Gardner scrambled to his feet, remembered to grab his lapels, and hustled his butt out of the restaurant. Hell… if Lucas barked at the three of us forever boot-camps, we would have grabbed our shirts, and marched out after Gardner. Boyle approached us with a grin.

"I'm sorry about Gardner. We're done here. We'll be in touch if we need your weapons or a question answered. I forgot to ask Gardner about being able to keep the sidearms. I'm senior on scene, so it's a judgement call. I'll be in touch. Please don't disturb the crime scene tape." He turned to Marla. "We'll have you back in business tomorrow afternoon, Mar."

"Thanks, Jer. I hope you guys can get over the loss of the old 'Warehouse', but the city put too much pressure on Alexi. We brought all the memorabilia we could keep without a fight."

Jerrod waved her off. "We all know that. It's a process. The heat's on us all the time now not to socialize anywhere. I don't know what the hell the future will bring. Without all of you working with John - Antifa, BLM, and La Raza thugs would have overrun the city a couple of times. We need you guys backing our play as a special unit, sanctioned by Homeland Security and the FBI. Just between us, do any of you know what the hell this appeasement of domestic terrorist gangs is all about?"

"Globalists selling out America, Jer," Lucas answered. "Chaos and the breakdown of law and order soften the populace to One World Order with the Sharia Law Mutants working enforcement. You've seen what's happened in Europe and Australia. We're very close to civil war all over the world to protect Nationalism and the rights of nations for self-determination."

"I read and researched the new colony you helped establish, where they shipped all the non-assimilating Muslims from the UK. It's thriving now, I hear, and they've disavowed Islam completely. The videos of the place are incredible. Look... thank you for this. I hope we can find out what happened here tonight and who the target actually was."

"No sweat, Jer," I told him. "We'll look into it too. If we find anything the OPD can use, we'll contact you right away."

"Thanks, John. It's good seeing you. I...I bet a grand against you beating Carl Logan."

I patted his shoulder as my companions hooted with muffled enjoyment. "I nearly bet on him myself, Jer. Don't worry about it. I'll talk at you later."

Boyle seemed relieved at admitting his fight bet. He gathered the Blue and left.

Marla decorated the bar with the Bud and Beam brothers. Oh my, it was tempting to make this an Uber night tonight, but we needed to be coherent when arriving at Pain Central. No doubt Lynn would be pissed if we arrived after she interrogated the driver, unable to process what she learned. We toasted to once more avoiding casualties.

"Lynn will have news. I'll have just one set before Clint and I join her at Pain Central. No need for you and Casey to go there, Pap."

"Call us if something important develops," Lucas replied. "I'd be surprised if that gang of cheap punks we handled tonight had anything to do with this shootout."

"Agreed. I don't think it had anything to do with Alexi's new restaurant either," Casey added. "Someone knew we'd be here. They sent Snow Whites instead of killers, unless their main purpose was to get the drop on us. If their purpose was to take us prisoner, it would mean they don't know shit about us."

"Clint and I will let you both know." I stood away from the bar with Clint. "We'll fix this, Marla. I'll send a contractor over tomorrow to assess the damage from those meatheads' firing into the ceiling and for cleanup once I get the all clear on the crime scene."

"Thanks, John. I'll let Alexi know what happened when I see him tonight."

We waved and walked toward the exit.

"Freeze, maggots!"

Laughter, as both Clint and I did exactly that. I turned around and Casey was recording us on his phone. Oh boy… Nick would be getting the uploads on my night back in boot-camp for sure. I better wash my Muerto t-shirt.

Chapter Two

Death Cult

The man groaned into consciousness, noting he could not move any limb or his head. Lynn's smiling face appeared over him. "Hi there, blondie. Nice dye job. My associate has a video for you to see. It may save us some time."

"Why am I restrained. I have done nothing wrong. Arrest me or turn me loose!"

Lynn frowned, while waving Gus Denova away as he moved into a position allowing their prisoner to view his iPad. "Wrong start, Betty. You have an interesting accent. We'll need to fix your attitude a bit so you can be more helpful."

"I am not helping you with anything. I will not say anything until my lawyer is present."

"He is Middle Eastern, Lynn," Jafar said. "I cannot place the accent though."

"He'll be glad to tell us soon. Hook the clips on, Sil."

"What clips... wait... you cannot torture me!" Suddenly, his entire world descended into pain filled agony.

Lynn stopped for a moment. "He's too loud Gus. Duct tape his mouth."

"Yes, Dr. Deville," Gus Denova joked as he followed Lynn's orders.

Lynn turned on both the heat and electrical into the acupuncture needles inserted into the man's nerve clusters in his feet. She varied the intensity with practiced care, making certain the man did not die. Five minutes, an eternity to the prisoner, passed with only brief instants of Lynn dialing back completely. After another ten minutes to allow sanity to seep into her captive's brain, Lynn removed the duct tape with a quick rip upwards.

"We're recording this, Betty. Tell me your name first. Remember, I ask the questions and you answer them."

"Rarsour! Kaed Rarsour! I am… a Palestinian."

"There are no Palestinians. You may as well just say you're a terrorist from the area of Palestine. Your name sounds familiar," Lynn said. "There's an activist bitch in New York who claims to be another phony Palestinian named… ah… help me out, Achmed."

"Minda Rarsour," Jafar answered. "She constantly plots in public for Sharia Law and the overthrow of the United States, including calling for the assassination of the President. She spews taquiyya (lying to the infidels) out her pie-hole about how wonderful life is as a woman in Islam. Everything, of course, offends her. She has ties with The Muslim Brotherhood and CAIR (Council on American-Islamic Relations), along with Hamas. Samira and I know much about her. She stated Samira and I should be killed for leaving Islam."

"Leaving Islam is… punishable by death!"

"Oh… Kaed… you are such a dummy." Lynn placed the duct tape over his mouth once again. "I think you need a quick refresher course on speak only when spoken to."

The frantic pleas for mercy turned into a ululating muffled, continuous scream for the next three minutes. Lynn again allowed Kaed a moment to gather whatever thoughts were left. "Okay, I think we have the ground rules clear. Who is Minda Rarsour to you?"

"My…my sister."

"Uh oh… I'm getting a bad feeling your sister has something to do with this nasty assault on our favorite bar. Since my associate, Jafar Kensington, knows of your sister and her threats, I'm betting he and his beautiful family were the target of tonight's travesty. Tell us what did your sister plan for them?"

"We…we were to take them to a place… ah… and… make a video of them either reaffirming their faith in Islam or killing them."

Lynn's face descended into the darkness. "Don't lie to me, Kaed. That's the line you feed the other brainwashed mutants."

Kaed now feared more than death. "Yes… we were going to kill them all, no matter what they did to save their lives."

"Where's your sister now?"

Kaed hesitated. Lynn grabbed his chin with her face a few inches above his. "No take backs, Betty… I will keep you alive until we confirm the place where your sister is. If it doesn't match what you tell me now, I will torture you until hell's eternity will be a welcome alternative. Want another sample?"

"No! She… she did this to me. Jihad… quickly and murderously she said… the family would be an example to others trying to leave Islam. We would be kept safely and get away without being caught. Where… where are my other brothers?"

Lynn smiled. "All dead, as you will pray to be, Kaed. Answer truthfully and join your idiot brothers in the afterlife painlessly. Lie, and I will guide you to hell on earth you have only had a mild taste of. Follow the truth, and you will have a pain free leaving of this plane of existence."

Kaed closed his eyes, with the realization his brothers were dead, and his sister would be no matter what he said. The people here were monsters. They were not the globalist dupes he had been told about. "Minda is on board a yacht in a Sausalito docking."

"Good. Go the extra yard for your departure on this earth," Lynn stated. "How many security and guests would be aboard this yacht?"

"Minda travels with three bodyguards. The yacht she will be staying on is owned by Ishmail Maniyeh. He is of the Palestinian and Muslim brotherhood… Allah forgive me for my betrayal!"

"It's a small thing, Kaed," Lynn told him with a pat on the cheek. "You Sharia Law Mutant idiots have caused so much death and dishonor, no amount of penance on your part can ever make it right. I can offer you penance here, for your blasphemous deeds, in helping thwart the evil your brain-dead species seeks to visit on innocent people. I cannot offer you forgiveness… you no good rotten-"

"Mistress!" Quays Tannous urged. "Don't do this! We'll find out the specifics and have Kaed for confirmation."

Lynn broke contact, stepping away. "Thank you. I...I had a feeling I could lose control here. We have enough to investigate. Let's get to it until Cheese arrives with the parameters of this cluster fuck. I believe you want to help now, sweetie. Don't ruin my perception. Let's go through this from the beginning. Talk with diligence and information. Fill us in on times, dates, locations, and contacts with realization this was an attempted killing of my family. Believe me when I say this. If Achmed finds one syllable wrong with what you say, you will be mine for an eternity you could not imagine in your wildest dreams."

* * *

Clint and I walked in on a prisoner so devoid of reality, he perked up as we approached. I knew beyond any shadow of a doubt, Cruella Deville plucked everything from this guy's brain matter even partially in our wheelhouse.

"Hi Lynn. I see our guest has been reconditioned. Were we the targets?"

"In a way we were, John. Meet Kaed Rarsour, brother of Minda Rarsour."

That stunned me a bit. "The Hamas infiltrator from Palestine who looks like Gumby with a hijab?"

"One and the same, Kaed and his deceased brothers assaulted the restaurant to capture Jafar, Samira and Mia on Gumby's orders. She petitioned Hamas and the PLO for permission to make an example of torturing and murdering Jafar's family, on the pretense they would again embrace the death cult before dying. Jafar confirmed everything he could with the cell and tablet you sent along with Kaed. They have been in direct contact, mostly by Arabic text, with Hamas and PLO leaders on our FBI watch lists. Jafar said the communiques cloaked the language in ordering what was to be done, but knowing what took place, Jafar broke the general code."

"Minda will hear of her brothers' failure quickly," Jafar added. "She's staying in the Alexandria Suite at Casa Madrona Hotel & Spa in Sausalito across the Bay."

"I've stayed there with Lora once. It's beautiful, but I didn't stay in the Alexandria Suite. That place costs thousands a night. We need to go get her tonight before she has time to escape. Did you have anything to drink, little brother?"

"No," Jafar answered. "I will drive. You are right, John. We must get her. Can we use our FBI credentials with some cover story? We can get Kaed to tell her anything we want him to say."

"I can get Kaed to tell her the plot failed, and he escaped," Lynn agreed. "Kaed will tell her he hired guards to escort her to the airport where she and her bodyguards can get a flight to New York."

"I like it," Clint said. "We can arrive in our big stretch limousine. Lynn can go in with you and I, John. We'll be the porters, while Lynn makes nice with Gumby. Once we get her and the bodyguards in the limo… well… you know, depending on the element of surprise, we may or may not need to do some interior work on the limo."

"That's a solid plan," I replied. "We have our MIB suits here at the Center. What will we need to do for Kaed to be coherent enough for this mission call?"

"If she calls, we'll have him ready. I am the devil incarnate to Kaed," Lynn told us. "We'll begin rehearsing now. You and Jafar get your MIB gear on. Clint reads and writes Arabic. He can study Kaed's style in the texts on his cell. Clint can draft a message, and then we'll have Kaed draft a message without seeing Clint's. We'll compare the two and see how we do. Once she gets the text, Minda may call to confirm, rather than text back. I'll have Kaed ready to answer."

"Sounds right, Lynn. C'mon, little brother, let's go look good." I led the way to our outfitting room. We keep all our outfits for working my detective business when we do escorting gigs at Pain Central. By the time Jafar and I readied ourselves for playing dress-up, Lynn produced the two drafts for me to see. Clint had matched Kaed's style nearly to perfection.

Jafar looked the drafts over too. "I cannot tell the difference other than a couple of words, Clint. You will be able to answer any text clarification without her realizing it is not her brother doing it."

Kaed hung on every word, to be ready when Dr. Deville wanted him to speak.

"Clint made sure Kaed knows he speaks Arabic like a native. He will be a good little helper, won't you Kaed?"

Kaed dropped his head into a slight bow. "Yes, Mistress of the unimaginable!"

Clint adjourned to the dressing room while I typed in Clint's message for Gumby. I finished with the text in time for Clint's return. Jafar was already checking it over. He gave it to Clint for final analysis. Clint sent it. She texted back in a panic, stating she had to call. Lynn shook Kaed's chin.

"Are you ready to be the helpful, grief-stricken brother, who simply urges your sister to be prepared to leave in two hours, when the escorts you hired will collect her at the entrance to the Suite?"

"I am ready. I will not fail, Mistress. My bitch sister, who killed her own brothers with this fanaticism, will pay for what she has done."

"Don't pull the outrage card yet. Be the grieved brother of few words." Lynn signaled Clint to text her it would be okay to call. "She always initiates the call."

I listened to Gumby's hysterical Arabic on speaker with Clint and Jafar, gauging how well the call sounded. Kaed kept silent, only uttering small acknowledgements of pain and grief, when Minda stopped for a moment. As she spoke less, Kaed began repeatedly urging her to prepare for departure. She finally quieted enough to acknowledge the time of her leaving. Kaed promised to meet her at the airport and disconnected.

"He did very well, Babe." Clint turned to Silvio, who had the duty tonight at Pain Central. Gus and Quays had already left for home. "Lock this guest away in our nice cell until we return, Sil."

Silvio restrained Kaed and took him to holding. Lynn dressed then as our more fashionable guide. I could tell Clint liked the way she looked in the thigh length off the shoulder black silk dress with burgundy highlights. I grinned at Clint.

"Jafar can drop you two at home with the dress, brother. Gumby won't be going anywhere. Silvio and I will bed her down until morning."

"I like that idea." Clint grasped Lynn's hand. "Do you want John to check Kaed into eternity tonight, Babe."

"Kaed can go virgin hunting tonight. I'm hoping we can take the bodyguards as if we're arresting them all as FBI agents once we get in the limo. We'll make them all think ACLU lawyers with halal meals will be waiting to hear how offended they are."

"Good one, Lynn. Clint and I will get the Colt .45 drop on them inside the limo, and you do the FBI special agent in charge thing on them."

"She has three Hamas bodyguards," Jafar said. "If they do not obey immediately, shoot them in the head. If they do obey, I will park down the street and get in the back to restrain them all, so they are never without a gun at their heads."

"Agreed, little brother. We want this takedown safe and secure. If Lynn can get a few more names, we don't need to go over in the Sand to get, we'll make a statement to be sent about the cost of coming after our family."

"What do you mean 'if' I get some names, Cheese. When I get done with Gumby tomorrow, we'll have all the names Minda has in her tiny brain. I've decided to play 'Truth or Consequences' with her."

"I have no doubt your game show will be most informative, Sis."

* * *

Jafar parked our stretch limo in front of the Casa Madrona Hotel's very wide street. We porters exited the limousine in professional manner, journeying to where we could gain access to the plush Alexandria Suite. Greeted at the door by the bodyguards, Lynn greeted them in passable Arabic, Clint had been teaching her in a crash course. It started during our tour of duty on the newly created 'City of Hope', where we deposited Islamic malcontents from the UK to be readjusted into civilization. She told the guards to let Clint and I handle the baggage, so their hands were free to protect Minda. They liked her suggestion and let Clint and I load the baggage on a cart we acquired in the hotel. Princess Gumby regally approached us with her patented serene look some people thought spoke of intelligent peaceful demeanor. Knowing what she was, that look blared stupid to me. After hearing her spiels on enabling Sharia Law, along with female genital mutilation, I figured they may have given her a partial lobotomy.

Lynn played the subservient helpful underling perfectly, guiding Princess Gumby with us minions hauling the bags down to the limousine. Lynn kept assuring Minda all was in readiness and there would be no delays of any kind in transport. Clint and I loaded the bags quickly as Jafar popped the trunk release. I opened the rear limousine passenger side door for the bodyguards and Princess Gumby to get in regally. Clint, Lynn, and I followed, sitting opposite of them with Lynn in the middle. Jafar drove away down Bridgeway a few blocks to where the street was less trafficked. Clint and I drew our Colts instantly as Jafar halted the vehicle.

"Grab your suit lapels!" Clint's order in Arabic gained instant adherence. "Do not let them go. If you do, we fire into your heads."

"What is the meaning of this?" Princess Gumby didn't like what was happening at all.

Lynn went right to her routine, showing her FBI credentials. "Special Agent in Charge, Lynn Dostiene. You and your cohorts are under arrest for coordinating an act of terror on American soil. Your underlings assaulted a restaurant tonight with the intent of kidnapping, torturing, and executing a family disavowing Islam. We captured your one brother, Kaed. He confessed to everything and agreed to testify against you in court. Be still. My associate will now restrain you all. Do not resist. We know your bodyguards are Hamas killers. The two men aiming weapons at them are special forces trained agents with many tours all over the Middle East."

Jafar entered the rear compartment, quickly restraining each of the bodyguards first. They wanted no part of Clint and I. Killers recognize killers. They probably would have drawn on us if they had known we planned to boat their eviscerated remains ten miles out to sea. Princess Gumby's usually serenely stupid face turned feral as Jafar began restraining her.

"You will not put those restraints on me!"

Lynn bitch slapped her so hard, she rebounded off her bodyguard into an almost erect position again. Minda covered her face with a cry of horror. Lynn grabbed her nose in a finger vice that elicited mewling snorts and pleas. "Put your hands behind your back to be restrained or I rip your nose off... your choice."

Jafar was able to restrain Minda without any difficulty. "Thanks for that first introduction to hell, Lynn."

"No problem, Achmed. It felt so good, I just want to keep blasting her." Lynn released Princess Gumby's nose with revulsion. "Yuck!"

Lynn wiped her fingers on Minda's dress as Gumby cried and sobbed. Lynn bitch slapped her again. "Shut your pie-hole, Gumby. We're here to get justice in ways you infiltrating, death cult zombies seldom see. Shut up and enjoy the ride across the Bay to what we call Pain Central. It's the last stop on your America hating tour, bitch!"

Then, the laugh-a-thon began in earnest. We heard all the demands stoked into these Sharia Law Mutants when caught red-handed. One of the guards recognized he would die soon.

"Shut your mouth, bitch! These people will kill us. I do not wish to die screaming because you are a moron."

Lynn patted his knee. "Tell us what little you know, and I promise you get a quick introduction to the afterlife."

The guard leaned back. "Thank you. I will do as you advise. I do not know much, but I will tell you everything I do know. I hate this bitch! She is allowed to treat us like dirt, because she espouses lies to the infidels about Islam they stupidly believe."

"I like this guy," Lynn said. "You shall get the ending you asked for: pleasure instead of pain."

Shocked by her bodyguard's betrayal, Minda Rarsour did an incredibly stupid thing: she spat at Lynn, who smiled and punched her with a straight right hand to Minda's left eye, bouncing her off the seatback. The fist strike also launched our Princess Gumby into a wail of hurt and outrage, earning her another bitch slap. This time, she clamped her mouth shut, closed her eyes and stared downward.

"You're learning," Lynn told her.

Jafar drove to Pain Central, where Clint and Jafar helped me get the prisoners inside. Silvio and I guided the bodyguards to their cells for the night. I gave them a professional frisk, including checking the linings of their clothes. I erred when I took their restraints off before putting them in a cell. By then, the two bodyguards who had been quiet in the car, now recognized we did indeed plan to kill them, as had their third more fatalistic cohort concluded in the limo. They tried to rush Silvio. He carries a stun-gun nightstick with so much power, one touch will knock a full-grown man flat on his back in a split-second. After Silvio's attitude adjustment, which the third fatalist bodyguard backed away from, we deposited them in their cells.

On the way back to our next duty, Silvio chuckled. "I wonder what those two figured to do, even if they could have overpowered me. They disrespected you, Dark Lord."

"They probably hoped to threaten me with your death if I didn't let them go."

My explanation amused Silvio. "I would have been toast."

"I didn't observe the rules closely, Sil. We know better than to take the restraints off before putting them in the cell. It's been a long day, including pole poking Rocky smashing the crap out of me in the ocean this morning. It's no excuse for me to get stupid. I won't let it happen again."

"No worries. I saw the lapse in routine and had my nightstick ready. Man, that stick can really put them down."

We stopped by Kaed's cell with his eternity shot. Syl restrained him through the bars. He meekly sat on his bunk. "Did you get her?"

"We did. She's being held upstairs for the time being," I told him.

"Good." Kaed turned to get his shot.

I didn't prolong the task. I'm certain he enjoyed his last few moments. Silvio and I stored him in a body-bag for disposal tomorrow. We had an empty storage freezer, so space was not an issue. Clint and Lynn stuck around with Jafar until we finished, while they entertained Princess Gumby. Her eye, already swollen, prompted threats of suing us, brutality, and the most humorous of all: reporting us to the World Court.

"We were going to leave, but Princess Gumby's complaint list grows every time she opens her mouth," Lynn said. "We've never been threatened with the World Court before."

"You laugh now, but soon you shall answer for this outrageous treatment," Rarsour told us. "I want something for the pain of my eye injury."

Clint nearly missed catching Lynn's wrist. Dr. Deville's painkiller was a left fist in Rarsour's other eye. "Don't, Babe. You'll hurt your hand. Syl. Give her ladyship a painkiller."

Silvio used his nightstick on Minda. The jolt knocked her off the chair and onto the floor. She twitched in spasms as the effects wore off. Jafar lifted her onto the chair again. He patted her shoulder. "Keep silent. Tonight, think of all the items you believe will make Dr. Deville happy."

Rarsour stared at Jafar with hatred. "If not for your kafir helpers, Kensington, I would be witnessing Islamic justice meted out to your blasphemous family. My idiot brothers should have captured you easily, while making a violent statement at the restaurant. You should be in chains right now, awaiting torture and death for turning your back on Islam, along with your kafir wife."

Jafar smiled. "On second thought, think about all the ways you can thwart Dr. Deville's interrogation. Show her you cannot be broken."

"I will not be broken. You kafirs cannot torture me."

"Oh… this will be so special tomorrow," Lynn said. "Take us home, Achmed."

"Are you sure you don't want to ride with us," Jafar asked me.

"Go ahead, John," Silvio urged. "I can take care of Rarsour."

"Nope. I'll see you three tomorrow. I'm stone cold sober now. I'll take one of our cars home. I made a mistake down in holding. I plan to lock Princess Gumby away by the book. Tomorrow's Sunday, so let's meet here at 11 am."

"Sounds good, John," Clint agreed.

After they left, we took Minda to our upstairs apartment type cell. I took her restraints off with Silvio ready with nightstick in hand. Women can be the most dangerous creatures on earth. Lynn Montoya Dostiene illustrated that point for us constantly.

"Strip down to your underwear," I told her.

Rarsour gasped. "You…you cannot be serious. I will do no such thing!"

I nodded at Silvio. He made her do the electric rumba. When she recovered, I yanked her to a standing position again. "Take your clothes off down to your underwear or Silvio will give you another gentle charge."

Sobbing, Rarsour stripped down to her underwear. I checked her body for bandages or anything capable of hiding a weapon. I then shoved her inside the cell. My thorough examination of her clothing revealed two razor blades inside the lining of the full-length body cloak she wore. I found nothing else in her clothing. I threw them to her.

"That would have been nasty, John."

"Yeah, Sil, it always pays to follow the rules." I locked the cell door.

"You will be killed for seeing my nakedness!"

"I doubt it. Goodnight, Princess. I'll see you tomorrow, Sil."

"Stop and get us breakfast, John."

"Will do. I'll stop by the Pantry in the morning. Want a little of everything?"

"Their biscuits and sausage gravy."

"Does your wife know about this?"

"I am in great shape. Being a Cruella Deville minion uses a lot of calories. Besides, I only get to have it once in a while."

"I'm kidding. Biscuits and gravy, it is."

* * *

Lora and Al binged on the Netflix series, 'Stranger Things'. I don't mind it, but they know I like 'The Punisher'. If I miss a couple of 'Stranger Things', it's no big deal. "Hi."

"You had a long day and night, DL," Lora said. "Lynn called and told me about the emergency op to get the woman plotting to torture and kill Jafar's family. She said you'd be tired."

I immediately thought of the YouTube video with the blindfolded Cheeseburger. "Did she mention anything else?"

"She didn't have to, Dad. We saw the YouTube video," Al lanced me. "What did you call Dad after we watched it, Mom?"

"Dodo... I called you a dodo bird... and possibly an idiot."

"I could think of worse ones. It wasn't as bad as it looked. I'll take a shower quickly. It's only midnight. I'll watch one of those 'Stranger Things' with you while I sip a Beam."

* * *

Later, in bed with Lora, she had more to say. "You won't ever do that again, will you?"

"Probably not. I already admitted it was stupid. Let's practice my other super power." For some reason, if I stared at Lora in a certain way, she shuddered.

"Don't. It won't work," Lora told me, and then shuddered. "Damn it! That's just disturbing. Okay... I'm ready now. You can't..." she shuddered again. "Damn it!"

She closed her eyes, face all scrunched up. I didn't know if it would work, but I stared at her, concentrating with intensity. The power of suggestion won out again. Lora shuddered. I enjoyed her failure to not shudder, even with eyes closed, rather enthusiastically. She hopped on top of me, playfully choking me while grunting in fake rage. It worked against her though as some of my other powers came into play.

* * *

I arrived at 10 am with breakfast for Silvio. We have one of those goofy insert cup coffee machines. They make one cup at a time, so I made Silvio and I a cup while he drooled over breakfast. The delicious smell of meat fat overpowered everything in the kitchen. I made some rye toast from our own food supply. Silvio would be going home before Lynn went to work on Minda. It's never a good idea to load up on rich food before a Dr. Deville interrogation. I have a cast iron stomach, but no one wants to eat something like biscuits and gravy before entering Dr. Deville's podiatry clinic with a prisoner.

Clint and Lynn arrived with the baby. Lynn sniffed the air. "Oh my! Biscuits and gravy from 'The Buttercup'! Yum! Did you save me some?"

I stand corrected. "There's plenty, Lynn. I have it in the warmer. I'll get it for you. Want some, Clint?"

"No thanks. I'll have some toast and coffee."

I placed a dish in front of Lynn. She ate hungrily. "I'll have coffee too, John."

I served everyone, including Silvio's second helping. The meal entertained too as Lynn gave Clint Jr little bits of gravy dipped biscuit. His face brightened in lip smacking need, reaching with both tiny hands when Lynn didn't serve it quickly enough. "Wow… the little bugger loves this stuff. Dannie and Amara will be over after church services. They love the way this new ministry uses music and plays to teach the word of God. After years of joyless Islam, Amara never misses a service or a chance to sing and act in the plays. Clint and I attend a couple times a month. It's fun."

"Where do you go?" This was a new side of Lynn. I would like to attend a service with Lora and Al, especially with the added music and spectacle. Al seemed to be outgrowing Justin Bieber, the infamous 'Beeper' and his voice like a castrated cat. I needed to go somewhere to give thanks to God in a formal venue for that blessing.

"They go to 3Crosses in Castro Valley." Lynn and Clint Jr finished their biscuits and gravy. "I needed that… and apparently, so did the baby."

Amara and Dannie arrived. Dannie and CIA Director Gilbrech's personal assistant, Clyde Bacall were seeing each other every time they could. Since our very own pilot supreme, Laredo Sawyer, married Dannie's mom, Sybil, he flies Dannie to meet Clyde whenever Bacall arrives somewhere in the Western States on business. Dannie took baby Clint in her arms.

"I smell biscuits and gravy, you little rascal."

"Would you and Amara like some," I asked. "There's still plenty in the warmer."

"I am starving," Amara said. "I would love some, John."

"Ditto," Dannie added.

After serving them food, Clint and I retrieved the very angry Minda after placing her iPhone and tablet in the interrogation room. Clint positioned our satellite laptop in place there to confirm as much of what Minda told us as we could. We avoided making a mistake opening her electronic gadgets. She would be glad to unlock the devices safely later.

"I am hungry, thirsty, and I need a shower. My needs must be met before I am taken anywhere. The meal must be halal."

"You had a sink in your room. Water is all you get," I explained as I opened the cell door. "As to food, we don't have halal food, and where you'll be going, you won't need a shower. Come with me. We're taking you into interrogation, where all your questions will be ignored, while all of ours will be answered quite earnestly by you."

Clint took her arm. "Don't make this part difficult. We're taking you easy or hard."

Although she accompanied us without further resistance, Princess Gumby peppered us with demands for phone calls, lawyers, the name of our superior… on and on, until it was a relief to get her strapped down in the podiatry wing of our interrogation facility. The Princess knew something bad was on tap when strapped motionless on our podiatry table. When we inserted the acupuncture needles into her heels, Minda began struggling in earnest.

"Release me this instant! What are you doing to my feet? I will not answer anything! I have rights! I am an American!"

"We know for a fact you are an Hamas infiltrator," Lynn replied calmly. "You say you believe in feminism, but you try to establish Sharia Law, the most misogynistic, woman battering blasphemy of laws ever created. While you're still coherent, we want to know everything about your fifth columnist actions, and all your terrorist contacts. We also want to know if it was you who singled out Jafar Kensington and his family for death."

"I will tell you nothing, other than Kensington's family deserves to die. They renounced Islam. That is punishable by death in the Islamic religion."

"You mixed a few words. Islam is a death cult, not a religion." Lynn gestured for the clips to be attached. "It doesn't matter what you believe. Soon, you will have only one thought in your mind – to please me."

"You are bluffing. I know you cannot torture me."

Clint pinched off Minda's nostrils. When she opened her mouth, I inserted the ball gag. Rarsour did not like that at all. Lynn patted her cheek. "Let's begin your reeducation, shall we?"

Dr. Deville played Princess Gumby like a big mouth bass, reeling in the pain, and then relaxing the line. Each time Rarsour appeared close to losing consciousness, Lynn allowed her bass to flounder in the waters of agony.

"I think we have Princess Gumby's attention. Remove the gag, Cheese."

I did as ordered, wiping her face a bit afterward. We allowed a brief time for Minda to regain coherence.

"You're going to be my good little helper, aren't you?"

"Yes! Yes… yeeeeesssssss… I… I will talk… anything… just please do not turn on the torture machine. Oh… Allah! I am on fire inside."

"You know what we want. Start from the beginning of how you became the female face of the death cult. Then, we want everything. We have your iPhone and tablet. I want you to unlock each one. If you goof up and lock us out, I will punish you."

She didn't. We spent the next hour listening to Princess Gumby recite everything Lynn asked for. Most importantly, we learned why she targeted Jafar. Hamas figured rightly, killing Samira would draw her father from the Saudi Arabia base. Badee Karim, an important figure with the Northern Alliance during our first incursion in Afghanistan, worked tirelessly through our contacts inside Afghanistan to create another secular state as we did with the 'City of Hope'. The last thing on earth terrorist leaders wanted was a follow up to our incredible success in establishing a secular refuge from Islam for Muslims seeking life away from the death cult.

Our CIA Assistant Director, Denny Strobert, met secretly with Badee, showing him the details of our 'City of Hope'. He connected him directly with Khan Eshieh, our leader in the secular refuge, 'City of Hope'. They became friends, with Khan sharing every success, and explaining all the problems in the initial creation. With his own daughter and son-in-law disavowing Islam, Khan's enthusiastic and commonsense points concerning the devastation caused by Islam, hit Badee at the right time. Badee's initial inroads with his followers in Afghanistan had even drawn the ire of the foremost terror enabling country on earth: Saudi Arabia. He was no longer safe in Saudi Arabia, even at an American installation. Hamas and the Muslim Brotherhood wanted him dead now before he could be relocated.

Clint and I worked diligently, crosschecking Minda's information with her communications on both the iPhone and tablet, in conjunction with terrorist watch lists around the world. "Her info checks out, John. Most of her contacts are Hamas and PLO in Palestine. I think we should give them over to the Mossad. They can decide how they want to handle the situation. Denny can probably trade for concessions, so we can get updates on Hamas movements."

"I agree. We need to depend on the Israelis for anything going on in Palestine. Our concerns should focus on the main guy contacting Minda: Khaled Hanniyey. He gave the order."

"She specified he ordered the restaurant statement," Lynn added. "Khaled wanted a blood bath the moment the Rarsour brothers captured Jafar and family. He rightly figured if they fired randomly, killing as many as possible, they would be able to escape in the aftermath with Jafar's family easily, without being identified."

"We've had bad run-ins with Mexico this past year," I replied. "Puerto Vallarta camouflages Hanniyeh's operation with the Saudi's bankrolling his yacht parked in the Puerto Vallarta Marina. We would need to get the Ranger on this."

"Lucas will be happy to hear that. If we took the Sea Wolf, Lucas wouldn't need a co-pilot," Clint pointed out.

"True, but Payaso told us he would crew with Lucas anytime we take the Ranger out. Besides, with the firepower and helicopter landing pads, we could give the Mexican Navy and Airforce a run for their money."

"Then... you're not thinking of hitting Khaled's boat in port?"

"Mexico isn't Iran yet, Lynn. Blowing the crap out of an Iranian port was so good, I'd like to do it every other day," I replied. "We can take the Ranger well beyond the twelve-mile International Boundary Mexico claims. If Khaled ever does take the yacht out, we can hit him hard and not leave a trace. I'm glad Minda's still alive."

"I get it." Lynn walked over to the nearly comatose Minda. "Hi sweetie. I have another question for you. You mentioned Khaled's yacht in the Vallarta Marina. Does he ever take the yacht out on the water? Take your time. Clear your thoughts before speaking."

Minda thought very hard. I could imagine the half dead squirrels running the mind wheel in her head. Her face brightened suddenly. "Yes...yes... he does. I...I have been on it during a cruise. Khaled often sails to Isla Maria Magdalena where he meets with other Hamas and Muslim Brotherhood members from the states. He owns an estate on the island."

Lynn's eyes narrowed. "You left the meeting place out of our discussion, sweetie. Why is that?"

"Oh... oh please," Minda sobbed. "I did not remember it... until you mentioned him leaving the port! Please... please do not... punish me."

Lynn smoothed a hand over Minda's brow. "Calm down. I can forgive you for this one omission. Tell us all about who he takes with him on these trips."

Minda became animated. "His companion at the meetings, who has ties... with Muslims of the Americas and CAIR – Mammar Rhahin!"

"The bearded troll preaching all Jews must die near Sacramento?"

"Yes... Mistress! And...and I have another... a woman accompanies them. Like me, she provides taqiyya for the infidels – Safia Sakaria. I was asked to accompany them on two occasions. Khaled... mentioned something about another cruise soon... but he said I should return to New York after the Kensington mission."

"What about guards and crew?"

"They are… handpicked from the Muslim Brotherhood and Hamas. Because he takes no one but a couple of important officials, Khaled travels with a crew of twenty-five, even though his superyacht would need nearly fifty if he entertained a full contingent of guests. They… are well armed."

In the middle of Minda's description of the crew, Denny Strobert arrived. He looked jet-lagged and generally on his last leg. Lynn saw him and gave Minda her eternity shot. Denny's fists tightened, and his lips formed a snarl line for a moment. He simply shrugged at our stifled amusement. We knew why he blasted in here like this, because we keep him briefed on everything. He thought to bargain for Princess Gumby – not going to happen. When they come after family, they die… badly.

"I love Maria and Brewster-John," Lynn said, shedding her gloves. "You, Denny, are on a day to day basis with me. We could have told you Princess Gumby wasn't leaving here except in a body-bag. On the other hand, we have an Hamas trained killer, bodyguarding for Minda, or Princess Gumby, as we nicknamed her. We can give him to you. His cohorts are dead meat. I know you like to learn the intricacies of how operations work. His name's Aled Kalil."

"I'll take him. Did you already blast his mind into zombie land, or can he still think on his own and reason?"

Even Lynn chuckled at Denny's backhand swipe. "He's good to go, Spawn. We have a new mission, Cheese can explain to you."

"It's so nice to get a reading on how things are going in my CIA black-op division."

"We need to organize, Den," I told him. "Go get something to eat and drink. We'll be with you shortly."

"I have a driver on loan from Paul. Clyde Bacall wanted to see his love, Dannie, so he's been with me this trip connecting threads overseas for Badee Karim. Clyde is very happy at this moment. It was a surprise for him to see Dannie here at Pain Central."

"Neato. I like Clyde. Paul and Nick turned him to the dark side. It seems to be working out real well for him," I replied, while Clint and I deposited our poor Princess Gumby into a body-bag.

Denny looked down at the faded flower of Islamic brainwashing with a jaundiced eye. "Rarsour doesn't look much like Gumby anymore. She looks more like Pokey."

Denny's ace hit a humorous note, as indeed, Gumby had metamorphized into Pokey after Lynn's information gathering session.

Clint, Lynn, and I went down to handle our three bodyguards with the well-fed Silvio. He would be relieved soon by Lynn's other minion, Quays Tannous. "We get them the usual way, right?"

"Absolutely, Sil," Clint deadpanned Nick McCarty's favorite reply.

We arrived at the cells. Lynn ordered them to stand and get restrained at the bars. Aled moved to the opening for restraints immediately with his back to us. Silvio restrained him. The other two did not move. I didn't blame them. They were killers. They knew this would be a death journey. We did make a mistake putting all three in the same cell because of my error the night before. The other two bodyguards attacked Aled a heartbeat after he was restrained. Figures that the one with some logic was also the toughest.

Lynn opened the cell instantly with Clint in 'shoot 'em in the head' form to back my play. We needed Aled. I streaked into the cell without restraint. I had no intention of breaking bones in my fists. I should have let Silvio stun-gun them into oblivion, but when the monster inside arrives, I need to get a taste. I did not pull punches. My left to the first troll's ribcage broke bones in an audible symphony of pain. The second took a knife hand strike to the neck. He croaked out his life on the cell floor, clutching his ruined throat. I grabbed Aled, looking him over.

"You look okay, Aled. This was supposed to go smoother."

"I know I must die. I would have killed these two if they had assaulted me last night. They knew it, so they stayed away. I am sick of this life in Islam's deadly embrace. I may as well have been one of the others they strapped bombs to."

"We have another course of life in mind for you," I said in Arabic. "My CIA Assistant Director arrived this morning. He would like your cooperation in a special project he formed a while back to counteract terrorism. Would you be willing to assist him in that capacity?"

At first, my words in Arabic surprised Aled. "If I could leave this death-style of life, I would do anything asked of me. I do not know how valuable I can be. Perhaps your Assistant Director knows how to make me valuable doing something other than enduring this blasphemy of life."

"Everything is valuable to Denny. Guide him upstairs to Denny, Sil. Clint and I will handle cleanup."

"Okay, John." Silvio guided the still restrained Aled away.

Clint and I fixed the remaining two for cold storage. By the time we joined everyone, Denny was happily discussing information with Aled. Silvio stood in attendance to watch over our new collaborator. Clyde and Dannie were off by themselves. Lynn and Amara played with the baby while sipping coffee.

"Let's go into the control room and investigate Khaled's ship," Clint suggested. "We can hack in to find notice of 'The Rigel's' movements in and out of the Vallarta Marina, along with ship's registry. I took a quick look while Lynn interrogated Rarsour. 'The Rigel' is a hundred-eighty-footer. That size boat doesn't move unnoticed."

"The Isla Maria Magdalena is over sixty miles from the coast, and uninhabited, way outside Mexican territorial waters. We can intercept 'The Rigel' the moment the boat moves towards the island. There's no way it avoids the Ranger's radar."

"Got it. I hacked into Khaled's communications with his hidden estate at Isla Magdalena. He and his guests will be anchoring near his estate at the north end of The Isla Maria Magdalena three weeks from this coming Saturday. Khaled pays a lot of money to keep his estate secret and protected. Caretakers boat to The Isla Magdalena from the larger prison Isla Madre when they know Khaled will be visiting on 'The Rigel'. They prepare the estate, along with providing a security detail if Khaled doesn't bring his own. Notice was given to Vallarta Marina, 'Rigel' will be leaving port the Friday prior to that."

"Nice work, brother. We'll need not only Gus, but everyone he can round up, including El Muerto. Gus will know how the sailing conditions are from Monster's Island at this time of year."

"It's the beginning of June," Clint pointed out. "College let out for our girls. Al's almost done with softball and school. I imagine the same deal happens down in 'Dead Boy' land. Last time I talked to Nick, he told me his daughter Jean's riding herd on the Unholies doing the Irish at Otter's Point every morning, after he sailed with the Unholies to Jamaica and sanctioned Tolo Whitt for us. They're training every day now to get Jean off their backs. I guess the wives were a bit worried too. Dead-Boy will probably jump at the chance to go if Gus can make the trip."

"I bet we can talk Muerto into entertaining too. Too bad this damn mission's so dangerous. You get to take your wife to dance the nights away, but the rest of us are out of luck."

"You're not thinkin', compadre," Clint replied. "Laredo can fly the dependents to land before the event. We'd have a nice cruise from Monster Island, pick the dependents up at our dock, and sail for Puerto Vallarta."

"Damn good plan." I grinned. "I'll get to work on my two. Do you want to sell Gus and Muerto on a Mexico cruise?"

"I'll do it," Clint agreed. "Let's not take chances though. We need to square this with our Monsters and Snow Whites as well. The Ranger requires a formidable crew to sail her safely. Don't forget fresh supplies for the trip need stocked. I'm glad Lucas and Gus trained us all on our last excursion. It was business and a lot of fun."

"I know Lynn will be on board," I replied. "I wonder if Clyde wants to go along with Dannie. I'm assuming you'll need Dannie and Amara along to fly off with the baby when it comes time."

"Yep. That's a good idea about having Clyde along, but I don't know if he should be on board when we hit 'Rigel'. Nick and Paul had some trouble with Clyde's priorities early on in their relationship, when Paul hired him as his driver and assistant."

I smiled, remembering the alternative for Clyde was either succeed and accept things, or get shot in the head. "I believe they cleared the gray areas from Clyde's mind. Muerto made him a rich man. If Director Gilbrech wants plausible deniability for his driver, he can fly off with the dependents."

"I'll call right away and learn what Dead-Boy is up to."

Chapter Three

Chicago Redux

A wet early June rain greeted morning commuters and pedestrians holding umbrellas to shield from both 'Windy City' rain and wind. Leia Zhoe watched the limousine slow near her father's old friend Lee Wu's store. She knew the new gang controllers planned to retake the city after El Muerto's winter devastation of the gangs. This one, sophisticated, cordial, with mixed race enforcers, arrived politely to threaten and cajole. They used professional killers. If refused, they burned and terrorized. The mob leader, Edgar Thurman, made the rounds of neighborhood shops, spreading what he called good will. Extortion, money laundering, and blackmail filled his tool drawer. He came always jauntily dressed, in expensive suits and a bowler hat, his close-cut beard framing a deceptively bright smile.

The passenger door opened in the back to allow Thurman's minion to lead a brutal enforcement party with a message. Instead, a bum like figure, with wild black hair and beard, dressed in used tattered clothing and black hoodie, streaked to the limousine, and slammed the minion back into the vehicle using the car door. He then opened it and tossed in something before lurching to the building's side with arms shielding head. The spectacular explosion, contained by the bullet resistant glass in the limousine, guaranteed no one inside could have survived. The black hooded man opened the blown door and tossed in a second grenade. Instead of huddling against the building, the hooded man walked away. Only the size and weight of the armored limousine kept it from being blown on its side.

Leia smiled. "That had to have hurt."

The older man shooed her away from viewing the dead. "Do not ruin this, child! The police will be here soon. Put on your game-face."

Leia smiled as Wu herded her behind the counter. The police arrived soon after, glancing into the limousine, but hurrying away as the fire department arrived to coat the smoldering vehicle in flame retardant foam before the gas tank exploded. "I think El Muerto called in an anonymous tip."

Only twenty minutes passed before a contingent of two plain clothes detectives and two uniforms entered the shop with an army out on the street. The black man who approached Zhoe and Wu, did so in a tired ambling gate. He showed them his shield.

"I'm Detective Patrick. What happened here?"

"A limousine drove in front of Mr. Wu's place. I have seen it before. It is the new gang moving into the neighborhood. The man trying to take over for the 'Black Souls' and 'Black Disciples' told us his name was Edgar Thurman, but if we did not want to die, we would forget we ever knew his name."

"You seem to know it now," Patrick retorted, surprised anyone on the street would speak with him. He was used to the mostly Chinese storekeepers and residents stonewalling him with no response to any of his questions.

Leia smiled. "It seems I have no need to fear Edgar Thurman any longer. We saw a hooded man throw something into the limousine before it exploded. He wore jeans and black hoodie. The hair sticking out from his hoodie was long and dark, along with a wild looking beard of the same color."

Surprised at the details, Detective Patrick jotted down hurried notes. "Can you tell me anything about his height or weight?"

"He crouched the entire time, including when he threw something in the limousine," Leia answered. "It looked like he was of medium weight."

"Do you think you could pick him out of a lineup?"

"Dressed as he was… sure… I could do it." *I'm never going to*, Leia mumbled to herself.

Detective Patrick handed Leia his card. "If you or Mr. Wu think of anything else, please call me. Thank you for your help."

"Thank you for coming so fast, Sir," Leia replied.

"We…we actually didn't. We believe we were called to the scene by the perp."

Leia pretended shock. "Why…why would the man do that?"

"He may be a psychopathic serial killer. It may be this killer either copies the vigilante, El Muerto, or the real Muerto returned."

"Wow…" Leia turned as if stunned. "He killed many bad people."

"A killer is a killer ma'am. Call me if you think of anything else."

"I will, Detective. Count on it." Leia smiled at Lee Wu after the police detective rejoined the crime scene. "The boys are back in town."

"I saw only one."

"You missed the van picking him up a block away," Leia told Lee. "Muerto did not return alone."

* * *

Nick walked away from the explosion, knowing Edgar and his posse would not be making their usual extortion rounds ever again. Leia kept him apprised of the progress since his last El Muerto visit to Chicago. Her community organized and fought back in secrecy, raiding potential gang and drug dealing hangouts with great success. When Edgar Thurman arrived on the Chicago scene, Leia recognized professional killers. She advised her vigilante force to hold off on any attacks.

Leia left a message at the internet drop link Nick gave her, explaining the situation, along with the surveillance pictures and videos recorded by her vigilante force. After identifying Edgar Thurman's mob, Nick drove to Chicago, using his Rosco Weatherby identity, checking in at The Grand Plaza Hotel on North State Street where he stayed before. He promised Leia to handle the situation, confirming Thurman's mob connections exceeded any typical gangbanger mayhem, petty crime and intimidation. Nick located Thurman's swank, heavily guarded office by capturing one of his street collectors. After showing Dillon Pratt his collection of El Muerto interrogation sessions, Dillon explained the exact location of Thurman's operation. Nick retired Dillon to a landfill.

Investigating Thurman's security procedures and number of guards, Nick decided to make the rounds with Thurman as he terrorized parts of Chicago, formerly terrorized by the 'Black Souls' and 'Black Disciples' gangs, Nick had destroyed. He decided to make a statement, because the murderous gangs of Chicago killed each other and innocent bystanders at a rate alarming to any intelligent person – not so the liberal leftist mayor of the undisputed murder capital of America. Nick's grenades in the limousine proved even mobsters like Thurman could be reached in broad daylight. The limousine Thurman ordered custom made with reinforced steel and windows incorporated special shielding around the fuel tank. Nick had checked. Nick made it into a human stew pot.

A van drove next to him as Nick readied his 1911 for quick action. Johnny was at the wheel. "Hey sailor… want a lift?"

"Crap!" Nick hurried around to the sliding door. Upon opening it, some friends awaited. John Harding, Tommy Sands, Clint and Lynn Dostiene, Casey Lambert and Lucas Blake waved at him from their bench seating. "Oh boy… this is going to be good."

       * * *

"Hi Nick," I greeted him. "Come on in, you pirate."

Nick glared at Gus after entering the van full of people. "I knew if I kept you briefed on this mercy mission, you'd share it for God knows what reason."

Gus made placating gestures at Nick, who hugged Lynn, and shook hands with the rest of us Monsters. "Johnny can tell you, Muerto. They made us an offer we couldn't refuse."

"You mean you couldn't refuse, Payaso," Johnny said as he sped through the streets away from the grenade attack. "They hit Payaso where it hurts, Muerto: his seagoing bones."

"Two ET-MP grenades? Damn, Muerto… who did you make extra sure about," Casey asked.

"Edgar Thurman. He decided to move into a neighborhood fighting back against the gangs. A young woman, leading the vigilante force resisting the gangs, contacted me for help. I inadvertently saved her when I helped Paul's goofy stepdaughter from getting her entire family killed. We became friends. I gave her my card. Enough about what I'm doing. Where do we take this discussion in comfort while you tell my alter ego, Rosco Weatherby, all about this Payaso enthusiasm for sudden adventure?"

"You're the expert on Chicago's killing fields," I joked with him. "You tell us, and I hope it's somewhere you can play and sing."

Nick's face brightened. "The Redhead Piano Bar. It's perfect – always crowded, live music, and they know me there. I confess I played at the 'Redhead' when I shouldn't have – on my Chicago gang bending adjustment. Really… what's this all about, I know you all well enough to know this didn't happen by accident, so why are all of you here? John could have called for me anytime."

"I have a gig here too," I explained. "When I heard what you were doing from Gus, I arranged a meeting with Ian Wolf, who wanted to have a coming fight negotiation at a neutral venue. When I mentioned Chicago, he was all in, saying when and where. He'll be here this afternoon. Can I tell him it's okay to meet at 'The Redhead Piano Bar'?"

"I'm good with that, although this Chicago gig is getting crowded. On the plus side, Lynn could get a knife fight on nearly any corner of the city."

"Very funny, Muerto. I have heard the action can heat up in a heartbeat," Lynn replied. "Tonight, I'd rather dance to anything you want to play."

"I'd like that too, Lynn," Nick admitted. "Are you all staying at the 'Grand'?"

"I flew us in this morning with Johnny and Gus. We did check in at the 'Grand'. Are you still mission enabled?"

"Probably," Nick answered with a shrug. "The mobsters don't do well with adjustments. They tend to lash out. In this case, I made sure to get the kingpin and a few of his worst enforcers. The old cliché about the head of the snake works in this instance. My vigilante contact has the resistance in place to record reaction to the horrible ending of Edgar Thurman. She will warn everyone to stay undercover for a few days too. I know a couple of his lieutenants were not with him. From prior experience, the lieutenants scatter to the wind because they're not getting paid. Unfortunately, Edgar has done this crap before in other cities, riding point when a problem arises. He does so with a crew that's been with him for quite some time. Al Castro and Rollie Patrona worked as enforcers for Edgar first, before becoming two of his most trusted lieutenants. We'll see if this crew takes a hint from what happened with the head snake. If not... well... you all know."

"Doin' right ain't got no end?"

Nick grinned at the Monsters who enjoyed my rehash of his oft told motto. "That is especially correct here, my friends. If the leftover mobsters go to war, I plan to execute their army. I leave no one behind to answer for what I do in an instance like this. If the bad guys want to play payback with my innocents, El Muerto gets the scalpels out until payback is forgotten."

Nick's declaration cut through the humor. "We need your crew on our cruise, Nick. Read us in on this tonight, while the bad guys stew, and we celebrate a rather impressive adjustment in snake behavior. I brought a squad no mobster gang can hang with for even an instant."

"I appreciate that, John, but this is a secret war, where we don't draw in the liberal leftist ass-wipes running this city and state. I initially introduced El Muerto into the mix this past winter to camouflage what my mission was – to save Paul Gilbrech's idiot stepdaughter and family. Her daughter Deirdre wanted me to wipe them all out, much to her mommy's horror. I didn't leave until everyone who ever had a design on that family was dead. I left others, like my friend Leia Zhoe, to fight it out for the community, but with a promise I would help if I could. I can... and I will."

Lynn gripped Nick's hand. "We all brought our Muerto pajamas this trip. We'll tear this fuckin' city apart, if need be, and leave no one alive amongst the thugs to accuse anyone."

Nick covered Lynn's hand with his free one. "Thank you. Rachel knew I had to do this. She understood I couldn't achieve my mission if I hit and ran. The last black op here to protect Paul's stepdaughter took weeks and drew in the Justice Department. Luckily, my two friends, Tim and Grace, led the strike force sent to end the corruption I found and passed on. It still turned into a blood bath at the end but left me with a cover and way out. If I'm hearing you right, this black op you Monsters have on the horizon will be going down quickly. I'm interested. Talk to me tonight. Perhaps I can do enough damage here to send the mobsters into hiding for a couple months. I can come back and finish covering for my fledgling vigilante force after we complete your black op."

"Fair enough," I replied, waving off Lucas's temptation to jump in with something insulting, and probably funny. "I see in your face you want some time to mull this over until we meet tonight. Until then, we'll stay clear of you. If nothing else, watching you rock the house tonight at the 'Redhead' will be worth the trip here. Thanks for the consult, brother."

"Anytime, John. Our crews are bonded now. I appreciate you giving me a chance to think this through. I'll be in contact with Leia shortly. She has her spies in all the right places. I can make better judgements once she gives me on site intel. I did see the demo of who really straightens your Hard Case ass into an at attention mode instantly. I'm glad I wasn't with you when Ahab put on his stripes again. I would have been in lockstep with you the moment I heard 'Freeze maggots'. It's damn disturbing."

"Yeah… brother… it is."

Johnny stopped near Nick's SUV. Nick exited, carrying his beard and wig in a bag. He didn't get two steps before, 'Freeze maggot!' shot out of our van interior and froze Nick like a first day boot-camp. There would have been more humorous appreciation besides that of Johnny, Gus, Tommy, Lucas and Lynn; but Clint, Casey, and I jumped with him. Damn it!

* * *

The Redhead Piano Bar has a dress code – business casual – no hoodies, t-shirts, sunglasses, flip-flops, or underwear showing. When we Monsters arrived, we dressed for a night of entertainment and a business meeting. In other words, we dressed in suits, and Lynn wore the dress Clint liked from our FBI sting operation to get Princess Gumby. The bar has an awning type entryway out to the sidewalk. A gang of five hoodies wearing sunglasses, argued with the man in a suit, blocking their entry. They wore their pants with attached underwear showing, even below their hoodies. They not only blocked our way inside, they were blocking other patrons. Cheers sounded as a couple of police officers arrived.

The lead hoodie showed outrage at the sight of police. "What you call Five-0 on us for? This racist dress code is bullshit!"

The officer in the lead was black, a little over six feet tall, and lean, probably in his late twenties. His woman partner, looked a bit older, Latino, and only an inch or two shorter than her partner.

"Move along," the first officer told them. "There are tons of bars in the Lakeview area. Go find one that likes looking at your underwear. I come here all the time. Go change, and they will let you right in."

"Oh good... we get the word from a 'house negro'. I think I saw your likeness on a lawn jockey. Maybe-"

I led our group waiting to go in, so I blocked their view accidentally in the narrow space. I saw the two hoodies, slightly to the rear of the second officer, begin slipping something bad down from under their loose tops. "Ambush!"

I rushed forward, bull-rushing the two accessing weapons, smashing them to the sidewalk. Uzis clattered next to them as I added mallet fist strikes to their heads. Clint, Casey, and Lynn followed my lead, drawing weapons to cover the other three hoodies. Lucas drew his while watching the street and people behind us. Tommy wisely slipped off to the side. Some of them ran for it. They were there for entertainment, not combat. I kicked the Uzis away from my two writhing hoodies, freeing my FBI identification for the stunned police officers. My Monsters did the same, with Lynn taking charge.

"FBI Special Agent Lynn Dostiene. Sorry about jetting into this without warning. Agent Harding spotted the ambush. We can help you restrain these thugs."

"Thank...thank you," the woman officer bent down toward the weapons on the sidewalk. "They're Uzis, Bill! Shit! This is an ambush."

"I'm Bill Raithman, and this is my partner, Willa Santora. We appreciate your help. Thanks for saving our damn lives."

The big mouth that did all the talking tried a fast draw. Clint pistol whipped him, bloody and unconscious to the sidewalk. The Glock he cleared slipped from his twitching hand. That was enough of this touchy-feely crap. Casey and I body slammed the two still standing and ripped their hoodies off. Clint did the same to his unconscious prisoner, while the officers stripped off the tops from the two men I bludgeoned. We collected quite the assortment of weapons. By then three more squad cars arrived, spilling out a half dozen more officers to handcuff and arrest. I spotted Nick grinning at us from the crowd. He didn't approach. So much for our being able to help him.

"Good Lord, it's a miracle your agents were here," Santora said. "Are you on a case or something?"

"No," Lynn replied. "We needed to refuel on the way to the West Coast. We're having a few things checked out on our plane. A friend told us how wonderful 'The Redhead Piano Bar' was, so we decided to give it a try. We stopped here for another reason. In an hour, Agent Harding will be meeting with Ian Wolf to negotiate defending his UFC Heavyweight title."

"I knew I recognized you, Hard Case. I love it when you do the Dark Lord in the octagon! Can we get a formal statement from you to corroborate our report," Raithman asked.

"Sure," I answered. "We'll do whatever you need us to do."

What they needed and wanted was a photo shoot, after loading the prisoners in the squad cars. I posed with all the police and bar customers waiting to get in 'The Redhead'. Raithman gave Lynn his card so we would know where to file our reports. A Lieutenant Anders arrived on scene to learn what happened and to interrupt our small celebration of life.

"What the hell happened here, Bill?"

"Those BLM thugs getting driven away ambushed me and Willa." He pointed to the confiscated weapons, now bagged for transport. "These FBI agents planned a night in 'The Redhead', waiting in line. They saved our lives."

Anders shook hands with all of us, pleased with what he heard, but angry as hell at yet another ambush of the 'Blue'. After they left, the bar manager welcomed us all in personally. "Damn… you all picked a bad night. We may need to do a canned karaoke music night. My piano player has the flu."

Lynn pulled him aside as the bar patrons streamed by. "We have a friend here on the down/low. He's a professional musician and singer who works with the FBI and Department of Justice. He's working undercover. We hoped to get him a chance to play tonight."

The manager looked skeptical. "Okay... I'd do anything for your team tonight, especially if I can get some pictures of Hard Case posing in the bar with us. Is your friend any good?"

"I'll send him over to your piano. You'll be able to see for yourself." Lynn gestured at Nick, and then pointed at the piano.

Nick took the hint and trekked to the piano. In an instant, Nick owned the joint with a gripping rendition of 'Blood, Sweat, and Tears' song 'And When I Die'. His pounding keyboard playing and singing won the crowd into singing along. He followed it with 'Lucretia Mac Evil' as the manager grinned in wonder.

"My God... I'll make a fortune tonight. Tell him he can play as long as he wants, whenever he wants."

"Will do," Lynn replied. The manager walked away clapping his hands with the crowd. "Well... that was a hell of a start to the evening. From now on, you're behind us in any line, Cheese. We hardly got a taste."

"Fine by me."

"Those BLM assholes were going to hose down the police and any civilians getting in their way," Lucas said. "They planned to get away in the chaos. I saw Nick searching for a getaway vehicle. He signaled me there wasn't one. I wish he'd forget about Chicago. I'm glad Johnny and Gus won't be here for another half hour. They figured the three of them together long enough could screw Nick's chances of keeping this war secret."

"Wolf won't be here for a while either," Tommy said. "I don't know about you bunch, but I could use a drink."

"Amen to that, brother." I heard Nick begin his specialty starter, 'House of the Rising Sun'. "I'll get a Bud and Beam for you, Clint, and a white zin for Lynn. Go dance. We'll stay away from the stools right in front of the piano."

"Thanks, Cheese," Lynn said, tugging Clint to the instantly crowded dance floor.

The manager waved us over to a table he had brought out for us. "Will this be big enough for your business meeting, John?"

"It sure will. My agent and manager, Tommy Sands, negotiates with me. My other FBI agent friends will adjourn to the bar. Thank you for this."

"Can I get a picture of me and you at the bar together?"

"I'll take the picture," Tommy accepted the manager's camera phone.

The manager and I posed at the bar with customers and bartenders photobombing us through the series. We all paused from our entertaining pursuit as Nick launched into a well-recognized classic, 'Nessun Dorma', in Italian no less. Good God Almighty... you could have heard a pin drop as Nick sang it in true Andrea Bocelli style. He throttled that piano into making all the base sounds in addition to the melody. At the end, Lynn and Clint went into a torrid embrace, before applauding like mad, tears streaming down Lynn's face. The standing ovation carried on so long, it stunned Nick. Instead of continuing, he stood and bowed.

"You have done a magical thing bringing your friend with you tonight to play, John. That was wondrous. Thank you for the pictures and your friend, Nick."

Uh oh. "I didn't tell you his name was Nick."

The manager smiled. "I have read every novel Nick McCarty has written. I recognized him from his book jacket pictures immediately. I shall not mention it again. After all this ends tonight, may I get a picture with him. I promise not to frame it in the bar for a few weeks."

"I'll ask him. Thank you for your understanding."

The manager returned to his duties as Nick performed some more slow tunes, in a Country Western fashion: 'When I Loved Her', 'Lovin' Her was Easier', and 'Help Me Make it Through the Night'. Stringing those three Kris Kristofferson songs together nearly wiped Lynn out. She clung onto Clint through them as if he were the main mast in a hailstorm. Nick ended the set with 'Sunday Morning Coming Down'.

He waved and shined like a new penny in its element as he received another standing ovation before Lynn intercepted him after the set. Not for the first time did I wonder about my brother-in-arms. I knew the story about his music mentor on a high-priced assassination, who was killed by a thug one night before Nick returned from his Paris assassination gig. Nick didn't talk about how the thug spent his final hours, when Muerto tortured and killed his way through town until he found out who did it. I would imagine it rivaled a few deaths by our own Cruella Deville.

Clint and Lynn escorted the music man to our table. I had the Bud and Beam brothers waiting for him and Clint, along with a white zin for Lynn. I felt like I was compromising his mission with my crew forcing him in with us.

"Man... I wish Dev and Jess were here," Nick said, after toasting with all of us and taking a long swallow of his Bud brother. "I feel in the mood to do everything tonight, including a nice wake for that bastard, Tolo Whitt. I'm doing 'Montego Bay' and 'The Banana Boat Song' anyway in honor of 'The Rain Maker' and my MC Hammer partner, Devon Constantine and Jesse Brown."

We all toasted once again. Lucas had been quiet, but he spoke in a quiet tone. "You are possibly the biggest mystery I have ever run across, Nick. God Bless you son. You can sure touch this Drill Sergeant badass right down to his toes with your music. Can you play 'It's a Wonderful World' like Louis?"

"I sure can, Top. I feel this night will be a special one. I wish all our people were here. Since they're not... I will need to do a repeat performance on the Ranger. My contact, Leia, told me Thurman's army headed for the hills. They didn't trust payment dealing with a force using grenades. His two lieutenants stayed though, planning to build an army from the streets. I need to find out who would be paying for something like that. It's all in control though for now. Do all the prep work. I already had words with Johnny and Gus. They left after my set to get home and find out how many of our dependents want to take a ride on the wild side."

"I wish we could have stayed with you to finish this."

Nick chuckled. "You probably cast a spotlight on all of us, but you Monsters saved a lot of lives. The damn BLM doesn't care what color skin wears the 'Blue'. That ambush was well done. They picked a bar they knew had a dress code. They dressed to break all the rules, played the race card to the hilt until the police arrived, then prepared to ambush the 'Blue' and kill as many civilians as need be to get away. I wish Lynn could get one of those guys for interrogation."

"We'll have all their names," Lynn replied. "Some ACLU or BLM lawyer will find a way to put the murderous bastards on the street again. We'll collect them quietly. I'll learn who funded and ordered their ambush."

"Count me in if you get word while I'm still here in Chicago," Nick replied.

"Your secret identity may be disappearing." I told him about the manager.

"I admit I've gotten careless. I should be wearing at least a slight disguise everywhere I go. Until I leave this trip behind, I will be extremely careful." Nick glanced at the entrance. "I think I see your possible UFC opponent. He's nearly as big as Tolo Whitt."

"We all know how that worked out for Tolo," Clint quipped. "Come with us to the bar so John and Tommy can discuss business. You need a few more minutes rest before your next set."

"Absolutely. Good luck with the negotiations. Can you check my bag with the barkeep, Case?"

"Sure." Casey took Nick's bag with him while Nick followed with their drinks.

Tommy stayed next to me. We stood to greet Ian Wolf. His companions, three guys in dark suits with 'wise-guy' stapled onto their features, glanced professionally at the 'Redhead Bar's' clientele. They seemed annoyed at the lights, probably because they were stopped at the door and told to take off their sunglasses. They paused in front of our table in formation.

"Ian? I'm John Harding. This is my agent and manager, Tommy Sands. He represents Alexi Fiialkov's UFC interests too."

"Good meeting you," Tommy said, extending his hand. It was ignored.

Wolf and his group sat down across from us.

"Please join us." My small play on words drew some chuckles from my crew at the bar. Tommy and I sat down. We were proficient at any pretense known to man. We never got offended.

"This is my manager, Donny Callan." Wolf gestured at the man next to him. "We didn't come here to be friends."

"Cordial would be nice. Since you're not, let's get to it," Tommy aced him. "What do you have in mind for a fight date, Mr. Callan?"

"We have a proposal accepted from both the UFC and MGM Grand for a heavyweight championship bout in four months," Callan replied.

Tommy glanced at me and I nodded. "The date is agreeable to us."

"We want a sixty/forty split. My fighter gets sixty."

Okay… now that was funny. Tommy and I, along with everyone listening in at the bar, enjoyed the split offer immensely. It was only after maybe twenty seconds we realized Callan was serious. Tommy shook his head.

"Tell me something. Did Ian fracture his head instead of his wrist before the Logan fight? I'm not sure whether you heard or not, but John Harding is the UFC Heavyweight Champion. You're not. I'll be generous. Your offer gave us a good laugh. You could have offered a fifty-five/forty-five split with your fighter getting forty-five. I would have turned it down and offered Ian thirty-five. We would have settled on Ian getting forty. Our split negotiation is done. Take forty or walk."

Tommy handled it very politely in my estimation, especially after the throwaway offer they made. Wolf got this stunned look on his face.

"I made that fight with you and Logan, Harding. My buildup sold out all venues. You merely collected a huge payday on my hard work."

I grinned at Tommy. "You need to fight and win the fight you contract for, Ian. I didn't want to fight Logan, for all the reasons mixing boxing and UFC can be damn dangerous. The UFC offered to clean my slate with them, so we gambled and took the Logan fight as a replacement for you and your fractured wrist."

"You're delusional if you think John will fight with you getting sixty on the split," Tommy explained. "John gets sixty. Take it or walk – simple as that."

"I will talk this over with Alexi," Callan stated.

Tommy took out his iPhone, hit Alexi's contact number, and answered Fiialkov's greeting with his own before explaining what was happening. Tommy smiled as Alexi laughed loudly enough to be heard by both Callan and Wolf. "Hand…hand your phone to this poser, Tommy."

"Alexi wants to speak with you." Tommy handed Callan the phone.

After a short burst of staccato words, Callan made as if to toss the phone. I plucked it out of his hand. "No damaging our equipment, Callan."

"Fine. We will agree to this travesty under one condition: the knife-hand strike is out."

"So that's what this sixty garbage was about. You wanted to negotiate the knife-hand strike out of the fight with the split ploy - not going to work," Tommy told him. "It's legal in the UFC. If you don't like it, become a boxer."

I could tell Tommy's immediate dismissal of their terms pissed off both men. I was beginning to wonder why the hell they even came here. I saw Nick heading to the piano to thunderous applause, which spooked the Wolf party at first.

"An acquaintance of mine filled in for the regular entertainment. Tommy told you the terms. If you're agreeable, Alexi will have the contract drawn up after speaking with the UFC and MGM Grand." As I finished my statement, I chuckled. Nick started his set with the old Simon and Garfunkel tune 'The Boxer'. I waved at him.

"Pay attention, pug," Callan ordered me. "We're not done here yet."

"I may be a pug, but I'm the UFC Heavyweight Champion and Wolf ain't. If Wolf wants a crack at taking my belt, you better agree to terms and forget all your other ridiculous bullshit."

Tommy grinned. "What he said."

Callan began standing in a huff but was pulled back down by the man next to him we thought was a bodyguard. "Sit down, Donny. I'm Tito Flores. My partners and I manage Ian. Your win against Carl Logan impressed us. We wanted to get a preview of

Logan's moves in the Octagon against you with UFC rules. We figured you would give him a good battle before being knocked out. Instead... we got a detailed look at you dominating Boxing's heavyweight champion."

"That was because Logan had to fight by UFC rules," I replied. "He would have probably cleaned my clock in a boxing ring. It's nice meeting you, Mr. Flores. The terms remain the same. I hate to use clichéd terms like 'take it or leave it'... but take it or leave it."

To his credit, Flores simply smiled. "I could make it worth your while to let us ban the knife-hand strike. What would you say to a hundred thousand dollars?"

"John doesn't do that," Tommy said. "We have money. You could make it a million and John would still turn you down. Please... either agree to the fight as we've stated or leave and allow us to enjoy the music."

"Remember the incident between Tonya Harding and Nancy Kerrigan?"

Tito was getting interesting. "First of all, Tonya's not related. Yeah, I remember Tonya's ex-husband hired a thug to baton strike Kerrigan's leg. Sordid story, Tito. What does it have to do with me, other than Tonya's last name?"

"I was simply pointing out the fact you never know what can happen in sports. I've heard you live a dangerous life outside of the UFC. You're an Oaktown Cartel enforcer. I saw your blindfold match recently. It proves you're in a position where anything may happen to you, ending in a debilitating injury. You take many chances."

Before we could continue this eerie discussion, Lucas approached the table and he was not happy. "I heard your little story. Let me tell you another one. If anything 'debilitating' happens to John, I will hunt your ass down. If you want a war, you'll get one. I advise you to play this straight. Make some money on the fight, enjoy Las Vegas, and get your fighter ready to win. Oaktown protects its own."

Tito knew killers. He looked at Lucas, with Clint, Casey, and Lynn behind him, smiling like sharks passing a school of tuna. He stood, Wolf and friends stood with him. "Very well said, Sir. I will take your advice. We agree to your terms, Mr. Sands. Please let Alexi know. Good evening."

Just like that, negotiations ended. Wolf and Callan followed Tito out like puppy dogs on a short leash. "Well... I don't think that could have been any stranger. Thanks, Pappy. I was wondering how to respond. I believe you stated our position perfectly. On the funny side, Tito used Tonya Harding in his parable."

"She's your mom, isn't she, Cheese."

"Very funny, Crue."

Nick began playing the first strains of 'It's a Wonderful World'. He lengthened the opening to give Clint and Lynn a chance to get on the dance floor. Lucas and Casey brought Tommy and I the Bud and Beam brothers. We toasted quietly as Nick launched into a very credible rendition of Louis Armstrong's classic. Nick followed with some other big Armstrong hits, 'Moon River' and 'A Kiss to Build a Dream on'. Then, it was on to Jamaica as the music man did 'Montego Bay' and 'The Banana Boat Song'. Oh my... the crowd did the 'day-o' loud and proud. He finished the set with the theme from the 'Titanic' movie and 'The Bodyguard' – 'My Heart Will Go On' and 'I Will Always Love You', followed by his jazzed version of 'Layla'. The groan when he walked to our table echoed around the room. We had the brothers waiting for him.

"Good Lord Almighty," Lucas exclaimed, hugging his protégé. "I'm goin' back home and wear my 'Muerto Pajamas' for a week straight. I'll send you pictures."

"Please don't."

Oh boy, we were all howling after that exchange. Nothing great and good ever goes on without the insertion of bad. Three guys in suits and attitudes made their way to our table. I figured they were there to compliment Nick on his entertainment. Wrong.

The first slimy looking guy with no sense pointed at Nick with a look of drunk distaste. "Man... you suck! What was all that crap? You need to be playin' in some elevator in Hoboken."

Nick cracked up at that line. His genuine enjoyment of the retard's ace made the rest of us laugh with him. "Hoboken... huh? Never played there, partner. What would you like to hear?"

"Heavy metal, ass-wipe!"

Nick stood, motioning the Monsters down only just in time. We were inebriated to a small extent, and tonight, Nick reminded us of why we love this cold-blooded assassin so much. He was unique in ways only us Monsters could comprehend. We understood the killer inside him. We understood the creative war raging in his head to play music, write novels, and build civilizations like our 'City of Hope' in the Sand. We waited like wolves in a pack.

"I don't do 'Heavy Metal'. I like a few things I've heard, but I can't play them on a piano." Nick reasoned with them in a level voice. "This bar actually advertises 'oldies' as their musical fare. Why would you three come to a bar where they tell you straight off your choice in music doesn't get played here?"

The slimy guy expressed humor like that character role Richard Widmark did in the old movie 'Kiss of Death' - a hideous laugh without emotion. It would have been creepy to normal folks. We Monsters just enjoyed the playacting. Yeah... as I felt the killer begin to surface, I wished I would have ordered snacks from the bar. I envisioned ripping 'slimy's' throat out. Lynn, of all people, moved to put an arm around my shoulder. She bent down to whisper.

"Don't Cheese! Let Muerto handle this. Clint and I want to dance some more."

I glanced up at her with understanding between killers. "I want some more music and dance too, Crue."

Slimy gestured at the rest of us, which definitely piqued our interest. "You think these folks can shield you, huh?"

Nick leaned forward with hands on the table. "They could... ass-wipe... but I don't need them to shield me from you. I see you don't like me. Let's go outside the bar alone. You can fix my attitude all by yourself. Tell your people though, to stay in the bar. If they follow you out, I can't protect them. Want to play... or not?"

Slimy had no sense. "Let's rock and roll outside."

"That's what I wanted to hear." Nick turned to us. Lucas, Casey and Lynn were already moving around the three idiots. "It's a trap, John. Can you entertain these three while I investigate this sudden music critique?"

"Absolutely." My Monsters filled three of our chairs with the suits, who suddenly weren't as drunk as they appeared before.

Lucas and Casey forced their two charges down painfully by their necks until they stopped struggling. Lynn entertained the one who had spoken with Nick, using the tip of her knife to caress his Adam's Apple. "Sit quietly, moron, or I take a slice of pie."

Clint dropped into a seat opposite the three, with a coat held over his Colt .45 with only the large barrel hole showing. "You three lucked out being the ones sent in here."

Nick briefly spoke with the manager, his welcoming smile disappearing with Nick's first words. He gestured Nick into the back of the bar.

I leaned forward. "Sit quietly. I can tell you boys haven't been drinking. Would you like to explain what you're doing here and who sent you?"

"You people don't know who you're dealing with," the guy Lucas held spoke for the first time. "It would be best if you and your crew get the hell out of Chicago. We saw what you all did earlier."

"So, you three knew the ambush would happen when it did?"

"We had other business, but Edgar Thurman's reach extends all over Chicago."

Lynn chuckled. "You mean the mobster that got blown up into red slime?"

"Edgar's lieutenants are in charge now," the guy under Lynn's relaxed knife muttered. "They know the piano guy is El Muerto. He'll pay for what he did."

I leaned back in my chair. "Hold that thought."

* * *

"Those dimwits should have coaxed Weatherby out here by now, Al."

"Give them a chance. They can't get the other crew involved, Weatherby's with. You saw that bunch smash down our recruits. If not for them, Weatherby would have been caught in the police ambush. Our guys knew to spray him in the crowd after the ambush. It was a first-class plan to get the cops thinking the usual Chicago street wars and BLM ambush, all tied into social justice crap. We know now Weatherby did the deed on Edgar. One of tonight's BLM gangbangers gave the lawyer we sent the message they spotted Weatherby looking for a driver before he got slammed. Lucky thing we planned to have the 'bangers split up and escape in the chaos. We'll give our guys ten more minutes. Relax, Rollie."

"I don't like us doing the dirty work again. We told Edgar to stay the hell off the streets until the empire got built. He screwed himself. Give me a smoke."

Rollie handed Al a cigarette and lighter. "I thought you quit."

"I did until the boss got blown up with a grenade."

"I hear ya'. Roll down the window though a little."

Al lit his cigarette and rolled down the window a quarter of the way as he exhaled a plume of smoke. Something rolled over the open upper glass edge, hit his leg and came to rest at his feet. "Oh shit!"

The explosion blew the unreinforced car on its side.

* * *

"I need to go out the back for a while. I'm a little light headed, Ernie."

Ernie Morgan's smile vanished. "Oh God... I hope you can return to play."

Nick patted his shoulder as they journeyed out the back way. "I need some fresh air, Ernie. I'll be back. I'm having a great time. I need to clear my head... that's all."

"Right through that door," Ernie pointed the way. "There's a street exit around to your left. Don't close anything. Otherwise, you'll need to return through the front."

"Thanks."

Nick threaded his way to the street without notice. He moved up the street to his right, finding a darkened spot near the buildings to search for a sign of foul play. Nick spotted the two-man team in a late model Chevrolet Impala only a hundred feet from the entrance to 'The Redhead Piano Bar', but across the street. Nick jogged down the block, circling after crossing the street. When he reached the Impala, Nick crouched down next to it, listening to the voices inside, while sitting with his head down and knees up, pretending to be wasted. The street was relatively devoid of traffic across from the 'Redhead'. When he heard Rollie tell Al to crack a window, Nick grinned and reached into his jacket for an ET-MP grenade. He looked at it with respect.

"Never leave home without it." Nick rolled the grenade in a split second after Al rolled his window down, noting there would be no innocent bystanders on this side of the street. Nick left in a hurry, making sure he didn't become one. He jogged down the block during the explosion with his windbreaker hood up. After crossing the street, Nick pulled off his hood and jogged to the door for the rear entry to the bar. With the utmost use of explosion panic, he slipped inside the bar without anyone other than the Monsters noting his arrival. In seconds, he was at the keyboard. Motown oldies made people forget the explosion.

Chapter Four

Hell on Wheels

I didn't see any further need to detain the minions of a dead mobster. "Give me everything out of your pockets. I want to see unlocked cell-phones, driver's licenses, and everything else of a personal nature."

They relinquished their belongings as ordered. I checked each one before scanning it for future listing.

"What was... that explosion? It...it rocked the bar."

"Let's see. You're Aron. Well... since I have your pictures and IDs for our database, you three can go and sin no more. If anything weird happens in the city, the first thing we'll do is pluck you three from the street."

Lucas sat next to me, watching the three leave, avoiding glances, glares, or any form of visual recognition when passing Nick. "The prick stalked out the back, used a grenade on the bad guys, and slipped behind the piano for another set before the sound stopped reverberating between the buildings."

"Yep. I bet he even wiped his feet before reentering the bar."

Casey delivered fresh drinks. They were most welcome. Clint and Lynn danced to Nick's classic style of 'I Heard It Through the Grapevine', 'Do You Love Me', and 'Reach Out, I'll Be There'. When Nick launched into his Barry White repertoire, complete with silky voice, the customers had to dance at their tables.

"Muerto is scary good," Casey said. "I think the only thing in danger here is his secret war. I wonder who he aced out there."

"He's probably finishing the set, so we may find out shortly," I replied. "The police ducked in here for a few moments, looked around at the enthralled audience, and left. I'm thinking as the night winds down, Muerto will need to ghost out the back. I bet he left them with a real mystery to solve."

Nick finished with 'Respect' and stood to a bar of groans, waving his thanks. Women tried to waylay him along the way while we watched the 'Silver Tongued Devil' laugh and defuse every advance until reaching our table. Casey brought him an ice-cold Bud but no Beam brother. Clint and Lynn only then managed to thread their way to our table, their drinks waiting for them.

We toasted once again to the music man, who we now awaited news from. He wasted no time after guzzling down half of his Bud brother. "Okay then, here's the deal. The occupants of an Impala across the way awaited my being tricked outside by the dopey music critic with MP10s. I'm speculating, but I think the guy wanting a fight was to lead me out to the narrow, covered awning entry passage and to the right of the restaurant entrance. He would then lead the way ten or twenty feet further. He runs. I get sprayed and no one is the wiser. I listened by their car. They worked for Edgar Thurman – the two lieutenants acting as his dual seconds. Those guys you took care of earlier were meant to ambush the police as a secondary cover. Their main gig was to spray the crowd while escaping, nailing me in the process."

"Well damn, Muerto," Lynn replied, as Nick quenched his thirst. "Maybe it's time for all of us to leave this PC hellhole. The bad guys have an arsenal and the citizens have nada!"

"The guys we spoke with only knew your Weatherby identity," I told him. "If the Thurman lieutenants know your Weatherby identity, they know where you are staying."

Nick grinned. "No, they don't. I checked out of there today. I knew I was overstaying my Grand Plaza visit. Al and Rollie had one of their street urchins watching my hotel. I have only the light bag I brought with me here. My SUV's parked at the airport long term parking. I think I made an error in getting into the van with you guys after I handled Thurman. I knew if I refused to get in, Captain 'Queeg' Nason would have jumped out and made a scene like we were back in our Pacific Grove whistle stop. That's where they picked up my trail. I'm glad I sent my two interlopers home. It appears I will need to make an incognito escape to my new hotel, 'The Holiday Inn Express' only a few minutes away. I had Cala back home make the reservations prepaid for me under her name. They know I'll be checking in late."

"This is mostly our fault," I told him. "Why not leave now. You handled the two hangers on."

"I can't until I make sure there's no blow back on Leia and her dad."

"How the hell do you make sure of that," Lynn asked.

Nick drained his Bud. "I'll go to work at their shop for a few days as a cleaning guy. I speak Mandarin. If the coast looks clear, I'll head to the airport, pick up my SUV and leave for home."

"One more set before you sneak out, Muerto."

"Okay, Lynn… name your poison. What would you like to dance to?"

"Clint and I discussed the list: 'Devil or Angel', 'Summertime', 'California Dreaming', 'Duke of Earl', and 'Proud Mary'."

"Oh my. I need another beer before that set."

Clint obliged. Ernie, the manager came over to check on his cash cow. He whispered near Nick's ear. "Are you okay to play, Mr. McCarty?"

"One more set, Ernie. Then I need to go. Thanks for keeping my novelist identity to yourself." Nick gave him what looked like a handful of hundreds.

Ernie was stunned. "I should be paying you."

"Don't worry about it. My newest novel, 'Hell Zone', is selling like hotcakes. I'll get started on my next set in a few minutes."

"Start whenever you want." Ernie walked away a happy man.

Nick finished his beer with a sigh of satisfaction. "I wonder how many patrol cars are outside. Al and Rollie set the ambush down the block slightly and across the street. I'm hoping when I do get out of here, they won't be looking for anyone exiting the bar."

"We'll cover for you. After you get situated outside the bar at the side entrance, we'll walk over to anyone there behind the crime scene tape. I'll ask for the officer in charge. When the officer assigned the case confronts us, we'll present our IDs. We'll have everyone's attention for you to slip out without being seen."

"Thanks, John. That sounds perfect. I'll go do my final set and then adjourn out the back. I will be in touch."

Nick returned to the piano. Thunderous applause followed. He did Lynn and Clint's musical picks in order, not rushing anything. Nick added his rendition of 'Piano Man', engaging every voice in the bar to sing along. He ended the set with 'Goodnight My Love'. The dancers mobbed him as he walked through to the back where Earnie escorted him through to the rear.

Lynn and Clint reached our table after a considerable time working their way through the crowd. I noticed very few of the bar's customers even peeked outside after the explosion. Better to dance when you can, in a city breaking all records for homicides, with the most stringent gun laws in the nation and citizens at risk – their rights to defend themselves ripped away by a city government of politically correct morons.

"We need to kidnap Muerto," Lynn stated. "We'll gather his kids, wife and dog later."

Everyone at the table shunned her, including Clint. "How many of us do you think would survive a play like that, my love?"

Lynn was too busy enjoying the in-sync shunning to answer.

    * * *

The Monsters and I approached the huge yellow taped crime scene with care. We drew the attention of everyone in law enforcement there. We stopped near two of the officers with our FBI credentials held in plain view. I asked to speak with the officer in charge of the scene.

"Wait here, Sir." The officer hurried into the middle of a chaotic crime scene, returning with a harried looking woman detective.

She examined our IDs, while we drew the attention of all eyes. We were an impressive looking bunch of killers, well-dressed, with a huge bridge troll fronting the group. "I'm Detective Kelly Winslow. Did someone from downtown call in the FBI, Agent Harding?"

"No, Detective. My associates and I were inside 'The Redhead Piano Bar' across the street when the explosion happened. We offer our assistance if you want it."

"Does your team have any expertise in explosives or car bombs?" Winslow decided to ask pertinent questions I didn't expect.

"We have extensive expertise in all manner of explosive charges. Four of us have done multiple tours in Iraq and Afghanistan. We are a special operations team."

"Then yes, I would like you to take a look at this mess. Follow me."

Lynn whispered to Clint, who chuckled, and grasped her hand for a moment. She remained at the taped perimeter. I glanced at Clint questioningly while following Winslow.

"Lynn just bought those shoes she wore," Clint answered my unasked question.

We all stifled amusement with difficulty as Winslow gathered and passed out high intensity mini-lights. They can brighten areas like daylight, or sharply highlight pinpointed targets of interest. Using such lights focuses the attention of an inspector. We took them and examined the crime scene with professional thoroughness. I noticed Nick decided to choose a concussive blast to help prevent fragments from causing a fuel tank eruption with resulting fire. The fire department was on hand and had foamed extensively to make the scene safe. We finished our inspection. Winslow awaited our findings with a suit standing near her - well groomed, arrogant, with a condescending aura about him. I smelled Chicago political stench. The twerp walked into my airspace.

"You talk to me from now on, Harding."

I backed him out of my face with a small hand shiver that nearly put him on his back. "I'm not sure who you think I am, but I don't take orders from you. If you wish to speak with me, stay out of my face. Who are you, and why should I care?"

"How dare you! I'm Alderman Briston Harley. This is my district. Never lay a hand on me again, you racist cracker!"

Lucas shot forward, gripped Harley's suit front and lifted Briston from the street, shaking him. "This man is a Recon Marine, as I am. He's my brother. Call my brother a racist cracker, or any other name, and I will bitch slap you until you cry! Do you understand me, Maggot?"

The other law enforcement officers and detectives didn't move during Lucas's attitude adjustment. I saw a few smiles, including Detective Winslow's, which told me everything I needed to know about Harley.

Although Harley could barely breathe, he managed a jerky nod of acknowledgement. Lucas tossed him on his ass. "Don't forget what I said."

While Harley gasped and skittered backwards away from us, we Monsters conferred, comparing what we'd seen and concurring. I then turned to Winslow. "We believe an ET-MP grenade was used. From the damaged interior with apparent ballooning effect, we're in agreement as to the cause."

"Interesting. We figured some kind of IED."

"If an IED had been used, the damage would have been extensive outside the vehicle with probable damage to the building near the car," I explained. "If an older style M67 fragmentation grenade had been used, the explosive fragmented charge should have pierced the vehicle's interior, spraying outward. The perpetrator used an ET-MP grenade, which can either be used in fragmentation or concussive mode. The grenade, set in concussive mode, killed the vehicle's passenger and driver, while shattering glass in an outward direction. The blast caused a slight ballooning of the interior from the concussive force. The victims were not lacerated as an M67 grenade would have done. Also, I'm sure you noticed the MP10 submachine guns in the car. It appears these men were not here innocently."

"I recorded your report, if that's okay," Winslow replied.

"I don't mind a bit. I hope it helps."

"It confirms my suspicion a gangland nemesis calling himself El Muerto has returned," Winslow stated. "Grenades are his specialty."

"Gangland nemesis?" I attained an award-winning look of confusion.

"He wiped out two gangs terrorizing their area neighborhoods, sending gangs into hiding all over the city. The city requested a Department of Justice investigation to get Muerto, but instead they nailed a corrupt Alderman. We're caught in the middle. Your report helps me make an informed case-"

"Why are you speaking with this man?" Harley approached carefully after forcing a couple of police officers to front for him. "You're black, Winslow! Why would you be siding with this..." Harley took one look at Lucas and altered course. "This interloper."

"Agent Harding leads an FBI special unit. They are explosives experts, Alderman. I asked for their help. They've already confirmed this incident may be linked to a return of El Muerto."

The stricken look Alderman Harley featured as he glanced furtively at the buildings around the scene, nearly caused the Monsters to lose their composure. Nick made quite an impression amongst the political hierarchy in the city. Harley began backing away from the scene. "You...you call me if there is any change Winslow."

Harley scurried off in a zig-zag pattern, which caused Winslow to turn away from us with her hand over mouth in stifled amusement. We Monsters enjoyed the show, as did many of the police officers. Winslow turned toward us again.

"Sor...sorry, but Harley and many of the other politicos in the city think it was Muerto who gave the Feds evidence leading to the ouster and convictions of Alderman Spike Kale and Alderwoman Meya Atwar. I doubt I need tell you how corrupt Chicago's political structure is. Thank you all for your help. I appreciate it. Agent Blake... that was entertainment."

"My pleasure," Lucas replied. "If we investigated a bit on the sly, would you be interested in Harley wearing an orange jumpsuit?"

"In a heartbeat. The US Marshal's service sent a US Marshal Nick McCarty here with their special investigations group. We found out he's a bestselling author and consults with the FBI and CIA. He blew away two gangbangers without blinking an eye, inside a restaurant, after the arrest of Alderman Kale. Do you know him?"

There was no ducking this question. "Yes, we do. We have handled a number of cases with him. He is a motivated and passionate law enforcement agent."

"Yes... he is. If you do get the Department of Justice involved, please send him back with whatever team returns for Harley, if you find anything incriminating about the Alderman that will stick in court. Nothing the lawyers could do fazed McCarty at all. Kale hiring goons to kill a federal marshal will get him life in prison."

"We'll make the recommendation," I promised, handing her my FBI card. "Goodnight, Detective. We're heading to our base on the West Coast tomorrow. Call me if you need confirmation on what I told you about this attack."

Winslow gave me her card. "Call me directly if you get anything on Harley. I know a guy in the State Attorney General's Office, DA Lancaster, who can help with the legal proceedings."

"We'll try and make it happen."

"It appears not everyone is corrupt in this city of death," Lucas said, while we were walking away.

"True, but we better be careful about involving Nick in anything else here. If we get stuff on Harley, we can maybe come back with Nick on a task force to do a legitimate investigation and arrest."

"I want that Harley guy, Clint."

"I'll get to work on it, Pap."

* * *

"Get to work, round-eye," Leia Zhoe ordered in Mandarin.

"I am working, you ungrateful little troll." Nick mopped the shop floor with his usual attention to detail. "I do not understand how you put up with this disrespectful tart, Lee."

Lee Wu hugged Leia. "You would not be here, except for the urging of my forceful friend."

Nick used black rimmed spectacles, a Chicago Cubs ballcap, and a high collared pullover sweater with apron to attain a nondescript appearance. He continued the conversation in Mandarin. "You are right, but may I remind you I saved her butt?"

"That is true, which means you are responsible for me forever. Get back to work before I get my stick." Leia put hands on hips for emphasis.

Nick enjoyed Leia's declaration along with Lee for a moment before returning to his mopping. An older Chinese woman came in, looked at Nick with disgust and handed her shopping list to Leia. Leia read the items on the list and handed it to Nick.

"Get a cart and retrieve these items, round-eye."

The old woman cackled and spoke in Mandarin. "List is in Mandarin. Heh…heh…"

"I speak, read, and write Mandarin," Nick replied in the same language, accepting the list. "I will return in a few moments."

The Wu store carried herbs, spices, medicines, and common grocery items. His clientele, loyal and numbered largely in the local area, returned steadily because of his excellent service. He also sold his specialty items on-line in numerous marketing avenues, including Amazon. The old woman, taken aback by Nick's nearly native use of her language, rattled off a string of questioning remarks to Lee Wu as Nick filled the order.

"Why is this 'gweilo' working for you?"

"It is not for you to insult my workers, Chunhua," Lee replied. "Trust me when I tell you this man defends all, no matter their race. He helps us in a matter our community cannot handle alone."

Nick returned with the small cart of goods and returned the list to Chunhua. "The Sichuan Peppercorns are out of stock, at least on the shelf, Mr. Wu."

Lee patted Chunhua's hand. "Leia will total your purchases while I get the peppercorns from the back."

Nick returned to his mopping. He never glanced completely away from the front entrance as the old woman watched him. "Why do you stare at the door?"

"This 'gweilo' has more than one duty," Nick explained with a smile.

His smile faded as the three men who baited him in 'The Redhead Piano Bar' walked in. Aron Bronte, Kevin Clowder, and Dee Ramos wore hoodies, ballcaps, and sunglasses, coupled with the 'prison pants and I'm available look'. John sent him the files on the three suits from the 'Redhead' he uncovered after scanning their IDs. Nick never forgot mannerisms or a plethora of other details about people. He thought humorously as they looked around the shop, if they paid as close attention, the three dupes would be running for their car when they saw Nick. Instead, they launched immediately into intimidation form.

"Get lost, you old crone!" Aron reached for the old woman.

Nick lunged from the side with his ultra volt stun-gun nightstick. The first touch dumped Aron in a jittering pile of flesh. Nick didn't hesitate. He swung the nightstick into Dee Ramos's temple, dropping him unconscious to the floor. His targeting brought him to the chest of Kevin Clowder, who was trying to clear a weapon from under his hoodie. Nick's full on zap, crashed Clowder in a heap. Nick put away his nightstick and guided Chunhua around the counter into Leia's arms. After restraining each man with wrists at his back, Nick dragged each into the backroom. He then gagged them with duct tape and restrained each one at their ankles. When done, Nick zapped the three men again with a full five second discharge. He frisked them with a professional assassin's thoroughness, producing cell-phones, personal items, weapons, and most importantly a vehicle remote fob. Nick reentered the main store.

"Please accept the store's deepest regrets for this intrusion on your buying journey. I see Mr. Wu has found your missing item. Thank you for your understanding." Nick returned to his mopping.

Chunhua glanced from Lee to Leia without understanding. "What…what has happened?"

"Nothing you need concern yourself with," Leia assured her. She bagged the woman's purchases while Lee finished the sale at the cash register.

On her way out, Chunhua stopped to put a hand on Nick's arm. "I see you do good things. I am sorry I called you a 'gweilo'."

"In Cantonese 'gweilo' is not an insult. In Mandarin, it may mean 'white or foreign devil', but it could be a milder label in Cantonese."

Chunhua smiled and walked toward the exit with her purchase. "I meant it in the Mandarin!"

"Lǎo tài pó (old hag)!"

Chunhua laughed on her way out.

Nick finished his mopping chore, while Lee and Leia enjoyed his Chunhua rebuttal. He kept watching, although he knew with the keys in Aron's pocket, it was unlikely they incorporated a driver. He would need to move quickly. *I missed too many things on this Chicago intervention. I'm getting sloppy.* Nick put away his cleaning gear after drying the floor and making certain no spots of blood remained. Activating the vehicle remote key fob outside the shop, Nick found his prisoners' car, a late model Dodge Charger parked down the street. Nick drove it to the front of the shop with black Nitrile gloves on. The car, registered to Aron Bronte, would work as a message.

Returning to his prisoners, Nick undid the ankle restraints on Ramos, slapping him and the others into consciousness. "I will help each of you up and take you to your car. You are under arrest. I am US Marshal Nick McCarty."

Nick Mirandized them as he helped Ramos to his feet. "Nod if you understand these rights as I've explained them."

The men nodded sullenly, not that it meant anything to Nick. He planned to torture any details not in evidence from them, before using an incendiary grenade on their car with the three men inside. His problem would be sending a message without being seen. Leia volunteered for anything he needed. He could use a timer on his improvised grenade from a spot out of sight, but Nick would need a ride from the area quickly.

Nick tightened Ramos's hoodie around his face with ballcap and sunglasses in place. Nick walked him out and placed him in the rear passenger compartment. He repeated his transfer method with each man, making sure the street was clear and Nick kept his head down until returning to the store. Nick took out his iPhone and uploaded a map to Leia's phone. He had already picked a spot along

North Streeter Drive, blocked by trees on both sides with no cameras anywhere.

Leia met him at the door as Nick stepped inside. "What time do you want me there?"

"It will be after dark. I will call you. Are you still okay with this?"

"Of course, round-eye. I know you will kill those men and find out many things before you do. Is there any chance they're the only ones left over from Thurman?"

"They arrived to terrorize and restart Thurman's extortion/protection racket. Someone paid the deceased lieutenants and these idiots. If a money source wasn't behind these incidents after Thurman died, then my only guess is they stupidly picked up where Thurman left off, hoping to get a quick score and get out. I will find out. Thanks for doing this Leia."

Leia gripped Nick's hand. "I wish you weren't married."

Nick smiled and patted her cheek. "I'm a cold-blooded killer. You're too young for me anyway, kid. Besides, mess with a 'gweilo', and make future tale of woe."

Nick left her laughing. He took a deep breath. Rachel must be protected at all costs, knowing in his heart there could never be another woman like her for him. He went through hell to save her, Jean and Deke the dog. They went through hell accepting what he could do and what he had done. *Actually, Deke didn't care how many 'gweilo' targets I kill, as long as he could sit on the deck with me and a beer bowl*. Remembering Deke putting his paws on the piano bench and swaying with him to the music and singing made Nick swallow hard. *Damn animals cinch your life into theirs, just by caring about you naturally*.

* * *

Nick turned right and parked in the small turnoff on North Streeter Drive, parking on the turnoff with muffled cries assaulting him. He knew his three prisoners reasoned with the way he took them, they would never reenter their past lives in any way, shape, or form. Nick turned off the engine. He motioned the three to quiet down.

"I'm El Muerto, boys. You found me, and I found you. If there had been a conscious logical thought in your heads, you would have run for the hills. You didn't. Now... it's too late. Let me show you your options."

Nick removed their gags and played the El Muerto classics for his captive audience on an HD iPad screen. "This could be you, or the three of you can talk to me with what you know like old friends. Like friends, I'll send you to hell peacefully in bliss. The alternative will obliterate your imaginings of pain. Choose wisely, my little gangbanger idiots."

"This is bull... shit!" You don't scare me, cracker! Take me to the cops and piss on your mama's grave. I know you can't torture us... except with fake videos you created. Don't waste my time! I want a lawyer," Aron Bronte declared.

"I think you need a doctor, Aron. Dr. Muerto is in the house." Nick moved to the rear passenger area, thankful he had guessed right who his example would be.

Nick made sure Aron was belted in tightly. He restrained Aron at the ankles once more, and duct taped his mouth again. Only the scalpel slicing his clothing, skin, and outside cellular membrane produced screams of horror, muffled to hideous bleating. Nick applied his Clorox to Aron's bulging intestines, hearing the crack of doom in Aron's muffled screams. After a fifteen-minute application into the darkness for Aron, his brain gave up the ghost. The stroke muffled his sounds and body forever. Nick turned then to his horrified audience.

"Dr. Muerto is in, kiddies. Who wants to die screaming and who doesn't? If you don't, I better hear you confirm your real names and who profits from this new mob action. Mobster chief, Edgar Thurman, met his doom challenging El Muerto!"

"Alderman Briston Harley! He been in bed with Edgar Thurman all along!" Ramos wanted nothing to do with Dr. Muerto. "Harley asked in Thurman at the beginning. He thought you gone, man! Harley fill the need. Why you do this?"

Nick gave them both a lethal dose of eternity syringe. "Because I'm not a useless, drug dealing pimp, with delusions of grandeur. Tell Eddie I said so when you see him."

Nick faced the camera planted on the side panel at the right angle. Nick wore his El Muerto mask and cape as he held the bloody scalpel in his hand. "El Muerto believes in America, not mob pimps, drug pushers, and Sharia Law Mutant refugee fakes from the Sand. I deal torture and death to America's enemies! Hear this, Alderman Briston Harley! Nothing will protect you from me. I will be at your bedside soon with scalpel and bleach for a proper cleaning!"

Nick shut down the recording. He uploaded it to Johnny, who called within ten minutes. "Oh my, Muerto… I believe you have tipped the law's scales of order back into alignment. I will bounce the signal everywhere before zeroing in on Chicago media, national media, and all the social sites."

"If I get the results I hope for, I'll be home sooner than I thought, Kabong."

Gus intruded then on the call. "You destroyed those men, Muerto!"

"I did indeed, Payaso. Thank you."

"That was not a compliment, you cold blooded savage."

"That is again of no matter. El Muerto… away." Gus's gagging noises rattled in his ear before Nick disconnected.

Nick planted the incendiary charge with timer in place and activated. He left Bronte's Dodge to walk along North Streeter Drive without his El Muerto costume on. Leia picked him up. Inside her car, Nick held onto his equipment bag with a smile. Leia noticed, even in the darkened interior.

"What are you smiling at round-eye?"

"What the future holds for at least one section of Chicago, kid."

* * *

At Pain Central, the Monsters enjoyed the morning national news on the big screen, where Jafar displayed a terrified Alderman Harley being led away in handcuffs from his office by Detective Kelly Winslow. The moment he saw the cameras, Harley stopped dead in his tracks. His lip quivered while he regained control of his emotions enough to speak.

"I…I confessed to it all, Muerto! I'm going to prison! Tell him, Winslow!"

Taking a moment before speaking, while the rest of us Monsters loudly banged the conference table in fits of loud amusement, Detective Winslow proclaimed only that Alderman Harley confessed to a number of charges - presented on a video recording by a deceased gangbanger named Dee Ramos.

"Tell what happened! Those boys… they got tortured and cooked! Muerto is a monster!"

Lucas pounded the luckily empty conference table with his fist. "Yeah, he is!"

The cameras zeroed in on Detective Winslow's face, as she tried desperately to keep from losing her grim look. "No further comment."

"It appears I won't need to investigate Alderman Harley any longer," Clint said.

"Best of all, we won't be going to Chicago for an investigation," I added. "Nick sure called that one. Those three idiots began making the rounds, thinking to start another protection sham. Briston should have resigned and made a run for it. Instead, the idiot thinks he can start his extortion ring up again with the three stooges."

My iPhone buzzed. El Muerto himself was on the line. I put him on speaker. "Hey, Nick… we watched your adventures this morning on the news. You saved us an investigation we wanted to coerce you into conducting with us of Alderman Harley."

"He didn't want to meet Muerto. This way I get to go home this morning and maybe stay away from Chicago for a while. I don't know what the hell they need to do short of a revolution in this town. Unless they get rid of the leftist gangsters running the Chicago political system from top to bottom, they're spitting into the wind. I'm in my vehicle, heading home. If you need anything from our blessed flyover country, call me. Otherwise, soon, I will be sitting on the beach at Otter's Point with an anti-Irish coffee, thanks to my daughter, the sobriety officer. Has anything changed on intercepting Khaled Hanniyeh on 'The Rigel'?"

"Nope. Laredo's flying us to Washington to get the Ranger from Monster Island once Hanniyeh confirms his leaving Puerto Vallarta. That gives us time before Hanniyeh leaves the Vallarta Marina for the Isla Maria Magdalena to get the Ranger in position. Achmed keeps track of Hanniyeh's usual passengers, named for us by Minda Rarsour. Both Safia Sakaria and Mammar Rhahin have flight plans coordinated for Puerto Vallarta. Mexico owns Isla Magdalena, otherwise we could assault Hanniyeh's estate there too. We could dump on a lot of Muslim Brotherhood types and probably some CAIR bigwigs he sails with."

"Gus can boat us close. You and I could hit the estate."

I didn't like the sound of an assault on a sovereign nation's island, unless it's inhabited by Sand Jawas. "That sounds like a Muerto grenade party to me Mexico would frown on."

"Maybe you should wear your Muerto t-shirt this week until you get your nerve back, Cheese."

Oh my. The Monsters loved that ace. It took me a few moments to get my voice back. "I'll check on the logistics. Thanks, I needed that… you prick."

"Anytime. El Muerto… away!" Nick disconnected.

"You have a fight to get ready for, Cheese," Lynn reminded me. "We don't want you losing to Ian Wolf. It's time to play with the sharks. You had your vacation visiting Chicago."

Just like that, a good laugh ended in a debilitating Sea Wolf excursion where most of the time I wouldn't be on the boat. "Okay… let's empty the freezer too."

"Thank God," Gus Denova exclaimed. "I think we still have Jimmy Hoffa in there."

* * *

In Lynn's able hands, Rocky kicked my ass at every point. I did get strikes in, but they were few and far between. I only got one good wrap around to snap Rocky out of Lynn's hands, stinging her a good one. Unlike Tommy, she refuses to wear gloves. It stings like hell and Lynn turns the air blue until the stinging goes away. To entertain her and my contingent of fisherman, I did my Flipper imitation, rising out of the water, and making dolphin sounds. I practiced them until I could be mistaken for a dolphin. Lynn hates it when I bait her, but it's my only weapon to lure her into hanging on too long. She knows if her grip can be maintained for a few more seconds, I would lose my spin on the pole.

We fed the fishes earlier, about fifteen miles off shore. We do it in such a way, the bodies do not need to be weighted down. After our dumping procedure spread out over a few miles laterally, I get to have my head beat in somewhere between the three and five-mile mark. The only exhaustion I felt was mental. I figured now, when I finished with some quality strikes, I've had a good day. Today, I phoned it in, but still navigated through a workout not meant for any human being to endure. As Lucas began another low speed start he called out.

"On the horizon! Get the range finders on it, Casey! Clint… get the M107. I ain't ever getting caught out here again. The rest of you break out the MP5s."

I stayed where I was. We had enough Monsters and Snow Whites to take out anything short of a destroyer. Besides, I had another twenty minutes to go, and Tommy would make me get back in the damn water.

"This is not a drill," Casey called out. "They are on intercept course and armed with automatic rifles."

I pulled myself up along the side. "Clint… stop the boat out of range for their rifles."

Clint didn't waste any breath asking why. The M107 sniper rifle has nearly double the range of anything they might have on board. Clint killed the pilot, then killed the controls with our spent uranium loads, rapidly fired into the cabin. The boat, a sleek looking speedboat, rocked to a halt. The men fired at us, but we were nearly two thousand yards away. We had no way of knowing who sent them, or which one knew anything useful. They weren't going to simply allow us to board the boat without casualties. Clint would need to pick off the shooters one by one until they surrendered. In doing so, we might miss the knowledgeable one.

"Lynn! Hand me one of those light breathing apparatus, my fins, and a knife."

Lynn handed the items over to me. "Don't get crazy, Cheese. I don't want new toys that badly."

"In this case, I do. Clint will watch them. Besides, Casey can probably pick them off with the MP5, tilting it at just the right angle."

"Oh man, I'd be Day-shot Casey too, if I could do that." Casey received a few laughs for that line except from a suddenly glowering Lucas.

"Don't encourage him, Recon. What do you have planned?"

"They ain't going anywhere, and they can't see me in the water from there. If I make a wide-angle approach, I can get behind them. Then, I'll think of something."

"Get out of the damn water, you dolt!"

"Listen, Lucas! I can do this. If I can't find a good place to board her and get the drop on them, I'll move away and let you all have target practice. If Clint fires a round into their hull above the waterline occasionally, it will keep their attention. I don't want their boat to sink with all their cell-phones and tablets."

"I'm going on record now as saying this is idiocy," Tommy said. "I don't need range finders to tell me there's at least half a dozen guys on there."

"I could wound them, John," Clint said. "You could wound them."

"They would make bad choices, brother, and we'd lose our chance to learn who sent the pirates. I'll remember to bring one of our new full-face communication masks with us next time. I left them all on the Ranger. My bad. I'll do a Flipper imitation if I want you to kill them all."

I left them laughing. I knew I had ten minutes of breathing time underwater with the compact breathing apparatus. I circled to the left, moving like I had a motor strapped on me with my fins. It did take some time to make a careful approach, popping out of the water to draw a quick breath. I had no intention of going under with the breathing apparatus until I wanted to make my final approach. Clint didn't hit anyone, but he comically shot pieces out of their railing every few minutes. That drew a barrage of firing from what I could tell by sound were AK 47s, the preferred weapon of our enemy. Lucas kept moving in circles at a distance well out of their range.

I moved around the bow of the boat with its blasted pilot's cabin, enjoying what an M107 Barrett with enhanced ammo can do. Clint and I were close order combat by choice, but we were proficient in sniper range weapons, and not adverse in the slightest to use them. If anyone ever came after either one of us, they would find out instantly how many casualties an opposing force can take from long range. We would strike and move constantly until we decimated them. Hopefully, we would have air superiority in our own land.

Putting in my breather, I dove straight down until my natural neutral buoyancy kicked in. I only had enough weight on my belt to keep me from being like a bobber on top of the water during training, to counteract the buoyancy of my dry-suit. I dived until I felt the freedom of floating without pull to the surface. The boat bobbed helplessly in the water. I inspected it front to back before hugging the side as I surfaced. The boat road low in the water, which helped considerably.

I shed my fins. The boat had a low fantail access. I ditched my weight belt and slipped my goggles down around my neck as I positioned for an assault. I waited until Clint fired another couple of rounds into the railing. I heard curses in Spanish before they tried a barrage of tilted rounds toward the moving Sea Wolf.

By the time the barrage ended, I was on board, knife in hand, like a yellow banana on the attack. Once amongst the six on deck, they never had a chance. I used the hilt of my heavy dive knife to stun my targets while beating them down with blows meant to maim. Only one managed to bring his weapon up on me, but Clint exploded his head like a ripe melon dropped from five hundred feet. God... I prayed he wasn't the one we needed to get to the bottom of this attack. I pumped my fist in the air for Clint, ending my spiel with a pointing finger jutting at the boat in the distance. I wasted no time in stripping away weapons and dragging the enemy combatants against the railing. I now carried a fully loaded AK 47 while I positioned them. They had broken faces, ribs, and knee joints. I took them all out with good old Rocky in mind, admitting to myself these poor dupes incurred the wrath of Rocky Poke-pole torture.

Casey leaped aboard the moment Sea Wolf closed in under Lucas's expert handling, with MP5 slung. "Hey, John... nicely done, brother. Lynn is already frothing at the mouth to get started. I bet you'd like to slip on board the 'Wolf', get a shower, and put on some clothes, huh?"

"And have the brothers Bud and Beam. You have the con, brother. I'll see if I can navigate onto the Sea Wolf without having to go by water route."

I eased to the side of the two bobbing boats, cursed like a proper sailor, and dived back into the water while Casey laughed his ass off. I attained the Sea Wolf deck easily through our divers' entry on the fantail, cold and alone once more. Lucas stopped me as I trekked toward the heavenly shower and change of clothes.

"I watched you attack that boat, Recon. You are the finest Marine I ever trained. You may be the most cement-headed one… but damn… you are the best!"

We gripped hands in recognition of the honor Lucas gave me. I then snapped to attention.

In yellow banana suit glory, I ripped off a stiff salute. "Thank you, Sir!"

Lucas didn't move. "I hope you don't think you're trekking down to the shower with the saltwater dripping banana suit on, maggot!"

Rats! I stripped out of my dry-suit without comment. The rest of my boat crew enjoyed Lucas's dress down. They waved with smiles on my way down to enjoy the shower and fresh clothes. Oh man… did that ever feel good. By the time I returned to the main deck, Clint, Casey, Tommy, Jess, and Dev had transferred our prisoners aboard, along with all their weapons and electronic gizmos. I saw the sharks hitting the dead pirate Clint blasted and recently gutted by Casey. They made short work of him. After the prisoner transfer, Clint secured them to the aft railing, moaning and griping about their boo-boos, until Clint popped one on top of the head with his Colt.

"Anyone else need some pain therapy?"

Silence from our unhappy guests. Lynn, of course, inspected her toys with intense interest, trying to decipher the leader without being told. It was a game we had time for now.

I went to the railing after getting a glass of Bud with one shot Beam, for a very tasty boilermaker, quickly erasing the lingering taste of ocean. Our Snow Whites had returned to their fishing after the prisoner transfer. I noted the ice chest nearly full of their catch. "It looks like you guys relieved the ocean of at least a couple days fish fry."

"I had my usual catch of nothing," Tommy replied, "but these two have been reeling them in. Between the blindfold episode and today's one-man pirate attack, I'm beginning to think these Rocky Poke-pole training exercises make you suicidal."

He probably came close in his analysis when I thought about it. "Calculated gambles."

"Tommy's right, brother," Dev stated. "You boarded the boat to idiot's island too many times lately. I'm workin' on a Latin spell of exorcism for you."

"Yeah, DL," Jess added. "You possessed, brother. Dev goin' to get the devil out of you, boy. Bring the Latin, Dev!"

Jess took Dev's pole. Devon Constantine raised his hands to the heavens with his eyes closed. The Latin floated on his thunderous bass voice with power and flair.

"Exsúrgat Deus et dissipéntur inimíci ejus: et fúgiant qui odérunt eum a fácie ejus!

Sicut déficit fumus defíciant; sicut fluit cera a fácie ígnis, sic péreant peccatóres a fácie Dei!"

(Let God arise and let His enemies be scattered: and let them that hate Him flee from before His Face! As smoke vanisheth, so let them vanish away: as wax melteth before the fire, so let the wicked perish at the presence of God!)

I nearly spilled my wonderful boilermaker, while enjoying Dev's attempt to exorcise my demon. Even our prisoners cringed against the railing. Oh my… he repeated the incantation three times. During the third, I merely bowed my head. Tommy, on the other hand, could barely breathe. He dropped to his butt, rocking back and forth in loud amusement. As if in solidarity, all the others stood with hands clasped and heads down. We didn't know what the hell he was saying; but when Dev brings the Latin, he sounds like Moses returning from Mount Sinai with the Ten Commandments in hand.

I toasted Dev when he finished and drained my boilermaker. Tommy waved me off helplessly as I tried to get him back on his feet. "Your Latin is scary good, Dev."

Dev smiled. "I get the kids all the time. If they start acting up or being disrespectful, I bring the Latin. They hide behind Rose."

"What does Rose do?"

"That's the funny part, John. Rose makes the sign of the cross and mutters, 'Madre de Dios'. She thinks I'm spooky. Do you feel lighter now that I performed the exorcism?"

Before I could answer, Jess grabbed me, staring intensely into my eyes. He released me. "I think the only thing DL is light on is boilermaker liquid."

"Right you are, Jess. Excuse me. Get up, T."

Tommy scrambled to his feet. "I'm joining you this round, John. Dev? You and Jess want a beer?"

"Sure, T. Sounds good since we don't need to do the mat work today when we get back. Heave a shot into mine too."

"Same here," Jess said. "This demon slaying tests the soul, my brothers."

Chapter Five

School Daze

"Honey… I'm home." I felt pretty good. I limited myself to only two boilermakers. Lynn, Clint and the minions were entertaining our guests at Pain Central. Clint felt it important to learn everything we could from their electronic gizmos before questioning them. They figured life was over as they knew it when we blew up their boat.

My two family members greeted me grimly, one with an ice pack over her left eye. Uh oh, trouble in River City. "First, how are you Al? I see by the scraped knuckles you fought back."

"A fifth-grade girl terrorized the Sparks twins at recess, Dad. When I stopped her by saying I would get a teacher, she called me everything you could imagine. I tried to simply walk away with Jim and Kara, but she sucker-punched me from behind. I turned and fought her off, nailing her to the body like you showed me. When she launched at me again, she did the windmill style you prepped me for. I ducked inside and hit her with an uppercut as we practiced. It knocked her down, chipped a tooth, and made her cry. Her two girlfriends tried to jam me, so I opened up. The fight was over by the time the teacher rushed over. I made those two babies cry too."

Elementary school fights are not my specialty. To say I was proud as hell of Al would be an understatement. I taught Al never to throw a punch, unless it meant something to her all the way inside the gut. "How opened up did you need to get?"

"One girl has a broken nose," Lora answered for her. "The other one got a straight kick to the ribs, coming in. They think her rib is cracked. Della and I went to the school together. The mothers of the three girls were screaming at Principal Duncan. When they saw us enter, they tried to approach, but Della told them if they came at us, we'd beat them down and kick their brains in. They took one look at Della and suddenly the attack was on hold. I had my stun-gun in hand, inside my purse. The security guards arrived in force then."

"I'm almost afraid to ask about the ending, since no good deed ever goes unpunished." I knew Principal Duncan. She's black, but knows the brutal truth, anyone of any race can be successful in America if they work their jobs instead of their mouths.

"Principal Duncan did the right thing. She made sure the hurt girls got medical attention first. Al Capone here refused medical attention. The teacher who finally arrived on scene told Duncan she saw the three older girls attacking Al, after calling her every vile name in the book. Once the twins told Duncan every detail, she suspended the three older girls."

"Ms. Duncan couldn't shut Jim and Kara up," Al added. "They told her everything those girls were saying, and that they were pushing the twins around, screaming in their faces. They backed my story about being sucker-punched from behind. Those two are like audio recorders."

I knew firsthand how formidable the twins' vocabulary was. Della home schooled them long before they entered kindergarten. "We'll tighten security for the immediate future. I'll install some extra cams tomorrow with views of Della's house too. You know the drill, Al. No one leaves the school building unless I'm there. We'll deal with the fallout as it happens."

"I called our lawyer. Harry didn't like the scene I painted either. I gave him the names and addresses of the three kids. He will be contacting the school board and Principal Duncan for updates."

Harry Bonavena represented all our interests. His firm came recommended highly by Alexi Fiialkov. We kept him on a large retainer because he took nothing for granted. Admittedly, we needed his large firm to represent us and Oaktown Cartel interests. He's been read in on our qualifications and credentials. Harry noticed the change in the city even though the politicos work against us at every step.

"Good. That's all we can do on the legal front. Al's safety will need to be protected until we figure whether she needs to switch schools or not. I know you have a lot of friends at Allendale. We won't pull you out of there unless this incident spins out of control.

The school should have acted more forcefully when that Muslim teacher tried to rewrite school policy."

"Couldn't we fight through this if I stay careful, Dad?"

"Maybe. I think you need to use your imagination as to how easy it would be to find a split second let down in security. We don't yet know how nuts these people are-"

That's when bad became worse. A rock crashed through our window in the front. "Get your gun, Lora," I called out as I streaked through our front entrance into half a dozen thugs. They never expected me. They thought throwing a rock through a Monster's window would frighten the Monster, leaving him cowering in a corner. I didn't think I killed anyone, not that I cared, but I did maim a few for life. I smashed knee joints, broke arms with knife-hand strikes, and faces with fists. Only one tried to run. He didn't make it. With all six bodies down, and me looking like a bloody ghoul from noses and faces I smashed, Lora came out with her Glock in hand.

"I called it in, John. Thank God, Earl and 'Rique are on duty. Earl told me they're five minutes away." She handed me a peroxide wet towel.

It felt good to clean my face off. "They'll need an EMT unit too, babe."

"I told them that already. I didn't get through to Earl's personal line before you smashed everyone into oblivion. Good Lord... if they ever need a real Hulk for the movies, you should make the top of the list."

I shrugged. "No one throws a rock through my window without a violent response. They're lucky they didn't pull a weapon. Earl would have needed the coroner then. I have this now. Take care of Al. I'll make sure these guys stay down until Earl and 'Rique get here. It looks like a down turn for safety in the future."

"Or the end of it," Lora replied, reentering the house.

Della and her husband, Frank, came out on their porch. "Are you okay, John?"

"I'm fine. Unfortunately, I think we've had a little fallout from Al's adventure earlier. One of these clowns threw a rock through my window in broad daylight."

"Lord A'mighty… are they mental? I'm sorry the twins and Al got mixed up in this."

"The parents who raised the three girls to be bullying thugs are to blame, Della. We may need to get the kids into private school if this all goes South. I have Oaktown's lawyer working on it. I'll make sure Jim and Kara go where Al goes if I can't fix this."

"Thank God for you in this town, John," Frank said. "From what the twins said, you've sure trained Al well. Thank her for us. That took guts to face off three against one."

"I'll tell her. I will keep you updated. I will be taking everyone to school and back for the immediate future. I'm glad the school year is almost over."

As they waved and went inside, Earl and 'Rique arrived with only flashing lights. They joined me in front of the six pack of moaning goons.

"Hey, John. Lora told me this may be an ongoing thing," Earl said.

"It's possible. Want some help with frisking these guys? I didn't give them a chance to pull a weapon on me, but I'd bet at least one packs heat. I've been watching hands. If they were in any shape to reach, they would have done so by now."

"Sure. Here. We can't get into trouble if an FBI agent assists at a crime scene." 'Rique handed me a pair of Nitrile gloves.

By the time the EMTs arrived, we had confiscated weapons, personal items, and drugs. 'Rique labeled and took pictures of each guy's face and evidence bag. The medical techs did triage on busted knee joints, fractured faces, and broken arms. Once they finished, they needed to take three in to the hospital. The other walking wounded went with Earl, while 'Rique escorted the ones going to the hospital, after taking pictures of my broken window and the rock lying on our floor amidst broken glass. He bagged the poor rock, an innocent victim of idiots. Another squad car arrived to follow the EMT vehicle.

"I'm certain a couple of the parents are in this bunch," 'Rique observed. "I saw a couple of names on the IDs we collected matching the names of those bullying kids at Al's school. I'll have

Lora text you the names of the families involved in the attempted beat down at the school."

"Is Al okay?"

"She's handling it, Earl. Lynn taught her the Cruella Deville motto: it is what it is. That's how we're dealing with it. I'm installing more video cams on the property, so I can keep the other victims of this crap protected. You understand what will happen if this escalates, right?"

"Believe me, brother, I know," Earl replied. "I will get the word out to check your neighborhood and street more closely for congregating thugs, especially at night. That they tried this in broad daylight amazes me. These dumb-shits really don't have a clue who you are. Your YouTube videos alone have millions of hits. I saw the latest goofy blindfold trick. Sorry... but that was just plain nuts."

"So, I've been told. If these jerks ever come at night, this will be over. You can tell the DA I'll be pressing charges. I don't mind if he makes a plea deal with these morons, but if something's not done, I'll open a few doors better left closed. I'm opening my own investigation. I'll know everyone involved and where they can be found by nightfall."

Earl grinned. "I bet you will. Clint and Achmed can find anyone or anything. I'll call you if our perps begin ratting each other out the moment they are interrogated."

"That would help. If they get let out back on the street, I may have a special interrogation for them. We have a cruise coming very soon I can't talk about, after school ends for Al. I'll be taking Lora and Al with me for part of the cruise. I may convince her to take Al for a visit with family back East. When I'm finished with business, I'll fly to Boston and escort them home."

"If they decide to stay, Lora has my number. 'Rique and I can be here fast to cover for you. If not for your team, those BLM gangsters would have decimated us, and a lot of innocent people injured or killed in the crossfire. Besides, the Homeland Security money you've directed our way for reporting gangster and terrorist problems really helps a lot. The least we can do is keep your family safe for a few days."

"Thanks, Earl. I hope it doesn't come to that. If I uncover anything the DA can use, I will call you with it, especially if I can make it from a confidential informant."

After Earl left with his prisoners, I went in to clean the mess and get the glass people to put in a picture window of the bullet resistant variety. I had told Lora to wait on cleaning until the police left. We three cleaned the glass shards and the framing. The glass contractor arrived within the hour, took measurements, and installed a neat roll down metallic cover until he could return with the glass. In the meantime, I called Clint to get him and Lynn up to speed.

"Damn… that's not good. Achmed's here now working with us on interrogation of the prisoners. Lynn has her target picked out. He and I will launch into this thug family dispute right after. Send me the file of what you do have. So, Al kicked three girls' asses, all older than her. Lynn will love that story. Your work with her sure paid off."

"Yeah, it did. I got the idea from Nick. He trains Jean and Sonny in everything they're interested in. Nick told me there's no use in trying to keep them out of our business. Training prepares them for life too. I doubt Al will be like Jean, but she can, at least, protect herself. She loves the bow."

"That is one silent, nasty weapon. If we need to move on your domestic issue before we leave on the cruise, then so be it," Clint said. "You stay inside today, John. Lynn and I will handle the workup for what we need to do about who sent the pirate boat after us. Achmed will work your case and our background checks for the prisoners' stories. Get something to eat and sip a couple more. It appears we're going to get busy again."

"No question about that. Thanks, Clint. Talk at you later." I disconnected and went into the kitchen where Lora was showing Al our tax file for the year. Al had a passion for numbers, especially after Lora explained break-even points, spreadsheets, and profit/loss statements. Taking the magic out of the business accounting end thrilled Al. I liked her new interest in something low key and much less dangerous. "I'm home for the day. Want me to order something for dinner?"

"Why don't we go over to the new 'Warehouse' and get something. I'll take my tablet and check our cams remotely. If you want, I'll get us a ride over and back. You can have something too.

I'll text everyone we're going over there for dinner at six. Anyone wanting to hear Al's blackeye story can join us. I'll call ahead to Marla too."

"That sounds great. I'll drive though. I won't have anything else to drink."

Al pumped her fist. "Yes! I get to be the badass tonight. I hope Lynn comes."

* * *

Lynn stroked the man's cheek they now knew was Otis Soterro. "This is my bitch. Quays? Cue up our interrogation hits for Otis, so he knows what lies behind door number two."

"Yes, Mistress of the Unimaginable." Quays knew these men recognized him from his days in the cartel. They were open mouthed stunned seeing Gus Denova, Silvio Ruelas, and Quays greet them at Pain Central. Although none of the minions knew the prisoners personally, they could tell the men knew them as former cartel enforcers. His subservience to Lynn helped to do the 'warmup' for what was to come. He had no problem with the ploy and needed very little acting to play Lynn's minion. The Monsters trusted the minions implicitly, made them rich beyond their dreams, and protected them as family. Quays now had a family he never dreamed of having.

Quays played the tablet video for Otis. Luckily, Silvio was standing by with the barf bag. Otis heaved within minutes. Quays experienced men being tortured by the cartels, but never had he experienced an imagination for torture like Lynn. They settled on the heel/nerve acupuncture needles because of the clean, no indication of any torture results. Silvio created a delivery system for the torture capable of delicate adjustments with horrific results, but the idea originated in the mind of Lynn Montoya Dostiene – the modern Marquis de Sade all others were measured by. The highlight video contained Lynn's complete repertoire of torture and the victims' agony. All ended in the same way, with Lynn obtaining all the information she requested.

"As you can see, Otis, this isn't a threat or a game," Quays explained. "There is no bargaining. If they keep you alive, it will have nothing to do with this. Cruella Deville, the 'Mistress of the Unimaginable' will make you tell her everything. The only difference in the procedure is how much agony you can endure before talking. Dr. Deville will find the mark. Believe that."

"Thank you, Quays," Lynn said. "Now then, Otis… what will it be, the hard way or the easy way?"

"Tito… Tito Flores! We work for him. He contracted us to eliminate John Harding, and as many of his crew as we could. Tito took money from some Arab named Khaled Hanniyey to kill Harding and his crew. He knew about the area where Harding's training is done. Tito owns Ian Wolf. He doesn't believe Wolf can beat Harding. Taking money to kill a man we wanted to see gone was… excellent… but we did not know about your group. You crippled our boat and sent a man on board who smashed us down like bugs."

Lynn grinned. "That was John Harding."

Otis blinked. "Ese amarillo diablo?"

Lynn took some moments to stifle amusement. "Yes… that yellow devil. He busted you bunch to pieces."

Otis saw amusement on his torturer's face. He hoped to get a painless flight into the beyond. Otis had looked into the eyes of death before. This woman embodied death beyond hope. "Exactly… he…he was like that old horror movie, 'The Creature from the Black Lagoon'. In moments, he had batted us down like flies."

"Good…good stuff, Otis." Lynn pinched his cheek. "Speak and explain every detail about this operation, and anything you can think of having to do with this Hanniyeh fellow. I have my best information checker on this as we speak. Keep talking, my little helper."

Lynn reversed suddenly to stare into Otis's eyes with promised retribution truly unimaginable. "I think we understand each other here… don't we, Otis?"

"Yes!" Otis cringed back from Lynn's unblinking promise of torturous death with passion. "I will tell you everything… 'Mistress of the Unimaginable'!"

Lynn straightened away from Otis with a smile. "You amused me, Otis. That fact gained you a pain free journey. Don't screw it up. If we find any flaw in your information… and we will…

we go back to the beginning. You don't want that. I give points for not knowing the details on the first round where we give you leeway. Mess with me at this point and I will stretch your ending into an oblivion of agony past hope, despair, or comprehension."

Otis nodded. "I am done now. I saw my ending much differently… in a blaze of glory. I am a drug whore enforcer. Tito still thinks of your crew as a target to be dispensed with. I have been around. Your crew took us down like lemmings running off a cliff. I will strive to provide you with as much information as I can to fuck Tito. He could have negotiated as he does many times. He sent us into hell… because of his own arrogance. We complied because… we trusted the asshole."

Lynn stroked Otis's cheek gently. "I think you have the full meaning in mind of our intentions. We're Americans, my little helper. We do not sell out America for any price. She flies her flag and we kill anyone who tries to prevent it. Please don't make the mistake of thinking we care about your personal or foreign country's woes. We don't! Speak with my assistant truthfully and you will gain escape from all this, pain free. Refuse, and all will be at risk, including your sanity."

"I…I understand."

"Tell me something, Otis. How did Tito tell you to communicate the success or failure of your mission to kill us?"

"I never call him. I text to a throwaway phone he has. On a kill mission like this, I…I would text one word: muerto – all small letters."

Lynn smiled. "Where would you and your crew be going after such a mission?"

"Into hiding. First, we would have steamed your boat far out to sea, and to the South at least twenty miles. After our return, we would have docked Tito's boat, then separated from each other and remained silent for at least a week, depending on the way your deaths were reported if your boat was discovered."

"I have a small job then for you and your phone. We want Tito to believe your mission was completed successfully."

"Yes… Mistress."

An hour later, Clint and the minions bagged the last body. Otis's information, confirmed by Jafar, pinpointed Tito's whereabouts at the Richmond Marina.

"The boat is an eighty-foot cruiser, titled 'La Belleza'," Jafar put the Richmond Marina on the big screen with 'La Belleza' marked by him on their hi-tech table control. "I hacked into their security system. I can clear you all the way to the boat if you want to avoid approaching by water. It has an end of the dock tie-up, so 'La Belleza' can't be seen easily by people on other boats. I checked by satellite. The boats at the end of the pier nearest Tito's boat are unoccupied."

"I think Lynn and I will handle this," Clint replied. "John's having issues at home. We're meeting for dinner. We'll need a driver at 1am."

"I will drive," Gus Denova volunteered. "Do you need a car with masked plates."

"Yes. It will need to be high end, Gus, so we don't attract attention. Once I run this by John, Lynn and I will go home, play with the baby, get a nap, and be ready for you."

"I will pick you up at 1am sharp."

* * *

Our dependents stayed at the table while I briefed the crew on my rock throwing adventure. Clint and Lynn updated us on who sent the pirates. I can tell you Tommy and I were surprised. If Tito meant us harm, why do it before the fight? It made no sense.

"I should go with you."

"No, John, you shouldn't," Clint replied. "Lynn and I will learn what this pirate attack was all about. The simplest motive is I believe Tito wanted you out of contention completely. I'm betting he doesn't believe Ian can beat you. Your disappearance opens the championship to rated contenders in the heavyweight division for a number of elimination bouts, all with big draws, and big money."

"I think you're right, Clint," Tommy agreed. "I don't see any other plausible theory fitting this stupidity."

"If this matches my hunch, what would you like us to do with Tito?"

"Good question, Clint. He'll have at least a couple of men there and maybe some women. This could be a bad idea taking him on his boat. I have a counter suggestion. Why not let Jafar track him when he leaves his boat. We could stop his car with sirens and arrest everyone in the car. We'll impound the car at Pain Central, along with its owner. Lynn can get answers for us in a more clinical way there."

"Agreed, Cheese," Lynn said. "Tito thinks we're dead. If he hears otherwise, who cares? We'll catch up to him sometime. Maybe Jafar will get a lead on him leaving the Marina tomorrow or the next day. I like the idea of arresting and restraining that bunch like we're taking them into custody for law enforcement."

"I can go along on this bust," Gus Denova said. "I will drive their vehicle."

"I'm glad Amara drove us over with the baby," Lynn said. "Barkeep? A glass of white zin please. If I'm not going on the hunt tonight, I'll enjoy a little pre-dinner beverage."

Clint ordered a beer too. While we discussed my slight domestic problem, three men and a woman entered the bar. One of them, I recognized. He used to be a professional football player, Koren Capricorn. The woman looked to be his current girlfriend, Lessa Riab. They scanned the room as the 'Warehouse' greeter readied a table for their party of four. I never was a big football fan. The small interest I had ended when the kneeling buffoons began disrespecting America, the Flag, and the Anthem. This social warrior stuff, always based on lies and leftist bullshit, pissed me off. I turned to my Beam brother for consoling wisdom. Then I heard Lynn chuckle and felt a hand on my shoulder. I turned. Capricorn stood there, staring at me. He was a few inches shorter than me, but with his poof-ball hair, we probably would match up back to back in height, with him being even a hair taller, so to speak.

"You're John Harding," he announced.

"Guilty as charged."

"I've been taking martial arts since I was a kid. What do you think my chances would be fighting in the UFC? Do you know who I am?"

"I know who you are. I don't know what your chances would be. Have you ever been in a real fight?"

"Sure… a few scuffles here and there, plus, I played pro football."

"Dancing around in full pads doesn't count as fighting. It may give you good stamina though. Why would you want to fight in the UFC? You would need to train hard for a long time to get proficient. I admit the money would be good because you have name recognition. If you won a few of your first bouts, you could get a nice payday, but the money's nowhere near what you got tossing footballs."

Capricorn smirked. "I can't get a job in the NFL because of my beliefs."

"You can't get a job because you suck as a quarterback," Lucas jolted him. "The defenses figured out you couldn't see downfield to hit secondary receivers. That's what ended your career, Kneeler."

Capricorn's girlfriend tried to tug him away because his friends were making tough guy poses at us, and Capricorn's face turned feral. "Let us leave this man. He is a non-believer who has blasphemed against Islam."

"That is true," I admitted. "Have a good evening, folks. Good luck with your UFC career."

I turned back to the bar, but Capricorn wasn't done.

"I want you to give me a match in Las Vegas. It would mean big money for both of us."

"I can't give you a fight. Those money bouts need to be sanctioned by the UFC. Even if you could bypass the rules, and you somehow won the fight, you wouldn't be the champion. Everyone in the heavyweight division has more of a claim than you for a title shot."

"So, you're afraid to fight me?"

"You're not listening," I replied calmly, as his accusation caused loud amusement amongst my companions, especially Jess and Dev. "The UFC and the MGM Grand make contracts for fights, not the fighters. Once a fighter is ranked and accepted by the UFC, a match can be negotiated between fight teams."

"We're negotiating right now. What if we came to an agreement to fight and presented it to the UFC and MGM Grand as a done deal."

Tommy spoke because he could see I wasn't as amused after hearing this chuckle-head. "Like any other sport, you need to do your time earning a place. The cage doesn't give fighters a license to kill. If the UFC accepted the fight, they could be liable for your death or maiming in the cage."

"Who the hell are you."

"Tommy Sands, John's manager and business partner. We're trying to keep you from getting hurt. If you keep pushing buttons, I imagine you could get a fight with one of the newcomers in the UFC on the undercard somewhere. Without training, you could still get killed."

"Man… you don't know shit about me!"

"Look," Tommy reasoned, "those are the rules. Talk to the UFC officials. They'll tell you the same thing. They won't allow you to commit suicide in the octagon."

"We'll see about that! You're just afraid, Harding!" He left my crew amidst wild amusement.

"Funny or not, I hope the UFC doesn't do something stupid and allow that dope to fight someone," Tommy said. "If he's lucky, he'll get submitted in the first fifteen seconds."

"Capricorn made me hungry. Let's eat." I received enthusiastic support for that idea.

* * *

Al gave a rousing, detail rich summary of her battle. I let her describe the rock throwing action too. Lynn enjoyed the fight scene the most. She loved the way Al fought back after getting sucker-punched from behind. Being able to take a punch means something. No one expressed amusement about the rock throwing. In Monster land, attacking family means death, which was still on the table. All in all, it was a fun night. We walked out together, with me explaining I would be going to the school in the morning for an update. Capricorn One was waiting for me with his friends. Jess, Dev, Tommy, Jafar, and the minions moved in front of our dependents, of which there were many there tonight. Only idiots would face off with my crew. One guy did the unthinkable, started pulling a weapon to keep us in line. Clint had his Colt pointed at the man's head in a split second with Casey and Lucas only a heartbeat behind.

"Reach for anything again and I shoot you posers all in the head," Clint told them.

"Are you stupid?" Tommy came forward. "These people are killers. What possible outcome did you expect out here in the parking lot?"

Koren pointed at me. "I want to show this chicken-shit I'm the real deal."

"School this America hatin' piece of shit, Recon."

I took off my jacket and handed it to Lynn. She knew they didn't have a cutter, so Crue hung back, enjoying the show. I figured to give them one. "Okay, Kneeler, bring it."

Capricorn One went through a slew of martial arts waving hands, feet kicking high into the air, accompanied by a Bruce Lee type wah-wah. Then… he stopped in sideways form and gave me the Bruce Lee come-on, gesturing me to attack with a hand gesture. I obliged with a behind the knee leg strike. Koren screamed as he went to the ground, hugging his knee to him, tears streaming down his face. Small shrieks of agony squeaked from his mouth every few seconds. He writhed from side to side with Lessa trying to comfort him, while ducking around his poof-ball hair. Capricorn One wouldn't be kneeling anywhere in the near future.

"Good Lord, Betty! You faced off with John Harding and this is all you got? Stop squealing like a stuck pig. Sing the National Anthem." Lynn had to take a few verbal shots while the Monsters enjoyed the show with restraint.

Lessa jumped to her feet from lover-boy's side, screaming, "kafir whore", while trying to bitch-slap probably one of the most dangerous women on the planet.

Lynn dropped my jacket, blocked the arm, and shot a left jab right into her nose. It exploded in blood. Then… the screams started in earnest, with Lynn laughing her butt off. Lessa landed on the ground in an unceremoniously revealing manner. She decided to pick tonight to go commando. I pointed at the two companions.

"Get your friends loaded for the hospital. Never come back here again. This is an Oaktown Cartel and police bar. If I see any of you here, I will take my pound of flesh. Are we clear?"

"Yeah… we clear," one of the lucid ones said.

We remained in place until the two injured screamers were loaded into the SUV they drove here with. Lynn retrieved my coat for me. "Short on entertainment value, but a nice ending note to the night. Tito's up next. See you in the morning, Cheese."

"Yep. Right after school drop off."

Lynn glanced at Al. "Watch your back, girl. Be aware of your surroundings at all times."

Al waved. "Absolutely."

* * *

It had been a while since the last time I walked Al into the school. When a girl has her very own bridge troll, kids, parents, and teachers notice. Lora and Della walked in with me. Della escorted her twins to the kindergarten room, while Lora and I accompanied Al to her class. We all then proceeded to Principal Rose Duncan's office. The school secretary smiled and waved us in.

Rose greeted us from her desk. "Sit down, folks. I've talked with the school board this morning. They're as stupidly clueless as always. Your lawyer setting them straight right from the beginning made an impression."

I explained what happened in the rock throwing incident. I handed her the file Jafar made for me concerning the men who participated, including their arrests at my house. "They are related to the three girls. Only one is a father: Derek Rains. They are all in custody, although three are in the hospital."

Duncan scanned through the file. "I take it they didn't give themselves up after throwing the rock, huh?"

"Ah… no, but they all survived."

"May I keep this?"

"Yes. I figured you may want to send the school board a copy. The memory disk I taped inside the folder has the file on it."

"We want to make sure our kids are safe here," Della said. "When older kids can terrorize kindergartners, the school has a problem."

"I agree," Duncan said. "I'm adding a teacher and security guard to our recess time watch. Just to explain how crazy the school board, PC morons are, they wondered if Alice should be charged with a hate crime."

"Oh my god! You're kidding me. Did you tell them my twins are black?"

"I did indeed. It was a conference call with two black men and a Latina. All they wanted to know was if the winner was white. They didn't care it was three on one, or that Al was punched from behind to start the fight. They know I'm black and they were on the verge of calling me a racist. I'm thinking the three girls' parents called it in. That one of the fathers participated or led an attack on your house frightens me. Those girls will always be thugs if they're raised as thugs."

"We know they're not taught thug behavior in school," I assured her. "Al's told us the school has anti-bullying assemblies all the time."

"For all the good it does," Duncan admitted. "I get reports from parents their kids are bullied on the internet. I tell them to keep the kids off the social sites and they look at me like I grew a horn in the center of my head."

"Thank you," I replied. "Finally, someone else who understands internet bullying is the easiest thing in the world to avoid. Go to school, keep your head on studies, and only use the internet for research. These kids are conditioned to Google anyone in the world who might be mentioning their name. It's parents' responsibility to limit kids' access to what's become a dangerous place."

"Every teacher in the school has been coached to correct any bullying type behavior, but we can't see or hear everything. I see those Facebook videos of black thugs and their 'knockout game'. It makes me heartsick."

A commotion in the outer office cut off the conversation as I heard the secretary trying to stop someone from coming into Duncan's office. I went to the door and opened it. A big man ran into me, bounced off, and fell on his side. Two more guys, accompanied by two trash-talking women trailed the first guy by only a couple steps. The first guy jumped to his feet and took a swing at me.

I moved inside the swing, gripping his sides and nailed him with a knee to the solar plexus. His day was done. The other two rushed me. I clapped my hands with one guy's head between them and stomped the other guy's instep. They joined their buddy on the floor. Lora stun-gunned the first woman trying to rush past my short entanglement. The other woman tried backing out the door, but security arrived to stop her.

"I called the police too, Rose," the secretary told her, holding a cloth to her bleeding mouth. "The woman on the floor punched me in the face. I'm pressing charges."

"I have an ice pack in the office, Sela. I'll get it for you."

I pitched each one of the groaning men against the office wall. "Stay still or I will hurt you."

"Slide over there next to your friends," Lora told the woman she zapped. "If you don't, I'll zap you until you do."

She did as Lora ordered her to do, still vibrating slightly from her first arcing. The security guards guided the woman they had in custody over to our group. Rose returned with the ice pack for Sela. When the police arrived, we told them the story. I had a passing acquaintance with the two police officers. I showed them my FBI credentials and they wrote down my information. A transport needed to be called in, because drugs and weapons were found on all the suspects. Although only the guy who I kneed carried a gun, the rest had knives, including the women. Sela, Lora, and I all agreed to testify if the DA prosecuted the case in court. With the charges these idiots had on them, a plea deal would be the only way they avoided prison.

Once they were transferred to police custody, I shook hands with the security guards and gave them my card. "Please call me if you need help."

"We will, John. Thank you," the first guard on scene, Stan Bridges said. "That guy with the gun is scary business. Ms. Duncan is lucky you were here."

"I think I was the lucky one. I don't know what those jerks had in mind. They may have planned to hunt for my daughter."

"Jesus! That is a bad thought."

"Yeah… it is, brother. Watch your backs."

* * *

In the principal's office once again, Della spoke first. "I think that incident should take care of what and who needs to be held responsible for the fight in school."

"Small doubt about that. I wish to hell our security guards were allowed to be armed. Stan was right. I heard him say I was lucky you were here, John. God knows what those people planned. I'm sure it wasn't a debate about what we should do about the fight. You can all go home. I'm doing a conference call with the board members right now."

"Thank you," I replied, taking Lora's arm. "C'mon, Della. I don't want to get detention for overstaying my welcome."

"I'm really sure you'll need to worry about that," Della retorted.

"Stay out of trouble, young man," Principal Duncan warned me jokingly… not for the first time.

"He's incapable of it, Rose," Lora lanced me.

Rose grinned. "I know."

* * *

I hung my head as I exited our vehicle of fate, seeing Jess and Dev waiting for me with folded arms over chests. Lora followed me, laughing her ass off. She shot out front to confront my brothers. "Don't you two be disrespecting the Dark Lord. He had to do crap you haven't even heard about."

Lora explained in detail what we just went through, including a humorous rendition of her zapping one of the women.

Jess and Dev enjoyed Lora's admonition and briefing with humor as they broke formation. "Damn… you getting into the meat of public school politics in Oakland will not end well for you, brother. What Lora described is exactly why."

"I know the corrupt processes at work here, Jess. The serious racist assholes who tried to invade Principal Duncan's office came with the promise of a lot more. They were there to either go after Al, or take over Principal Duncan's office in the hopes of fifteen minutes of reality TV. I thought maybe you two came here this morning to protest the harsh treatment I gave Capricorn, the Kneeler."

"That'll be the day. We want in on this thug bullshit against Al," Jess said. "We need a front of real black citizens ready to defend what's right. These BLM assholes gained a foothold because real black Americans don't get any media."

"Okay… how do I make this right, my brother? I can't change our pixels. Lora, Al and I are white. I could do the old 'hey, some of my best friends are black' cookie."

Oh my… they enjoyed that addition to the mix. It took a while, with Lora joining them in amusement, to acquire a response. Dev spoke then. "You need us with you when this stuff happens at school or anywhere else."

"I admit having you two with me would have been great. I'm sure we can agree a three on one situation looks better for me than having you and Jess in the mix, my brothers."

"I get your point. You're right as usual, John. From the way Lora described it, you needed to be alone in this." Devon Constantine stated. "We want a piece though when we can make a difference. You've stood with us many times. We don't know how to even make a stand with the media backing BLM traitors."

"Draw a line and put it behind you, Dev. Some things can't be undone or altered. The media won't ever be on our side. I will factor you two into these kinds of messes when I have something positive for you both to add. The ones responsible this time really screwed up. One had a gun. They all had knives and drugs. Karma caught them in this instance. I'm glad school's out this week."

Then it struck me. "You two didn't come to commiserate with me about the Dark Lord's dilemma. You guys already know I would call you both in a heartbeat if I needed help. I know what you're here for. Go away, and sin no more."

"You know we can't do that. We have our orders," Dev said. "Crue called and told me there's no movement on Tito. We need to empty the freezer once again. Last, but not least, Tommy wants you in the water this morning."

I knew it! I turned away in disgust while my wife and brothers-in-arms enjoyed my discomfiture. I shunned them. "Dead to me. If we fix Tito the way we should, I won't have a fight to train for."

"T believes you should fight Wolf anyway. Alexi said the MGM Grand and UFC showed interest in the fight the moment he mentioned it," Jess said.

I kissed Lora. "If you have anything to do at the office, do it from here. Do we have anything on the schedule?"

"Jess and Dev are escorting a group of Chinese businessmen in San Francisco tomorrow. They claim to speak English, but it wouldn't hurt to have you along," Lora replied. "Besides, they asked if the UFC Heavyweight Champion would be with them."

"Do they just want to hit the tourist spots?"

"That's their plan. They want to see Pier 39, Fisherman's Wharf, Union Square, Ghirardelli Square, Golden Gate Park... the usual."

"If it keeps me out of the water tomorrow, I'm in."

Chapter Six

Escort Service

Everyone loved the trip out on the Sea Wolf today. After feeding the fish, we moved in to the ten-mile mark and the Cheeseburger hit the water. I didn't get to skip the water. I didn't want to train. I wanted to fish and drink beer all day. Instead, here I was with Lynn busting my butt with Rocky the poke pole. I worked out, but I got my head handed to me, with only a handful of hard strikes. Tommy called time. I swam around to the fantail. Lucas met me at the back.

"After that performance, I should make you swim behind the boat to port."

"Gee… thanks, Pap. I don't even know if I'll get a fight with Wolf after we take care of that prick, Tito."

Jafar called Clint from Pain Central. He hurried to the fantail with our crew and put Jafar on speaker. "You're sure it's only Tito and three of his men, along with the crew to run the boat?"

"Absolutely sure. I lucked out and got solid images of the people boarding. I have him locked on. I'm streaming his location to you now. Best of all, his course will bring him within sight of the Sea Wolf."

"Thanks. I will network with you. John's here. We need to discuss this."

"I understand," Jafar replied. "He wanted to kill you all. I'm a junior Monster, but to me, that means light the fires, cue 'Ride of the Valkyries', and send 'La Belleza' to the bottom of the ocean."

"Your opinion is respected, Achmed," Lucas said. "We don't discount your input. Stay on the network. Clint just indicated you're on with us right now, from bridge to fantail."

"I'm tracking and scanning the vessel for anything I can talk you into vaporizing it for – this Tito comes out of nowhere and hires a kill mission on the most dangerous team on the planet. It… wait one… shit… Tito's heading for you - no doubt about it and at flank speed!"

Casey came out of the hold with our airburst EMP gun. He passed it to Lynn. "Say hello… to my little friend!"

"Tito must have our position locked too," I said. "We'll need a full speed sweep-by to get him in range of the EMP gun, Lucas, but not so close we get caught in our own weapon's airburst fire. I know we have our equipment shielded from electromagnetic pulse attack. I just don't want to take a chance of something going wrong."

"I hear you. Get into battle gear, Recon! I hate killing beautiful ships, but this dog needs put down without casualties on our side. I'll pace him and race him. Those cruisers ain't got shit for a full power confrontation. He has something aboard he plans to boink us with. His boys must have gotten word to him we were eating them alive. He knows his killers are dead. I'll jet out further from the coast as far as he'll chase us."

I was already stripping out of the banana colored dry-suit. Lucas wasted no time. He went to the bridge with one thought in mind, get as far out to sea as we could without discouraging Tito. The rest of us prepared for the attack of an unknown variety. When it became apparent Sea Wolf gained on the larger ship, Lucas slowed to allow Tito to close the distance. Jafar would transmit anything lethal they showed on deck in real time. We became Monsters. We knew many would die aboard the 'La Belleza' who probably only slept with the dogs, never figuring to be punished for the fleas they woke with. I did not see a positive outcome for the crew of 'La Belleza'. I rushed down to get a quick blessed shower. When I came on deck, I was ready for what would be done.

I brought the XM25 rocket launcher from below deck, placing it on the deck with ammo near Lynn. Dev, Tommy, and Jess were armed with MP5s, but we don't ask them to participate in a kill mission. Our upgraded XM307 pop-out mount with its M2 Browning, Ma Deuce .50 caliber counterpart, would be manned by Casey and I. Lucas slowed more, allowing 'La Belleza' to come within sight. He started the combination 'Jaws' and 'Ride of the Valkyries' theme songs while swinging around in a zig-zag pattern. Then things got real.

"Jesus… God in heaven…" Jafar exclaimed. "They have a pop-out rail gun!"

"Calm the hell down, Achmed," Lucas called out for all of us to hear. "Coming in range, Lynn. Ready the EMP gun. On my mark… now!"

Lynn fired the electromagnetic pulse, airburst weapon multiple times, targeting the boat's control bridge, along with randomly selected targets, until 'La Belleza' became a floating piece of debris.

"Rip her, Case," Lucas ordered.

Casey sang out the 'Yellow Rose of Texas' while firing with expert precision from stem to stern on 'La Belleza', shredding everything with the .50 caliber depleted uranium loads. He did so at the water line, so no matter what the crew did, there would be no rescue for the poor 'La Belleza'. I sighted in the rail-gun, which is one powerful weapon, capable of reducing the Sea Wolf to atomic dust. With 'Ride of the Valkyries' singing inside my soul and blasting everything else into silence, I blew the rail-gun into pieces, the force of my 25mm barrage pitching what was left of it into the sea.

Lucas circled the Sea Wolf around 'La Belleza' like a we were a pack of wolves completing the kill, which we were. He circled with our death anthem blaring while we visited death upon any crew stupid enough to get within sight. I probably mentioned we're Monsters. Like El Muerto, we don't like being hunted, and we tend to destroy our enemies without hesitation or mercy. As the ship sank, what we had hoped for happened. The surviving crew abandoned ship, waving their arms in surrender. We held fire for the time being. I spotted Tito on one of the life-rafts put hurriedly into the water. I made sure everyone knew which one was Tito, so the one we wanted alive would be around to talk with Lynn. We killed everyone else. Clint wounded Tito, who drew a weapon out of desperation.

Lucas eased the Sea Wolf near Tito's small life-raft, he shared with two other dead men. Clint had clipped a piece of his shoulder. Tito sat holding his shoulder while glaring at me. I waited for Lucas to nudge the Sea Wolf's fantail ramp near Tito's life-raft. I then hung onto the railing and held out a hand. Clint kept his MP5 trained on Tito's head. We don't take chances.

"C'mon aboard, Tito. If you force me to come and get you, it will be a very painful transfer."

Tito, thinking he would be taken prisoner, decided to take his chances with us. He let me help him aboard our fantail ramp. "You killed my crew in cold blood!"

Everyone within hearing of that gem greeted it with loud amusement. I guided him to a seat on the main deck. "We know you planned to kill us. Did you plan to do it in warm blood? Don't make any more stupid comments."

"You doctor him, Cheese. We'll blow everything into pieces. Lucas can work the XM307, while Casey turns the bodies into mush. I'll get my practice with the XM25. All Snow Whites go below. This won't be pretty."

Lynn did not get an argument from Tommy, Jess, and Dev. They went below. Clint stayed with me while the fireworks began in earnest. We didn't want any bodies or bits of debris still floating on the surface. I grabbed our medical kit and stripped off Tito's coat and shirt after doing a thorough search for weapons and his phone. I knew he would have the phone on his person instead of throwing it overboard. By the time I finished doing a patch job on his shoulder, the Monsters finished making human sushi in the water. The sharks arrived to get some fresh human. The only sign of Tito's boat were random bits. We could then speak in normal tones.

"First off… where the hell did you get a rail-gun?"

Seeing no reason to lie about it, Tito made a flippant gesture with his hand. "I had it, and the hidden mount, made in Mexico from a Chinese design."

"Ever get to use it," Clint asked.

"Twice. They never knew what hit them. How did you stop my boat?"

"With a prototype airburst electromagnetic pulse weapon. Why the hell did you want us dead? We had a fight agreement."

"Ian believes he will tear you apart in the octagon. After you beat Carl Logan, I lost confidence in Wolf's ability to beat you. With the title, we could get grudge matches with Logan going again and make a fortune. Plus, I believe Wolf can beat Logan. You destroyed Carl. With you gone, we had easy sailing. I don't like you, Harding, but not enough to kill you over a goofy UFC match, even if it meant Ian Wolf would be champ. I took a twenty-million-dollar contract to kill you, and your crew, from Khaled Hanniyey."

By then we had quite the audience with Lucas guiding the Sea Wolf in a slow parallel course to the shore, away from the wreckage. "How did Hanniyey even know you?"

"We have similar smuggling interests in Mexico: weapons, drugs, and people. I have helped get some of his Isis dupes into the country. Can I buy my life with their names?"

"No, but you can achieve room temperature without screaming for a long time," Lynn said. "We'll also need all your bank account information. These operations cost time and money. You'll be pleased to know we're going after Khaled next."

Tito thought hard for a moment. I could tell he had been dealing death to others for a long time. He knew how bad it could be for him. "I imagine you have someone networked in to check what I tell you and transfer the accounts."

"We do. Let's get started." I opened the line to Jafar. "Tito wishes for you to check his information, little brother."

"Ready to go, John."

"One other thing, Tito," I said. "Did Ian or his manager know about the contract?"

"No. Ian thinks he's king of the world. His manager has been with him since the beginning. It was my idea to have him fake the fractured wrist. He was pissed at me after you beat Logan. I paid him what his cut would have been from the fight to shut him up. Ian could upset you for sure. He's excellent at ground and pound. His jujitsu holds can submit in an instant. I am sure you have seen his punching power with both hands."

"I have. He's impressive. Thanks. I'm glad he didn't have anything to do with this."

* * *

We docked two hours later with much more information about Khaled's operation and a lot more money in our accounts. Dev stopped me as we all separated on our own.

"Lora told me you would be going with Jess and me to San Francisco. After today, are you still interested in going?"

"I get out of going in the water, Dev. What do you think?"

Tommy overheard the conversation. "We'll need to leave the dock sooner, so you can get back in time."

"Forget it, Snow White Sands. I need to take Al and the Sparks twins to school tomorrow morning, making sure everyone knows the kids are under the protection of a giant bridge troll."

"Okay… I'll give you that. We need to stay ready, John. This Ian Wolf is no joke. Forget about the bloody handler. He's dead and gone. Wolf doesn't need Tito to sign for the fight."

"Stop worrying. I'm in the best shape of my life. I may not be dedicated enough to beat Rocky, the poke pole, but that doesn't mean anything, other than a few lost bouts with that stupid pole."

"DL's right, T," Jess said. "That damn pole is hell on earth for him in the water. Logan and Wolf would kill themselves after one training session just to avoid having to do it again."

"I counted twice if Crue hadn't let go of Rocky, she would have been sailing into the water," Dev added. "You let go so quick, it's hard to tell when you're in danger, chicken-shit."

We shared amusement over Dev's statement on Tommy's less than brave pole handling, including Tommy. "I admit it. I ain't ever getting catapulted into the ocean again… ever!"

Lynn joined us with Clint following. Her Cruella Deville antennae perking to attain all audio reception. "I heard my name being blasphemed over here, Devon."

"Don't start on me, Crue," Dev retorted with a wave-off of his hand. "I know your emotions run wild when you don't get to torture someone. Tito was no dummy. He earned a painless passing. Wasn't it enough with you blasting all kinds of shit into little pieces? We all know if you hung on to the pole every time, you're goin' into the ocean at some point."

Lynn ignored the dig about letting go of the pole. "You're right about one thing: I do enjoy blowing stuff to bits. Tito was old school. He knew what was coming. He probably deserved to get at least an hour of pain penance, but he sure filled in some blanks. What do you guys protect this tourist group from in San Francisco?"

"Mostly, the sacred homeless," Dev answered.

"The damn bums have gotten aggressive as hell," Jess added. "When they spot foreign tourists, they annoy the hell out of them, or worse. We also guide their decisions on what to see. Some tourists think it would be great to explore the Tenderloin district."

"Lately, we've seen the gangs showing in the business areas. The Surenos and MS-13 gang members hooked up a while back," I explained. "They're battling the Nortenos for more territory. They've been drifting away from the lower Mission District areas around Dolores Park. Our group tomorrow has a business meeting at one of those rent-a-meeting-room places on California Street. They want to go sightseeing in the morning before attending their meeting in the afternoon."

"Can Clint and I get in on this? I know we'd need to drive separately, but we could take Amara and the baby with us. We don't get into the city much."

"I don't see why not. We're meeting them at the Mark Hopkins Hotel at 10am."

"You guys wear all black, right?"

"Yep. We do the MIB imitation, any style," I answered.

"I don't think Crue should go," Jess bravely declared. "She's a trouble magnet. We do these guide gigs without anyone getting hurt. Sure as hell, the trouble magnet will generate some confrontation with who knows what."

As Lynn started to slow boil, Jess and Dev launched an MC Hammer 'You Can't Touch This' rendition. Despite Clint enjoying the show, Lynn pointed at our musical duo. "I'm going. Want to touch that?"

"No Mrs. – I'm done," Jess stated. "We got the Dark Lord with us, and Dev can call down the Latin if need be."

Lynn latched onto Tommy as he tried to slink away. "Snow White Sands. Get your stuff together. Clint and I will pick you up for a San Francisco visit at 9am. Wear your MIB gear."

"I know what you're doing, psycho. You want me along in case some idiot wants to pitch pennies with the knife. Can't you ever just enjoy some place you pick to visit."

"C'mon, Tommy, it'll be fun. You're on the clock with the 'Oakland Dark Lord Office'. We're not on bond enforcement. We're guiding tourists. What could go wrong?"

"Only you, psycho… only you. Fine… I'll go, if for no other reason than to help keep John alive for another MGM Grand date."

"Gee… thanks, T."

* * *

The jinx happened at of all places, Union Square, in the open area in front of Macy's where they light up the Christmas Tree every year. We introduced the four extremely nice Chinese businessmen to everyone. They loved us right from the start. They were big UFC fans, so our conversation stayed in the octagon, training, and the MGM Grand. Tommy and Lynn captivated them with tales of Rocky the poke pole.

Union Square was what they wanted to see first. Surrounded by big name complexes, the Square shines, especially at Christmas time. The Politicos don't let the police keep the vagrants out of anywhere, unless they have a rally for their own personal wealth. The vagrants in San Francisco urinate, defecate, and inhabit private and public property throughout the city. They vandalize and harass tourists, citizens, and property. The cure would be 'chain gangs'. When vagrants are apprehended tearing the city apart, the proper treatment would be 'chain gangs', cleaning up the messes in the city. No one has the guts to do that, so we're stuck with the 'homeless' – a dipshit label for able-bodied people too lazy to work, who spend their time either getting drunk or stoned.

It happened suddenly, because Amara stopped with Clint Jr at a spot where she could look up at the giant Macy's building in awe with Clint Jr happily giggling. The rest of us had walked ahead with the businessmen. We thought at this time in the morning, our relaxed, happy-go-lucky attributes would put them at ease, and create a welcoming atmosphere for the day. Fail! A big woman, pushing a shopping cart full of homeless crap scraps, blocked off Amara.

"Hey… bitch… I seen you eyeballin' me. You think you better than me?"

"I never looked at you, ma'am," Amara answered politely. "I have no idea what you are referring to."

"Don't talk down to me, bitch! I pound you into the pavement!"

Amara has been trained, like her coworker, Dannie, in the combat arts. No one touches or comes close to Clint Jr without a response. Amara silently stepped between Clint Jr's buggy and the fat homeless cretin, gesturing wildly at Amara in rage. "I wish you no harm, but I will not allow you to come any closer."

"I'll show you closer!"

When the woman attacked, Amara side-kicked her knee-joint. The woman pitched sideways in a heap to the cement, screaming in agony. A host of her brethren, waiting in anticipation of anything they could join in on, streamed toward the scene. I signaled our main crew to stay where they were. Jess alertly began taking a movie with his iPad. Clint, Lynn, and I ran back to confront the 'vagrant army'. Clint is a black belt in many martial arts. He prefers deadly force. He allows some interaction with casual acceptance. When the interaction becomes violent, Clint loves a final solution. I speeded in to prevent multitudes of idiots lying dead at our feet. I gestured at the ones charging in to stop. My size helped.

"That's far enough. Go back to your cardboard boxes, or wherever you came from."

A big guy launched at me with a sucker-punch. I hit him so hard in the chest, I think birdies sang from his belly. He hit the deck, gasping for breath and life. Another big dude pulled a knife. He advanced on me, with what I'm sure he thought was horrifying intent. I simply sighed with acceptance as Lynn rushed in, gesturing for the dummy to stop. He wasn't going to stop until looking down the barrel of Clint's Colt.

"Hold right there, Betty! Tommy! I need you, White Sands."

Tommy came forward reluctantly. I saw him glancing around, hoping for a policeman on the scene. I knew he imagined blood and bodies on the Union Square surface. The vagrant army, restless because things were not going their way, started moving in a semicircle. I put on my leather gloves and began decking the ones beginning to circle us. That stopped the circling vagrants. The woman who started it all wailed like a banshee. The guy with the knife saw Clint turn to pistol whip one of the guys maneuvering on his side and lunged. Lynn sliced him from wrist to elbow. The knife clattered to the pavement, followed by the guy, cradling his bloody mess of an arm.

Lynn was so mad about being cheated out of a show, I thought she'd start cutting random vagrants. Instead, she took out her stun-gun and zapped the wailer into unconsciousness. The silence was welcome. "Damn it, Cheese! I thought I'd lucked into some entertainment."

"C'mon, babe, let John handle this," Clint urged. "We'll rejoin our group with Amara and the baby."

"Okay… you did good, kid," Lynn told Amara. She wiped her knife on the bleeding arm guy, and walked away with Clint and Amara, pushing the entertained Clint Jr along.

I turned to the vagrants, who stupidly stayed in place, milling around, commiserating with the wounded. "Follow us at your own peril. If I see any of you bums on our tail, I will break pieces off you slime-balls."

I backed away, watching for anyone reaching for something, but the ones with broken faces, along with the bleeder, acted as cautionary notes against stupid moves. Curiously enough, no police arrived on scene. Granted, regular citizens headed for the safety of the stores, leaving the open mall area populated by only the vagrants. I debated whether to make a full report to the police with a copy of the movie Jess took, but I was afraid someone would only doctor the video to show our reaction to the attack. The businessmen, of course, thought the violent confrontation so entertaining, they asked if we had staged it for them.

Jess expressed his theory quietly out of the businessmen's hearing. "We brought the trouble magnet. That's what happened. Anyone else surprised about no cops being around?"

"I've heard they've gotten thrown under the bus so many times while enforcing the law, they wait for orders, rather than patrolling," Dev said.

"All I know is I'm glad we got away without a bloody mess on our hands," Tommy said. "Broad daylight in Union Square ranks last in places hosting knife and gun fights. It's one thing for Crue to slice and dice in a back alley. It's insanity to do it in Union Square. You better get out in front of it, John... maybe with our FBI contacts, Sam Reeves and Janie Labrie."

"I'll do that when we get done today. We won't take any more chances on this trip either. They want to go to Golden Gate Park next. There's seventy-five hundred vagrants in this damn city, and around two hundred nest in Golden Gate Park. Let's stay together and avoid trouble, right Crue?"

"I know Tommy was right, Cheese," Lynn admitted. "We'll strictly do our sightseeing gig without endangering your clients."

* * *

Golden Gate Park represents both beauty and danger. Renegade vagrant campers make the park a place to avoid at night. The beggars during the day aggressively annoy people with their panhandling. They cannot be completely avoided, especially the areas of the park near Haight Street. We escorted our clients through the Academy of Science, the Conservatory of Flowers, Queen Wilhelmina's Tulip Garden, and some genuine Dutch windmills. We saved the Japanese Teagarden for last. With Jess, Dev, and Tommy leading the way, we avoided all but a few of the beggars.

Near the Teagarden, three nasty looking vagrants plied their aggressive panhandling techniques on a family of four, I could tell were foreign tourists with two small children. We don't stand by while crap like that happens in front of our eyes. Lynn stayed with Amara and the baby, while Clint and I went to help the tourists. I put on my gloves to handle the physical stuff. Clint would watch for weapons. The children started crying as they huddled behind their mom. Their dad tried to reason with the men. He spoke broken English with a heavy Russian accent. The three bearded bums took a step back as Clint and I approached.

"Get away from these people," I told the bums. Clint sent the family on their way.

"We got rights!"

"Not with me, you don't," I told big-mouth. "You three ass-wipes help make this park into a cesspool. If I ran this city, bums like you would be wearing leg irons, digging ditches, or cleaning the streets."

"You can't tell us what we can or can't do," big-mouth's friend told me.

"I just did, Porky. Walk away or taste some pain."

The friend was nearly my size and a mean looking tramp. He tried to sucker-punch me. I blocked the punch with a knife-hand strike that snapped his wrist. The big baby fell sideways to the ground, holding his now floppy paw, sobbing for help. His two buddies, too stupid to take a hint, produced leather billy-clubs, and rushed Clint and me. I smashed a left hook to the lead attacker's belly that nearly drove his stomach out through the back. He dropped without a sound, writhing on the ground in silence. Clint grabbed the arm used to swing the billy-club at him. With a quick twist, he popped the man's shoulder out of its socket. The guy screamed bloody murder, so Clint chopped him in the throat before popping the shoulder back in.

"It's a great day for regular people and a piss poor one for the vagrants, brother," Clint said. "That first dude's wrist sounded like a rotten tree branch snapping under your knife-hand strike. It's no damn wonder all the UFC guys want your use of it banned."

I nodded as we rejoined our very entertained group. "My kicks are what set up anything I do with my hands. I admit the work with Rocky the poke pole has nearly made my speed with the knife-hand strike as fast as my left jab. I need the speed. I can't talk to Tommy. He'd want to toss me overboard from 'Ranger' and shoot arrows or something at me during our cruise. I want to dance with Lora while Muerto entertains."

"That's all Lynn talks about lately. She's primed for nights of dancing. Dead-boy really got to her the last time. When Dead-boy can make tears run down her cheeks, he's in a land beyond space and time."

"Agreed."

Humorously, the Chinese businessmen were shadowboxing what Clint and I did, speaking so fast, I had to shift concentration, or miss what they said. When I laughed, Clint gestured questioningly. "They think we're superheroes. They wonder if we go out at night righting wrongs, catching criminals, and then tying them up for the police to find – like Spiderman."

"They don't know our justice system very well," Clint replied.

Lynn met us. "What do you guys want to do when we take them to their meeting on California Street. We could walk the baby down to Dolores Park."

"Dolores Park hosts gangland brawls for territory between the Surenos and Nortenos," I explained. "It's one of the reasons we need to guard our clients even on California Street. The gangs keep pushing and the city keeps letting them."

"I know what Muerto would do with this situation," Lynn replied.

"Yep. He'd find their hangouts and toss in some grenades. Nick does that sparingly where he lives though. I admit… this has been the worst interaction with the bums we've ever had. Those three dirt-bags hassling tourists with kids in the daytime means the city has lost control." I looked at my watch. "We need to get our group to California Street. You and Clint can take Amara and the baby home. We'll finish the guide tour."

"I think we'll do exactly that," Lynn replied. "We saw enough San Francisco sights. You be careful with the Snow Whites, Cheese."

"They're only Snow Whites compared to us Monsters. I'd go into combat with them anytime, and anywhere."

"The combat has to be too well defined," Lynn replied. "Snow Whites hesitate. Clint knows what I mean."

"Lynn's right about that. I love Jess, Dev, and Tommy like family, but they have a conscience capable of freezing their trigger pull. We don't. If alone in a secluded spot, you, me, and Lynn would have killed the vagrant army we faced at Union Square."

Boy, was he right about that. "We'll be guarding these guys on California Street, not Kandahar. You go home and enjoy the rest of your day. The Snow Whites and I have this."

     * * *

On California Street, we waited outside the building for our clients, who were in their meeting. Large decorative planters ringed the well-maintained plaza area. Jess, Dev, and Tommy seemed much more relaxed. We frankly felt less stress without Cruella Deville accompanying us. The weather: mild, with very little wind, and the sun peaking in and out, made for a pleasurable moment.

"You can kick Wolf's ass, John," Tommy said suddenly. "I have no doubt about it. The part that scares me is when you start playing around. That was never like you."

"You're full of shit, T! I carried guys until you gave me the sign to put them down. It's different in the UFC. I admit I may let the Monster out, dancing at intervals, but so what?"

"Those were backstreet brawls," Tommy rebutted. "Hell… you whupped these two without complaining about the entertainment factor I signaled to you."

Uh oh. I was already waving my hands at Dev and Jess. "Don't take that to heart, brothers. Tommy and I were on the edge with the street fighting. Sometimes, because of the odds, I couldn't go full bore."

"We know," Jess admitted. "Even when you told me you went full on, I knew you didn't. It's okay. Dev and I know you carried us for the bettors on the fights. It helped us get to a much better place, earnin' big time money, and having a blast doing it. I can't wait to get back to the MGM Grand. That is fun shit. We rocked the house when you fought Logan."

"Our feelings ain't hurt, John," Dev added. "This fight with Wolf will go according to plan. You and the Monsters killed the bad element. Wolf will concentrate on the fight and not appeasing his Tito master. Tommy keeps pushing you for your own good… but damn… no one else could endure your training regimen."

"Thanks, guys, I…" then we got fronted. Half a dozen guys sauntered into our airspace, two of them with those dumb-shit MS-13 tats on their heads. Since they were aligning themselves with the Surenos, I figured these guys were all Surenos.

"Hey… ain't you John Harding, the UFC champ?" A lanky guy, a little over six feet tall, wearing the usual loose-fitting gang-banger dress, peered up at me through his sunglasses.

"Yes."

"We hear you head the Oaktown Cartel… that bullshit bunch breaking down the gangs in the East Bay."

"We do absorb the gangs when they move into our territory, running drugs, extortion rackets, and weapons."

"What you doin' here? This Sureno territory."

"We're escorting tourists doing a business meeting." I didn't see any harm in the truth, but I watched gang-banger hands.

"You need permission to do business here. There's a toll."

"We don't pay tolls, and I don't need your permission to do anything."

My response drew loud amusement from the Surenos. Lanky finally caught his breath after a period of hand gesture crap and muttering threats. "Maybe we absorb Oaktown right now."

"You're welcome to try. Do you know the rules?"

"What rules?"

"If you want to absorb Oaktown, you need to beat me. Normally, it's a one on one challenge. Since this is your territory, I'll take on all six of you."

Tommy took over as my challenge sobered them up. "The champ doesn't fight for nickels. How much money do you bunch have? We'll cover the bet at five to one odds."

The gang-bangers huddled together when we remained silent, waiting for their answer. Lanky waved some cash. "We got three hundred."

Tommy always carried two thousand. He showed Lanky the money. "You're covered."

I stripped down to my t-shirt, handing my Colt and clip on holster to Dev. I put on the leather gloves I brought. My guys backed away, leaving me facing off with the six, who began spreading out. I ran over Lanky in the center, with a flying left knee to the chest, using a side-kick with my right to crush the guy's knee joint next to Lanky. Continuing to my left, using the push off from the screaming knee-joint guy, my right hook smashed the one on

Lanky's other side square in the face as he turned, shattering his nose.

Dropping down, I leg whipped busted nose to land heavily on his back. I caught the one on my blindside rushing in with a heel kick in the stomach. Blocking a wild haymaker from the last man standing on the left, my uppercut lifted him clear of the ground, busting a bunch of his teeth. He hit the ground with a cry of agony, spitting teeth and blood. When I turned and made sure to stomp my stomach kick recipient in the face, the last guy ran for it. I caught him within twenty feet. He waved his hands when I yanked him backwards to the pavement.

"I'm done, man!"

"Calm down. Do you have a car?"

"Yeah… it down the street."

I helped him up. "Go get it and clean your boys off the street. If you show a weapon, we'll kill all of you. Do you understand?"

"I get it… I get it." He ran off to retrieve their punk-mobile.

Although pasty white, Lanky managed to sit up, trying to gasp air into his lungs. Tommy crouched near him. "You got owned by Oaktown, punk. Pay up, or John schools you again."

With a shaking hand he retrieved the cash from his pocket. Tommy accepted it and stood. The guy I sent for the car arrived. We threw the wounded inside. They drove away without another word spoken. Tommy inspected my hands after I removed the gloves. My strikes, tight fisted and on target, showed no damage. A small crowd of people, who stopped to watch the quick action, while recording it on their ever-present cell-phones, hurried away.

"You got your workout in," Dev said. He handed me my clothing first. Once I was dressed, he handed over my Colt and holster.

"Not much of a workout," Jess added. "DL put those suckers down so fast, it didn't even amount to a minute in the water."

"I think we should move inside the building," I replied. "We make easy targets out here. Someone in the crowd may have called the police too. If they don't see anyone on the street, they'll figure it's a done deal."

The building had a lobby and greeting personnel who watched the outside altercation through the many windows. I checked in with them, showing my FBI credentials, as did my companions. "Sorry about all that outside. Do the Surenos come around here often?"

One of the women with Nancy on her nametag answered. "They usually spread out along California or Fremont, selling drugs while keeping a low profile. I admit we have a lot of their customers working around this area. That was the most violent rumble I've ever seen. Why didn't you arrest them?"

"They confronted us about another matter. They didn't offer to sell us drugs," I answered. "We're here escorting clients. Did anyone call the police?"

"We didn't," Nancy's coworker, with Claire on her nametag replied. "It started and was over so fast, we never thought of it. I'm surprised those gangsters started the trouble. They acted like they knew you."

"They did in a way," Tommy said. "The leader knew John is the UFC Heavyweight Champion, and he was still stupid enough to start trouble."

"I don't watch that stuff," Nancy said. "Make yourselves comfortable."

"Thank you." I started to walk away, but Claire hurried around the counter to stop me.

"I know very little about the UFC, but could I get a picture with all you big guys around me. I'll get it enlarged and put it on the wall."

"Sure." We posed with her while Nancy took the picture. Jafar called while we were getting seated.

"Khaled confirmed with the port authority in Puerto Vallarta on 'The Rigel' departing port. He contacted his guests traveling with him about the departure for anchoring at Isla Maria Magdalena. I'm checking flights to Puerto Vallarta to see how many bad guys are going. Safia Sakaria and Mammar Rhahin have already left to join him on 'The Rigel'. Nick texted me. He made it home from Chicago without a Department of Justice investigation. He's tying some loose ends in the Grove. He agreed to another book-signing in

Pacific Grove tomorrow. School ends for Jean and Sonny the same time as Al on June 7th."

"Great. He can fly with us on the Gulf Stream. Laredo and I will pilot. We can take Gus, Johnny, Jian, Casey, Lucas, Clint, Lynn, Jess, Dev, and Tommy with all our personal weaponry. We sailed with a skeleton crew before with Gus. We'll take a launch out to Monster Island and sail the Ranger immediately to pick up all the dependents for the cruise."

"I'm not sure how I feel about mixing pleasure and combat cruises together," Jafar said. "I know we have the new AW101 transport helicopter capable of flying everyone off, but I'm still a little shaky about having Samira and Mia on board."

"If Samira feels the same way, you're under no pressure to bring her and Mia along. I hope I didn't sound like the dependents were a mandatory deal."

Jafar chuckled. "No one makes Samira do anything she doesn't want to do. We're considering it all. I hope it's not mandatory that the dependents get off the Ranger when we are mission enabled."

He froze me there. "I never considered it, little brother. We don't force anyone off, but they need to understand the danger. If Mia decides she wants to stay on board, no one will object. Pass your thoughts around on the subject. Like Lynn says 'it is what it is'. We can alter anything in our cruise plans except the actual combat."

"Thanks, John. I will post something for all of us to think about. Achmed out."

After our disconnect, I explained things to my companions. It surprised them too.

"No way do I crab this deal with my Rachel," Tommy said. "I finally get her to join me on an excursion and alter the exit? I don't think so."

"Yep. Maria and the kids will fly off," Dev agreed. "Maria knows what we do, but she wants no part of it. I wonder if Nick's Rachel feels the same way."

"Rochelle will probably want to go along," Jess said. "She always wantin' details of all the interactions we get into. The good thing is… we get to ask."

I grinned. "I can foresee one glitch in this down in Pacific Grove. Nick will be hung out to dry when he tells his Rachel and the kids there's a stay aboard option. He has another book-signing too, at the place he revealed the fake Marine at. I know Jean and Sonny will be trying to convince Rachel it's no big deal staying on board. She knows better though."

Chapter Seven

Hometown Business

"Play that crap again one more time, Muerto!" Rachel leaped to her feet with fists clenched as Jean and Sonny danced around in delight.

Deke scurried behind Nick's chair on the deck. "Calm down. You're scaring Deke. Jafar sent a text, saying it would be okay if dependents stayed aboard during our combat ops. Laredo will fly off anyone who doesn't want to be there. I will force these two minions aboard the helicopter on your decision."

"Dad!" Jean stopped celebrating and fronted Nick. "Don't let the Momster screw this trip up. Sonny and I want to crew aboard the boat before and during combat."

Nick stood and hugged Jean. "Sorry, kid. What your mom says goes. I love you and Sonny like I do my own son, Quinn. Remember… he would be with your mom."

"Send Kong and the Momster to shore!"

"That's not how families operate, kid. Your mom loves you, Sonny, and Quinn more than you can even imagine. This is dangerous business. Do not push your will any further. Your mom knows your preference. She decides."

"Why don't you get a voice in this, Dad?"

Nick gripped Jean at her shoulders gently. "Because I am a psychopathic killer, Viper. The only part of my life that sees beyond that is you and your mom. Don't make me choose, because I will choose your mom every time. She anchors me in reality. I have shown you what I will do to protect our goofy family. God help anyone attempting to hurt you, Sonny, your mom, Quinn, or Deke. You have only a vision of how far I would go. Do not badger your mom about this. Allow her to reach a decision without screaming repercussions."

Jean relaxed in Nick's hold. "I hear you, Dad. It's hard... so many things only turn out right when we react to danger violently. I'm not a spoiled brat. I understand what you're saying. Kong, Sonny, and I have our lives ahead of us. That's what mom sees. I hope she knows we'd rather die with you than live without you."

Nick released Jean and turned away. "C'mon, Deke. We need to take a walk before I lose control over everything. Thanks, Jean. That was the best. I will be back with you here no matter what. I'm with a team of professionals unmatched in ability and passion. I would never risk your Uncles Gus, Johnny, and Jian, along with your Aunt Cala unless I smelled victory without casualties."

Nick hugged Rachel on his way out. "Sorry... I should have talked to you in private about the option first. I thought of you spotting for me on the cruise ship when we took on the terrorist pirates. This will be different. If a plan I have in mind falls into place, our ship may not need to be part of the combat at all."

"You surprised me, and I overreacted a bit. Jean and Sonny dancing around like it was a done deal hit me the wrong way. Are we going to the North Bay as soon as school ends? I need to let Joe know about our time away, so he can get a substitute at the Monte."

"That's the plan. We're flying a skeleton crew to the Ranger with our personal weaponry. Gus and Lucas will pilot the Ranger to the North Bay with the skeleton crew and board the dependents. Even Dannie and Clyde may be going, although I'm not sure if Paul will let Clyde go with us on this black op."

"I'll think it over. If the Salvatores smell black op, secrecy will go right out the window. Your bribe has kept them quiet lately, but you know as well as I do, they can't be trusted," Rachel pointed out, lowering her voice. "Except for short periods of time, Sonny's already living with us."

"I know. We'll cover the trip as a vacation in the North Bay at our new house. Phil and Clarice don't need to know about a cruise. You're right though. I didn't even think about including them in any decision. I can't tell them about it."

Rachel became animated, gripping Nick's hands. "You could tell Phil and Clarice, but then you'd need to kill them."

"Very funny. I'll be back shortly." Nick turned to Sonny and Jean, who had returned to studying for final exams. "Do I need to worry about anything out on the street that happened while I was in Chicago?"

"Nope. Sonny and I have been very quiet at school. The end of the year calms everyone down. Off for the summer vacation and no more school for a while makes everyone a little friendlier."

"Just checking." Nick led the way with Deke following.

Outside, the fog moved slowly upwards toward their house. Crisp, cool June weather in the upper fifties energized the fog bank on a regular basis in the early evening. Nick walked on the level street above his house, not wanting to give Deke the long uphill return from the ocean. A car engine started down the street. He saw the brief flashing lights of a squad car. Neil Dickerson drove alongside of Nick and Deke with a wave.

"I was hoping you'd emerge for the walk with Deke. I didn't want to call and bother you. I know it was you tearing Chicago crime out a new asshole. What sent you on a return mission there? That Alderman Briston Harley confessing so he wouldn't meet up with Muerto was the funniest justice I've ever heard of, Nick. What's your CIA Director Gilbrech think about you going rogue in the Windy City?"

"So many questions, Chief. Are you writing a book? A contact of mine was in trouble there. I don't abandon my friends... ever. Gilbrech sent me to Chicago in the first place to save his stepdaughter and step-grandchild. He knows what I do often has unintended consequences. What can I do for you, Neil?"

"I have a problem on 14th Street. Can I park and walk with you?"

"Yep. I need to tell you I'm going away with my crew soon. If this problem needs long term surveillance type attention, I'll need to put you off for a time."

"Let me park and see what you think." Neil crossed to the right side of the road and parked his squad car, locking it and hurrying to join Nick and Deke. Neil did so with some trepidation. He knew being a friend to the most dangerous assassin in the world had consequences, including personal ones where he nearly died, along with his family. Only one solution ended the threat: Nick McCarty.

They walked half a block in silence as Neil gathered how he wanted to present his case. Nick noticed. "Spit it out, Neil. You know everything there is to know about unintended consequences. I'll warn you of them if there are any."

"There's an older retired couple living nearly parallel to you on 14th. A new jackass invaded the neighborhood. It doesn't happen in the Grove often because it's expensive as hell owning a house here. Apparently, this guy's parents died in a car crash on Interstate 156. They had thrown his ass out of the house years ago because he went nuts on drugs and booze. They didn't leave a will, so he claimed and received the entire estate, including 401Ks and annuities worth over a million dollars."

"I'm a writer with a vivid imagination. I don't like where this is going."

"Me either," Neil replied. "He's terrorizing the neighborhood, especially this older couple, because they've called the police to complain about his partying style with loud music, drugs, booze, and even fights in the street."

"I get it. The police arrive to quiet things down, warn this clown, and then they trek off, only to have this imbecile begin again. What did he do?"

"He vandalized their cars and house. Naturally, there's no proof. I tried talking with the couple, urging them to buy a first-class home security system. They did what I suggested. Now, they have recordings of a black hooded man vandalizing their yard, cars, and house front in HD format."

Nick chuckled, gripping his friend's shoulder and shook it. "This is a rough business outside the law, huh?"

"In the old days, a few cops would stop by and kick the livin' crap out of this wanker, warning him if he continued making problems for the neighborhood, he would end up floating in the ocean."

"Yep. When the justice system lines up on the side of criminal sensibilities, Chicago is what happens to it. When law and order are enforced, there will always be some aberration, where violence messes with Snow Whites' minds. Remember the old saying – 'People sleep peaceably in their beds at night only because rough men stand ready to do violence on their behalf'."

"I'm handcuffed, Nick. I see the looks of terror on this couple's faces, and I want to go to this guy's house and shoot him in the head. He bought a high-priced lawyer to file grievances with the city on his behalf about harassment. Now, the mayor ordered us not to invade this man's privacy. We have a complete dickhead as a mayor. In a way... I commiserate with him. I know the city settles instead of fights in court."

"I believe you have a grasp of the legal system nowadays, Neil. What is it you want me to do? I don't warn wankers off. I'm a final solution you recognized when muggers terrorized walkers along the beach path, and you asked for my help. We have no secrets between us now. You know what I do."

"You're going to make me say it," Neil replied, with head down while walking. "I deserve that, because the damn law doesn't work anymore. I want this prick dead. He has a sister, the parents loved. She wouldn't challenge his claim because she knows her brother would kill her and her family."

"Let's enjoy the fog and the June evening while we walk Deke. Send me everything, including all the sister's details. I believe I can convince this prick to do what's right."

"You are one very dangerous resource, Nick."

"Never forget that, my friend. I'm not a tool to be used haphazardly, and I want to distance anything we do from you and your family. Believe me when I tell you I don't want to ever see your wife and kids at my door next to death... ever again."

"I caused that through carelessness, Nick. I won't ever make that mistake again. I wish our families could be closer, have dinner together, play ball in the park... it cannot be. I know that now. How does your crew handle it?"

"One day at a time... one day at a time."

After Nick returned to the house, he found everyone awaiting him on the entertainment deck. He fixed Deke with a beer bowl and sat down with his own concoction. "I found out local law enforcement needs a dark side bolstering of justice. I never underestimate you two adolescent monsters, so I figured you saw Neil approach me."

"We always follow you and Deke's trail on walks, Dad," Jean stated. "We never know when someone will be waiting to be shot in the head."

"Gee… thanks for that bright spot."

"Okay… what did Neil assign you," Rachel asked. "I know he wasn't stalking you for the fun of it."

Nick explained the parameters of their meeting. "It's nearby and dangerous. I'm taking it on. I don't want a sociopath expanding operations. He chose his path. Guys like him never have security systems because they figure everyone else around them never pose a threat… until they run into a law enforcement agent who embraces alternatives."

"What are you planning for this assignment?"

"Enforce the law, Viper… enforce the law."

"I don't like that answer, Dad. It means nothing works in law enforcement. I wonder how Neil can arrive at work every day, knowing he's not allowed to stop the bad guys."

"It means reality. I don't sugarcoat what exists in reality. Neil follows the course dictated by leftist traitors and idiots, who know nothing beyond getting elected. He accepted me as a counterweight to injustice. I need to fulfill what he asks for… but only if I know in my psycho mind that what he asks for is just."

"Vigilante justice," Rachel stated.

"Yep. That is what it amounts to, now that oblivious human beings cannot abide the darkness within the actual enforcement of the law. Does any thinking human being side with a criminal in the act of visiting violence and misery on another human being? No… they don't, but regular everyday citizens vote idiots into positions of power who allow it and champion it. Justice is something tentative, held in the hand with knowledge of what can happen when it disappears… like now, for that old retired couple living in fear for their lives."

"What will you do then, Dad?"

"I'm goin' there and set things right."

"That's 'Outlaw Josie Wales' talk again, Muerto. You can't deal with reality in movie terms," Rachel retorted. "Everything can't be black and white. There must be some middle ground where you can reason with people."

"Neil tried reasoning, Mom! Why do you think he asked for Dad's help? Some folk just need killin'.'"

Nick enjoyed Jean's statement with loud amusement at first, followed by snorting wave-offs of Rachel's tightlipped angst. "Jean's right. Where the hell do you think you two and Deke would be if I let the law dictate our course?"

"Dead in a landfill somewhere... I imagine," Rachel admitted, as visions of the actions outside the law Nick had done to save her, Jean, and Deke, knifed into her consciousness. "God knows I caused it too."

Nick embraced his soulmate with a grim smile. "You embraced justice outside the law... just as Neil is doing. Think about that old couple having their retirement lives destroyed by an animal that should have been beaten into submission."

"You could do that, Nick." Even as she said it, Rachel knew different.

Nick's lips tightened on his mouth as he looked into the eyes of his only love. "No... I can't. I'm not that kind of angel," Nick quoted from the movie 'Michael'. "Neil asked for justice. When he asks that of me, it's because he knows beyond any doubt innocent lives will be lost or tortured to death by a brainless idiot without conscience. Someone who thinks they are above any law. Not so, this time, bucko. I accepted the contract."

"Really... what does it pay, Muerto?"

"My honor, and what little human commiseration I have left."

Rachel shrugged and hugged Nick. "Done deal."

"C'mon, Sonny. I better get you home. I need to drive by a house on the way."

"Yes, Sir."

* * *

Todd Stewart awoke in a sweat, his heart pounding, and his chest feeling constricted. He thought at first, he way overdid his drinking the night before. Sitting up in bed and swinging his legs over the bedside, dizziness and blurred vision assaulted his senses. Todd leaned against the headboard of his bed, panting for breath. A light across the bedroom came on, silhouetting a figure dressed all in black. Todd pawed in panic for the Glock 9mm he had in his nightstand.

"It's not there, Todd."

"What...what are you doin' in my house? Get out! I..." Todd tried to stand. Instead, he crashed into his nightstand and lamp, pitching headfirst into his dresser while grabbing his chest.

"That looks just swell, Todd," the man said. "You only have another five minutes of agony left. I would have liked giving you a cleansing, but we need to keep up appearances. This way, it will look like you passed on a moment after signing a deathbed will, giving everything to your sister."

"I...I ain't signin' anything," Todd croaked in a dry rasping snarl.

"Yeah... you will. You won't be alive when you do it, but the pen will be in your hand."

"Who... are you?" Todd gasped, clawing at the neck of his t-shirt.

"I'm a concerned neighbor. I live a couple streets over. We have a nice neighborhood here. It changed when you moved into your folks' house and began terrorizing the people around you. You wouldn't listen to the nice police officer who asked you politely to leave your neighbors alone, so the police officer asked me to set things right again. My name is Nick McCarty."

Todd writhed on the floor in earnest, soaked in sweat, his chest heaving. "Get me... to a hospital! You...you can't just... kill me!"

"I already did that, Todd. It was the least I could do for you... the very least."

Todd reached out to the man in black as his vision faded with his life.

* * *

"Thanks for reaching out, Todd."

Nick used Todd's hand to print a shaky apology to his sister, saying he knew he was dying, and he wanted to make things right by naming her his sole heir. Nick did a decent forgery of Todd's scribble at the end. He then slipped the magazine out from under the paper, allowing Todd's hand with pen to relax on the paper. The pen dropped away.

"See, I knew you would do the right thing in the end. You've made your sis a very happy woman."

* * *

Rachel felt Nick's weight easing into the bed. "I'm awake. How did your neighborhood improvement plan work?"

"Excellently. After a stern talking to, Todd left a will making his sister the sole heir to the house. Wasn't that nice of him?"

Rachel squirmed, feeling Nick's hand gliding softly over her side. "Are you murderous goofballs really cruising into combat with dependents aboard?"

"I imagine so. There will be a choice as I explained." Nick began using his lips and tongue along Rachel's back. "Cala's pregnant and she's going into combat."

"Reaper is not a dependent... oh... no... it's too late... for... oh, God!"

* * *

With his new novel 'Hell Zone' on book shelves and the Amazon digital market place, Nick worked on his new manuscript. Although thirty thousand words into it already, the book title still escaped him. Nick first thought to use Fatima in the title, but he didn't like it. Always before, the title popped into his head within the first couple of chapters. He didn't worry about it, but his agent wanted to start marketing for when he finished. She wanted a title and a brief outline so as to get a cover artist working on the book jacket. Nick loved the early mornings, but the lack of inspiration on the title plagued him. His assassin, Diego's adventure, would be loosely based on a contract he did in Russia.

"Hey, Dad… last day of school," Jean announced as she entered the kitchen. Deke glanced at her from Nick's feet but didn't move. "Al texted me. She took on three girls at school and kicked their butts."

"John had a few run-ins with the parents during the aftermath. He's glad school is ending too. Did you and Sonny get ready for the two finals you have today?"

"Yep. We'll ace them. You have a book-signing on Saturday, right?"

"Rhonda confirmed it yesterday. She knew 'Hell Zone' hit the shelves already. It's nice doing one within walking distance. I won't be a mystery author this time at the 'Book Works'. Your mom, Tina, Cala, and Jian's girlfriend want to visit the café there. Joan told Jian she's never been to a book-signing. She'll probably be bored out of her mind like your mom and Tina."

"I think your book-signings are great. Joan might really like them. Mom and Tina like the people watching a little bit, as does Cala. They're not into grammar Nazis, and people who hate your writing, the way Sonny and I are. The people who talk about the US Marshal's service always entertain too." Jean filled the tea kettle and turned on the gas burner. "I want tea and toast this morning."

"That sounds good to me too. We have rye or sour dough bread."

"I want rye. Did you go out last night?"

Nick smiled. "You know I did. Otherwise, you wouldn't be asking. Yes, I finished with the neighborhood business, left the front door unlocked, and let Neil know this morning he should find a reason to visit the house in question."

"Thanks for letting me in on this. It means a lot to me."

"You would be impossible to deal with unless given legitimate options and alternatives, Jean. I know that, and I think your mom does too. I know you're leading to the question of whether you and Sonny can stay on the 'Ranger'. Rachel hasn't decided. It's important you accept her decision."

"I know." Jean turned off the kettle. She put teabags into separate big cups and filled them, only adding creamer to Nick's cup.

Nick noted the sugar and creamer she added to her own cup. "Still liking the sweet taste, huh?"

"Yep." Jean put four slices of rye bread into their toaster. "I love it dark brown with butter. I still like slurping all the tea down afterward, especially when mom is gagging at the sight."

Rachel entered the kitchen, noting the toast Jean busily buttered, the tea, and Deke showing an interest by moving to Jean's side. "Not tea and toast! Oh God… gross!"

Jean giggled, while putting more rye bread into the toaster. "Deke's half comes out of your slices, Dad."

"Okay… but I'm doing it under protest." Nick fed Deke a half piece of rye toast, before dunking his part in the tea.

Rachel went to the coffee pot while shunning her breakfast companions so as to block the sight of their slurping goop. Jean made the loud sound effects for her benefit. Rachel sat with her coffee across the table, keeping her head either turned or staring downward. Nick ate quietly, getting up to butter the next round of rye toast, and delivering it for Jean to annoy Rachel with. At the end, Jean did her slurping of the tea mush without pity for poor Rachel, who finally ducked out of the kitchen with coffee in hand.

"Disgusting, you two… disgusting!"

A few minutes later, Nick called Rachel back in. "C'mon in, Rach. I'm washing dishes now. Jean's going to brush her teeth before school."

Rachel reentered the kitchen, passing a smiling Jean with goopy crumbs all over the inside of her mouth. Rachel hid her eyes. "Gross!"

Sitting down across from Nick, busily typing another scene, Rachel pointed at him. "She annoys me like this because you encourage it."

"That's a stretch… even for you. Jean made breakfast. I never mentioned toast and tea, but it was mighty good."

"As good as this?" Rachel stood, pulling her robe open. Nude in more than a clothing manner, she posed provocatively.

"Oh… my… you brat! You know I'm taking Jean and Sonny to school."

Rachel chuckled. "Yeah… so what's your point."

"When I get back, there will be a torture session of unimaginable proportions."

"Oh no… not that. Whatever will I do?"

Nick made gestures causing Rachel to blush and close her robe again, as she plunked down on her chair. "I won't let you, Muerto!"

"We'll see."

* * *

A balmy June morning with only a slight wind escorted the group on the way to school, with Nick putting Deke through a series of commands. Gus walked along with them, listening to the plan for Nick's book-signing. Jean showed him an impressive profile outline, she and Sonny followed for picking out unruly people in the line. At the end, Gus shook his head in wonder.

"You two are something else. After being at other book-signings with your dad, I can tell you that profile illustrates nearly a hundred percent of the grammar Nazis, unhappy readers, and ding-a-lings looking for trouble. Well done. I want a copy for Kabong and Dragon."

"Great! It's a lot of fun meeting the people who come in with this profile," Jean replied.

A car slowed. Nick drew his Colt, still making sounds at Deke, but with .45 caliber death pointed in the direction of the slowing vehicle from under his windbreaker. Gus noticed, moving in front of the kids. The vehicle, a very new Mercedes, halted next to them. The back window opened. Author Hardin Travers, the guy Nick disgraced at the last 'Book Works' book-signing as a 'Stolen Honor' fake veteran, gestured at Nick to come over to the car.

"Say what you need to say from there, Travers. I have instant messenger, an email address, a Facebook account, Twitter,

Instagram… the whole social site smear. Why would you front me here on the street while I'm walking kids to school? You could have Googled me and received at least five pages of contact information."

"Have you ever Googled my name?"

"I don't have anything I want to say to you, so no, I've never Googled your name. Really… I don't think of you at all."

"I'm here to reason with you. I read 'Hell Zone'. It's full of Islamophobic crap! It should be pulled from the bookshelves. You should be censored. In the UK, you could be put in prison for hate speech. Your book would not be publishable in Canada. You need to pull the whole thing for a complete rewrite!"

"That's what you're wasting my time here for? Are you mental? I write about true Islam, the home of pedophiles, wife beaters and enslavers, female genital mutilation freaks, honor killers of their own children, people who belt bombs onto their kids, abuse animals… in other words, Sharia Law Mutants who wash their faces with camel piss. If you want to hang with the mutants, be my guest. Stay the hell away from me."

The driver's side door popped open and a huge, chin bearded, wild-eyed guy with black stringy hair raced around the hood of the car, screaming in Arabic about blaspheming Islam. Deke leaped to meet him, all teeth, and hackles raised. The man stopped in his tracks, reaching into his jacket.

"You pull a gun, I shoot you in the head, Mutant," Nick told him in Arabic, revealing his Colt. "Get in your car and drive this dunce in the backseat away to wherever you idiots hold your hootenannies."

"You will pay for this insult to Islam!" The man returned to the driver's seat and sped away. Deke moved again to Nick's side.

"That didn't look like one of the same guys Travers had with him at the signing," Gus observed. "I didn't think you went too far with 'Hell Zone'."

"Travers may have skimmed through the novel, but I doubt those other jackasses even know I wrote anything about Islam, except for what Travers told them. C'mon, kids, let's get you to school for this last day." Nick entered something on his phone before beginning to walk Deke again. "I have their license plate number. Maybe I can learn a bit more about them. I don't like threats and I'm tired of having this walk to school interrupted."

"We'll be leaving for the North Bay in a couple days. By the time we get back, I'd bet Travers and his trolls will be protesting somewhere else," Gus replied.

"For his sake… he better be."

* * *

Nick drove his Ford down the hill with Rachel, Quinn, Jean, Sonny, Gus and Tina. Johnny and Cala would be meeting them at the 'Book Works' with Jian and Joan. "Sorry, we didn't walk today, but I don't want to take chances with all of you along today after our Travers incident."

"I don't like walking up the damn hill anyway," Tina said. "I notice you guys haven't been haunting Otter's Point as often in the morning. It wouldn't have anything to do with Jean thinking you Unholies, now numbering five, should have a hand related title, like the 'Drunken Hand', would it?"

"We cut back a bit," Nick admitted, as Jean giggled. "Mostly, it had to do with my Chicago trip."

"I thought of one too, 'Five Sheets into the Wind'," Rachel added.

"Very funny." Nick parked the Ford down the street from 'Book Works', near the Monte Café. "Are you working for a while today, Rach?"

"I'm working the afternoon shift. Joe has the back room fixed for Quinn. He loves seeing the baby, so I'll take Quinn with me."

Johnny drove alongside as Nick set Quinn's carriage on the walkway. Cala and Joan exited together from where they had been talking in the vehicle's backseat to greet Rachel and Tina. Johnny and Jian joined Nick and Gus. Jean and Sonny walked over to the sidewalk, checking the crowd forming near the 'Book Works'. Rachel took charge of the carriage.

"We'll walk over and see if we can get a seat inside the café. I think it would be easier to do so without the great Muerto."

"Gee, thanks, Rach."

"Should I stay here in solidarity with my 'Drunken Hand' companions," Cala asked.

"Go," Johnny ordered with amusement. "We shall be the 'Drunken Paw'."

Cala nodded in agreement. "Very clever, my husband – I am like the toe separated from the rest on the paw."

Cala hurried along to catch Rachel, Tina, and Joan. Jean and Sonny followed the women, as Nick gestured for them to protect and watch. Nick's phone buzzed as he began filling in his partners on the neighborhood adjustment, so they would have the same story – a small gathering at Nick's house until nearly 3am.

"Hi Neil. Don't talk on this line. We're in front of the Monte. Where are you?"

"On the other side of Lighthouse. I'm driving from an apparent heart attack call. I'll be there in a moment."

"See you then." Nick disconnected. "Neil found a reason to check my handiwork. He can fill us in on how I did with the letter."

"We'll go set things in place for the signing," Johnny said. "We came prepared this time for anything, like Jean and Sonny do, with iPads, cell-phones, and writing implements."

"Thanks, guys." Neil drove alongside Nick a moment later. Nick slipped into the squad car. "Are we okay to talk?"

"Yep. I use the gizmo you gave me for detecting bugs the moment I get in the car. Your setting was perfect. The coroner already concluded an apparent heart attack. No one will be questioning it, least of all the only surviving family member. She was the only one the least bit suspicious about the note."

"I thought she might be reluctant to believe Todd would do anything right for her. I hoped she'd consider it a miracle and let it go."

"Elaine admitted the chicken-scratch job you did on his signature sold her on Todd having written the note. She even thought maybe he had a brain tumor. Did you watch him, Muerto?"

"Of course. I need to be precise with the stuff I use. Otherwise, it will appear too obvious. I mix it a bit light, according to estimated weight. Then, the only real question is how long it will take to work. I have a book-signing to do. Thanks for briefing me. The cartoons have our story – a gettogether at my house until 3am."

"As things are now, that'll work without question. I'm glad Todd knew what was happening. The prick deserved it."

"It's a better day in the neighborhood. We're going to the North Bay probably tomorrow, visiting our other house there. We will be there for an indeterminate time. I'm hoping for just a few weeks. My satellite phone you have the number for will be on all the time if something happens needing an urgent response."

"Okay… see you when you get back. Thank you for Todd."

"It was a pleasure." Nick left the squad car. At the 'Book Works', people were streaming in and out, not actually there for the signing in an hour. Nick had worn his windbreaker with a ballcap and the hood over it. Inside, Rhonda met him at the door.

"I'm so glad you could do this, Nick. Cassie stocked me with 'Hell Zone' and 'Blood Beach' on consignment. She says your digital sales are way up."

"That's because my publisher kept the price at a reasonable rate, instead of doing what the other New York publishing houses do: jack the prices of the digital books to what they charge for paperbacks. The people who buy the digital copies are usually voracious readers. They have limited space in their houses, so a reading tablet helps considerably. You've done well here, catering also to children's reading material. Digital children's books do not make a very good bedtime story with young readers. I'm certain that will change at some point."

"The changes do worry me," Rhonda admitted. "We have the café and internet availability. We may need to expand those with specialty items."

"Agreed. It's never a good idea to not try new ideas. Workshops for different home repairs, vehicle maintenance, and computer tech can be done in coordination with various repair facilities. Writing workshops may interest people. You had a nice crowd when Travers and I talked before the book-signing. They asked some very good questions. I like your place. It's in a very nice position on our main drag, Lighthouse Avenue. The locals and tourists stop in and your shop always looks busy."

"Thank you," Rhonda replied. "I must admit, I like your idea about do-it-yourself seminars. We have many customers from the building trades and automotive repair shops. They could coach people on what they can do safely and what would be better left to professionals."

"Exactly. I think it would be a great bond with the community. I'm not much on the idealists who think no one should make a buck sharing knowledge, but a little sharing and advice would keep some folks out of trouble."

"We should have a great turnout for your signing. Everyone wants to be on hand in case you need to shoot someone or beat them up."

"Ouch!" Nick hung his head as the amused Rhonda pulled him towards where his partners, Gus and Johnny, worked setting the books on display with Jean and Sonny's help. "I'll mention we have five US Marshals in our group, three of whom also hold FBI credentials. That should dissuade people from acting out in public."

"It didn't the last time. That's okay... notoriety sells books. I only appeal on behalf of our building. We would like it in the same shape as when you entered... when you leave."

"I'll do my best, Rhonda, but you drive a hard bargain. How do you like our uniform of the day?"

"I love it. Black leather jackets, black shirts, black pants, black everything... including the kids – very eye-catching."

"I borrowed the idea from our friends in the North Bay. They're more impressive wearing them than we are by a wide margin. The leader's John Harding."

"The UFC Heavyweight Champion?"

"Yep. I bet when he visits me, I could get him to come in and talk UFC and the bond retrieval business. We can take pictures for your walls. I look like a midget next to him, but it would be fun."

Rhonda could hardly speak. "Oh...oh my God... that would be incredible, Nick! Please, do so if you can."

"I promise. You should think about getting a piano in here. I'll even buy you a great one."

"Why… why would you do that for us?"

"I sing and play piano," Nick replied. "It would be fun to entertain so close to home."

"Are you any good?"

Nick grinned. "My partners and I have been working on a number with the kids I wanted to surprise my friend John with up North. It may get our book-signing off to a great start."

"Do it! I don't care if it bombs. I want to see it."

"Done deal. Stay tuned." Nick walked over to his book-signing crew. "We're on. I told you I could do it. I snuck it in the back door with promises of John Harding, the UFC champ. We need Cala to stream it directly to Pain Central for the Monsters. We worked hard on our routines for the music and the grammar Nazi salute. Let's have some fun."

"Yes!" Johnny pumped a fist. "Ever since you did that at Alice Harding's softball game with Jess, I wanted to do it. We're good too, if Payaso doesn't screw us up."

"I'll be fine," Gus said, putting on his Ray-Ban sunglasses. "It's Dragon breath you should be worrying about. He has about as much rhythm as a spastic gerbil."

Jian rushed the table from the family seating in the first row, already fumbling his Ray-Bans in place. "That is a lie, hater Payaso. You are jealous because I have better moves."

Sonny and Jean, ready to go, stifled amusement at the usual 'Drunken Hand' banter. Nick gestured for order while putting on his Ray-Bans. Cala had them covered for video recording, trying not to shake so much in laughter, she messed up the recording.

Nick suddenly started it, with a quick turn toward the gathering crowd. "Day-O…. Da-a-a-y-O."

It was on from there. Each one knew their place with Gus, the tallest moving in rhythm to Nick's right as he sang the lyrics in perfect pitch. Johnny, Jian, Sonny, and Jean joined in harmony on his left, doing the backbeat harmonizing, their movements in perfect sync with Nick. They did the hand raising, jiving version through the second chorus with the crowd around them mesmerized, video recording, and swaying with Nick. When he finally ended the song with 'daylight come and I wanna go home', the people applauded, whistled, jumped around in enthusiasm and yelled for more.

Nick grinned. "One more."

Nick launched into 'Montego Bay' with his crew in instant harmony and movements. An entertainment frenzy captivated everyone in Rhonda's store, with every customer crowded inside, to the people gawking outside on the street, ten deep in places. When Nick and company finished, the applause thundered out to the street.

Nick stepped forward as the crowd quieted. "Thank you very much. I am US Marshal Nick McCarty. With me are US Marshals Gus Nason, Johnny Groves, Jian Chen, and Cala Groves. Three of us also have FBI credentials. Gus Nason is a master ship's pilot, Johnny and Cala Groves fly helicopters and co-pilot jet aircraft and small planes, as do I. Any, and all questions are welcome during this book-signing. We want to make this as entertaining as we can. Security has indicated the start of the line. Rest assured, I will get to you all."

Chapter Eight

The Usual

After their performance, they settled in at the table. Nick signed and shook hands, while his partners answered questions about everything, including their parts in the novels. Jean and Sonny watched the people, politely greeting anyone who spoke with them. An hour passed before Jean texted Gus and Johnny to check out the middle-aged woman - very thin, short dark hair, wearing glasses and a flowered dress, only five people away from the table. She carried only a Kindle Fire tablet in hand. Jean labeled her a grammar Nazi or nut-ball, because she fit both profiles. Gus texted back an animated nodding emoji.

Nick smiled at her when the woman reached him, noting the pinched look on her face. "Hi, how are you? Do you have anything you'd like me to sign?"

"In your novel, 'Blood Beach', your bad-ass woman character, Fatima, humiliates and smacks down a transgender in a dress going into the women's restroom at a sporting event, where Diego poisons the gangster he took a contract to kill. I want to know where you get off with this racist attitude against members of the LGBTQ community."

Nick chuckled, remembering the story of Lynn Dostiene doing what he wrote, in real life, at John Harding's UFC match. Lynn was protecting John's daughter Alice, who used the women's restroom. "I based the humorous scene on a real-life incident. By the way, I thought the proper term was LGBT. What does the Q stand for?"

The woman's face turned red. "It stands for those who identify themselves as queer, or are questioning their gender or sexual identity. Never mind that! Answer the question, and don't call me a 'Book Killer' for asking it."

"I would never call you a 'Book Killer'. When drive-by, one star, hit piece 'Book Killers' strike, they usually get the novel correctly identified when slamming it. The scene you describe happened in my new novel 'Hell Zone', not 'Blood Beach'."

Nick's correction drew amusement from the people within hearing of the exchange. He heard some women muttering in line that they didn't want men in dresses entering the women's restrooms either. The woman spun in a fury for a moment, before turning back to Nick.

"Answer the question! Never mind your twisting, snide comments."

"I can only answer it in one way: if you want an author who thinks it's okay for a man to put on a dress and enter the women's restroom, I'm not him. Find a different author. Another thing - the LGBTQ community as you call them are not a race, other than the human race, of which I'm a member."

"Your novels offend the community! They are never presented in a favorable light and you refuse to include gays in your novels!"

"You're right about that point, I choose not to write characters into my novels simply to appease some offended segment of humanity. I offend all manner of people in my novels. I also use my writing to make political and social commentary on something in real-life that bothers me. If you want to represent the LGBTQ community in a novel, write it yourself."

Applause sounded behind her, enraging the woman further. Jean stood. "If I'm ever in a women's restroom, and some guy in a dress tries to enter with me in front of my Dad, he'll get his butt kicked."

The woman smirked, folding arms over chest. "I see you're raising children to be homophobic just like you."

"Phobic means fear of. I'm not afraid of gays," Jean retorted. "I sure don't want a guy in a dress with me in the restroom. That's not fear. It's common sense."

People in line quieted, looking around guiltily, recognizing a subject they could be ridiculed or labeled for in taking sides. Jean sat down. The woman gestured at the line with sudden assurance.

"Right now, there are people in this line and store, who are members of the LGBTQ community you've offended with your disgusting behavior."

"Hey, lady," a guy ten people back in line, dressed in a business suit, holding a copy of 'Hell Zone' called out. "I'm gay and you sure as hell don't speak for me. The scene you're complaining about, from the wrong book, was hilarious. The guy in the dress tells Fatima he identified as a woman that day. Fatima tells the guy to identify as a rock, then he wouldn't need the bathroom at all."

The man in the business suit's scene description caused loud amusement because of who described it. The lady was none too pleased, but security arrived to escort her out of the store. She did not go quietly. People were telling her to 'get a life' as she struggled while being guided out of 'Book Works'.

As Nick happily returned to signing books, many of the women in line assured him they felt the same way as Fatima. Jean and Sonny returned to their duties. While watching the line, Sonny noticed another prim-faced woman, who didn't laugh at anything said, nor did she react to what the woman escorted out of the shop complained about. Jean agreed when Sonny explained his sighting. She passed it on to Gus with only one label: grammar Nazi and received the nodding emoji back.

The businessman who defended the Fatima scene reached Nick and shook hands enthusiastically, setting his book open for Nick to sign. "Would you put to my friend, Oscar?"

"Sure. I'd be glad to." Nick wrote the requested words and handed the book back.

"I heard you say the funny scene with the guy in the dress really happened. Did a woman like Fatima handle it?"

"Not exactly," Nick replied. "The woman who handled it in real-life makes Fatima look like a campfire girl. She's probably one of the most dangerous women on the planet."

"Wow... thank you for that. I love your series, Nick."

"Thanks, Oscar." Nick glanced at Gus and Johnny. "Damn... I didn't offend everyone today."

"Maybe you should write a gay into your novels," Gus responded.

"You're right. I think your character Jed needs a boyfriend."

"I'll shut up now." Gus elbowed the very amused Johnny.

The next lady put her copy of 'Hell Zone' in front of Nick with a big smile after stopping to greet both Jean and Sonny. "I hope you don't ever change the way you write your novels, Mr. McCarty. I just want your signature with, 'To Carmen'. I'm like your daughter. I don't want guys in the bathroom with me. I laughed my butt off when Fatima smacked that guy down."

"Humor was what I was shooting for, Carmen. Thanks for stopping in today."

Then it was the woman's turn Sonny picked out. She strode to stand in front of Nick with her copy of 'Hell Zone'. "You have many grammatical errors in this novel, Mr. McCarty. It should be edited and rereleased."

Nick signed the novel. "That won't be happening, but thanks for stopping by."

"One of the worst errors is your use of 'honing in' on a target, instead of using the proper phrase of 'homing in'."

"In point of fact, both phrases fit the usage and are accepted in 'Writers Digest'. I prefer 'honed in' because it means to sharpen focus. 'Homed in' became popular because of 'homing pigeons' and the phrase was extended inaccurately to missiles. A sniper like Diego 'hones in' on his target because he sharpens his focus on target. In any case, it's accepted."

The woman's mouth tightened in repressed angst at Nick's explanation. "I use a dictionary, not some digest."

"Many dictionaries also accept the phrasing."

"Not the one I use extensively."

"Too bad." Nick signaled his companions to perform as practiced for grammar Nazis. Everyone at the table stood and clapped their hands, including the kids, and then sat down.

"What the hell was that?"

"That's our salute to grammar Nazis visiting on signing days, done by a Pulp Fiction storyteller who doesn't care."

The line laughter enraged the woman. She reopened her book to a section where Fatima is described as waiting with 'baited breath'. "What about this, McCarty? I hate it when an author misuses a line like this. It's not 'baited breath', as in bait for a fish, it's 'bated breath', as in eager or anxious!"

Nick chuckled. "I baited you, as you waited with 'bated breath' to spring another of your fanciful treasures on me. Well done."

Nick signaled, and his crew stood, clapped, and sat down. "Thanks for stopping by."

The woman stormed off with laughter accompanying her from the line of people.

"I'm sorry. This is a public service announcement," Nick stated, standing momentarily, to address the other people in line. "I am a storyteller, rather than a grammar enthusiast. Dialogue and obscure phrases will always be subject to taste and obsessive people. Let me apologize in advance for any other grammar technicians in line. I tell stories, in my own way. If you don't like the occasional typo or grammar alteration to fit my preference, read someone else's stuff. Don't make it your life's work to edit my stories, thinking I care. I don't."

Nick's words drew the amusement he hoped for. "Let's sign some books and answer some entertaining questions."

The next hour proceeded without incident, with many US Marshal's service questions, and boating enthusiasts' probes into Gus's knowledge of boats. One, in particular, struck the rest of the line into silence so they could hear what was said in answer.

An early thirties man approached the table without a book. He didn't fit the kids' profile of anyone. Hair cut short, dressed in jeans, boots, t-shirt and blue windbreaker, the man seemed like an ordinary guy. "Hi, Mr. McCarty. Would it be okay if I ask Mr. Nason a rather complicated boating question?"

"Yes, Sir. Gus can answer anything you have a question about, and since we live on the ocean, I'll bet many in the line would like to hear the answer."

"Thank you. I'm trying to find a cheap place to live down here. The rent on anything exceeds my means, at this time. A guy I worked with up North has a boat in dock at the Monterey Municipal Marina. It's a sixty-footer with everything, but it needs engine work and maintenance. He figures it's worth between twelve thousand and three hundred thousand, depending on how it's repaired. I know the price gap is suspicious. The slip costs nearly a thousand a month. Do you think it would be a good investment for living on?"

"Boats are a blackhole where money in large amounts disappear, never to be seen again," Gus answered truthfully. "If you are not proficient at boat maintenance, engine repair, and have a day-job, a boat will break you physically, mentally, and financially. There is a reason large boats are owned by rich people or professionals who do all their own work. Are you one of those?"

"No, Sir, I'm not. I suspect my friend wants to be shed of his boat for all the reasons you stated. I checked on line, and those engines are expensive to service or repair, even if it's possible to fix them on board."

"I believe you have a good grip on reality, my friend," Gus replied. "Go to Gilroy for work, or if you're interested in boats, sign on to do anything in the boat repair business. Be on the other side of expensive boat repair and maintenance. I worked it for many years before ever owning my own. I became proficient at every aspect of piloting a craft and repairing it before investing in one."

"Do you still have the boat?"

Gus stared at the chuckling Nick with laser like retribution before answering. "No... it blew up down in the Caribbean mysteriously. You need not worry about such a thing if you pick the people you pal around with carefully."

"Understood." The man shook Gus's hand. "Thank you. That's great advice. Good luck with your book, Mr. McCarty."

"Thank you. I hope you find a way to get the boat you want someday." After the man walked away, Nick engaged Gus. "You just had to mention your unfortunate craft incident."

"I did indeed," Gus responded. "We've lost all our dependents, except for Jian and Cala. I thought your signing today was very entertaining."

"Me too. It may be Quinn began to act up. He's teething. Tina doesn't like this stuff anyway."

"True, she came for the café part. Uh oh... look who walked in."

Nick shook hands and signed the next person's 'Hell Zone', glancing at what Gus referred. Hardin Travers, and his little troop of Sharia Law offended, entered 'Book Works', getting into the back of the line. "Oh goodie."

"I will text Cala to be ready to record," Johnny said. "Jian sees them too."

"We were almost done too," Gus added. He showed Nick another text from Jean, indicating a guy with a mustache, five people back in the line. Jean ended the texted message with the word 'nut-ball'."

Nick smiled at Jean. "She's really good at this stuff."

The next four in front of Jean's choice of nut-ball, all wanted to talk about the US Marshal's service and the rumor of a special unit Nick headed with his squad. They had shared ideas while in line, all nearing the table together with the questions. The three men and a woman asked specific questions concerning how Nick's unit receives their assignments, and what rules of engagement they follow. Nick answered as vaguely as he could with Gus and Johnny's help, knowing some details about his sniper duties had leaked to the public.

"Local law enforcement can request our unit, or the Department of Justice, through our contacts in Sacramento," Nick explained.

"We have great resources for outlining the best course of action, including satellite imaging and access to criminal databases all over the world," Johnny added.

"Usually, we're not asked into a case unless a hostage situation or a dangerous escapee is involved," Gus said. "We try to prevent casualties. Our unit examines every possibility for ending a violent situation without the public or law enforcement being involved in a gun battle."

"Do you have permission to take the shot without an order," the woman asked.

"Yes," Nick admitted. "We only enter extremely desperate situations where hesitation means injury or death."

The four walked away with their signed copies, while still debating what they had been told. Nick signaled for the guy Jean indicated to come forward. "I hope the talk about the special unit status doesn't piss off our law enforcement community."

"So far, they're happy with the results," Gus replied.

Nick greeted the mustache man. "Hello, Sir. Do you have something for me to sign?"

"I do not. I've attempted to read your nauseating, right wing crap. Your writing, banal at best, indicates overwhelmingly you should be in a different profession. The repetitious dialogue and situations cast doubt you even had a formal education."

"Thanks for stopping by." Nick looked toward the next person in line.

"Wait a minute! What do you have to say about my observations?"

"Nothing. You don't like my writing. Read a different author. I imagine you feel better having delivered your critique on my shortcomings as a writer, so enjoy the rest of your day."

"You are a disgrace to the writing profession!"

Nick grinned. "You're being repetitious, banal, and you're beginning to bore me."

The 'Book Works' hired security officers moved in as the man lurched closer to the table. "Why you… let me go!"

"Knowing what Mr. McCarty can do, I should let you go, but we're being paid to make sure Nick doesn't need to kill anyone today. Come along now."

As the security officers guided mustache man toward the door, he shouted out idle insults. Nick waved at Jean. "You sure called that one right."

Rhonda ended the line as the last of the patrons entered to get in line. To her surprise, Hardin Travers and his companions moved to the back of the line. "What is this, Hardin?"

"Nothing at all, Rhonda." Travers lifted his copy of 'Hell Zone' for her to see. "My associates and I are here for McCarty's autograph."

"I have security here, so that better be all you came for. I'm surprised after your last unfortunate interaction with Nick, that you would seek another."

"As you've stated, you have security."

Rhonda walked to the café section, wondering if she would need to call the police.

Nick noticed the interchange between Rhonda and Travers. "Best text Jian to sit with the kids. I don't much like this."

"On it," Johnny said. A moment later, Jian joined Jean and Sonny behind the greeting table.

When Hardin's group reached Nick, the big half-beard man Nick ordered back inside his car early in the day, took the lead with a scowl. "Well... well, look who came to our humble book-signing. If you've come to do anything other than get your book signed, it won't go well for you, Travers."

"We are here on behalf of the Council on American Islamic Relations," Travers replied. "Your blatant racism and bigotry toward Islam cannot be tolerated any longer. 'Hell Zone' references Islam, the religion of peace, as being a terrorist organization."

"You came here under the banner of a terrorist organization: CAIR. Islam is not a race or a religion, so your accusation is false. Islam's Sharia Law is terrorism. 'Quran Verse (9:5) States: So when the sacred months have passed away, then slay the idolaters wherever you find them, and take them captive and besiege them and lie in wait for them in every ambush, then if they repent and keep up prayer and pay the poor-rate, leave their way free to them' – that's not a religion of peace. Besides, everyone with half a brain knows Islam means surrender, not peace. Give me your book. I'll sign it and you can leave."

"I don't want your stupid signature. I want you arrested for hate crimes."

"Using the truth about Islam in Pulp Fiction form breaks no laws." Nick motioned the security officers to stay where they were as he stood to face Travers' group. He didn't want them injured. "I have a feeling your bearded buddy here came into this place of business with an illegal weapon. That didn't end well for you the last time. It won't end well this time. Walk out now, and I won't arrest you. We will take you all into federal custody if you do anything else."

The big bearded man reached for Nick. "Kafir!"

Nick's hand streaked inside the man's reach to his neck, gripping his throat with hand strength that brought the bigger man gagging across the table, unable to move without the feeling his throat would be ripped out. His companions noted four automatics pointed at their heads. Nick leaned into his captive.

"I'm going to release you. Get on your knees with fingers locked behind your head. That goes for you others too, including you, Travers."

The bearded man collapsed choking to the floor, with Nick's drawn Colt .45 pointed at his head. "All of you get on your knees now! Otherwise... this will be the bloodiest book-signing ever."

Cala, who was still recording the incident, put away her weapon when Nick drew his. Gus and Johnny walked around the greeting table, covering the now kneeling men. Jian smiled, flashing a set of plastic ties he retrieved from the inside of his coat. He quickly secured the prisoners as another crowd formed to see what happened.

"You're getting to be a regular boy-scout, Jian," Nick said.

"I must be prepared for anything when attending a gathering with you, round-eye."

The bearded man, pretending to still be choking, inched his hand inside his coat. Nick kicked him in the face, following it with a kick in his groin as he rolled on his back in agony. The man forgot all about his face. Gus put on Nitrile gloves, the always prepared Jian handed him. Gus found a holstered Sig-Sauer 9mm on the downed man. Johnny and Jian disarmed the other two. Both carried 9mm automatics. Travers was unarmed.

"These men are my bodyguards. They have weapons permits," Travers said. "Release me and let me up."

Nick pointed at one of the other men. "Do you have a permit to carry a concealed weapon?"

"No."

"Didn't think so," Nick said. He took out his iPhone and called Neil. "The Chief will be less than pleased at this mess."

Cala held her iPad up. "The Monsters loved it."

* * *

The fact our meeting ended the moment Nick began his performance at the book-signing bothered us not at all. Watching his crew, all in black, moving in perfect sync, drove us all into a swaying, clapping enjoyment of the goofiest world class assassin of all time. We continued our finalizing of what we needed to bring for attacking the Isla, where Khalid built his estate in isolation. After surprised acknowledgement of Nick's plan of attack, outlined in a detailed text from him, we decided his approach to be much better than another at sea assault, Cala popped in another video of the signing adventures.

Lynn loved the confrontation with the LGBTQ woman, hearing for the first time that Nick used her intervention in defense of Al outside the women's restroom in his novel 'Hell Zone'. When the guy in line amused the rest of his fellow readers with the 'identify with a rock' line, Lynn enjoyed the moment thoroughly. Cala kept streaming the grammar Nazi adventures and angry reader guy. The fun raced on into an 'offended' encounter, ending in arrests.

"Muerto exists in a cartoon class all by himself," I stated. "His plan to stay away from Khalid's ship completely, makes a hell of a lot more sense."

"We'll still be attacking a sovereign nation's property, but it won't be the first time in Mexico's case," Lucas said. "They take anyone's money, even if doing so puts terrorists in their backyard, plotting terrorist actions."

"Laredo and Cala landing us inland away from the estate, allows us to go in overland, do our business quietly, and then get the hell out of there," I replied. "With Tonto along, I like our chances of a complete surprise attack."

"Nick's finish to the mission will turn Khalid's people and the Mexican authorities inside... out," Clint agreed. "Once we kill everyone at the estate, Laredo flies in, and we load the bodies for disposal way out to sea. We clean the place like it never happened, leaving a mystery no one will solve. Lynn gets Khalid to transfer his money to us, thereby making it appear even more likely Khalid went into hiding."

"Best of all, we get to cruise with the crooner assassin entertaining us nightly," Lynn added. "Luckily, Ranger incorporates those small built in boats to launch, so Cheese can get his poke training in."

"Not happening!" I listened to all the comical arguments highlighting why my ocean training needed to go on, before cutting them off at the pass. "Tell you all what. If any of you can force me into the water, I'll train."

That caused general amusement, because no one here, or combination of those present, could force me into the water against my will. "I think that ends the training in the ocean talk. If you ever held onto Rocky the pole poke, Betty... I'd have you dancing across the water every day." I ended with my imitation dolphin sounds.

Everyone enjoyed my swipe at Lynn. She took it in stride. "Remember, Cheese... we have the final game to play tomorrow morning with the Bobcats for the trophy."

Damn! I had forgotten completely, and Al hadn't mentioned it because of our fight problems at school. We were rained out last weekend in the first inning of the championship game, going for the first-place trophy, second year in a row. The downside to playing for the championship: Hector, Jill, and their Bobcats would be our opponents, second year straight.

"I see in your face the school fight and parent thug fest wiped your memory banks clean concerning our game. Maybe we should have held practices this week. I bet the Bobcats did."

"I know they probably did, Lynn. Our girls cheered when I gave them the week off, along with the parents. They played five tournament games the same day. We'll meet today for a short tune-up practice and sharpen them up for the game. I bet they'll be fresh tomorrow for the matchup. Let's see how many we can get to show for a little scrimmage with us playing them. They'll love taking us on."

"That's a fresh idea," Clint said. "We have enough to play if all the Monsters and Snow Whites can come. We'll even have enough for a couple of umpires."

Denny Strobert, our assistant CIA Director, newly arrived from a meeting in DC, raised his hand. "I'll umpire."

"I'll text the girls and see who can meet," Jafar said. "Want to make it at 4pm, John?"

"That sounds good. We'll warmup for fifteen minutes and play for an hour. We'll bat the balls just like we do for them in practice. Swing at everything pitched, and just meet the ball so we can give everyone some fielding practice. Samira pitches well. Can she play, little brother?"

"Sure. We'll set the playpen in the dugout for Mia and Clint Jr. Tonto and Naji can sway back and forth together. I'll text Nick too. His signing ended at noon. I believe he was heading our way tomorrow morning anyway."

"Try him. Even if he can't make it today, maybe he can make the game tomorrow. This should be a blast. I'll ask Lora to coach the girls in the dugout."

* * *

We lucked out and didn't need to go far. Allendale Recreation Center had a field open. We practiced for about twenty minutes. The girls looked so sharp, I think we could have played the Bobcats without a practice. They loved the idea so much, all of them showed, along with many of our dependents, who hooted at us no matter what we did. Dev opened our practice game with a Latin protection spell. The usual hilarity ensued as Jess eyed the skies for darkening clouds, and the dogs swayed in sync during the Latin. Casey played first, Clint second, Jafar shortstop, Lynn third, Lucas left field, Jess center field, Dev right field, Samira pitching, and me catching. Tommy was our coach and babysitter with Amara, Tonto and Naji. The minions handled equipment and base coaching.

Al pitched first for our hometown A's. She pitched, varying fastballs and changeups, nearly striking out our first hitter, Lynn, who managed a weak comebacker to the mound for an easy out at first. Our girls, who never taunt the other team, were encouraged to do so today. Jafar hit a hard grounder to the shortstop, getting thrown out easily. Jess roped one to the fence in right field, making it into third with a chorus of boos. Dev got under Al's changeup just right, lofting a fly to the fence in center, where the girl's centerfielder caught it.

By then, we'd drawn an appreciative crowd, including Nick's Unholies and dependents. Deke joined his canine partners in the dugout. Just as they had done on the cruise ship, their movements became as one, except when one of the babies wanted to play with them. Three fur-faces then hung over the playpen railing with Amara on hand to wipe hands, while the babies stroked them. We really got the business in the field from parents and our dependents. Dubbed villains and thugs, the crowd really gave it to us, with catcalls and chants.

Samira pitched down the heart of the plate, varying her two pitches as Al had done, only to the chant of 'pitcher has a rubber arm' etc. Mary hit the first pitch into right for a single. I could tell she planned to test me and Clint. The moment Samira pitched to the girls' next batter, Callie, Mary streaked for second. I threw her out with five feet to spare, Clint allowing Mary to slide right into his glove. Denny called her out. We received a veritable audio deluge of boos. Al then hit a homerun over the left field fence. Lucas comically threw his glove into the air at it. One of our spectators threw it back on the field as Al coasted with one flap down around the bases to thunderous applause.

Sherry bunted a beauty down the third base line, but Lynn pounced on it and threw her out with a perfect throw to Casey. Kelly hit a screamer past Jafar into the left center gap for a double. Samira provided the entertainment as she belittled her husband in three languages. He kept his head bowed while scuffing his shoe in the dirt. Jan then hit the next offering straight up the middle between Samira's legs, ticking off Clint's glove as he dived for it. Kelly scored, but Jess held Jan to a single. Jafar went wild with comical gestures in the air, followed by throwing his glove into the ground. Samira enjoyed the show, shrugging with a smile. Ellie took the next pitch, a changeup, for a strike. I had no throw. Jan slid into second just as I came out of my crouch. It was then my turn to get it in three languages from Samira. Dora hit a long flyball to Dev in right field, who endured the wall of boos on his way to the dugout, smiling and waving.

A seesaw battle developed when Al, on Lora's orders, I found out later, hit me with a pitch on the shoulder. I naturally played it as if someone cut my arm off with a chainsaw. We tied the score, but the A's pulled into the lead with a good series of ropes and perfect bunts. As we headed into inning four, two runs down, a gang of hoodies arrived, slapping hands and deriding us. We lost a lot of spectators who were not family and dependents. The gang of nineteen were delighted they could belittle us from the stands. When they started in on the girls, Lynn walked over with her minions scrambling into their special equipment bag to back her play.

"You girls are welcome to rake over the adults if you keep your language in bounds. Lay off our girls on the team."

"Who you callin' girls, bitch?"

"I'm calling you a girl, Betty. This area belongs to the Oaktown Cartel. We don't let little hobo tramps like you disrupt our neighborhood. Who the hell are you bunch, and why should I care?"

"We Twelfth Street Lobos! We heard all 'bout you bad-ass Oaktown posers. Heard you all came here to play with the girls. Guess you didn't think you'd get fronted out here where we maybe end Oaktown forever... bitch!"

Some of them began reaching. Things changed then, because the minions: Gus Denova, Quays Tannous, and Silvio Ruelas flanked the thugs. They chambered rounds into MP5 submachine guns. Gus stepped forward. "I am Gus Denova, Oaktown Cartel, with my associates Quays Tannous, and Silvio Ruelas. We have full auto, MP5 submachine guns. Grab the fronts of your hoodies with both hands or die where you stand. I will not tell you twice."

When the leader didn't move fast enough, Gus aimed at his head and began to squeeze off a burst.

"Wait! We good... we good." The leader grabbed his lapels. His companions followed his lead.

"Now," Gus said. "Get on your knees!"

They dropped to their knees instantly.

I joined Gus. "I'm dismissing the girls and their parents. Kill them all if they make another move. I don't want any of the girls hurt in any way, Gus."

"Absolutely. They take a hand off their hoodie, we will mow them down."

I rejoined the girls and their worried parents. "Great game. You girls whupped us. We will see you all tomorrow an hour before game-time. Don't give this interruption a thought. We had a wonderful time. I'm sorry it was interrupted. We'll get a rematch sometime in the future after the championship game."

"Did your adults let us win, Coach?"

I don't lie to anyone. "Look, Kelly, we don't try and smash the ball as hard as we can. We could really hurt you girls. Other than that, we played full bore. Ask Jan. Did I look like I was throwing the game when I nailed your stealing butt at second, Jan?"

Jan grinned. "You got me good. I thought I had it stolen. I wasn't even close."

"See you all tomorrow. Remember to put on your game-faces. We need to play the worst two poor sport coaches in the league. Don't take anything personally. Let Lynn and I intercede when they get out of hand. Manny's umpiring behind the plate and he's the best."

After the girls left, twilight time arrived in a slow fading of light. Nick sent his crew to their new North Bay home to get ready for our party tonight. He let Jean, Sonny, and Deke the dog stay, mainly because his drinking buddy didn't want to leave Tonto and Naji. I released everyone but the Monsters. Lora allowed Al to run back with Jean and Sonny, making a gesture as if she were shooting herself in the head. It would be an opportunity to see if Al would react in the same manner as Jean and Sonny. It's called Monster parenting from hell, but Nick's way with the kids seemed to be the only logical path in our situation. We greeted each other as brothers, one big happy, horrific family.

"Hell of a game, John. I enjoyed the heck out of it," Nick told me. "When these punks interrupted it, my first thought is best left to the imagination."

"We all carried a taste of that with us, Dead-Boy," Clint said. "Samira swearing at Achmed in three languages for missing an impossible ball, and then having the next batter hit one between her legs... man... that's entertainment."

"She got me good too," Achmed admitted. "I would be a liar if I said I didn't enjoy her miss. What do you want to do with these guys?"

"I'd like to cut this one's throat," Lynn said, pointing at the leader.

The leader spit on the ground. "I heard Oaktown has some girlie 'cutter' who thinks she's the baddest thing ever. I cut before people can blink, bitch!"

A universal groan went through my crew as Lynn crouched near the lead guy, stroking his cheek. "Oh my... aren't you just the sweetest thing, Betty. Hey, Nick, think you can fill in for Tommy? We have an Oaktown challenge. You can be the guest host."

Nick chuckled, gesturing for Jean and Sonny to guard. Their knives snapped open out of sight instantly. With one gesture from Nick, Deke streaked over to Jean and Sonny, hackles raised, fangs drooling. Al noticed. She stayed by Jean. I noticed her acceptance of a reality she wanted no part of. Nick approached the front as Tommy would have done.

"Well, ladies, here's the deal. You have a sissy-boy who thinks he's a 'cutter'. We have a 'cutter' second to none. She doesn't cut for quarters, kiddies. How much do you gangland posers have to bet? We're giving ten to one odds. I'm covering all bets." Nick took out a wad of cash. "You can all stand now, but keep those hands grabbing your hoodies, or die. Talk it over. Let us know what kind of money you got to back your big mouth talker."

The gangbangers stood carefully, grouped together for a few moments, muttering amongst themselves. The leader turned to Nick. "We got two-fifty."

"Smalltime, but acceptable. Since you claim to be a 'cutter', I assume you have a knife with you, take it out slowly. Bring out anything but a knife and Mr. Denova puts a burst through your head."

The leader shed his hoodie, and a few seconds later he held an impressive switchblade knife in hand. "I ready."

Lynn drew her knife out, flicked it open, and motioned for her opponent to get started. "C'mon, Betty, show us what you got."

He streaked toward Lynn, willing to take a wound in order to stab Lynn fatally. It probably was the only way I figured he had a chance. At the last second, Lynn dropped to the side, and leg whipped the charging gangbanger. He tumbled head over heels, losing his knife after stabbing his own arm. Crying out, he grabbed his wounded arm, rolling over on his back. Lynn straightened, walked to him, and kicked the gangbanger's ribcage. It jackknifed the wounded man into a fetal position.

"Pathetic," Lynn said. "On the other hand, you did knife someone."

"Pay up, kids." Nick put away his own money. "Be extra careful getting the payoff out."

Once they had the money together, including retrieving their wounded companion's money, Nick collected it. "Next... I want to see IDs. Hold them out for scanning after you pull your hoodies off. Do it nicely and you dummies might just live through this act of stupidity."

Clint and I accompanied Jafar as he scanned in the IDs, checking each one to be sure the faces matched the ID pictures. Once that was done, I took over from Nick. "Okay, this is the delicate part. I know you idiots brought guns to the field to shoot us down. Extract them with thumb and forefinger slowly. Then, place them on the ground in front of you."

They completed the task without getting shot. Jafar then took a picture of each man and the weapon he put on the ground, again accompanied by me and Clint. Oh my, they did not like that. One decided to make a run for it. I ran him down in a matter of a few steps, yanking him backwards to the ground.

"You'll be coming along with us. Sit there." I turned to his buddies. "Gus will explain to the rest of you what being absorbed by the Oaktown Cartel means. I'll give you a brief rundown. Stay away from Oakland's citizens. Do as we tell you to do, or we will kill all of you. Did I miss anything, Gus?"

"You hit the high points, John. I will show them the Cruella Deville highlight show."

"Good one." I began bagging the weapons, while Gus showed off Crue's biggest hits with Silvio and Quays keeping the gangbangers covered.

"Hey!" A big meathead pointed at me. "Ain't you supposed to fight six of us, and we get twenty-five thousand if we beat you."

"Yeah... what about that, Cheese?" Lynn gestured at the gangbangers. "These guys are getting the short end of the stick. Besides, the only thing Betty did was stab himself. What kind of entertainment is that?"

"We got six dudes bust you into pieces, prick!"

"No... you really don't, meathead."

"Recon! Make this punk and his friends cry or I'll do it for you! Then, I make you wear Muerto pajamas for a month," Lucas warned.

Oh boy, the Monsters, Nick, and the kids enjoyed that rip from Lucas. "Okay, I'll do it, but we're not taking them all to the damn hospital. Do you morons even have a car?"

"We got wheels," another slickster told me. "For twenty-five Gs, it be you need an undertaker, fool."

The Monster inside perked up. I immediately didn't like this lanky piece of crap. "I hope you're volunteering to be one of the six, Urkel."

"Damn right... I be one of the six." He started stalking toward me, thinking I wouldn't snatch his Adam's Apple out and feed it to the dogs. Lynn intercepted him with knifepoint to his throat.

"Be patient, sissy-boy, your time's coming. Go get with the big troll and pick your guys. We don't have all day."

I noted Nick moved the kids back with the dogs. The Troll and Urkel picked out four other goons to get me. I took out my MMA fight gloves from my bag and put them on. I had no intention of even getting a bruised knuckle. I had a plan for a workout I wanted to try. Once we faced off, I stood with my hands at my sides.

"Would you like me to attack, or would you tools like to attack me? I don't have a preference. It will end the same way no matter what you pick."

They charged me. Bad move, but they had no good ones, so the charging made them feel good about their chances for a moment. Their happy charge turned to dust in the wind. I threw a left and right combination at the first two to reach me, catching them coming in. I smashed both their faces to mush. They hit the ground, gagging blood. I moved around the other four, stunned that both the Troll and Urkel already hit the ground, writhing as they held their poor face boo-boos in bloody hands.

I worked then, moving fast to stab my left jab into the faces of the rest, giving them no way to escape as noses busted, teeth got knocked out, and eyes swelled. Then, I switched to left hooks and overhand rights. In minutes, the six hit the ground with busted faces, tears, and cries. I moved to kick in ribs and groins until I heard Lucas.

"Recon! Well done. Let's wrap this up and get to the party at Dead-Boy's house."

"I hear you, Top." I plucked Urkel off the ground, still holding his ruined face. "If I ever see you again, I'll rip your throat out. Nod if you understand, flea brain."

Urkel nodded enthusiastically. I pitched him onto his partners. "Get these ass-wipes into your cars. Poor babies will need medical and dental attention, especially the poser who thought he was a 'cutter'. We kill people, girls. Gather your casualties, get in your cars and sin no more. You're all on our list. If we match your weapons to crimes, we'll be back to get you. We have FBI credentials and assets. Our friend is US Marshal Nick McCarty, with special unit access into the Department of Justice. We will find you. Get the hell out of here."

I didn't need to expand on my order. The goons plucked their fellow thugs to their feet, urging them on their way with help. I grabbed my prisoner off the ground. "Come along with me. I'll drop you off at the local precinct station."

"I'll do that," Quays said. "Sil and I will be going in the precinct direction, John. We'll take him and the weapons. We'll all be at Muerto's place later."

"Thanks, Quays. You can bet this is a murder wrap, so stay focused."

"We will." Quays smiled. "You are one dangerous hombre, my friend."

I shrugged. "Thank you! No one believes it. They think I'm a poser. The six-guy thing is the limit. I could probably take on more, but I don't think it's a good idea."

"For me, I do not consider any of this a good idea, hombre. We will see you later."

"We'll be partying tonight, brother... in moderation, of course. Are you bringing the new baby?"

Quays smiled. "Of course."

"Outstanding. Have you slept at night yet?"

"An hour or two at a time."

"That doesn't sound like fun."

"Nope... it is wonderful."

"I hear you, amigo." I left the weapons runner to Quays and Silvio. The rest of the Monsters were with Nick, the dogs, and the kids.

Nick shook hands with me. "You and Lynn are the whole package, brother. I know Lynn was disappointed, but the ending with the clown stabbing himself entertained more than a bloodier one. Did your workout suit you?"

"Lynn saved the lanky one's ass. If he had reached me, I would have ended him. He nearly ruined my workout plans. I'm sure my performance wouldn't have pleased Tommy. He would have to admit I did try to avoid any killings though... with Lynn's help."

"You did, indeed," Nick agreed with me. "I think Lucas stopped you from turning a workout into a 'Missouri Boat Ride'."

Remembering the scene from Nick's favorite western, 'The Outlaw Josie Wales', I shrugged in acceptance. "You're probably right. Lucas started it though. I was going to have Lynn bitch slap the big baby until he cried, but no... Lucas was out for blood.

Nobody makes me wear Muerto pajamas. Besides, Lucas's wife says she can't get him to even wash his Muerto pajamas. Romance is like out of the question. The bottoms are getting hell of smelly, and…"

Clint and Casey grabbed Lucas, holding on for dear life, while laughing their asses off. Lynn interceded. "Oh… so the rest of us have to take crap, but you get to try and whup on Cheese because he aces you, huh?"

Lucas relaxed, but pointed at me threateningly. "Yeah… okay… but I owe this young punk a dress down."

"I followed your orders, Pap. Let's break this up and go get ready for some Muerto music. You and the Unholies acting out the calypso songs caused pandemonium at Pain Central. I almost went home to get my Muerto t-shirt."

"Plenty more entertainment waiting at Casa del Muerto," Nick replied. "I hear we have a championship game to attend tomorrow too. You beat the Dark Lord already, Al. The championship will be like an anti-climax."

"My arm felt great today. Kelly's pitching tomorrow for the first few innings. I get to come in and finish it off. I'm glad you're all coming."

"We loved everything, the game and the gangbanger faceoff," Jean said. "Tonight will really be fun. Sonny and I want to visit your house, so you can show us the work you've been doing with the bow before we go on the cruise."

"We'll have time before the Ranger arrives in port," Al replied. "I'm glad you're not bored watching the game. The coaches for the Bobcats tomorrow are nearly as entertaining as the gang arriving at the ballpark today. Dad doesn't need to beat them up, but Lynn and Dad have to listen while they complain about everything. One of the coaches, Jill, stays in the dugout most of the time now. When she leaves the dugout to argue something, Lynn dances out to meet her, doing different moves, while listening to her drone on about nothing."

"She makes the umpires start laughing. After a time, the ump just shouts, 'Play Ball'," Clint added. "It's the only thing that's ever worked to silence Jill."

"We're trying to get Cheese to do the robot as the Dark Lord when he needs to face off with Hector," Lynn said.

"I want him to do his Justin Bieber imitation in Dark Lord voice," Casey chimed in. "It's hilarious. He doesn't do it much, because it tends to make Al's head explode."

"Does not," Al replied. "Justin doesn't sound anything like Dad."

I naturally had to start doing the Dark Lord robot, while singing the Beeper song that sounds like two cats in heat going at it. Only a couple of minutes into it, Lucas and Lynn couldn't breathe, Al was beating on me, and the dogs were crooning. I stopped, but it was many moments before the amused audience could speak again.

"That…that was the funniest stuff ever," Nick said. "I could picture you going to meet with the ump and your opposing coach doing it."

"Manny would be forced to toss me," I explained. "Lynn plays it out perfectly. My doing Beeper and the robot in DL sound would be judged inappropriate taunting."

"I've been working on new moves for Jill," Lynn said. "You know Jill and Hector will be stopping the game every few minutes."

"Can we bring anything tonight, Nick," I asked.

"Nope. I'm ordering catered in stuff from the local 'Olive Garden Restaurant' near the house. I already have the refreshments stocked. It will be a come-as-you-are party."

"Can Sonny and Jean come over to the house now, Dad? We want to work with the bow a little."

"I don't have any objection."

"Can we, Dad?"

Nick turned to his two young charges. "It's okay with me. I know you two will behave."

Chapter Nine

Preparations

Al impressed Jean and Sonny. I made sure she didn't overdo the demonstration. The A's needed their pitcher to play the game without a sore arm. It turned out Nick had worked with Jean and Sonny when they asked if he would teach them the bow. I built an enclosed target range of soft backing to catch errant arrows, covering the entire distance with the strong green mesh they make fences from. The nearly thirty-yard distance, enhanced with solar lighting, even enticed Lora into actively participating. Al made me do my Robin Hood trick. I hit dead center on the bullseye, rapidly firing another arrow to split the first one.

"Show off." Lora gave me a nudge, which amounted to her nudging me and bouncing off.

The kids loved the demonstration. Jean and Sonny detailed the training Nick took them through with the knives and at the range with weapons. I could imagine how intense his training regimen was after seeing the skill Jean and Sonny had. I witnessed Nick put his stiletto blade through the UK Labour Party's lead representative, Gemy Borebyn's eye socket, on Alexi Fiialkov's tanker at a meeting with world representatives. The Borebyn dunce started to draw a weapon on the number one assassin in the world. Our ex-Muslim 'City of Hope' had a rough start until everyone understood what violence we Monsters bring to a mission.

Both Jean and Sonny showed a knack for the bow. I could tell they didn't like the bow as much as the knives. They could carry the knives in secret. Nick updated me all the time on what he put the kids through, knowing I dealt with Al in a more open way too. The instance where they were surrounded by gangbangers, led by billionaire Tark Ruban's security guy, made me glad I trained Al in martial arts and weapons too. Jean and Sonny were blooded in the incident, wounding men as instructed by Nick's order instantly, without hesitation. They also shot a man in the incident when Rachel forced Nick into protecting the Santa Rosalia statue, wounding as Nick ordered. Al would make a great law enforcement officer if she chose to, but Jean and Sonny were Monsters in training.

I didn't get fancy with the knife training. I bought the best throwing knives I could find, so well balanced, after showing Al and Lora proper techniques, they began to hit their target. Al showed Jean and Sonny how far she had progressed. Jean showed her the intricate training exercises Nick encouraged them to practice. The two young Monsters demonstrated throwing with both hands, moving in either direction, making Lora gasp. I noted with a smile, the two of them felt the balance of my blades before making their throws.

"Wow… I'll work on it," Al told them. "Thanks!"

"We're family," Jean stated. "When we get older, we'll be Monsters together."

Al shook her head with a smile. "I know Lynn Montoya Dostiene very well. I might be a Snow White someday, but not a Monster. I can tell you two will be. I've thought about being an FBI Agent. I'll go through law school, maybe do a military stint in service, and then apply to the FBI or Secret Service."

"Monsters need law enforcement contacts," Sonny replied. "We have the Chief of Police on our side down in the 'Grove'. Chief Dickerson consults and asks for help when we get the occasional gang infiltration."

"We have the US Marshals who helped during our flight across the country," Jean added. "Tim and Grace are like family to us. They know what Dad is. They also know never to cross him. They knew it was him in Chicago and accepted what he did because it was right. He keeps them on a need to know basis though."

"We have Sam and Janie," Al replied. "They're FBI Agents who consult with the Monsters. Clint worked with them. They help when someone can be taken into custody. I want to work cases and solve crimes like Clint did with Sam and Janie. He tracked serial killers, because he could outthink the serial killer. He didn't limit himself to the handbook."

Al giggled. "He caught Lynn."

"Really?"

"Yeah, Jean," I answered. "She was killing serial rapists and abusers. Sam and Janie couldn't come close to catching her. Clint tracked her, let her finish the job, and then arrested her. Like Lynn promised, she beat the rap. When they got stuck again with a horrific serial killer team mutilating women, Sam and Janie had to go into the mountains and recruit Clint. The only reason he agreed was because they told him a Cartel captured Lynn. They agreed to get him satellite surveillance to help Clint plot her extraction. Denny Strobert put us all together and we went down to get Lynn. She could conceivably be the most dangerous woman on the planet."

"Do you really pitch her into the ocean during training, Sir?"

"I do on my good days, Sonny. Most of the time, she beats me like a redheaded stepchild."

"Hey… I resent that," Lora, my redhead, chimed in. "C'mon. Enough Monster stories. Let's get ready for the party. I plan on making Mr. UFC dance with me all night long."

"Speaking of partying, I heard you've been ragging the Unholies about their Irish mornings," I mentioned, grinning at Jean. "How's that working out for you."

Jean delivered the answer with a straight-faced delivery. "They killed the messenger."

Oh boy, we enjoyed that answer for a time. "Okay, then. Like Lora said, let's get ready."

* * *

I noticed one thing at the party immediately. Jean did not like Sonny dancing with Al. She kept it to herself, but after this, I planned to bring a boy Al liked on these family gettogethers. They were just kids, but Nick noticed too, as Sonny was assigned by Rachel and Lora to dance with both girls. I felt like allowing him to have a couple shots, because he looked a little stiff while performing his duties. The rest of us Monsters, Snow Whites, and dependents had a blast. Jian's girlfriend, Joan, drove from Pacific Grove with her violin. Nick and Joan did 'Ride of the Valkyries' in a 'Dueling Banjos' type adlib that was amazing. Adding the violin created a musical masterpiece. Joan had soul. She could play jazz with the skill of a concert violinist.

In the middle of Joan and Nick churning out a beautiful rendition of 'As Time Goes By', someone knocked, banged, and rang the doorbell repeatedly. Lynn, who was three sheets into the wind, ran over to her bag. Extracting her Glock, she gestured for all of us to stay where we were.

"I got this. I will shoot whoever is at the door in the head. My minions will drag them into the bushes for the night."

The funniest part happened when Gus Denova, Quays Tannous, and Silvio Ruelas dropped to one knee, head down in deference, then stood and proceeded to her side. Clint blocked the way before Lynn could streak through the doorway.

"Babe… calm down. You're feeling good, but it's not a smart thing to mix the good stuff with the bad stuff. Nick's been playing piano with just a beer. John has a hollow leg for booze. Lucas and Casey have been dancing all night with only a beer or two. We'll handle this."

Lynn relaxed in Clint's arms. "It just seems like the moment we get a little buzzed, with music playing, some dildo shows up to ruin the moment. I'm coming along. I'll only bring my knife and minions, right Quays?"

Quays glanced at his brother minions with a grin. "We are here and armed, Mistress of the Unimaginable, to follow you to 'Hell's Gate'."

By that time, Nick and I were already at the doorway with Lucas and Casey. We Monsters can get into primetime at a moment's notice. Gus, Johnny, Jian, and Cala all joined us, with Cala recording the incident. Nick stared into their eyes and nodded as the banging on the door increased. "We're good to go, Dark Lord."

Nick answered the door with a big smile, and no hesitation. This guy was a Monster. He showed no hesitation, no caution, and no physical acceptance of danger. It was Capricorn One, Koren Capricorn. He was on crutches, with his knee in a cast. A horde of people were behind him, possibly thirty, including media.

"Hello," Nick said. "Whatever you're selling… I don't want any, but thanks for thinking of me."

Nick shut the door. He had seen the media cameras amongst the crowd. "Well... this will be entertaining, Lynn."

The banging started immediately, in conjunction with the doorbell ringing. Nick answered again. "Oh my... apparently English is your second language. Whatever you're-"

A huge body slammed against the screen door. He looked like someone not to be faced... unless you're a Monster. "Get that bitch, Harding, out here for a stomping!"

In a flash faster than most people can think, a Colt barrel popped the man's forehead hard enough to buck him back a couple of steps, while pawing at his head. "If you slam into my screen-door again, I will put a round right between your eyes. Back the hell off my stoop, tell me what you're doing here, and why I should care. I bore easily. If you bore me for too long, I start shooting."

For added clarification, Nick put a hole through his screen, and two inches away from a guy's foot, who was reaching. "Everyone grab your hoodie and shirt fronts with both hands. If you don't, I start shooting now. I haven't missed in years, and that was from a leap over a waterfall. Grab the cloth! Now!"

The crowd quieted, doing as Nick told them. "Good! Spit it out, Kneeler. I know you, Koren Capricorn. To me, you're nothing but a penis headed, anti-American dolt. You believed all the BLM lies and liberal crap fed to you without even a single attempt to find out the truth. You disrespected this nation that made you a multi-millionaire with no talent, no honor, and no common sense. You dishonored men and women of our military who gave their lives for the flag and its anthem. You should be stripped of citizenship and deported to whatever hellhole you think would accept a useless piece of shit with no real-life talent other than sitting on your traitorous ass."

Capricorn One started to bleat threats about what he would do to Nick if his knee wasn't damaged. Nick waited for him to finish shooting his mouth off. Nick pointed at him with disgust.

"You? Kid... you're a joke. John Harding put you down crying for your momma with one legitimate UFC kick. You don't belong with men, not even these football men posers, who don't know how to do anything of real use except play with themselves. Get the hell off my lawn!"

To say the Monsters were lapping up that Muerto tirade with relish would be an understatement. It caused an unhappy circumstance... unhappy for the crowd. The big bulldozer, whom Nick popped in the forehead, tore the screen door off. There had been enough noise, especially Nick's warning shot, that we had all the Snow Whites and Monsters ready for action. I smashed the bulldozer so hard in the middle of his face, he shot back into his brethren, spewing blood everywhere. Oh my... did that ever feel good. Nick ended the confrontation with one righteous pistol whipping across Capricorn One's face, back and forth with light gouges making an X across Capricorn One's features in blood. He fell on the stoop's surface, bellowing in anguish, holding his busted face.

"Oh, for God's sakes, Betty." Lynn kicked him in the groin. He stopped screaming. "Show's over, posers."

I went down the stoop to the guy spitting out blood and teeth. "How did you and the Kneeler know I was here?"

"Guy at the park... with the Lobos... followed you... and called Cap."

I straightened and nudged broken face with my foot. "You owe my friend for the door. I'll cover the debt. Leave now, or I take payment in blood. Help the Kneeler get on his feet and take him with you."

Bulldozer stood with some help from his friends. They helped the jackknifed Capricorn One to his feet, getting his crutches under Koren's shaking arms. He sobbed at every step, as they inched him away. The crowd with him glanced at the Monsters and decided wisely that tonight was not their night. They left. The media didn't.

"Koren Capricorn is being blackballed by the NFL! He's taking a stand for human rights!" The woman yelled as the media moved in. They tried to invade my airspace. Lynn blocked her.

"That's close enough, Crumcake."

"My name is not Crumcake!"

Lynn shrugged. "It should be."

"He's not being blackballed by anyone. Capricorn One only began kneeling when the other teams started kicking the crap out of him on the field because he couldn't see secondary receivers down field." I thought what the hell, we can banter for a few moments until the news audience at home has something other than the violent confrontation to think about.

"Do you watch the NFL, Harding?" This question came from a guy standing at a more comfortable distance.

"Not since the Kneeler and the other members of the National Felons League began disrespecting the flag and anthem over lies by a racist organization paid for by a billionaire Globalist."

"So, you're another one wanting to force these Americans to stand against their will," Crumbcake continued.

"Even if the NFL makes these anti-American ingrates stand, it won't change them inside. They'll still be anti-American thugs. My advice to the NFL - fire every kneeler, sitter, and fist in the air freak. Hire players loyal to America, proud to stand with hands over hearts, who know the flag and anthem represent an ideal paid for in blood across the world's battlefields, by patriots – each one worth a hundred of these NFL traitors. NFL - dead to me. Goodnight."

They began to shout other stuff until Nick slammed the door in their faces. They fortunately knew better than to begin pounding on the door again. I halfway strung out my interaction with the media because I knew what would be waiting for me inside. Lucas didn't disappoint. He poked his DI face up into mine.

"So... boot-camp... you got tailed from the park like a nine-year-old girl-scout selling cookies?"

"Yeah... I did. I was talking to the kids. I forgot to check my six – stupid and dangerous."

"C'mon Lucas," Lynn urged. "We need to hit the dance floor. If the dummy follows Cheese again, he'll be going on a boat trip."

"He will indeed," I agreed. "We'll be at the park for the game tomorrow. With this media attention, we'll need to be on guard to keep the girls safe. Anyone suspicious gets yanked for a conversation."

"Jean and I will watch everyone, Mr. Harding," Sonny said. "We have a formula for profiling at the book-signings. Jean can probably figure an adjustment we can make to our checklist."

Jean became animated. "Yes! Great idea, Cracker. We'll network with Jay. Predator always has a few quirks people do we don't think about."

Then it was Al's turn. "Could I stay overnight, Dad. I'd like to help them."

"It's okay with me, John," Nick said. "The kids do an excellent job at the book-signings. We have extra guest accessories for Al. What time does she need to be at the game?"

"Noontime for warmup. I like the idea. I'll swing by at eleven with her uniform and leave from here for the game. Don't stay up too late, Al."

"I won't. I promise. Winning tomorrow means a lot to me."

"Time's wasting." Lynn yanked Nick toward the entertainment room.

* * *

The girls practiced with eagerness, their movements confident and fluid. We coaches hit and pitched to the team in groups, until satisfied we took the edge off competing in the championship game. Our entire crew attended, along with Nick's. We spread everyone out, so all parts of the field were under observation. Nick sat with Sonny and Jean, conferring with them on their newly made profiling sheet. Rachel, Tina, Cala, and Joan sat in our ladies auxiliary section. Baby Quinn joined Mia and Clint Jr in the playpen under Amara's watchful eye. Deke, Naji, and Tonto sat together at the cage, unless one of the kids wanted to pet them.

The tedious part began with Kelly's pitching warmups before the game's start. Hector and Jill watched with exasperated mutterings and head shakes at each pitch. They did so in a position close to our catcher, Jan. Kelly knew the two did it to mess with her head, so she concentrated on Manny, our umpire. Manny would nod if a pitch was a strike. He did so for both teams, so the girls knew where the strike zone was. Fast pitch softball can sometimes take a dangerous turn if people don't pay attention.

The danger part happened a moment later, when a slightly high fast ball ticked off Jan's catcher's mitt. It pegged Jill in the eye, flattening her. I grabbed one of our ice packs. We rushed over from the dugout. Lynn and I don't care much for either Jill or Hector, but we certainly didn't want her hurt. Hector knelt next to his stunned wife, cradling her head. He pointed at Jan.

"You did that on purpose!"

"Did not." There was a reason Jan was our catcher. She had an edge, and she was one tough girl. "You and Jill shouldn't be standing so close. John and Lynn don't stand there gawking at your pitcher when she warms up."

"You watch your mouth, young lady!" Hector entered dangerous territory.

Our parent fans all knew to not run their mouths off or get into personal beefs with either the umps or the opposing side. They knew Lynn and I would handle any matter with the girls' wellbeing utmost in mind. Manny knew it too. One look at Lynn's death face and Manny moved right into Hector's wheelhouse.

"Jan's exactly right. It's dangerous this close to the catcher. From now on, you two stay in the dugout during warmups."

"What?!" Manny's order brought Jill leaping to her feet. "You can't do that!"

"I can, and I will. John and Lynn leave your pitchers to warmup without trying to intimidate them. You two will do the same. One more outburst at Jan or anyone else on the A's, and I'll throw your butt out, Hector. That was an idiot remark. Jan tried to catch the ball. Get over it. Play ball!"

"Here, Jill." I handed her the ice pack. "It will keep the swelling down."

She took it reluctantly, placing it against her eye. Lynn and I waited until Hector and Jill walked away before encouraging both Jan and Kelly to concentrate. "You two are doing great. Thanks, Manny."

"Those two make it hard for all of us, including their team," Manny replied. "We don't normally do it, but on close calls, we umps will confer to make sure we get the call right."

"Good idea, Manny. That should calm the parents and players down in a tight ballgame. Lynn and I won't argue the game no matter what."

"I know, John, but could you come out and join us a little quicker when Hector storms to the plate?"

"Sure, but you know if I say anything in your defense, he'll protest the game, right?"

"Don't defend me then. Do something funny, like in your UFC matches."

"Yeah, John! That would be so cool," Jan piped in.

"Al's a Justin Bieber fan," Kelly added. "She says you do Justin in Dark Lord voice while doing the robot. Do that!"

"Oh my… I have to see that, John," Manny urged. "Please."

"John thought if he did funny stuff, you'd toss him for taunting," Lynn said.

"You have my word, John. Do it at a moment where Hector has his exploding head face on, practically spitting in my face. Once you crack everyone up in the stands, when I can breathe again, I'll say 'Play Ball'."

"Hey," Hector called out. "Get a room. Break up the love fest and start the game!"

"Have a good game, Blue." Lynn and I walked to our dugout. "You were right, Lynn."

"Yeah, but don't do it when Al's pitching later. Unless the Bobcats are at least six runs ahead of us, Hector gets his exploding head face on in the third inning. That should give Al a chance to recover."

"Okay, I'll robot and Beeper to the plate. That should be long enough to either drive the crowd away or end a Hector tirade."

* * *

Nick returned from the concession stand with nachos and sodas for the kids. He had already delivered three meat-soaked rawhide chew toys for the dogs. "Did I miss anything?"

"Kelly walked a couple, and they drove in both runs before she got the third out," Jean said. "It's two to nothing still. You caused bad karma by leaving at a crucial time."

"You get more like the Momster every day, tulip."

"I'm Viper."

"Not anymore. Any luck on the surveillance?"

"This guy fits our profile, Sir." Sonny held up his iPad, showing a rough looking dark-haired guy in regular street clothes, but bundled up like he planned on flying to the arctic circle. He didn't have his hood on, but he did have a thin black pullup, lower face mask, covering his mouth and nose like an old-time bandito.

"I think you two are on to something. Where is he now?"

"He went behind the bleachers on our dugout's side," Jean answered. "He hasn't come back yet."

"I'll go look for him to be on the safe side. I don't like that he went behind our dugout. Even if you're wrong, good catch."

        * * *

Taylor Fredricks watched the bleacher crowd move and flow, waiting for a shot at John Harding. With the noise, he didn't believe anyone would notice his silenced Glock. After ten minutes, he had a clean angle to fire. Taylor opened his coat, under which, he was sweating profusely. As Taylor gripped the Glock with attached silencer inside his coat, he felt the barrel of something poke into his back.

"Don't turn. Grab the front of your jacket with both hands. That's it. Walk with me. I'm US Marshal Nick McCarty. You're under arrest for attempted murder of a federal agent. Come along quietly or I blow your spine in two. I have a Colt .45 with hollow point slugs jammed in your back. Do anything but what I say, and I empty the mag in you."

"Okay… man… don't shoot. I wasn't doing anything. Man has to protect himself here in this neighborhood."

"Walk me to your car. Keep clutching the front of your jacket. Move now."

Fredricks led his captor to an old Mazda SUV. "This mine."

"Unlock it at the passenger side and open the sliding door."

* * *

Nick took the keys. He helped Fredricks inside the vehicle and followed him into the interior. No one paid any attention to them at the street side. The sidewalk, empty of pedestrian traffic at game time, was shielded by trees from the playing field.

"Stay kneeling on the van floor. Don't lose your grip on the coat or you will have a very painful death." Nick shut the sliding door. "I am going to get your weapon. I will do it slow and easy."

Nick reached inside the jacket he witnessed Fredricks drawing from with his right hand. "A Glock with silencer, huh? Yeah, everyone in the neighborhood packs one of these for protection. Whose idea was this?"

"I did it for the Lobos. I figured with Harding dead, Lobos be back."

Nick set the weapon on the van floor with his gloved hand. "Hold very still."

Nick jabbed Taylor in the neck with a syringe of his special morphine mix. Taylor struggled briefly with Nick forcing him face down on the van floor. "That was just to relax you a bit. We have a scene to stage. I can't have you wrecking my small play plot."

"Oh man... what did you give me?" Taylor sluggishly rolled to his side before Nick lifted him to a sitting position against some cardboard boxes lined sloppily along the van's interior wall.

Nick retrieved the Glock with silencer. He waited as Fredricks dozed and his eyes shut. Nick put the Glock in Fredricks' right hand, pinched off his nostrils, causing Taylor's mouth to pop open.

"Open wide. That's it. Dr. Muerto needs to insert his tongue depressant."

Nick carefully put the silencer barrel in Taylor's mouth, ducked away slightly, and helped Fredricks pull the trigger with his right index finger. Nick quickly released the weapon as blood and brain matter spattered onto the van wall and boxes. As Taylor slumped to the van floor, the Glock dropped first from his hand, onto his lap, and then slid off to clatter against the metal floor. Nick examined the scene.

"Perfect, my friend." Nick took a picture of Fredricks, placed the key into the ignition of the SUV, locked the front doors, exited the vehicle, and made sure the sliding door locked.

Nick texted Jean and Jafar everything was okay. He included a picture of Fredricks for Jafar with a request to scan for identity. He immediately walked toward the ballpark. *I hope I didn't miss anything important… like a Dark Lord robot dance and song.*

＊ ＊ ＊

"I saw Nick talking with the kids," Casey told me when we reached the dugout. "Afterward, he went around the bleachers. He's not back yet."

Clint moved around Casey. "I'll check on him."

Jafar met Clint at the entrance to the dugout, while the Bobcat's pitcher warmed up to start the bottom of the second inning, with the score still two to nothing. He smiled. "Quick huddle."

The Monster coaches huddled in the corner by the playpen. Jafar showed us a picture of the bad guy with his brains on the van wall behind him. The text requested an ID and a typical Muerto remark, 'bad guy so depressed about getting ready to kill John, he walked to his van and committed suicide'. Oh boy, we enjoyed Muerto's update. I heard 'Play Ball' and returned to my duties. Dora was first up in the inning. She gets a little tight.

"Relax and meet the ball, Dora. It's just another softball game with a pizza waiting at the end no matter what."

"Thanks, John." Dora grinned up at me and headed for the plate.

"The kids identified the guy for Nick," Jafar said on his way out. "They're the real deal."

"No question about that," Lynn remarked. "Do you have enough electronics to really ID him?"

"I do. I'm sitting in the middle of everyone, so no one can see me or what I'm doing."

"Thanks, little brother. Text me if you find something serious. I'll turn my phone back on." I always turned off my phone, because we didn't allow the girls to sit in the dugout with their eyes glued to small screens like adolescent zombies.

"Will do."

Dora nearly got beaned with the first pitch. She dropped back on her butt to avoid it, the bat falling at her feet. She looked at me and waved she was okay. The next pitch, Dora dropped a perfect bunt down the third base line. The girl playing third reached the ball, but her pitch sailed high into right field. Dora reached third before the right fielder hit the cutoff. Lucas signaled her into a slide and stop. The pitcher, Jenny Franco, visibly angry about the way she started, walked Mary. She threw two balls to Callie, drawing a visit from a tightlipped Jill.

I signaled Casey to send Mary on the next pitch. The moment Jenny let go of the ball, Mary streaked for second. When the catcher leaped to let go a throw to second, Lucas sent Dora in for our first run. Mary slid into second under the tag. Callie, having struck out swinging the first at bat, took another pitch for strike two. She took a deep breath and swung evenly without overdoing it. The ball roped into center, scoring Mary for the tying run. Al dropped another bunt beauty, so unexpected because of her hitting prowess, it didn't draw a throw. Sherry hit a double play ball, the Bobcats turned perfectly. Callie scored during it. Beth hit a comebacker for the third out, but it was a great game at three to two in our favor.

During Kelly's warmups, Jill marched out to go through a litany of things Manny missed in the first inning. Lynn danced to the plate, comically doing the twist, line dance shuffle, and ended at home plate with a modified Macarena. The applause was loud and long, allowing Manny to simply shout 'Play Ball'.

"Did you hear a word I said?"

"Yeah, Jill... I did. Did you hear me say 'Play Ball'? That's the signal for you to return to your dugout... now."

Lynn returned to more applause. Kelly and Jan had enjoyed the opening interruption of the day so much, they teamed for a three up and down inning. Kelly struck out one and got two more ground outs. Callie playing shortstop and Dora playing second, made perfect throws to Al at first. Hector argued both calls at first. Manny conferenced on both, and the plays stood as called. That began the boiler going inside Hector Torres. Jenny returned as the Bobcat pitcher for a third inning.

Kelly hit the first pitch to the fence, where the Bobcat left fielder made an over the shoulder catch so good, even our kids applauded, along with us. Kelly shrugged on her way by. "I was robbed."

"You smashed it," Lynn replied. "It'll give you a longer cool down before you start the third inning."

Jan went out and hit a screamer over the center field fence for a four to two lead. Jill made an idiot of herself asking to inspect Jan's bat. Manny didn't bother to answer her. He shouted his usual 'Play Ball' and waved our Ellie to the plate. She bunted, deadening it two feet in front of the plate. The catcher's throw sailed into right, allowing Ellie to reach second. Jenny walked Dora, bringing Jill to the mound. Mary hit a dribbler between the pitcher and third base. Mary crossed the bag safely. Hector ran out to question the call, screaming the Bobcats were getting hosed. Even the Bobcat parents groaned. Manny conferenced with all the umpires. When the Bobcats play, the umps knew better than to not pay attention. They unanimously said the call was correct. I thought Hector was going to have a stroke.

"Do it, Cheese, before he blows a gasket."

There I went, doing the Dark Lord Robot up the first baseline. Out came Beeper's cat-scratch song. If you think it's easy doing a Beeper song in Dark Lord voice, try it sometime. By the time I reached first base, even the Bobcats had dropped their mitts, howling in amusement with the fans and our dugouts. Beeper was good for something. Manny couldn't speak or breathe, least of all yell 'Play Ball'. Then Hector did a bad thing. He sucker-punched me. I caught his fist, holding him at arm's length away from me in a tightening vice. He realized suddenly what he had done, and the sudden silence.

"Sor…sorry, John."

"It's okay, Hector, but put this back at your side. Let Manny umpire in peace." I released his hand. He hurried into the dugout.

"I can toss him for that, John."

"I don't want the game to go on like that, Manny. He can't hit me anyway. It may help him think about what he's doing though."

"Thanks, John. That was the funniest thing I have ever seen. Play Ball!"

Just like that, the party ended. I received applause on my way to the dugout, where Al gave me the silent treatment. You can't please everyone.

"Great restraint out there, Cheese," Lynn said. "I think Hector lost it before you started. When you did the approach, he lost his mind."

"That's what I thought too. No big deal."

Callie and Al both hit ground outs. It was Al's turn to pitch. She would finish the game if she could. Naturally Jill stood out of the dugout to study our lefty, but she did so from a safe distance. Then the interrogation and retribution started on Manny for allowing aberrant pitching. Lynn stayed in the dugout. She knew Al thought Jill was funny. Her pitching was spot on in the warmups.

"Do you hear me, Manny?"

"Everyone in the park can hear you. Al pitches lefthanded. It's not illegal. She's coming set. Her release is fine, without deception or hesitation, and I don't know why I'm even telling you this again. Play Ball!"

The rest of the game was a pitcher's duel. Both Hector and Jill's daughter, Felisa, and Al, were strike throwers. Each had a good changeup and moved the ball up and down at will. The score remained unchanged. The defenses played excellent ball behind their control pitchers. The Bobcats had their last chance at the top of the seventh inning with the top of the order batting. Al, in a groove, struck out the first batter, and caught a popup to the mound. Then Felisa hit a homerun, and I mean she knocked the proverbial cover off the ball. Al did what I told her class acts do. She tipped her cap as Felisa rounded third. Unfortunately, for the Bobcats, Al struck the next girl out, swinging, and the game was over. Out came the protesting Hector and Jill show, but other sounds ended the poor sportsmanship.

Nick launched into a pre-planned 'Banana Boat Song'. His tenor voice in harmony with Jess and Dev 'Day-O' stopped everything else in the park. When Gus, Johnny, Jian, Sonny, and Jean joined in formation with sunglasses and black attire, the game passed into history. With the lyrics harmonized perfectly, combined with the rehearsed dancing movements, no one even remembered the game. The Bobcat and A's girls streamed to the front, dancing with the rest of the fans. Nick did a repeat of 'Montego Bay' with his crew that literally transcended the sporting moment. I even saw Hector, Jill and Felisa swaying at the side, and laughing at Nick's synchronized dancing crew. Dev and Jess harmonized perfectly with Nick's crew. When 'Montego Bay' ended, Nick straightened. At his signal, everyone in his dancing cadre put hands over hearts. He sang the National Anthem as well as anyone I had ever heard, without musical backup. Some moments are unfathomable. Here, we had the world's number one assassin, having killed and decked out a suicide scene an hour ago, entertaining a large audience and singing the National Anthem. Oh… hell… yeah!

After the Anthem ended in thunderous applause, Nick sang Lee Greenwood's 'God Bless the USA' song to finish one of the most spectacular endings of anything. It made me feel like crap we had to fly to launch our Ranger cruise warship for a task ahead. On the other hand, The Ranger had an entertainment and dancing room we planned to enjoy for our sailing days, intermixed with a deadly dangerous mission. Such is Monster vacation time.

"I want to invite everyone to Red Boy Pizza. It will be our treat." Cheers went up, so I figured we might not have a bad trophy ceremony.

We gathered all the equipment into my soccer mom van. The trophy ceremony was short and sweet. The dogs were taken home before our pizza party. Everyone was in the mood for pizza. The two teams and parents filled Red Boy. I gave the manager my debit card to run a tab. Nick's crew all came. Jafar explained in detail the threat taken care of by Nick personally, so everyone would remain on guard against any other unhappy Lobos. One more incident, and we would make the Lobos extinct. We toasted Sonny and Jean, although we didn't spell out why. They went into a huddle with Al, showing her the way Fredricks became a suspect.

"Wow… you two did great," Al said. "Thanks for keeping me updated when you're at home too."

"We need to keep our FBI contact apprised of all situations," Jean replied.

"Uh oh." Tommy was staring at the entrance.

I turned. It was Ian Wolf, his manager, and three other very grim looking men. "Excuse Tommy and me for a little bit. We'll go find out how Ian knew we came to the Red Boy, and why he decided to come."

"We'll be watching," Clint said.

The Monsters and Unholies shifted to positions where they could observe. Dev and Jess came along with me and Tommy. Ian waited at the door. Only two tables were left unoccupied. I motioned for Ian to join us. We put the two tables together and gathered additional chairs.

"Would you like a beer?" Tommy took over the official business with a polite offer.

"No. We want to know what happened to Tito," Ian replied.

"Tito? You mean the guy who accepted the fight conditions?"

"Yeah. You know damn well who Tito is," the manager, Donny Callan, said.

"Why should we know where he is," Tommy ducked the question. "He's your boss. I assume he's with his guys."

"His men are gone too," Wolf said.

"There you go. He's a gangster. He and his men are probably off doing gangster things."

"We think you know where they all are, Sands," Wolf stated.

"Well gee, that's too bad, because we can't help you with your Tito problem. Have you gone to the police? Maybe they can help."

"No… we didn't go to the damn police and none of them are answering their phones," Callan retorted.

"Like Tommy told you. We can't help with the Tito problem," I told them. "Do you still want the fight to go on. Alexi is working on the legal parts and taking it to the UFC and MGM

Grand. If you're backing out of it, say so, and we'll get in touch with Alexi."

"Hell no, I ain't backing out! Maybe it would be best if we leave, Donny. We ain't finding out anything from these bozos!" Wolf stood, and his companions joined him. "You got anything else to say, Harding."

I stood too, along with my guys. "You got a pretty mouth."

I smiled as it was a full scale 'hold me back' exercise, with Callan and the two grim guys holding on to Ian 'Death-Claw' Wolf, so he wouldn't attack me before the official papers were signed. I didn't care. Ian noticed I hadn't even moved into a defensive posture. It looked for a moment like maybe Wolf might get away and take a shot. It would be his last. Then Dev shot his fists in the air, head thrown back and eyes closed. I recognized the Latin exorcism spell. Man, he quieted the whole place down in an instant. It was Moses again with the 'Ten Commandments' voice – beautiful. It stunned Wolf and his companions. Dev finished to wild applause from our crowd. They had been treated to the Latin before.

"What the hell was that?"

"Your signal to get the hell out of here before the Dark Lord snatches your throat out," Jess answered. "Take the hint and save it for the cage where you can make some money for doctor bills."

"C'mon, Ian. He's right," Callan said. "You can get Harding in the cage."

"I'll maim you in the cage, Harding!" Wolf spun around. He stormed out and his buddies followed.

I waved. "Let's get a beer. Great Latin, Dev."

"I saw Wolf get pumped enough to make a fatal error, John. We want back in the Sin City lights. We're going to really perform this time, even more than we did when you took on Logan."

"Yeah, Dev caught it just in time," Jess added. He grinned. "I glanced over and saw Rose making the sign of the cross, brother."

Dev laughed. "I think she's a little freaked about my Latin."

"That makes two of us," Tommy agreed. "It sure stopped Wolf. Did you have to tell the prick he had a pretty mouth, DL?"

I shrugged. "It seemed like the thing to do. I'm not fond of being called a bozo."

"I hate clowns," Jess said. "He meant bozo like Bozo the clown, right?"

"He probably meant stupid and insignificant, like the definition," I replied.

"You'll need to hurt him, DL."

"I believe I will, Jess."

Chapter Ten

Isla Maria Magdalena

Nick told Rachel on the way home about the way Sonny and Jean found Fredricks. "They may have saved John's life."

"That is incredible, kids," Rachel said. "Do you think they'll find the guy?"

"Eventually," Nick answered. "It does appear he was acting alone though. They're tightening security to make sure the Lobos' movements will be covered. Did everyone decide about what they wanted to do regarding the Ranger cruise?"

"I'm stayin' with Gus," Tina said.

"Ripper and Kabong will always be together," Cala said.

"Dragon is in," Jian said. "Joan understands we're a special unit. I doubt she understands how special. She went with us when we protected the statue of Santa Rosalia. I have been trying to figure out a way to tell her everything. This may be the perfect time to keep her on board. Like you said, the ship won't be part of the battle. She will see us leaving for battle."

"I agree," Nick said. "She'll see both sides of the Unholies. She's coming to stay after we pull into Oakland, right?"

"Yes. She will be boarding with the other dependents."

"We're in," Rachel stated. "Jean's right. Living without you would be too much, but I don't know how staying on board helps. We're not flying onto the Isla with you."

"Denny, Gus, Cala, Clyde, Jafar, the Snow Whites, and Lynn's minions will be remaining with the ship. Between them and having Laredo ready with the helicopter, we will have all emergency contingencies covered. The dogs are all going, but only Tonto will be going with us to the Isla," Nick explained.

"What about if something bad happens and Gus needs to sail the Ranger home," Tina asked. The looks she got set her back. "Hey… someone has to ask the tough questions."

"I'll have enough people to sail Ranger to home port," Gus answered. "Muerto and the Dark Lord will bring everyone home. These people are terrorists who love sending other people out to die. They don't do so well in life and death situations. The Monsters and us Unholies defeated everything in our path during the formation of the City of Hope."

"We'll have Jafar relaying minute by minute satellite data to us," Nick added. "Our approach will be over rough terrain, but we've all done it before. We'll halt our approach when I have visual sighting of the estate from a higher vantage point. Lucas will handle sniper backup with Jian as his spotter. He will have line of sight on all movement at the estate. Frankly, the cleanup afterward to present the scene as I picture it will be the hardest part of this. We're killers without peer. We don't make mistakes in combat. I'm not too crazy about taking Lynn with us, but Clint told me she's done a mission like this before. That's good enough for me. Everyone with Gus on the ship is combat ready too, especially the minions. They have weapons aboard the Ranger to combat anything coming our way. Laredo will be on board to fly the Harrier jet we will be taking with us. Nothing will be left to chance."

"I guess it's wrong that I wish the ship was attacked and we could battle pirates, huh?"

"You little brat," Rachel said. "I might have known if I agreed to stay on board the Ranger, you would be praying for an attack."

"Calm down, Momster," Jean replied. "I should have said we'll be ready. I went too far with the 'I wish' part. Dad's explanation fired me up."

"I realize that, Daughter of Darkness. I'm always glad to have you and Sonny around me when I have Quinn, even when all we're doing is walking down to Otter's Point. Like Muerto said before, you two are blooded. Cala gave me a complete description of the knife incident. I know you shot on command when protecting the Santa Rosalia statue. I have no doubt you both are up to the mark. We don't raise victims in this family."

"That's for sure, Mom. Wait until we start training Kong from the moment he can walk."

Rachel gasped as everyone else enjoyed her shock. "You leave my baby boy alone! How many times have I told you not to call him Kong."

"You can't protect him forever, Mom. Cracker and I need another member for our squad in the future. Jay's good, but Kong carries Muerto DNA. He won't be a Snow White."

"Muerto!"

Nick sighed. "Yes. I am to blame for everything. Quinn carries your DNA too, Momster. That should mean something. Maybe he'll be an accountant."

Rachel glanced over at the special baby seat carrying the sleeping Quinn in the second set of seats. "Crap! Fat chance of that."

Rachel pointed at the smiling Jean. "I see that look, young lady. You are not turning my little boy into a Monster."

"I won't have to. With Sonny as his older brother and me his Big Sis, Kong will rule."

"Sonny! Don't you dare turn Quinn into Kong."

Sonny shook his head, uneasily seeing he had only amused observers around him in the big Ford. He shrugged with his head down. "Sorry, Ma, I'm a minion of the Daughter of Darkness."

"Damn it!" Rachel shook her head at the loud humorous appreciation of her plight. "Quinn will be different. I will guide him into the arts, philosophy, accounting, the legal profession… or even medicine. You jerks need lawyers and doctors."

"Dream on, Mom," Jean replied. "Kong will have his own mind. Sonny and I will train him. He'll still be getting corrupted in school, so if he really chooses to be a doctor or lawyer, we won't stop him."

Rachel relaxed against her seat. "He's doomed."

* * *

We landed on the other side of the Isla Magdalena. Laredo chose the landing zone with Cala copiloting. The terrain would be a small inconvenience to traverse for us. We carried the most up to date GPS networking available, along with satellite guidance from Jafar. Humorously, it rained as we rappelled down from the copter.

"Not the rain again!" Lynn was none too happy. "This shit pisses me off. Every time I go on a combat insertion, I get rained on."

As Clint released Tonto from his insertion harness, Tonto padded over to bump into Lynn. "That's Tonto's way of saying quit whining or we'll stick your butt back on the helicopter, Betty."

We weren't in sound range of anyone so a moment of amusement at Lynn's expense proceeded until Lucas waved a hand in front of her face. "This rain is a blessing. It will keep any guards outside the estate under cover, while covering our approach both in sound and sight. Tonto will pick a pathway in the direction we want to go. This will be slow going. We can't afford a casualty on the approach. Be aware of your footing. We have the best footgear money can buy, but it can't save you from missteps off a cliff."

"I know, Pap. I'll keep my mouth shut this time to target."

"Good. Let's get 'er done."

We checked each other's packs and gear. The combat helmets we wore incorporated networking, GPS, and night-vision features. We have money and government contacts, which put us into the space-age of combat gear. Lucas suggested trying out the Heckler & Koch UMP45 submachine gun with noise suppressor after our last outing. Clint and I liked it, as did Lynn. Lighter than the MP5, we liked the larger caliber and advanced noise suppression. Everyone else, including the Unholies, carried Night-shot Casey's favorite, the MP5 with noise suppression. Nick and I both packed M107 .50 caliber sniper rifles in case we needed a coordinated sniper action on the guards. Clint packed our XM25 grenade launcher with ammo. If we wanted to make this a mystery, the XM25 would only be used if the mission went to hell in a handbasket.

Laredo and Cala would fly air support from the Ranger once we neared our objective. Satellite coverage revealed twenty-two bodies at the estate, including our primary targets. Jafar isolated ten soldiers with weapons. He also identified our main targets: Khaled Hanniyeh, Safia Sakaria, and Mammar Rhahin. The others belonged to Hamas and The Muslim Brotherhood. They all flew into Puerto Vallarta to board Hanniyeh's ship, 'The Rigel', for a cruise and extended estate stay. We knew they weren't meeting to discuss peace in our time. They all shared a common goal: the death of Israel and all Jews. In addition to their desire to exterminate the Jewish people, they wanted to establish terrorist cells in the United States. Their main agenda would be how to get trained operatives from their bases in the Middle East and Europe into the States.

Clint took point with Tonto, keeping our early warning canine heading in the right direction. He picked along, making sure we encountered no booby traps or dangerous patches of terrain. The weird landscape, a mixture of vegetation, brush, and thin tree lines, stretched on endlessly. Some mountainous patches overlooked the inlet and beach where Hanniyeh's estate incorporated a pier and small boat access. The small boats, taking the passengers from 'The Rigel' to the estate's pier, returned to 'Rigel' rather than chance being swamped in rough weather. One of our main objectives centered on jamming all communications going into and out of the estate. Johnny packed the most powerful jammer available, capable of blocking wifi and cell-phone communications instantly.

It took us nearly two hours to get line of sight on the estate from our chosen high ground. As the satellite feed revealed, the area around the estate, cleared of all vegetation, provided a custom paving stone surface for twenty yards all around the estate. Lucas scanned his target area and decided we were in a perfect position for his sniper's nest. With the other nest set on slightly lower ground across from us, Casey would have a good portion of the estate in his sights from there. He would also have the XM25 with him. During the initial sniper action Lynn would spot for Casey, while Jian spotted for Lucas.

I went with Clint, Tonto, Johnny, and Nick to work around to the unguarded beach side. Although an awning type overlay bordered the estate to give the guards cover, they were still visible underneath it from both sniper nest positions. Five guards sat at small tables in intervals around the estate's perimeter facing the rest of the Isla. They took turns walking the perimeter, two at a time, which suited our purposes perfectly. We hoped to get positioned to intercept a couple of them, possibly the right size for Nick and Johnny to switch into their uniforms.

We took our time avoiding the guards as we moved around to the beachfront. The rain, steady on our approach, opened into a deluge of water. We enjoyed some muttered profanity from Lynn over our network. The estate's huge open patio could be accessed from the house through sliding glass doors. Fortunately, the blinds were drawn closed. Clint stayed with Tonto at the side of the estate building. After positioning ourselves in the patio recess, Johnny found a good spot for our jammer, and turned it on to check. After making sure it jammed us, Johnny turned it on again.

"In position, Pap," I said.

"Two guards strolling around to the right front of the estate as you face out to sea. Those rain ponchos they're wearing should be enough of a disguise."

"Understood."

As Lucas described, the two guards strolled past, glancing out at the ocean. Nick and Johnny double-teamed one of them with Johnny hugging the man's arms to his sides. Muerto broke his neck. I did the same to my man, plucking him off the walkway to prevent his rifle from clattering onto the stone paving. Nick and Johnny quickly pulled on their caps and ponchos. Our camo pants, much the same as theirs, would not be detected until it was too late.

"Guards are down Lucas. Nick and Johnny have their uniforms on. I will stay with the jammer until Nick and Johnny get around the estate. The moment you spot them, let me know, and I'll turn on our jammer. Take out the remaining three guards. Nick and Johnny will try to position them before any detection. We'll be off-line."

"Understood," Lucas said. "Everyone will move down for the assault. I'll remain alone here. I have excellent visuals. On my mark, Case. I have the two on the right."

"Ready," Casey acknowledged. "Double tap, center mass."

"I see Muerto and Kabong. Fire." Listening to Lucas, I could imagine he and Casey guiding the three into eternity before they knew what hit them, within seconds.

"All down." Lucas continued control. "Our guys have them in their chairs already."

"Clint and I have the rear access with Tonto. Move on the front with Muerto and Kabong leading, after I learn whether the rear access door is unlocked."

I tried the rear sliding door gently. I could not hear voices. It was unlocked. "We're good to go. I'm turning on jammer. Switch to walkie-talkies. Let me see how far we can get into the back."

"Understood," Nick said at the front. "We are ready. When you're shooting at soldier looking guys, Muerto and Kabong have cuter pants and boots."

"Right... cuter pants and boots. Got it. Moving in now." I opened the sliding glass door enough for Clint to send Tonto in slinking mode through the crack.

Clint trained Tonto to enter a room, kill if attacked, and if not attacked, to stay low against the perimeter walls in stealth mode, while scouting for the enemy. He then will continue until sighting a human. Tonto returns then to guide us. We could tell by the length of time, he needed to scout deep into the estate house, before making contact, we were in an unpopulated area. Tonto poked his head out to glance at Clint with his 'what are you waiting for... an invitation look'. I opened the door widely enough to allow Clint and I in full combat regalia to slip inside.

"Gee, Tonto," I whispered, "you sure took your time."

Tonto looked up at Clint, who nodded, and Tonto pissed on my boot. Damn it. With Tonto padding in the lead, we scouted the entire rear of the estate. Once we reached a point where walls and ceiling expanded into ballroom type size, Tonto halted. We needed to stay in place and allow the bad guys to retreat into our ambush.

"We're in place," I whispered into our walkie-talkie.

"Going mission enabled," Nick answered.

* * *

Nick looked around at his cadre of killers, a smile vibrating on his lips. "Johnny and I will walk in like we own the place, as I hope the guards actually do in reality. We'll continue until we get stopped. Then we kill. We all know what Khaled looks like. If we can separate him from his pack while killing the rest... then great. If not... he dies, and we write off the mission on our taxes."

"We'll lag behind a bit and spread for better cover fire," Casey replied. "We've done this a thousand times. They will hesitate. We won't. Good luck to Khaled. If he's lucky, he'll die in the first volley. Otherwise, the poor sap meets Cruella Deville."

"Hey... all he needs to do is give us all his money. I'd like to take this estate too, but we'd probably need to declare war on Mexico. Anybody we see looking like him, shoot them in the gut. If you get a chance to blow a couple pieces off that Safia bitch, I'd like to play with her too."

"Understood," Nick replied.

Nick and Johnny entered the house without hesitation, simply moving toward party sounds, where it seemed the Muslims threw away the rule against alcohol consumption. Rounding the entry way into a large dining area, Nick noticed happily, the five other soldiers stood like sentries against the same wall. In front of them, with music playing and drinks being guzzled, were most of their identified targets. The chef and two men from Khaled's ship cooked for the estate. Jafar identified them first, letting John know they were not innocent lambs, hired to make meals. They were cold blooded killers who had been with Khaled a long time. Nick moved toward the soldiers with Johnny at his side, stitching them with short 9mm bursts from their MP5s. Lynn, Casey, and Jian covered the room, including the guests at the dining table.

Screams of anguish from the guests froze the more violent ones in the group. Lynn shot Khaled in both shoulders as he sat at the head of the table. The ACP .45 rounds pitched Hanniyeh backwards, chair and body flipping to the floor. Lynn knew Casey and Jian would be careful to cover her. She walked over and smashed Safia Sakaria in the face with the butt of her UMP45 submachine gun. Lynn grinned as she turned her UMP45 on Mammar Rhahin and fired a burst into his head. Their companions knew they were in trouble. They reached for weapons and died. The kill mission finished in short order, as Nick and Johnny joined in. Nick used his walkie-talkie.

"Main room and targets secured! Possible cooking staff fleeing through the back towards you, John!"

* * *

Clint motioned Tonto between his legs as three guys ran toward us, firing into imagined targets around them. No shots were fired at us directly. We shot them in the head. They fell in the same spot.

"Secure in the rear," I said. "We'll let Tonto scout the complex."

Tonto went on hunt. We were cut off from Jafar for the time being, holding position. Tonto returned a short time later, after being acknowledged by our front assault group. Clint and I joined the Muerto group in the dining area. It was a mess. I called in Laredo and Cala to land near the open front of the estate. They arrived in short order while we limited blood mess.

"Johnny, Jian, and I will start cleaning the premises, if you Monsters will bag the bodies for disposal. Cala's copiloting so she'll fix them for disposal at sea if you want to toss them out, John. We can give Khaled and Safia a shot to make them comfortable for their flight to the Ranger after the disposal at sea. We should seal Khaled's wounds with antibiotic, surgical pads, and duct tape for the time being."

"I'll take care of that, Muerto," Lynn said. "I want the player to know me. Get him sitting on his chair, Cheese. I'll get our med kit out of Clint's bag."

"I noticed you didn't really care to talk with Mammar Rhahin," Nick remarked.

Lynn shrugged. "The only thing he knew how to say is 'kill all the Jews'. Imam hate mutants are a dime a dozen. Safia, on the other hand, can be used with Khaled."

"Understood." Nick went to work on cleaning.

I righted the groaning Khaled in his chair. After stripping off his jacket and shirt, we cleaned wounds with peroxide. Lynn applied antibiotic and surgical pads. Clint had plenty of surgical tape, so Lynn and I wrapped the shoulders tightly. I gave him a syringe of happy juice. The Unholies started cleanup immediately with the three Clint and I shot in the other room. Laredo landed five minutes later at the front. We covered the inside of the helicopter with a tarp. I took only twenty minutes to load all the bodies. Cala copiloted, so she and I stripped and prepared our fish food while Laredo flew us way out over the ocean. I then tossed a couple bloody ones out for bait. Once the bait started getting ripped into, I disposed of the rest. I dumped the clothing a mile away from the bodies. By the time we returned, Lucas had joined everyone else in the house. Nick, Jian, and Johnny were busily cleaning blood and flesh, while my Monsters stayed away in one area with the drugged Khaled and Safia.

Clint gestured at Nick and crew. "Dead-Boy pointed out it would be better if the rest of us didn't contaminate the scene."

"It makes it easier if I know exactly who was where and what was touched," Nick added. "Why don't you all fly back to the Ranger? Lynn can get started on her toys. We'll finish cleaning and patching. I'll call for pickup once we finish."

"We're partying when you get back on board, Muerto," Lynn said.

"Of course. I think it would be better though if Gus and Lucas get us steaming North. Our luck's holding with Mexico. We could probably tear them out a new one if they attacked the Ranger, but I promised Rachel we wouldn't be riding the Ranger into combat."

"Nick's right," Lucas said. "I'll never get my wife on another cruise if she hears even one shot fired."

"Let's leave Muerto and the cleaning Unholies to their work," I agreed. "See you when you finish. Did you find my jammer where I left it, Nick?"

"Yep. I went over the entire estate, checking every room. I cleaned up what Tonto left behind while decorating your boot too. The people on 'The Rigel' know Khaled would never have a dog here, so I need to be thorough with anything Tonto was around. See you all on board."

Everyone appreciated hearing about the Tonto adjustment I endured. "Okay. Were there any stray bullet holes to patch?"

"Very few. I'll deal with them."

"Muerto always packs his patch kit," Jian explained. "He is sick and twisted, but artistic in his final touches. This scene will be exactly as he wants it."

"Thanks, Dragon Breath."

"I am Dark Dragon."

"Not anymore."

* * *

Jian and Johnny waited by the door as Nick did a final once over, scanning the scene. He decided during their cleaning to wash and put away everything, rather than leave the dinner and drinking scene intact with food and dishware. Nick insisted on cleaning the kitchen by himself, leaving no room for error. All the cleaning supplies were returned into storage and bloody rags bagged for disposal elsewhere.

"I must admit this place appears to have never hosted anybody or anything," Jian said.

Nick joined them in the entryway with the disposal bag. He put on his combat gear. "We killed ten Mexican regular army guys. Their disappearance will not go unnoticed. It's still raining. That will help in smoothing out any sign of the helicopter landing. We'll have Laredo pick us up in the back."

"We can do that now, right," Johnny asked.

"I'm done in here. I won't call Laredo until we finish outside." Nick led the way to their landing zone.

The storm pounded rain into the ground where Laredo landed with enough force to completely erase where the landing gear and footsteps had been. Nick kept Jian and Johnny on the paving stone walkway while he examined the area. Nearing the point where he felt it safe to call for pickup, a light appeared on the horizon. Nick could also hear a boat engine's roar getting louder. He hurried over to his companions.

"Damn... we have company. Talk about close calls – we finished barely in time to avoid this. I'm calling John and tell him to have Gus and Lucas get the Ranger moving. Laredo and Cala can fly from further away for our extraction. I'm beginning to wonder if they can even fly in here safely in this storm. I'd rather be hiding out on the Isla instead of bobbing all over in a helicopter."

"I agree," Johnny said as they rounded the estate to move into the surrounding terrain.

"You mean we may need to wait in the wet, cold darkness until daybreak?" Jian made an amusing whine noise while they walked.

"Maybe longer," Nick replied. "We'll hang out on the ridge we came down from, where Lucas covered us with his sniper nest. We can see who arrives for a visit, and whether they stay or head back to 'The Rigel'. They might make a distress call to the Mexican authorities on Isla Maria Madre where the Islas Marias Federal Prison is located. I suspect that's where Khaled recruited the guards from. Let's double time to the ridge where we can watch without worrying about being discovered."

The three did as Nick suggested without further comment. The treacherous footing, because of the storm, slowed their assent. Nick wanted to be in position before the boat tied at the pier. He did not want, however, an injury to any of them in the process. They barely made it to the ridge top before the boat arrived. They each packed high tech Steiner binoculars. Four men led the way from the boat with six women huddled under umbrellas.

"They expected to have the women brought after the dinner meeting," Nick said. "We just missed a blood bath."

"No way we could have cleaned out the place like we did if the party had been in full swing," Johnny agreed. "Call it in. We will need to trek back to the insertion point."

Lucas answered the satellite phone. Nick explained what happened. "We'll watch from our vantage point, but I think you and Gus need to move the Ranger North immediately."

"Agreed," Lucas replied. "Laredo has been fretting over going out again in this storm. He won't be happy about leaving you three there. I'm certain he will believe it's safer to wait until the storm breaks. This could be bad. You know that, right?"

"I know. If they get troops from the prison Isla to come here with dogs to search for the mysteriously missing people, we'll need to dig in somewhere. We're heading for the insertion point after we gather intel. I'll update you from there."

"Okay, Nick. We will get you out of there."

"I know that. My t-shirt and pajama line won't be worth a thing if I'm dead." Nick disconnected with Lucas's laughter in his ear.

Ten minutes later, the men rushed the women outside toward the boat, scanning their surroundings with fearful eyes. Only moments later, the boat left the pier, heading at full steam toward 'The Rigel'.

"That did not look good."

"Not so bad, Johnny," Nick replied. "Think about it. They left a bunch of people on an uninhabited Isla, with ten soldiers guarding them. They return to stock the party, and the place looks like aliens arrived to beam everyone aboard a UFO. The boaters may believe Khaled and his bunch are already passing Mars, heading for Pluto."

"Mickey Mouse's dog in the Disney cartoons?"

Nick grinned at Jian while Johnny enjoyed Jian's lack of astronomy knowledge in stifled amusement. "Forget Pluto. They'll be passing Mars, heading for Uranus."

"My anus? Is this round-eye humor?" Jian glanced from Nick to Johnny suspiciously. "This joke is meaningless. I like Mars Bars, by the way."

Nick put his arm around Jian's shoulders. "Never mind, Dragon. The insertion point's a long way from here in this weather. I think I have a Mars Bar in my pack. I'll give it to you when we get there."

"Really? Thank you. I am starving." Jian let Nick guide him on their way. "What does Johnny think is so funny?"

Nick glanced back at Johnny, who could barely breathe. "Easily entertained."

The storm plastered the three men all the way. Nick led at a steady pace, but slowly with great care. They needed to keep on the high ground because Nick could see where the storm caused flooded valleys of dangerous muck. When they reached the insertion point, they stayed on a rocky slope above the beach. Nick retrieved the candy from his pack.

"Sorry, Dragon. They're Three Musketeers Bars, just like us." He passed a couple to each of his friends.

"That is okay, Muerto. I like these too. Yes, we are the Three Musketeers."

"Two Musketeers and an astronomy idiot," Johnny retorted.

"Huh? That is mean. I do not believe in those signs. You are an Aquarius, but you act like a Libra. I bet you were born in the Year of the Rat."

After another bout of intense amusement at Jian's mixing of astrology with astronomy, Johnny gave Jian a small head shove on his helmet. "You are the best. If I must be stuck in the middle of nowhere with rain pounding what little sense I have left out my ears, I am glad it is with you, my friend."

"Thank you... I think," Jian replied. "What should we do if they bring dogs and soldiers, Muerto?"

"They will only search for a short time. The rain erases any evidence of our being here. They will have no starting point. Even if they bring bloodhounds, the soldiers will be having them sniff the Khaled group's clothing. We know they won't be able to go anywhere with that. I like our chances of not being discovered. What we need to watch for is patrol boats searching the Isla coastline. In the morning, we'll find a hideout inland, hopefully amongst the rocks, where we can stay out of sight. I'll take first watch. You two doze off if you can. I better call Lucas."

"We're hanging out in the rocks, near the insertion point." Nick briefed Lucas on the situation with the frightened boaters, who fled after learning Khaled's group vanished without a trace. "They may send patrol boats from the Islas Marias Federal Prison Isla. We'll look for a hideout in the rocks in the morning. Sorry, but tell Laredo it's storming like hell, and the wind is picking up."

"We have Jafar scanning all communications from 'The Rigel'. You nailed it. They're scared. They called Khaled's people with no theory other than the group vanished. A call went out to the prison Isla. They will be sending a couple of patrol boats out in the morning if the storm dies down."

"Good to know. Anyway, we're fine. We ain't warm and cozy, but we have the best gear known to mankind. We're dry. Did Crue have fun with her toys?"

"No. She's pissed. The minions showed Khaled and Safia Crue's hit parade of podiatry videos. We couldn't shut them up. When we asked for the account numbers to get our fee for all this, Khaled suddenly got silent. That brought a smile to her face. She's letting them stew overnight. Crue's mad because she wants to be celebrating with the Muerto Master of Music."

"We'll get to that, Top. Have a couple for us tonight."

"We don't touch the stuff until we have you three on board," Lucas stated. "We'll blow the prison Isla and every patrol boat they have into atomic dust if we need to. Jean wants to talk at you. Rachel already told her there aren't enough guys on all three Islas bad enough to take out Muerto. She still begged me to let her speak with you. Here she is."

"Dad!"

Nick's mouth tightened. *Some psycho I am.* "Viper! Are you keeping Deke out of trouble?"

"He's fine. I want to know if you're okay, or these Snow Whites are telling me what I want to hear."

Nick listened to the Monster's loud amusement at being called Snow Whites with a smile. "They're being straight up with you. The storm's too strong. We need to hang out here for a time. We're safe and sound. You probably heard what our two prisoners spewed. You and Sonny get into that with Al. Give me some fresh ideas on anything connected."

"Yeah! Okay… we're on it. Thanks, Dad. I love you."

Jean was gone before Nick could say goodbye. Lucas chuckled. "Now that was funny. I see Jean's been assimilating the Muerto humor."

"Lucas… all kidding aside. If things go to hell, get Laredo to fly the dependents off before you think about anything else."

"Did you just insult me?"

Nick grinned. "Yeah… that was stupid. It's a rainy night in Georgia."

"I want to hear that one when you get back on board, maggot."

"Absolutely, Top. Talk with you in the morning." Nick disconnected. "At least we know what they'll be sending to check on us."

"If Mexico gets involved, they probably have equipment for detecting heat signatures," Johnny replied. "We will need to go roll around in the mud or find some rocks to hide under."

"I spotted a few likely places, but I didn't want us to try and reach them in the dark with this rain." Nick paused for a moment. "The patrol boats worry me a bit if they land search parties. In this case, with no evidence to suggest foul play, they should be looking for survivors trying to be found. You're right though. At dawn, we'll find a better place."

* * *

Lora helped me think about something else besides our guys trapped on the Isla. I held her in my arms while she slept, which I rarely do. My mind drifted to the Isla with Nick, Johnny, and Jian. I hated being the one lying in a bed on a luxurious cruiser. I wanted to be on the rocks with them. A light tap on the door ended what little chance I had of sleeping. After moving the sleeping Lora aside, I quickly dressed in jeans, t-shirt, and boots. Clint and Lynn awaited me on the other side of the stateroom door.

"C'mon, Cheese. I thought of something. We need to hook Khaled up for some information gathering. I don't want Denny to wake up. He's already making eyes at Khaled, plotting to keep him." Lynn led the way to our makeshift jail, guarded by the minions. Quays stood as we approached. "We need to take Khaled some place quiet for a talk, Quays."

Clint and I went in. Both Khaled and Safia were drugged so they wouldn't disturb our dependents. We dragged the groggy Khaled off his cot. I held him while Clint duct taped his mouth and restrained his hands. We marched him away between us while Quays remained with Safia. I didn't bother questioning Lynn. Anything other than inaction suited me. Below decks in the engine room, the minions had already constructed a gurney with restraints for the coming interrogation in the morning. Clint and I strapped Khaled in tightly. He became aware through the drug haze this was not a drill. Lynn gave him an injection to counteract the daze while Clint and I installed our needles in his feet. Khaled began making mewling sounds as we attached the clips from our portable pain machine. Clint retrieved his satellite laptop, getting it ready for action.

"I have a question for you about something troubling me about your Isla estate. You mutants love to stockpile weapons and other things detrimental to the human race. I gave you an opportunity last night to give us your account numbers the easy way. For some reason, you think you'll survive this and keep your fortune. Before I ask my question, I need to teach you a lesson in truth telling so we don't waste any time."

Lynn revved Khaled into the stratosphere of pain in varying cycles for ten unimaginable minutes. She waited until sanity began seeping back into Khaled's features. "Now then, when I ask my questions, I want truthful answers immediately. Do you understand?"

Oh boy, did he understand. I removed the duct tape from his mouth while making shushing sounds. "Don't waste Dr. Deville's time. Stay silent and ready."

He stopped trying to speak. Lynn patted his cheek. "I want to know if you have a hidden underground weapons storage area on the Isla."

"Yes! Yes… you… you did not need to torture me to find that out."

"Yeah, I did. We'll start with how well you've learned your truth lesson. My associate will use your instructions to transfer liquid assets into our accounts. After we confirm that, you will explain exactly where on the Isla your weapons cache is."

Twenty minutes later, Clint had transferred all of Khaled's holdings into our accounts. We unstrapped Khaled so he could pinpoint where his hidden bunker was on our topographical map. He explained how to approach it from Nick's position. The access panel hydraulically released the hatch.

"You did good, my little helper. We will make you comfortable until our men on the Isla find the bunker. If you've given us the wrong info, I will make you regret the day you were ever born. How many people know about the bunker?"

"Three, but you killed two of them at our meeting, Mistress of the Unimaginable. I am the only one alive who knows where it is located. My... associates in Saudi Arabia know it exists, but their leader died in your attack. He...he should have been the one to live and be tortured. I...I assumed you came after me because of his order to take Badee Karim's family to draw him out."

"So, you're saying we killed the man in charge who ordered it, huh?"

"Yes, Mistress. His name was Saladin Al-Ayubi. He was a very powerful man in the Saudi hierarchy. We knew if Badee Karim could establish a secular state in Afghanistan, based on what Khan Eshieh is building, all of Islam could be at risk."

"I like the sound of that. Okay, Khal, let's get you tucked in."

* * *

I called Nick to confirm he received our pinpoint directions and map for the bunker. I put him on speaker with the Monsters and the Unholies' dependents.

"Isla Magdalena of muck... how may I direct your call?"

Jean giggled. After the greetings with loved ones, Nick got down to business.

"Great map. On our way to the bunker now. We need to make small detours because the rain has turned the place into mudslide heaven. The rain stopped intermittently, so if we avoid the searchers for a time, it may be safe for Laredo and Cala to come get us. I imagine Jafar will be able to tell when the search ends and they vacate the Isla."

"I have everything under surveillance, Muerto," Jafar told him. "They launched two patrol boats from the prison Islas Marias. Fifteen men are on board each boat, so they will be looking. I will be able to see every move they make."

"Excellent."

"If we see them nearing the bunker, we're coming with the 'Ride' and all guns blazing," Lucas told him.

"Thanks, but that's not necessary. There's only thirty of them."

The Monsters and Unholies' dependents appreciated that bit of Muerto humor for the next few moments.

"Thanks for thinking of the bunker, Crue," Muerto said. "We found a rocky overhang we planned to use for cover. The bunker will be much better. We'll call when we get inside. Muerto out."

"If Muerto accomplishes this mission without detection, it will give us all the time we need to relocate Badee Karim," Denny said. "I think the City of Hope with Khan Eshieh would be perfect for Badee. He could work from there to change Afghanistan around. Broadcasts by Badee from the heart of the city would possibly change everything in the Middle East."

I stood. "Let's man the monitors. Until we get our guys back, I want all eyes on what Jafar can conjure."

"God knows what he'll find in a hidden island bunker," Casey said.

* * *

"Here it is!" Jian stood near a hatch, completely hidden by vegetation. The three men had been searching the exact coordinates for nearly an hour.

Nick put in the code to release the hydraulically operated hatch. It swung open without a problem. "I'll go down and find out what this bunker is. It seems as if they buried a complete tanker or shipping container."

Nick descended the ladder to the pitch-black bottom. The switch at the base of the ladder turned on a series of battery operated lanterns, illuminating the interior. "It's a large shipping container with enough arms, explosives, grenade launchers, and rocket launchers to start a small war. There are even bomb vests stored here. C'mon down, my friends. It's dry. The hatch closure panel is at floor level."

Johnny and Jian joined Nick at the floor level. Nick hit the hatch closure the moment they were inside. "We'll need to empty this place out or blow it to kingdom come." Nick inspected the lighting first after closing the outside hatch. "I can tell this place needs maintenance."

Nick shined a flashlight on the battery container. "This power source would rot without maintenance and it appears close to doing exactly that. No doubt Khaled planned to provide maintenance for this bunker, but had a tough time trusting anyone to do it. We'll need to confiscate or destroy this stuff. I spotted an open area, where the vegetation looked manually removed, probably serving as a perfect landing zone to stock this hellhole."

"I think I'll take a moment to enjoy the quiet of not having rain pounding on my helmet." Johnny stood with hands outstretched, his face uplifted, and eyes closed.

"Enjoy Kabong. I'll see if our satellite phone will work in this joint." A static filled connection greeted Nick's attempt. He sighed, taking a video recording of the interior bunker contents. "I'll go pop the hood for another moment. Take inventory of what's here with an eye toward transport trips to Ranger, where we confiscate the major part of this weapons cache."

Outside the hatch. Nick sent the recording before calling. The connection cleared beyond the hatch. Lucas answered. "Neat place, Top. I can't broadcast from within. I think we need to fly away with a lot of it or blow the thing up."

"Understood. We have everyone on the monitors, tracking the searchers. Last position of an insertion came within two hundred yards of the hatch, but we can tell they're blind to the location of the hatch. Stay inside for the next four hours and then reconnect."

"Will do. That way we have enough time to do inventory and make suggestions for confiscation. We need to blow this bunker once we get what we want."

"I will pass that on, Nick. It may also be possible to flood the bunker with saltwater. Take care of yourselves. If the damn hatch opens, kill everything trying to gain access."

Nick's stifled amusement set Lucas off. A few moments later, Lucas responded. "I played that goofball comment in my head for a moment. Talk with you in four hours."

Nick rejoined his companions with hatch closed. They looked at him with anticipation. He shrugged. "It's still raining. The searchers made it to within two hundred yards, but nothing to indicate they know the location of the hatch. Lucas told me to kill anything that opens the hatch."

Both Jian and Johnny laughed at the statement Lucas couldn't help but utter. Nick gestured happily during the amused greeting of the obvious. "We need to use our time wisely here."

"How will we do that in your humble opinion, Muerto," Johnny asked.

"I think we need to send them a music video." Nick smiled, thinking about a perfect one to do as a trio. "I have it! Watch me, guys."

Nick stood away from his companions. He began the main melody of 'I Can't Help Myself' by the Four Tops which had the secondary recognizable lyric of 'Sugar Pie, Honey Bunch'. Nick did it like he remembered the Four Tops doing it, with hands palm outwards waving from side to side in clock ticking form at chest level, with feet moving in rhythm from side to side. He did the whole song with Johnny and Jian laughing and beginning to mimic his movements. After getting the beat and movements down, they took positions on either side of him. Nick began the song again as they rehearsed. Johnny and Jian learned where to harmonize with 'Sugar Pie, Honey Bunch'. The rehearsal and recording took only an hour and a half to complete. Nick, without regard to danger or giving away their position, opened the hatch, and sent the recording. Johnny and Jian with MP5s at the ready, guarded against unexpected arrivals as he did it.

* * *

Jafar, on watch for the phone, took the call, with all of us watching him laugh his ass off while sending it to our big screen with full enhanced audio. The three Unholies did the Four Tops song in synch with perfect execution and voice. When we weren't laughing and joining in, I sent Jafar to get everyone. Soon, we had our entire crew doing 'Sugar Pie, Honey Bunch' with Nick and the Unholies. God... it was so good, I wanted to lay waste to the Islas Marias to bring Muerto back to the ship immediately.

Chapter Eleven

Las Vegas Business

After twenty-four hours, Nick checked in for his regular contact every four hours. Jafar answered. "Achmed… give me some good news."

"They recalled the boats. 'The Rigel' sailed for Puerto Vallarta two hours ago. No one has any idea what happened to Khaled's group. Laredo will leave for extraction once I confirm the patrol boats are ported. Gus and Lucas turned Ranger towards you. We have detection radar all on and set. If we get pinged by anyone, we will cruise by as if sailing for Mexico. Laredo knows exactly where the landing zone for the bunker is. If communications and radar detection stay clear, John will bring Clint and Casey with him to load as much of the bunker horde as Laredo feels safe hauling."

"Sounds great. Marooned Muerto over and out." Nick disconnected. He called down for his companions. "C'mon up. The search ended a couple hours ago. The sun is shining, birds are singing. It's a wonderful day in the neighborhood. When the Monsters get here, we'll form a Conga Line for loading what we want on the copter."

"It is beautiful being out of the bunker in the sunshine," Jian said. "I wonder what Joan thinks of all this."

"I doubt you will need to explain much to her," Johnny remarked.

"My advice… take a shower before you talk with her for any length of time, Dragon," Nick said.

"You do not smell like fresh roses either, Muerto."

* * *

The reunion on the ship, once we off loaded our cargo, took place on deck where the sea breeze cut down on the odor. Spending a few days in full combat clothes inside a closed bunker gave the

Unholies a distasteful ambience. They stripped down to pants and t-shirts on the helicopter ride to the ship. I bagged their clothing for cleaning at home. They cleaned their weapons inside the bunker. We each carried a basic cleaning kit into combat where we had unknown weather and terrain conditions.

While the Unholies showered, the rest of us stored the weapons cache we took from the bunker. We froze the bomb vests in the reinforced freezer. Before leaving the Isla, we filled the bunker with salt water and debris as Lucas suggested, above the height of what remained. I closed the hatch and buried it under rocks, dirt, and brush. The salt water would rot everything left inside. Tommy took a call while we finished storing the last crates confiscated. He came back to sit with me on deck, where our work party enjoyed a beer while steaming into United States Coastal waters.

"Alexi called. Ian Wolf and his manager pushed through a deal with the UFC and MGM Grand. The fight will be on in two weeks. They added it to a UFC event already planned."

"How the hell did they pull that stunt off, T?"

"The much-advertised light heavyweight championship was scrapped due to injuries suffered by both fighters in a pre-fight publicity meeting."

"Sounds like one of your publicity meetings, DL," Jess said.

"They went at it with fists, feet and furniture until their handlers and security finally got them under control," Tommy added. "They got pulled apart like a couple of rabid dogs – a bloody mess. The UFC suspended them both. UFC officials welcomed Wolf's proposal and Alexi agreed to it. I'm glad you've been getting your work in on this cruise."

"John's ready," Dev stated. "His left jab is enough to end a fight. I wouldn't mix it up with him if not for the head gear."

"Dev's right," Jess added. "Getting hit with that left jab feels like being hit in the face with a fence post. If DL mixes in his leg kick, he opens everything up for either a takedown submission or knockout."

"I'm not taking Wolf lightly. We will bring the whole show with us into the cage though. I say we work on our dance moves tonight if Muerto entertains. I'm talking the MGM into doing the 'Exorcist' theme in the background with Dev doing the Latin, and all of us in black inside the cage with heads bowed. We couldn't get it done the last time. We will before this fight."

"We should do 'Montego Bay'," Jafar suggested.

"I'm down with that," Dev said. "I love the 'Four Tops' song, but I don't want to be doing the 'Sugar Pie, Honey Bunch' song in the cage."

While we enjoyed Dev's humorous input, the Unholies joined us on the Ranger's spacious deck, except Gus. All three dogs joined the deck party too. Tommy told Nick about the Wolf fight. I filled him in on our pre-fight plan.

"Excellent! We need to make sure to be there. Do you think we can scalp some tickets?"

"We'll get it done, Nick," Tommy replied. "Being inside a sellout at the arena surpasses anything I've ever been involved in. If we can keep John from fighting pugs in the street blindfolded, this Las Vegas trip will be the best."

I shrugged at Tommy's ace. "I promise no street fights blindfolded. I don't know about the other kind."

"We'll polish all your dance moves tonight for the 'Montego Bay' opening in the cage," Nick promised. "John needs to be in the center with black robe. Save the Dark Lord robot for in the middle of the fight."

"We want you to go with us when we take the Ranger to port in the North," Lynn said.

"I'd be glad to. I don't see Clyde and Denny. Are they trying to smooth things over somewhere?"

"They're conferencing with Paul," Clint answered. "We need to be briefed on anything our intelligence agencies learn regarding the Isla operation. Plus, Denny sent the inventory of weapons found in the bunker. Jafar told us nothing concerning Khaled's group disappearance came out in the regular news."

"I can imagine the stories Khaled's people traded back and forth on the way to Puerto Vallarta," Johnny said. "We created a first-class mystery with a perfect op."

"What exactly was first-class about being marooned on Isla Magdalena for days while armed troops searched for you?"

"We survived without casualties, stopped a threat to our nation, and dealt with some very bad people," Nick replied. "That's called a perfect op, Rach."

"They even made a dance video," Jean added. "I hope Clyde and Denny hear something the intelligence agencies gathered about the mystery from their sources. I bet the stories will be wild."

"Where's Joan," Nick asked.

"She's processing information learned about our group," Tina said. "She knows the two prisoners were not flown off to an inland holding facility."

"I have told her about my past. I think she understands how much being with the Unholies means to me," Jian added. "I am glad Muerto will be entertaining tonight."

"I wish we had more days on the cruise than just the two getting back to port," Jean said. "I like working aboard ship."

"If it's okay with your mom, you and Sonny can sail with us to Monster Island," Nick told her.

"No combat, right?" Rachel endured the beseeching eyes of her daughter.

"Nope. We'll just be porting the ship."

"Will Al be going, John?"

"I'm letting her go along. Al asked already. I think there may have been some collusion between our kids." Lora answered for me.

"I figured as much. I knew the next words out of her mouth would have been 'Al's going'," Rachel said.

Al giggled. Jean immediately gave her a dirty look. "Oh… you did not just give us away to the enemy, maggot!"

Jean's drill sergeant lexicon entertained everyone, especially Lucas.

     * * *

We steamed Ranger north to Monster Island with a skeleton crew of Unholies, Monsters, and kids. Jean, Sonny and my Al earned their keep on deck and in the galley, intermittently taking lessons in captaining a ship Ranger's size from Gus and Lucas. Cala accompanied us, along with Lynn. They represented our female branch of Monsters. Joan came along at the last minute to continue playing violin with Nick's piano-man nights. She was in love with Jian, and she had shed all reservations about Monster truth. When Nick and Joan entertained, Lynn and Cala danced the night away with their husbands, Clint and Johnny. Sonny studiously and uncomfortably danced with both Jean and Al. The rest of us Monsters and Unholies practiced our synchronized dancing moves for the cage in Las Vegas, as well as impromptu entertainment at softball games or book signings. I admit we had so much fun, Gus anchored Ranger for the night on the way to Monster Island.

Because we're Monsters, we always have someone on watch during any time we're anchored. The Ranger incorporates the most sophisticated radar available to anyone, including the military. I had the duty on the bridge that night, when two boats we marked before on radar continued to close in on us. At over a hundred miles, I didn't really give them much thought. They were now at twenty miles and closing. Gus tracked them earlier, noting we couldn't expect to be alone on the water, especially in a common sea passage along the United States coast, leading to both Canada and Alaska. I hit the alarm for General Quarters, the Navy's term for imminent danger on board a ship.

Gus and Lucas arrived on the bridge in an instant. "Those two boats we noted on our same passage, closing on us, are now inside of twenty miles, headed right for us. I hate coincidences in the middle of the night aboard a ship. I believe we need to haul anchor and get Ranger moving until we can learn the threat level."

"Agreed," Gus said. "We have the bridge, John. Do you want us to move slowly, allowing them to close until we see who they are?"

"I wish we had the Harrier or Stealth on board still. I decided on a commercial flight back to the Bay because of the kids."

"We know that, Recon," Lucas retorted. "Get together with our teams. We'll need a combat strategy. Call Achmed. Tell him to get us satellite coverage. Maybe he can figure out who the bandits are and what they're packing for weaponry."

"On it." Lucas was right. I needed more intel and a plan.

Most of my crew had been dancing, rather than drinking. I explained the situation in stark terms. We were a long way from port. Bandits hunting us would not care whether we neared a port or not. At the rate they were gaining on us, we would not make port before they intercepted us anyway. Ranger had speed, but not patrol boat speed. I could feel us moving, so we would have mobility to turn or engage. I alerted Jafar. He launched into our threat immediately. Brother Muerto listened, smiled, and instantly suggested a course of action. His 'I don't like being hunted' motto flashed into my head.

"We have two speedy pontoon boats. We load two teams into them with sniper rifle capability, along with our air burst grenade launchers. If they are on an intercept course, we let Lucas and Gus steam toward Monster Island, while our two teams remain dead still in the water, under the radar. I gave my word to Rachel that Ranger would not be in combat with Jean aboard. I say we take these bastards out before they even get close."

Unanimous agreement to the plan rang out immediately. Jafar called in, his tone worried and formal. "I contacted Director Gilbrech. He immediately put every available coverage asset on the craft. Both boats are combat patrol craft. They have 20mm guns, machine guns, and I'm certain they have individual weapons with a dozen crew on each boat. I'm receiving updates from satellite. They're flying no flags and the ID numbers are blotted out."

"Great job, little brother. Stay with us. Muerto has a plan and we all like it."

In ten minutes, we were in combat gear, with the kids on the bridge under Gus and Lucas's protection. Ranger incorporated 20mm guns too. Lynn and Cala would be staying with the ship, in case Ranger turned into combat mode. On one pontoon boat, Clint and I carried UMP45 submachine guns, with Casey armed with his MP5. We also had an M107 sniper rifle with night-vision scope and two XM25 airburst grenade launchers. Nick, Johnny, and Jian carried the same equipment with MP5s instead of the UMP45s. Our combat helmets networked us with Ranger, boosting signals to maintain connection with Jafar.

After launching and splitting up, we sped to our separate positions while tracking the assault craft. Clint spotted for me as we shut down the pontoon boat engine. Nick and I would take out the bridges on both boats with M107 .50 caliber bursts of uranium tipped slugs. I brought enough ammo to cut the bridge in half. Once we stopped the boats, Casey, Clint, Jian and Johnny would fire the 25mm airburst rounds before the assault craft could detect us or return fire. Nick and I would fire on the boats simultaneously when the craft reached the five-hundred-meter range.

"I'm in position, DL," Nick told us.

"Ditto," I replied. Clint would call the firing strike.

"I have our boat in sight," Jian said.

"Same here," Clint reported. "They're confident. The boats are traveling only fifty feet apart. Two thousand meters and closing."

I readied my M107. Nick and I had created sniper nests inside the pontoon boats with some stability. We would each be in a comfortable prone position on mats with Johnny and Casey anchoring our stands until we finished. I watched my target craft loom larger with Clint calling out range information, which affected sighting for my planned bursts.

"Five-hundred-meters! Fire!"

My bursts tore through the bridge on target like tissue paper. I continued fire as Clint called out slight targeting adjustments. In minutes, the two craft were adrift. Nick and I fired under the waterline then after obliterating the bridges on both vessels. Our guys fired at will with the 25mm airburst rounds, raining death on what remained. We didn't stop until the craft sank, literally blowing them to bits. The fuel tanks exploded, finishing the job for us. Once our range finders ascertained only a couple bodies moved on top of the water, clinging to wreckage, we started our engines and moved in. Each of us picked out a live survivor in the best shape.

I recalled the Ranger and checked each of the three guys floating near our target. Only one seemed relatively unhurt. I yanked him aboard and restrained him while Casey and Clint shot the others, making sure nothing living survived on the water surface. Jian and Johnny did the same. We then turned toward Ranger for pickup. Lynn would finish turning the boats into mush with the

20mm guns on Ranger. We enjoyed the Ranger's approach with sound system alternating between the 'Jaws' theme and 'Ride of the Valkyries', lit up like Christmas in Times Square. We waved while passing, moving beyond the final stage, to give Lynn a clear field of fire. She fired the 20s until only cosmic dust remained in the darkness. Like Nick, we Monsters don't like being hunted. If we are hunted – no mercy for the hunters.

We reloaded our pontoon boats and took our prisoners to the area of the ship where Lynn would be conducting an investigation – the Ranger's engine room. Sullen and Middle Eastern, the two men with dark hair and chin beards probably thought they would be getting three hots and a cot. Clint and I strapped in the first contestant in Lynn's truth or consequences game, installing the needles in position. Casey clipped on our podiatry torture machine as Lynn arrived. Nick left for the bridge to check on the kids, while Johnny and Jian controlled our other prisoner. The prisoners lost their sullen looks fast. They were still wet, which made them good conductors. Lynn didn't waste any time. There would be no questions yet. I gave Jian a barf bag for their prisoner.

"You may need this for your bearded buddy there."

Jian accepted the bag distastefully. "Understood."

Before Lynn could begin, our strapped in guy gave us a laugh with the 'you cannot torture me' line. Lynn gave him ten minutes of hell, varying heat and amps with precision, taking into account the wet body. Jian did need the barf bag for our other prisoner. After he threw up, he began crying. Whatever started this sea attack would be common knowledge very soon. Once the strapped in guy could speak, Lynn smiled and patted his face.

"I need to know who sent you after us."

"We…we are innocent! I do not even know who you are! Do not-"

Lynn gave him another ten minutes of hell. The sobbing guy had enough. He spoke in Arabic before the other man regained coherent thought.

"Amir Mohammed Kostler's uncle hired us to find and kill you all! He suspected your people murdered his nephew. We had the port under surveillance, saw some of your people leave the boat with armed men. Gamar Kostler spotted the ones he wanted to kill staying aboard this ship. When you left the port, we followed, thinking it good fortune. We…we are dead men instead."

"Where can we find this Gamar Kostler," I asked.

"He was aboard my vessel tonight on the bridge. Gamar died in your first strike."

"Is anyone else tied to the Kostler clan after us?"

"I…I do not believe so. Gamar sought out Khaled Hanniyeh in Mexico to obtain the boats and help with money. He is on the Isla Maria Magdalena. Some sort of meeting was to take place there. Please… that is all I know… do not torture me."

"Your explanation has the ring of truth." I nodded at Clint when Lynn indicated she thought so too.

Clint gave the talker a syringe of death without pain. He then relieved the strapped in guy of life. "It makes me wish we could kill Amir all over again. Let's leave these two down here. We can dress them out and feed the fish tomorrow morning. Lynn and I are going to the bridge and talk Dead-Boy into entertaining again. I hope Joan didn't get too freaked out. She plays violin incredibly well. The two of them could get hired on in Vegas. Speaking of which, we need to find a venue for those two in Sin City, maybe away from the Strip."

"Agreed. I'll clean up here. Go recruit Joan and Muerto. I'll be along soon." I took the barf bag from Jian. "I hope Joan's okay, Dragon."

Jian shrugged. "I will find out shortly. Thank you."

"We'll have the Bud and Beam brothers awaiting you," Lynn said.

I unstrapped our first contestant. "That sounds mighty good."

* * *

I shook Nick's hand in port before he left for the 'Grove'. "I hope to see you in Vegas, Nick. That was fast thinking with the pontoon boat ambush."

"Thanks. You'll see us there. No way do I miss the act you guys have cooking for the show. Your rehearsals looked great. The MGM Arena will rock out when the crowd sees you all doing

'Montego Bay'. I'm glad we're going inland. I'm getting worn out with the sea assaults."

"The land assault wasn't real comfortable for you either. You should be able to rest enough at Otter's Point to enjoy Vegas."

"I plan to sneak in a few Irish mornings there with the Unholies since my sobriety guard doesn't have school. Jean sleeps in. I'll still hear about it from her."

I glanced over where Jean and Sonny were saying goodbye to Al. "Those three did great on the cruise. I hope you don't need to discuss our Gamar Kostler problem."

"It's always best to tell Rachel the truth. That way, if one of my cohorts blurts it out by accident, I'll be out ahead of it. Hey… no more blindfold fights."

"Scout's honor."

"You, my friend, were never a boy-scout."

"I always wanted to be, Muerto."

"Yeah… me too. See you in Vegas."

"Absolutely," I replied.

* * *

I answered the phone on the first ring, hoping the 6 am call wouldn't wake my sleeping ladies. Although in the kitchen, sound carries in my house. I didn't recognize the number on the caller ID pad. I decided to go with a hardened gumshoe greeting. "It's your nickel."

Alexi chuckled. "You probably didn't recognize the number. I'm using Marla's home phone. The UFC wants to do a contract signing with both you and Wolf in a ceremony at the MGM Grand Arena tonight. They know interest in the fight through their Pay-Per-View sales will soar if the two of you do the signing in person with some highlight films playing. ESPN agreed to play it live. It's at 5 pm."

"We can make that. It's only a little over an hour to get there. I'll bring Jess, Dev, Jafar and Tommy with me. We'll stay overnight so the guys can have some fun. You're coming, right?"

"Yes. I anticipated it would be okay with you, and who you would want to come along. I have six first-class tickets on Southwest, leaving Oakland International at noon. We have five suites booked for the night. Thanks for taking this on short notice. It will mean a big bump in the Pay-Per-View sales."

"I'll call the guys and meet you at the airport at 10:30." I immediately texted the guys and told them I'd call them in two hours. I went in the bedroom to awaken Lora in a gentle but passionate way. She would definitely not be angry at being awakened unexpectedly.

"Wait! Wha…what? Oh God!"

An hour later, I held my auburn-haired beauty, confident for at least a short time she would not be angry with my Vegas trip. "The UFC wants me and Wolf to do an MGM Grand signing to promote Pay-Per-View sales because we're a fill-in fight. We're a great fill-in, but the fans need to know. ESPN agreed to air it live."

"What was the wakeup call all about, penance?"

Sort of. "I love you. I needed to explain things early. I chose this way."

Lora moved against me in the manner she knows turns me inside out. "More penance please."

Well… okay then.

* * *

Alexi hired a limousine to take us all to the airport, so except for the usual security nonsense at the airport they could have solved with a couple of nukes, our flight in first-class involved a nice sipping of the Beam brother while in flight. Commercial flights always awakened me to the fact 'One World Order Globalists' ran our nation into a quagmire of third world shit-sand without any reason, other than selfish bullshit and money. Farces, like global warming and peaceful Islam, allowed the Globalists to enhance global wars, while ripping the world's populace of money and sanity. If that wasn't enough, they flood the world's civilized nations with Sharia Law Mutant zombie parasites, hell bent on destroying everything in their path. Dev saw me drain my iced Beam and signal for another from the stewardess.

"Something wrong, John?"

"Nothing we can do anything about, Dev. I'm just pondering conspiracy theories and the Illuminati."

"Oh man, brother," Jess broke in as I received my drink, "you can't go there. We got a President now who can't be bought. Stick with that thought."

"Trying, brother, but I've been in this war so long, I'm beginning to wonder why we can't go to the dark side and win the damn thing - devil take the hindmost."

"I believe as you, brother," Jafar added, proposing a toast. "I do not want Mia growing up in danger of Sharia Law. I will be dead before that ever happens."

We toasted, probably frightening some of our other first-class companions. A weird coincidence happened then. I heard a guy gibbering in Arabic while forcing his way into the first-class section. I had no idea what was going on, but when he pushed aside our very nice stewardess, he sealed his fate. I planted him with an uppercut, smashing his half beard nearly into his upper lip. He landed in the aisle with blood seeping from his shattered mouth. I didn't spill a drop of my Beam brother doing it. I drained it and handed the plastic cup to Jafar.

I helped the young lady to her feet and then settled her into one of the seats. "Are you okay?"

"I think so."

I showed her my FBI credentials. "My friends and I are FBI agents. They'll restrain this jerk and make sure he doesn't choke on his own blood and teeth. Can you find them some towels to do so?"

"Sure." She stood and hurried to get the towels, conferring with the other steward and stewardess at the back.

"We got this, DL," Tommy said.

"Thanks. I'll go check and see who this goon was traveling with, if anyone."

I addressed the full plane load of people in the back with my FBI credentials in plain sight. "Does anyone know why that guy charged the front?"

"He's been chanting in some language with that man there." The older lady pointed at another half beard looking at me with surly defiance.

"You'll need to come with me, Sir. The good news is you'll be flying first-class. The bad news is you'll be restrained until landing."

He immediately began calling me everything but friend in Arabic. When I told him to shut his pie-hole in Arabic or I'd rip his upper lip off, he shut-up. I yanked him out of his seat, guiding him into the first-class section. He tried to struggle, but I'm not a security guard. I clamped his neck until he became cooperative. The passengers loved every second. We have become a populace of citizens ready to explode. At the front, my guys had the other one in a window seat with his hands restrained and an iced towel in his mouth. They had put a towel over the bloodstained aisle. I sat his buddy down next to him after restraining the prick with plastic restraints the plane stocked. I grabbed his chin in a vice.

"Don't speak. We only have another twenty minutes of flying time. If you speak, I will make you look like your buddy, toothless Timmy. Do you understand?"

He nodded. I rejoined my companions with a shrug. "See what I mean?"

They appreciated my sarcastic phrase as the stewardess placed another iced Beam in my hand. "Thank you for helping me."

I toasted her and sipped. "Believe me, it was my pleasure."

"Are...are you John Harding, the UFC Heavyweight Champion," a guy at the back asked.

"I am. Sorry about all this."

"Don't be! Wow, what an uppercut! You didn't even spill your drink."

My guys enjoyed that observation. I sipped my Beam. "Thanks."

"I recognize your whole cage crew. Can I get a picture with you guys?"

What the hell, I may as well be supportive of any UFC fans, as well as American citizens, who loved someone doing something to thwart these mutants. It's great word of mouth publicity. We posed with him, and nearly everyone on the plane after that, with the stewardess volunteering to take any, and all group photos. It lightened my mood, and theirs. We were in an untenable situation in this country. The problem would not be solved instantly, because the Globalist ass-wipes continued in their Illuminati scenario no matter what. The rest of us hunkered down and decided whether to root hog or die.

The posing and interaction sobered me and my guys to a point where we met with the authorities on the ground in a somber mood. I flashed credentials, along with my compatriots. The welcoming authorities breathed a sigh of relief. I insisted and oversaw the video questioning of the two bearded mutants. It turned out the mutants originated in Pakistan, which did not surprise me. They demanded all the ACLU coached crap they did not deserve. I had Jafar working them on a side investigation with our host CIA assets. Once we ascertained they had falsified documents, the game evolved. I called Sam and Janie. They took the first flight to Las Vegas they could arrange. We left the authorities at the airport with holding instructions.

The guy who seemed to be in charge gave me a look of disinterest. I grabbed the sucker by the entire front of his suit. "Listen to me carefully, Chad. I know you and your identity. If you screw up this transfer to the arriving FBI agents, I will come to see you off book. Believe me, you do not want that. Nod, if you understand."

Chad nodded virulently. I released him. "Those FBI authorities are personal friends. I hope you're smart enough to know I will be checking on your performance."

"I…I understand!"

"Good." I joined my other FBI friends with less than happy thoughts.

"I think it would be a good idea to get to the MGM, clean up, and get a short nap before the signing, DL," Tommy suggested.

"Agreed. I am sick of this shit. Let's go do what you suggest before I go rogue. None of us want that."

"Don't make me get Dev to slap the Latin on your rogue ass, DL!" Jess pointed as Dev instantly got into a fists-up position, threatening the Latin.

I loved these guys. "I'm good for now. Save the Latin, brother. You may need it for the contract signing."

* * *

The little things bring us back from the precipice of life. A nap, shower, shave, and toothbrush will nearly always change a guy's outlook. I thought about wearing my Muerto t-shirt to the signing, but I knew that would be just wrong. The fact I brought it hinted at trouble in my head. I knew Lucas would be entertained. I didn't consider the fact wearing it would mean an extra half hour of interrogation, not to mention hinting the fact I actually knew a YouTube famous assassin. Nick would not be appreciative. It made me smile knowing he and his cartoons started the whole Unholy Trio channel because Kabong's videos were being displaced by cat videos.

My cage crew looked rejuvenated too. Jafar kept us grounded with his news update. Apparently, I missed the fact nearly everyone on the plane recorded my Pakistani interaction. A variety of angles on it now existed on the internet public record with a bunch of eye catching titles. Our cage crew garnered a lot of pictures and videos while we posed for pictures on the plane.

"They all look good, DL," Tommy said. "Fighting whacko terrorists with falsified papers on an airliner can't be a negative for us."

"I'm glad Jafar found their real names. We need to keep track of them," I replied. "Sam and Janie will update us on where they get placed."

UFC officials met us outside the arena. They escorted us inside to a raised podium setting. More people than ESPN news and camera crews filled the seats near the podium. Apparently, the MGM Grand allowed fans interested in seeing Wolf and I complete a boring contract signing attend the meeting. People applauded when we came into their view and climbed the steps to take our seats at the table. We waved and enjoyed the party-like mood.

"DL, there's Rock Costigan and Rutger Northman in the front row on the left," Jess said.

"Northman's still under suspension," Alexi replied. "I am surprised the UFC allowed him to attend this meeting."

"ESPN probably allowed them to attend to build up the event," Tommy remarked. "Since they turned political, their viewership declined in combination with the NFL kneeling thugs causing people to tune out football. They need a little notoriety. The UFC can give them that."

"Oh crap." Dev shook his head. "Here comes the little jerk from the fake news network and his camera guy. I bet the plane incident hit the news already. We only just heard about this signing today, right Alexi?"

"Only this morning, but as you point out, the plane incident probably enticed this nitwit to sell his network on attending. Here comes Ian's retinue."

Wolf and his manager, Donny Callan, led his cage crew to the other side of the podium. They took their seats and the lawyers took over. Wolf and I signed the papers after Alexi and Callan looked them over. Ian kept staring at me like he wanted a date. I began to suspect he may have invited Costigan, Northman, and the little twerp that haunts my after-fight press conferences.

"What's that idiot's name who keeps referencing my cage deaths, T?"

"Carey Hillman. I bet you're thinking Wolf invited our enemies, huh?"

"You've added reading minds to your list of skills," I replied. "It does seem likely. Can we leave now?"

Alexi and Tommy expressed amusement at that remark. ESPN didn't agree to stream this live, so people could watch us use ink pens. The host announcer appeared then.

"John Harding and Ian Wolf will take your questions now. Be polite and keep your questions concise. I will be the one pointing out whom the next question comes from."

He pointed at the twerp first. Oh good. Hillman stood. "Is it true you beat up two Pakistani refugees on the plane coming here, Harding?"

Jafar stood. "I am FBI Agent Jafar Kensington. Qais and Kabir Khosa were arrested by FBI agents after landing. They had forged identification, attacked a stewardess, and tried to rush the cockpit. John Harding stopped them. I have learned since then, they were on a no-fly list under their real names and were wanted by Interpol on suspicion of responsibility for an attempted bombing in the UK. What you just accused John Harding of is fake news, but I believe you already know that. I hope your media cohorts will stick with the truth."

"How dare you accuse my network of fake news? We have the right to investigate any controversy and get at the truth."

"When you start reporting the truth, I will stop calling you fake news frauds."

The audience applauded Jafar's answer and statement. He sat down. The twerp was allowed a follow-up question, which convinced me this signing was meant to be controversial. "Why didn't you restrain the man, Harding? You broke his jaw."

"He attacked a stewardess, twerp. I broke his jaw. Boo hoo. Light a candle."

The audience laughter and applause caused the ESPN guy to move on to the next question. The twerp sat down reluctantly. The question was to Wolf from a woman reporter in the front row. "Mr. Wolf – is it true you faked your hand injury to duck the Logan fight?"

"That is an insult! I have x-rays to prove I fractured my hand in training."

"The hospital that supposedly did the x-ray has no record of you ever going there," the woman persisted.

"Why would I fake it? I wanted to fight Logan."

"A persistent rumor claims you did it, so Mr. Harding would soften up Logan. When Harding beat Logan, did it shock you?"

"I don't need anyone softening my opponents. Logan tried to be a UFC fighter. He should have stayed with boxing."

"Thank you." The woman sat down to Wolf's relief.

The rest of the question and answer session passed with only questions concerning strikes and training regimen. Wolf and I posed together. He left right after, ignoring the fans asking for autographs and pictures with him. I stayed and had a blast posing in comical pictures with the fans, pretending to land knockout punches. I signed everything. My guys kept watch on the Rock and Rutger duo. They waited until the audience interaction ended. When they approached, the ESPN cameras started recording again.

"We want to know if you'll fight the winner of a match between Rutger and me," Costigan said.

"Mr. Northman is still under suspension," Alexi answered for me. "He twice attacked John, once in my restaurant, and the second time after a fight. Both were cowardly acts. Why in the world would John give either of you a title shot. He beat both of you decisively."

Northman didn't move. I could tell Alexi calling him a coward pissed him off, because his face tats began glowing. Costigan must have warned him not to say or do anything.

"We are the top contenders. Rutger is petitioning the UFC for reinstatement. If he gets it, we're going to fight in the next UFC event in Boston. We want Harding on record either agreeing to fight the winner or ducking us."

"I'll fight the winner. I'm not ducking anyone. I promise you this, it would be a bad idea to attack me away from the cage… a real bad idea."

"Understood," Costigan replied. "Do we have a deal then?"

"Yes." They walked away, knowing better than to shake my hand. I planned to crush Rutger's. The ESPN cameras stopped.

Tommy smiled. "You were hoping Rutger would shake hands with you and get crushed."

"Get out of my head, T."

The ESPN guy walked over to join us as his camera crews packed it in. "I'm sorry if it seemed like an ambush in here today. That was a great thing you guys did on the plane. I never thought Hillman would pursue a line of questioning relating to stopping those brothers inflight. We thought he'd ask something stupid like he usually does. Agent Kensington did a great job."

"Yep. Jafar kept the facts straight, instead of fake news Hillman running off with a fantasy story. We had a good time doing it. Wolf got the tough question."

"He sure did. Do you think the woman had it right?"

"Yeah, I do. I don't think ducking Logan was Ian's idea though. He had a handler who admitted he didn't think Wolf could beat Logan. Wolf has a great ground and pound game. I think he would have won unless Logan clocked him."

"Do you think he can beat you?"

"Sure. He has a chance. I don't think he can knock me out, but he could submit me. I've seen his moves. He's as fast as anyone in the division on the mat."

"Thanks for taking time with me."

"No problem." We shook hands and left. "That wasn't so bad either."

"I'm usually the pessimist," Tommy said, "but I don't like Wolf's chances."

"He won't have Tito Flores around to fake any fractures," I replied.

Outside the arena, Hillman awaited us. I looked around for a garbage can to stuff him in. Unfortunately, I didn't see one nearby.

"Harding! Are you using the knife-hand strike against Wolf?"

"If I see an opening, I will. It's legal."

"That strike should be illegal!"

"When you get to be the UFC commissioner, maybe you can get it outlawed. Until then, you'll need to rely on dishing fake news and asking stupid questions." I began walking away and the punk grabbed my arm.

"I'm not done with you yet, Harding. You believe you're above the law. One of these days, it will be you killed in the cage."

"If you don't get your hand off my arm, I'm going to throw you head first into that wall over there."

He backed up then. We brushed by. "There's never a garbage can around when you need one."

"I will say goodbye for now, my friends," Alexi said. "I need to meet with my associates at the Venetian. I will have the limousine pick us up at 11 am for the airport. Do not overdo your night in Sin City."

"We won't, Alexi. I'll keep these pugs in line," Tommy joked.

"Yes, but then who will watch you." Alexi walked away after the parting shot.

My phone rang. "Hi, Sam, did you like our gift?"

"Very much so. I have a favor to ask. It's volunteer only, John. We learned the Khosa brothers are members of a six-man cell. They were on their way back from a meeting in San Francisco. We busted their two cohorts there. The brother you punched out was high on Khat. They were not supposed to cause a problem on the plane. We are holding them incommunicado until further notice."

"I know that drug. It causes euphoria and acts like a stimulant. I guess that explains why two weasels flying with false identities would do something so stupid."

"We could contact the FBI office in Las Vegas, but you guys all have Homeland Security credentials too. Plus, Janie and I got called in to explain why the brothers weren't delivered to the Las Vegas office. We played the HS card because of the Interpol warrant. The electronics we confiscated from the brothers pinpointed the location of their cell in Las Vegas. These others are killers, John. I called Clint. He and Lynn are in the air. I told them to wait until I checked with you, but Lynn was adamant you would want in on it."

"She's right, but we're not packing anything other than sidearms."

"Laredo's flying them in with complete armaments. Here's the favor. Lynn wants her Hollywoods to turn them over to us in Vegas making a Hollywood Bounty Hunters episode. Laredo flew down to LA with Clint and Lynn to pick up the Hollywoods and are in route to you as we speak. The problem, as I see it, is taking them alive. I heard Jafar accompanied you to Las Vegas. We'll open everything for him to use."

"You're right about the alive part. Jafar and I will investigate this. I know one thing, our taking of the brothers hit the news all over. The rest of the cell will be aware of their capture. We'll need to move on this tonight."

"That's what we think too. This is big and dangerous. Our analysts are breaking down the data. They know the cell planned something for Vegas on July 4th."

"We'll work it. Are you and Janie flying in?"

"Yep. We'll be returning on a late flight. It goes without saying this cell ends anyway you need to end it. The Hollywoods understand Lynn. They act on her orders and forget anything she tells them to forget."

"Understood. We'll do what we can, Sam. See you soon." I disconnected. "Achmed, my friend, we have work to do. Enjoy Vegas, guys. I have Monster business with Lynn and Clint to attend to."

"Will you be flying back with us tomorrow?"

"I'm not sure, Dev. Lynn wants to do a Hollywood Bounty Hunters segment, so she's making Laredo stop in LA to pick up her actors and film crew."

"You still have a fight ahead, DL," Tommy said. "Don't be gettin' shot before we do our show in the cage."

"No shootings, we hope. We need to turn the banditos over to Sam and Janie by way of the Hollywoods. I'm not certain if we can, but we'll try. You can bet Lynn will have the minions with her helping warm the guest stars to the acting task at hand. Go on and have a good time. I'll call if I have trouble you can help with."

"Be sure and call," Jess ordered. "We ain't all Snow White."

"I will, Jess."

Chapter Twelve

Hollywood Handover

I received my orders from Cruella Deville. I met them with two big, black, E350 vans with Jafar and I driving. We left the Hollywoods off at the MGM Grand. Their part would not come until later. We had a good crew with Clint, Lynn, the minions, and Tonto. Jafar would network us for the task ahead.

"I almost stopped to get Johnny and Cala, but I remember what being pregnant at her stage felt like. She did a bunch of work on the cruise and copiloting with Laredo."

"I know you'll miss them during filming. You made the right decision though. Jafar did his homework on the house they're using on Pecos-McLeod Interconnect. We have some items to work out. They have a low masonry fence around the place. I have the keys to Nick's place here in Las Vegas in case we needed to tune your guest stars, but I believe we could use their place if we need to. It's more isolated than Nick's. The approach worries me."

"You think because they have a solid fence barrier, they may have boobytraps inside, huh?"

"I do, Clint. I wonder if we can draw them out to Nick's house. If Jafar and Lynn dress in the appropriate garb, what do you think of Achmed in a suit with briefcase and Lynn in dark robe and hijab. These guys have had no communication with their captured cell mutants. Jafar can be a lawyer working for the ACLU with connections to the Council on American-Islamic Relations. Lynn can play Kabir Khosa's girlfriend he met in San Francisco, who hired Achmed to defend the brothers. Jafar received the file from Sam with contact numbers and an email drop they use for secrecy."

"We play Nick's old ruse of Kabir's girlfriend seeing and speaking to him for a moment before they locked him away. Achmed can warn them they must leave the place they're in and meet at Nick's safe-house. Our well-dressed lawyer and hijab wearing girlfriend greet them at the door, lead them inside, and we subdue them. I like it!"

"Thanks, Clint. What do you think, Lynn?"

"I think Achmed will require a very craftily phrased message to make this work. He'll need to word it in a way warning the cell they are in danger. An explanation their house has been compromised follows the initial warning. Urging they vacate the house they're in would be next. Then, tell them not to head out of the city because Homeland Security has road blocks everywhere. He can then offer the safe-house with directions how to get to Nick's place while avoiding main avenues. End the message saying they will need to remain at Nick's place until the danger dies down."

"Good input, Crue," I told her.

We arrived at Nick's house a moment later. After unloading our gear, we settled into Nick's huge kitchen around Jafar who arrived with the other van. He created the message to be sent in Arabic type. Clint and I read it over, editing and suggesting small changes. Jafar sent it, along with a burner-phone number for them to call if they wanted sanctuary in the safe-house. One of them called almost immediately. I could tell in his voice, the Khosa brothers apprehension about the San Francisco contacts disappearing made them more than a little fearful. The man rambled a bit and Jafar cut him off, advising silence until they were inside the safe-house.

"Yes... of course... that is best. We will leave immediately with our gear and follow your map. Thank you."

"I will open the garage the moment you arrive so drive inside immediately. We must keep your vehicle out of sight. We will be awaiting your arrival." Jafar disconnected.

We picked the den as our reprogramming room. The minions set up the full gurney restraint system they brought with them. This would be intricate work, because we needed a complete picture of what these mutants rigged at their base-house. We could not use Nick's place for the Hollywood Bounty Hunter action. Enough of us would be on hand to make the scenes safe for the Hollywoods, but Lynn needed to make sure her terrorist cell actors complied. Tonto would play a big part in accomplishing that goal.

Clint and I moved the vans away from the house. Ten minutes later, a BMW arrived. Nick had a Cadillac Escalade stored in one bay, but the other side was empty. I opened the garage and the BMW advanced inside. I closed it behind them. Jafar and Lynn opened the connecting door to the house, standing to the side, dressed as a high-priced lawyer would dress with dark tailored suit. Lynn's garb with open-faced hijab hid her stun-gun nightstick. She kept her eyes on the floor. After solemn greetings, the men came inside the house, where Jafar guided them to where we awaited their entry.

The men cleared the doorway into the living-room and Lynn stun-gunned the rearmost guy. Clint and I, along with the minions, stun-gunned the rest into unconsciousness. It ended in seconds. Now, the hard part would begin. We restrained them all, except the one whom we strapped onto our information gathering gurney. He was not happy. Lynn shed her slave costume. The minions attached our first contestant to the needles, while the rest of us made sure the other three could watch without interference.

"Wait! What are you doing? We have done nothing wrong! Where is my lawyer?"

"That would be me," Jafar explained. "I only play one though. You'll see."

"Listen to me," Lynn said. "I know you all speak English. If you pretend not to understand, we'll take you through this in Arabic, but you will be punished. You boys are lucky. If you act out your parts properly, we will eventually turn you over to the FBI. On the way, we'll make you TV stars for a day. Let's begin."

Over the next hour, Lynn conducted her reeducation program with cold expertise. By the time she finished, no doubt existed as to what our new stars would be doing. They understood if we heard of them complaining about their treatment, which would be undetectable, we would get them back from the FBI, and toast them to death with the needles. Eager to please, our new stars memorized what they needed to do at their house. As it turned out, they did not boobytrap the house. We learned their fourth of July plan involved an IED outside the Wynn Casino. After the IED exploded, they would kill at random in the chaos, and escape before the police could react.

Before we brought over our film crew and actors, Lynn ordered our guest stars to wander all over with silenced MP5s and UMP45s covering their efforts. Once inside the house, Agent Tonto escorted one man around the entire house. Director Deville took over from there with her minions. Believe me when I tell you these guys wanted to please Crue more than anything in the world. Our camera guys, Sigried Kandelus and Calvin Douglas, filmed the arrival of Kensy (Buffster) Talon, her husband Kevin Halliday (ex-felon), Les Tavor (ex-Hell's Angel), Jet Lemarkus (ex-gangbanger), Daniel Atkins, and Jerry Sooner. The opening arrival, filmed down the street, would include them doing last second equipment checks, followed by stealthy movements to the terror cell's house.

When they reported for duty, they knew their lines, their positions, and altered anything Lynn wanted altered. The romantic part of each action show depended on the right looks of determination and affection Kevin exchanged with his wife, the Buffster. Kensy had a black belt in Taekwondo karate, but she was so tiny of frame, her strikes hurt no one. Kevin lovingly tested Kensy's pack and weapon, while their companions did the same. Because they would be going after terrorists, Les, Kevin, and Jet would be armed with unloaded MP5s. Sam and Janie arrived then to take over the scene for the FBI once the terrorists were in custody.

Lynn loved the opening. She made the cut sign to stop the cameras when the Hollywoods arrived at the door, and Jet picked the lock, or pretended to. "Perfect approach. Go inside, Cheese. Make sure everyone's in position."

"Yes, Director Deville." I moved past the Hollywoods into the house and shut the door.

Agent Tonto, positioned out of sight, took his cues from Clint, who was positioned on the other side of the room with silenced UMP45 pointed at the terrorists. The minions busily spaced the terrorists with startled looks of terror on their faces. Once they satisfied their creative instincts, Silvio Facetimed Lynn, showing her the living mannikins. She gave the scene her blessing. We moved out of sight.

"Anyone who screws this up will die on the gurney," I promised. "Make your Arabic angry, startled, and clipped. Understand?"

"Yes!" They chorused together.

In charged the Buffster with her MP5 armed squad. "On your knees! Hand's locked behind heads!"

The terrorists played their stunned surrender with believable movements and language. While under careful observation by the MP5 squad, Jerry Sooner and Daniel Atkins restrained the men. Sam and Janie approached the men from outside as they joined the bust, showing their FBI credentials to the men.

"FBI Special Agents Sam Reeves and Janie Labrie! You four are under arrest for conducting terrorist operations on United States soil. I will now read you your rights."

The arrests, aftermath, and joyful repacking of equipment took the episode to its hoped for ending. Hollywood Bounty Hunters still maintained the best ratings of any half hour reality show. Sam and Janie loaded the prisoners into an FBI van driven by four other agents. They left immediately with our guest stars.

"Thanks for this," Janie told Lynn. "Busting this terror cell is huge for us. The Hollywoods looked good too, very professional."

"It made for a great episode." Lynn hugged little Kensy. "My new little mommy, and her crew, did it all in one take. How's the baby?"

"Wonderful... but still keeping us up half the night."

"It's early. You guys take the van and go back to the MGM. We're officially turning this house and everything the terrorists have over to Sam and Janie."

I saw the lights first rounding the corner in a big winged fin car. "Get down now!"

Lynn grabbed everyone in her reach, hauling them flat toward the ground. They waited too long in the car to fire. As a single burst chattered, sparking in the darkness, Clint from the house, and me from the sidewalk, raked across their open windows with UMP45 hollow point .45 caliber slugs. The minions joined in with MP5 fire until we turned the inside of the big fin vehicle into a red slushy. It drifted across the road, horn blaring from the driver's head. I fired one more burst and pulped his head off the steering wheel. I hate car horns. The vehicle bumped to a halt against the center-divide.

"Sam's hit," Janie shouted.

"Stay there, Janie. We have a med kit," Lynn told her. "Clint and Cheese will secure the scene with my minions. I'll come to you."

We did just that. The minions covered our approach to the car, spreading in a three-pronged defense. Nothing was alive inside the red slushy mobile. I circled the car and turned off the engine. We didn't run to check the wounded. We retreated with weapons at the ready. Combat brings us right back into combat mode. All of us had seen casualties. We don't take more casualties while running around like Snow Whites. I was glad I gave our Snow Whites the night off. Clint and I reloaded magazines, as did the minions.

"Clint and I have the watch. Help Lynn check for wounded, Gus."

"On it." Gus, Silvio, and Quays retreated to Lynn and our remaining party.

Vans of FBI/Homeland Security agents arrived to investigate the terrorist cell house, only to find an active battle zone. Janie took charge, ordering armed agents on a perimeter guard around the house and our vehicles, while Lynn and Silvio worked on Sam's side wound. No one else was injured. Jet Lemarkus moved to my side.

"John… I know that vehicle. It belongs to one of the gangs we no longer negotiate with, the Surenos 38th Street Gang. We film in their territory once in a while. We stopped because they don't want to negotiate. Les and I considered calling you guys in because they've been stalking us. LA is less than six hours from here. I think they followed us to the airport. Lynn had a limousine pick us all up. If they saw Laredo's plane numbers, they could find out the destination. Lynn is famous for cuttin'. I'm certain they recognized her. They could have busted ass gettin' here, staked us at the MGM, and then here."

"Come with me. Take a look at the dead people. If you can confirm their identities, we will need to make this right again in LA. Nobody hunts us, Jet. If they do… they die."

"I…I know that, John." Jet walked over with me. A couple in the car didn't have faces left. Others still had enough to recognize. "They're Surenos… no doubt. That guy with his chest blown out was the leader. He's the prick we couldn't talk to – Victor

Rosario. He thought he owned LA. I told him take the money and go along with the show, because killers backed us. He wouldn't listen to anyone. Vaya con Dios, prick."

"I'm afraid we're in for some extended questioning. Thanks for letting me know about the Surenos. Go ahead and help get your stuff packed. I'll see how Sam's doing. I will explain the situation with the Surenos."

Lynn finished wrapping Sam's wound with Silvio supporting him. Clint joined me along with Janie. I related what Jet recognized and the theory he had. "I know with the perps dead, there won't be a case to build against the Surenos 38th Street Gang. It may be with Rosario dead, there won't be any further trouble."

"You don't believe that." Sam grimaced in pain as he shifted position with Silvio's help. "You're right about our side. If we obtained permission to investigate, it would be surveillance teams, and some extended sting operation lasting years."

"We'll be looking into it," Clint said.

"You Monsters work with a security company in LA, don't you," Janie asked.

"Red Dragon Security," I answered. "I'll give them a call. They may know some background on the gang. We hire them as security on large photo shoots with the Hollywoods. I'm sorry this turned into a combat zone and you got winged, Sam."

"I'll be okay. Your crew saved a lot of lives helping us bust the terrorist cell. Thanks for the patch job, Lynn. If my reaction time was as fast as yours, I wouldn't be lying here."

"Get well quick," Lynn replied. "Janie will need you back on your feet. Any chance of our gang getting out of here without an interrogation?"

Sam leaned his head back against the equipment bag and coats Silvio put under his back. "I wish."

The ambulance arrived. We helped the EMT's load Sam and adjourned into the terrorist house, so Janie could get our statements individually. I called Red Dragon Security's number and left a message for either Chuck or Sal to call me. Jafar texted an update to our crew. We didn't get to our rooms until 2 am. Tommy, Jess, and

Dev were done playing around by then so we all had a drink together before heading to our rooms.

"I would like to face off against Surenos 38th Street Gang with our entire crew."

"We're with you on that," Jess said. "They sent poser assassins after real killers. At least the leader decided to commit suicide along with his gang buddies. My mom's decided to run for mayor of Oakland instead of City Council or something like that."

"Great news, Jess! We need to get this campaign in full gear fast. November will be here in the blink of an eye. When we finish with the Surenos, we'll change over our office into Florence Brown's campaign headquarters. The Monster accounts have plenty to back her run, but fundraisers draw voters and interest. I'll get Lora to scout around for a place where we can hold one."

"You really think Mom has a chance, DL?"

"Absolutely."

"She's running against the sanctuary city championing mayor, Tibby Quafe," Dev added. "That means every illegal alien they can bus in from a hundred miles away will be voting in our election."

"We'll need to get every actual Oakland citizen to the polls," Tommy agreed. "It's an uphill battle. The blue-collar workers in Oakland vote like leftist street bums looking for handouts. Flo will need to change minds and get people thinking logically. That will be one tough task."

"If anyone can do it, it'll be Flo," I replied. "Let's get some sleep. Dev can bring the Latin and Nick will entertain with Joan at the fundraisers."

Jess grinned. "That might just do it. Don't mix the spells, brother, and make it rain on Mom's head."

It took us a few extra humorous moments before we could move after Jess's warning.

　　　* * *

Chuck Buchholz and Sal Sallaz watched the warehouse the Hollywood Bounty Hunters used as a headquarters. Sal pointed, and

Chuck nodded, switching his rangefinders to check the area Sal indicated. Three beat-up old vans approached the darkened area near the port of Los Angeles. They parked nearly a hundred yards away. What appeared to be twenty black clad figures emerged. I straightened from my spot next to Sal. I motioned Jafar up.

"C'mon, little brother. I believe we have business."

"I'll film it, in case we can use the footage," Jafar replied.

"All hands, on deck," Sal told our network. "That's the vans our guys have seen do drive-bys the Hollywoods' filming headquarters. It started the same day you hired us to watch the Hollywoods after they returned from Vegas. Rumor their leader was killed in a gun battle made the news today."

"We contacted them and explained the situation with the Oaktown Cartel," Chuck said. "One of the women up in Oakland, Crue killed in a knife fight, was a cousin of the Rosario brothers. Victor's dead now. Deacon Rosario recognized Gus Denova's name. He knows Gus, Silvio, and Quays worked as cartel enforcers. Deacon knows six of their guys, including his brother, tried to assassinate your team, and now they're all dead."

"They think this absorbing the gangs in Oakland is a joke, even with the facts," Sal added. "We did as you asked and set this meeting up with them. They say they understand the rules, but I think they're too stupid to even be allowed to drive cars."

"What the hell do they want?"

"They want a permanent position extorting money from the Hollywoods," Chuck answered. "They want twenty grand a month to protect the stars."

"We better get down there." Jafar and I walked down the steps of the warehouse we watched from. "On my way to the front, Crue."

"On our way. I have Tommy and Clint with me, along with the minions."

"In position," Lucas announced from his sniper's nest. "Clear to targets."

"In position," Casey said. "Clear to targets."

Dev and Jess were with Lucas and Casey as spotters. With this many targets, they needed a second set of eyes. I reached the warehouse front at the same time as the gang. My companions from inside the warehouse joined me. It stopped the gang, because the minions carried their MP5s in plain sight.

"I'm Deacon Rosario," a tall, lanky tattoo faced guy at the front said. "You killed my brother."

"And five of your other gangbangers," I replied. "We don't like being hunted and we don't take prisoners."

"Your cutter killed my cousin, Consuela."

"What the hell is this, Betty, a history lesson?" Lynn crossed her arms and tapped her foot. "You're boring the hell out of me so far. You lost some family. Big whoop. If you don't want us to vaporize your street thugs like your brother tried to do to us, you'd best make a deal... now."

"We saw all those fake fights on YouTube, Harding. We want a one on one with our best fighter. We have five large to put on him at ten to one odds, and you need to wear a blindfold."

"Bullshit!" Tommy stepped forward. "The champ has a fight in Vegas within a week."

"Easy, Tommy. Where is your guy?"

A guy an inch or two taller than me and probably fifty or sixty pounds heavier stepped around from the back. He pulled off his hoodie. "I... Cull Tiner, pussy. You fight me blindfolded, I rip yo' head off."

Slicked back black hair, a black goatee oiled into a point, steroid muscles bulging under a strapped t-shirt, and a shit-eating grin with gold teeth. I smiled as he walked into my airspace. I recognized a familiar scent from way back. My dad wore a cologne called Brut. This guy smelled like he bathed in it. Nothing like the scent of my old man to get me thinking violent thoughts.

"Just say no, Cheese," Lynn said from behind me.

"Don't do it! Honest to God, John. I'll make Dev shiv you with the Latin," Tommy threatened.

"Yeah, pussy… back the fuck down. That UFC shit's just fake wrestling," Mr. Brut told me.

Clint looked at my face, smiled and shook his head. "Anybody got a clean blindfold."

"I got one right here," Rosario produced a black blindfold with elastic. He handed it to Clint.

"It looks new." Clint inspected it carefully, including smelling it for something soaked into the material. He gave it back to Rosario.

I handed Clint my Colt and stripped out of my jacket. Turning my back to Rosario, I allowed him to put the blindfold in place. He spread the front material, so it covered part of my forehead and the top part of my nose.

"Do we have a deal, Harding? We get fifty large, and you get your asses out of our territory… if you're still alive."

I shrugged and grinned. "Deal. Say when, Tommy."

"No… and hell no!"

"On three," Clint took over. "One… two… three!"

Brut rushed in. I dropped at the last second, leg whipping him at ankle level. The trip sent him pitching head first into the pavement. I followed the scent instantly. With the blindfold on, I could picture my landing atop my old man with elbows blasting the Brut scent right off his face. I caught his chin and hammer fisted Brut into oblivion. I quit when Tommy yelled 'time'. I stood. Clint's voice rang out loud and strong.

"Go on, kiddies. Pull them pistols. We have snipers, so none of you reaching will live through a .50 caliber, spent uranium slug. My friends and I will also fire with automatic weapons. Your whole gang will be dead in ten seconds… but… go ahead… draw."

I took off my blindfold with a bloody hand. Mr. Brut was a mess, but still breathing.

"Listen carefully, kiddies," Clint said. "Grab the cloth of your hoodies and jackets high up under the shoulder where I can see all hands. My snipers will be looking for kiddies who disobey. You will get a nice .50 caliber slug right through your idiot head. Now… grab them."

They hesitated. Clint smiled. "Make an example of this other Rosario, Lucas."

"Wait! Do as he says! Do as he fucking says!"

Just like that, we had an understanding. "Pay up, Deacon. You'd best have the cash, or I plan on getting a little more work in on you."

"Wait… I… I mean we have a cutter."

A squeal of delight sounded behind me from Lynn, as I heard Tommy's groan. "C'mon, T. You're up and no ducking the call."

Tommy stepped forward, comically humming the 'Dark Lord' theme song from 'Star Wars'. "Oaktown has the premier cutter of all time, moron. She doesn't show her skills for peanuts. Get the five grand you already owe us out. Then… we'll talk about what you want for a secondary bet."

Rosario, out of his element, rushed around collecting money. He gathered the five grand easily enough, but only had nine hundred dollars to back his cutter. "That's all we got, man."

Tommy didn't need permission. He knew Lynn very well. "We'll give ten to one odds for you pikers. Bet accepted. Try and negotiate, and I have my friend here put a round through your junk."

"Okay… okay…" Rosario gestured at his group who were in stunned, lapel gripping form. "Carmen."

"About fuckin' time!" A woman stomped out of the group, pushing aside her companions. "Posers! I tol' you to let me go first!"

This woman was about six feet tall and looked like the proverbial fireplug. Her hair, tied tightly back in a stringy fold, revealed a thick lipped, puffy face, glowering around her as she strutted forward. Tommy took a step back in revulsion. "That's far enough, lady."

Lynn grinned and waved happily at her opponent. "My, oh my, you're a big one. Are you sure you're a cutter, Melba. Did you think Tommy said chopper? We're not having a log riding or ax throwing contest."

"I been insulted by little white bitches before, skank. My name's Carmen. You can call me 'Death-stroke'."

"Yeah... like in the comic books! Oh, honey, I think if you're looking for a comic book reference, 'Baby Huey' would be perfect."

Oh my... Carmen did not like that at all. I could tell she was a pro. After the initial look of blind rage, she smiled slowly, her lips drawing back into a grotesque caricature of a smile.

"I won't slice you quickly, bitch. I'll work you like I slice ham loaf, one thin slice at a time."

"Honey... that definitely is the only time you ever get close to a thin anything," Lynn replied.

"Oh... I will enjoy this cuttin'."

Carmen flicked out a long-bladed switchblade. She stooped low, moving with cat like quickness for a big woman. Lynn smashed a roundhouse kick to the side of her head. Carmen went down in a pile, losing her knife from nerveless fingers. Lynn plunged her blade down through Carmen's eye socket into her brain. She pulled out the blade while Carmen danced the final jitters of the dead, before relaxing into open mouthed, frozen surprise. Lynn wiped off her blade carefully on Carmen's clothing before straightening away from the dead woman.

"Damn, Melba... it looks like you didn't enjoy that as much as you thought."

"No fair!"

Deacon's outrage nearly made us Monsters lose sight of our watchfulness around so many targets. When Tommy could speak, he took over the show. "Pay up, punk!"

"Fuck you!" Rosario reached for his weapon, and a .50 caliber slug pulped his head, spraying blood and brain matter in a hail of red rain. Deacon's companions lurched away from him.

"Someone better get us our money, or there will be another accident," Tommy told them.

One of the men gestured with his palms out at Clint, who motioned for him to proceed. The gangbanger searched Deacon's hoodie pockets and withdrew the bet money. He handed the wad to Tommy.

"That concludes the challenge business." Tommy counted the money and put it in his coat. "Now then, here's how the rest of this works. Oaktown Cartel owns your asses. Do not come near any production or cast member of the Hollywood Bounty Hunters. If anything happens to them on your turf, we will hold your gang responsible. You will be hunted down one by one until your bunch cease to exist. My advice is disband your gang. Become working, honest citizens. I know better, so at least find a smarter leader."

I went over and kicked the groaning, flat-faced Mr. Brut in the side. "Get your cherry-ass up. Help drag Melba and Deacon away. We're not cleaning your mess, and we better never hear about your mess. If I ever see you again, punk, I'll snatch your throat out. Get moving... all of you." Mr. Brut stumbled to his feet, keeping his eyes on the ground.

The minions came forward with MP5s at the ready to keep anyone from making a bigger body pile. The gangbangers dragged their dead back the way they came. Tommy joined me to look over my hands. They were fine. I only used a hammer fist.

"Okay... I want to know how you did it this time, Cheese," Lynn stated, with Clint next to her. "That guy was no crusty bum, emitting waves of body odor."

"You didn't get close enough. He bathed in Brut... that old cologne... just like my dad used to put on. The damn stuff is on me now. I hope I remembered my Febreze can. Otherwise, I'll need to take a shower in the Hollywoods' clubhouse before we have a drink somewhere."

Chuck and Sal had joined us while the gang retreated. Chuck came over and sniffed me. "Yep... that's Brut. It's an improvement, kid. I think I have an old bottle for you to take with you."

"Very funny. Are you guys coming to Las Vegas for the fight? We scalped a block of tickets so Muerto and his crew could see the fight."

"Hell yeah," Sal answered. "We want to see you in the arena, marching to the cage with the Marine's Hymn booming out. They put you and the MIBs on the big screens. We rented your fight with Logan. Great stuff."

"Does Muerto have any business in Vegas?"

"Not that I know of, Chuck. He takes contracts again now. Plus, the moment his CIA Director friend, Paul Gilbrech hears of a Muerto destination, he starts hunting for targets."

"I wish he was here entertaining," Lynn said. "I thought you weren't going to pull that 'Blind Fury' crap anymore, Cheese."

"When something reminds me of my dad, I get violently stupid sometimes."

"We need to keep you incommunicado until the fight, John."

"Thanks for filling in when Snow White Sands decided to dump me, Clint."

"It was for your own good, Cement-head," Tommy replied.

"Oh shit... Achmed... you didn't... crap!" I saw with one glance at the exasperated Jafar that he uploaded the fight to YouTube already.

"We have an agreement. You tell me beforehand not to upload a video, and I don't upload it," Jafar replied with some frustration. "We use them to keep other gangs we've absorbed in line. It has thousands of hits already with 'Blind Fury 2' as the title."

"Cheese will be on the couch for a month after that one," Lynn explained to Chuck and Sal. "His wife Lora blew a gasket when she saw the first one."

"Oh my," Chuck replied, rubbing his hands together. "Too bad we can't get a picture of that. Maybe his daughter, Al, can be persuaded to put one on Instagram."

"Maybe this would me a good time for me to mention John just hammer-fisted a man into the pavement... blindfolded," Sal cautioned. "Smartass suggestions are not cool at this time, my friend."

"I heard Muerto called Dragon 'Whipped Dragon' when Joan hinted at owning Jian's ass," Lynn remarked.

"Don't say it," I told her.

Lynn ignored me, of course. "John can be 'Whipped Cheese'. We'll need to make him wear his Muerto t-shirt when he gets exiled to the couch."

"I'm going to get a drink somewhere." I walked away with my so-called friends enjoying Lynn's unfunny remark... unfunny to me anyhow. I would need to be Don Juan Cheese when I returned home, so I won't get exiled to the couch.

We took a stretch limousine to 'The House of Hayden', a nice saloon Tommy and I visited when we came down on a bond skip. They have a beautiful long bar. We all fit at one end. I already toasted with a couple of the brothers Bud and Beam. Our crew arrived just in time before a large group came in. They seemed in a jovial mood. Someone asked for autographs, but they stiffed him. We heard something about the autograph seeker being a lifelong Chargers fan, so I guess they belonged to the football team. The disappointed fan glanced at our end of the bar. His face lit up when he saw me. He hurried over with notepad in hand.

"You're John Harding, the UFC Heavyweight Champ, right?"

"I am."

He lowered his voice. "I just saw a YouTube video of you fighting a huge guy blindfolded. It was incredible. Did that really happen tonight?"

"Yes, but we'd rather not broadcast it to the bar."

"I understand. Can I have an autograph and a picture with you guys? I'm Ron Zanning." We shook hands.

"Sure." I signed the notepad with what he asked. We had been tipping big, so the bartender hurried over to take the photo. We posed for promotional bar shots too once the manager heard who I was. I noted the football players got surly during our photoshoot, glaring at me.

"Those guys don't seem to like you much, Cheese," Lynn remarked as the happy fan and manager returned to what they were doing. "They must be 'Capricorn One' fans."

"Screw them," Lucas said. "This fan stuff was fun. Let's enjoy the evening without any interaction with football thugs. We get our pictures on the wall of another bar. In a couple years, we'll be famous."

"We keep forgetting to get some for our office too," Chuck said.

Naturally, Chuck's remark led to another photo shoot.

"We need a photo without Chuck's mug in it for the front office," Sal joked.

Lynn retrieved her phone. "Hey guys, I bet you haven't seen the picture of Lucas in his El Muerto pajamas."

Before Lucas could snatch the phone, she tossed it to Sal. It was comic chaos in a split second. Lucas gave up and downed his Beam.

A few of the football players ambled down to join us. One three-hundred-pounder, maybe an inch or two shorter than me, led the way. "Hey! How about keeping it down over here."

"They're hardly making any noise, Mr. Ofung."

"You stay out of this, Manny."

"We'll quiet down," I told him.

"He's another one of those NFL kneelers," Lucas said. "His name's Hussel Ofung. I used to watch him play, until I stopped watching the traitorous dogs, disrespecting America. We'll be quiet, punk. Wave your fist in the air and go back where you were."

The Monsters, of course, yucked it up at Lucas's response, bringing Ofung's head to near explosion. "Better watch it, old man. No one punks me!"

Lucas turned with a smile, while holding his Beam brother. "You cheap punk, kneelin' and fistin'. Go join the Marines if you want to show me how tough you are. They need a few good men. You ain't one of them, but I'll sponsor you. Maybe you can turn into one."

Even with two Beams in me, I caught Ofung's reaching arm. I twisted him against the bar, with his companions looking down the barrels of 9mm and .45 caliber autos. "No one touches my Pap. You look like you want a piece. Show me you're worth a few moments of my time."

I released him and put out my hand. "Shake, big guy, but bring it when you do."

"I'm left handed, Harding. I heard what you did to Koren with your pussy kicks."

"He received exactly what he asked for." I held out my left hand. "You can always take your friends and return to your drinking."

Hussel got that smirking look on his face I can't stand. He probably crushed guys' hands as a joke to prove how tough he is. Hussel put out his left hand and gripped mine with a big grin. I let him start squeezing first, matching each escalation until Ofung ran out of escalations. I kept on clamping until Hussel dropped to his knees and grabbed my wrist with his other hand, snorting in pain. The bones in his hand began to crackle.

"Recon!"

Damn it. I was just about to make him scream. I released his hand. Ofung dropped on his ass, rubbing circulation into the hand, yipping quietly while gasping for breath. I motioned to his buddies. "Get this poser down to your side of the bar. Stay quiet and friendly or I'll make you quiet and friendly."

They retreated to their end of the bar, whispering compassionate sweet nothings into Ofung's ears. Tommy put five-hundred-dollar bills on the bar from our winnings. "Sorry for the disturbance, Manny."

Manny picked up the money with a stunned look. "This… this isn't necessary."

"Don't worry about it. It's a small thing, brother."

"Thank you." Manny returned to filling drinks.

I patted Lynn's hand. "Thanks for not doing any cutting, Crue."

"I thought about it, but those posers weren't worth the effort. Why didn't you let Lucas nail the big punk?"

Lucas chuckled. "Recon knows I don't fight. I kill. I've had a little too much to drink. I should have kept quiet like I advised everyone else."

"You right about one thing, Lucas," Jess said. "I used to watch this NFL scum play until they sided with the damn billionaire backed BLM traitors and their lies. No more! Dead to me."

"Same for me," Dev agreed. "I don't care what the league forces the treasonous assholes to do now. They'll still be the same inside their skin, all the way to the bone, ugly and traitorous."

"Dev!" I was suddenly hoping to get out of this downer incident. "I bet you know a Latin blessing spell."

Dev jumped off his barstool, nearly dumping his drink. "Oh, hell yeah... I do, John."

I signaled Manny over. "Give us all another round. Do you have any objections to my friend doing a Latin blessing on the bar?"

Manny grinned in incomprehension of Dev's power. "Ah... sure... I don't care."

"Do it, Dev," Jess said with fierce, closed eye concentration. "Damn... I feel the power buildin'."

Devon Constantine raised his fists in the air. The golden voiced Latin King dished the Latin blessing spell with a slight lilt to his voice, making a melodious adjustment to his already impressive delivery. It was spellbinding. He ended it with a bass-voiced harmonious 'amen' in 'High Mass' form. Dev got a standing ovation. Even some of the NFL thugs applauded. We swarmed him after Dev finished our evening on a high note.

Chapter Thirteen

Campaign Business and Death Claw

Nick allowed Jean to stay overnight at Jay's house with Sonny. The three planned a networking extravaganza with Al on Messenger. Nick cautioned her to observe all protocol when speaking to her face to face. Their absence from the house, coupled with Nick already reaching his writing goal for the day, along with giving Deke a long training exercise stint, enabled Nick and Rachel to have an uninterrupted date night. Quinn slept peacefully in his portable crib on the balcony.

Nick sang and played for her first with Deke swaying on the bench next to him and crooning comically on certain notes. Rachel sipped her wine, singing along, while enjoying Deke's accompaniment. Nick finished playing and put Quinn to bed in his room. He rejoined Rachel, looking out over the ocean from the enclosed balcony, sharing intimate touches, initiating a lovemaking interlude without the urgency of their daily passionate trysts.

Cooling slowly from a heated and nearly violent coupling in their room, Nick massaged Rachel's shoulders, his hands alternating to a spinal journey of his thumbs along Rachel's back to the base of her spine. Rachel moaned, reaching back to grip Nick's side when he reached the base before returning to her shoulders. His phone buzzed on the nightstand. Nick glanced at the caller ID.

"Let it go to voice."

"I can't. It's the Director of the CIA. He can send a Reaper Drone if I ignore him."

"I've seen Paul's reactions around you. That's fear, not authority," Rachel replied. "Go ahead and answer it."

"Assassins R Us. Muerto the magnificent here. How may I direct your call?"

After a brief humorous recognition of Nick's greeting, Paul Gilbrech opened a business dialogue in short order. "Clyde told me you're attending the UFC event in Las Vegas to see John Harding fight."

"Big mouth must have heard the news from his lovely Dannie. Yep. I'm going to Sin City. The family will be with me along with my crew and their families."

"I wouldn't bother you with this, but Senator Rory Cooker will be in Searchlight, Nevada at a hideaway owned by The Muslim Brotherhood. I've had him under surveillance overseas, because of his being an apologist for terrorist groups like CAIR and The Muslim Brotherhood. He's on the Committee for Foreign Relations."

"I know who the bald headed young worm is," Nick replied. "Spit it out, Paul."

"He made a trip to the United Arab Emirates. Our assets in the region have proof he met with Isis agents there in a private mansion, owned by Khaled Hanniyeh, where we believe he passed state secrets to Hanniyeh. I believe Khaled organized the terrorist meeting on the Isla Maria Magdalena, to pass on the information. His convenient disappearance luckily ended the threat."

"A lot of things were involved in the Hanniyeh sanction. Luck wasn't one of them," Nick replied.

"Granted, your teams did an incredible job Khaled's associates can't begin to trace. You and the cartoons getting trapped on the Isla did not get mentioned in any mission statement. I think some luck was involved."

"Did you call El Muerto merely to insult his valiant expertise in avoiding death?" Nick paused while Paul briefly enjoyed Nick's humor. "I get it. Khaled's people need to go to the source with big bucks and pay Cooker directly. El Muerto bets the worm extorted a fortune to meet with the buyers again. What stuff is wormy selling?"

"Commerce and Transportation logistics and security protocols."

"Crap! Picture Muerto with his fortune telling hat on, mind melding with you in this situation. You want El Muerto to somehow kill everything at this Searchlight, Nevada meeting, including a sitting United States Senator, and make it look like a terrorist's deadly squabble."

"El Muerto nailed it the first time."

"If you have proof, why not turn the evidence over to the DOJ?"

"We suspect too many shadow government morons inside the FBI, DOJ, and Homeland Security," Paul answered. "I want Cooker dead before he can pass the information in some other way. The only thing stopping him now is he hasn't been paid. Someone emptied Khaled's bank accounts before Cooker got his cut."

"Oh no," Nick chimed in. "The no good dirty rats stole Khaled's money too? Horrible... just horrible. Did you like the donation you and Clyde received?"

"Yes... indeed. I'm contracting you and the cartoons because your ploys using the alias's Ebi Zarin and Amin Jutoh worked extraordinarily well in the past. I took the lead on this. I put all resources concerning the Jutoh and Zarin names on our networks. Rumors still abound you are both dead, but others claim you are building a nationwide network of cells. It appears everyone who knows, or suspects differently, died at some point along the way."

"Send me everything you have. What's the window on this?"

"Cooker meets with the terrorists two days before the fight. Cooker will be booked at the MGM Grand during the time. He has tickets to the UFC event as a cover. I appreciate you taking a look at this op."

"No problem. I can't stand the sight of wormy. I've seen his self-important hissy fits when grilling some poor government position holder. It doesn't surprise me the prick sells out his country. Why would anyone in their right mind vote for a Sharia Law Mutant enabler and apologist?"

"You answered your own question, Muerto – no one in their right mind."

"Time's short. I'll brief the cartoons tomorrow. I hope your file has all the info on anyone even vaguely connected to wormy and his buddies. I'm going to need a volunteer to help everyone into the afterlife."

"Don't tell me you have another bomb vest."

Silence.

"Muerto?"

"You said don't tell you. Okay… yeah… the bunker Lynn found for us to hide in on Isla Magdalena stocked a few. I naturally asked permission from the Dark Lord to confiscate them for future use. If this works, you'll still need to nail Cooker in the eye of public opinion with hard evidence, so the leftist media buries it like they did 'Pedophile Island'."

"We have enough to shut up any liberal leftist media conglomerate. Besides, we have the flash drives you confiscated from Moronas before his passing. Believe me. The leftist media and snowflakes will be glad to sweep Cooker under their rug of deceit and traitorous dealings."

"I will call you tomorrow. Thanks for ruining my vacation, you prick."

"I merely enhanced it, Muerto." Gilbrech disconnected.

Rachel pounced on Nick before he could even put the phone down. "You stored more suicide bomb vests in my house? Are you mental!"

"First off, it's not your house. It's our house. Secondly, the vests are stored safely in my interrogation bunker at Johnny's place. Thirdly." Nick clamped Rachel's hips.

"No… don't… oh crap! Muerto!"

* * *

"You promised not to do the blindfold fight stuff ever again!" Lora stood at the kitchen counter with Al next to her. They decided to double team me.

"Yeah… I did, but there were extenuating circumstances. The guy took a bath in Brut cologne. I knew where he was every second. The fight lasted about five seconds. I need to call Nick. Jess found out his mom talked the Oakland Marriott City Center into volunteering their Grand Ball Room for her first Campaign Fundraising Event. I'm hoping he can entertain with Joan at the event."

The icy atmosphere warmed almost immediately. "Yes! Al… go text your spies in the 'Grove'. Ask them to sell the Unholies on a trip North for a Muerto/Joan entertainment night."

"On it!"

I drew the reluctant Lora into my arms. I made my case with hands and lips to the point I believe Lora would vote for the blindfold the next time. She pushed away, drawing ragged breaths, knowing her own visible desire would wreck any statements of outrage at this point. "Ca...call, Nick... you...you beast."

I grinned as the beast with the taste of a hunt ahead. I called Nick. He answered a few more buzzes later than normal. I heard fumbling of the phone on his end. "Nick?"

"Uh... yeah... sorry, DL. I saw the signing. Did you know that was coming?"

"No... it was a last-minute deal to stir interest. I was wondering if I could interest you in entertaining with Joan at Florence Brown's mayoral campaign fundraiser tomorrow night."

"Jesse Brown's mom, Flo? Hell, yeah! We need to get her elected. This will make it a little tight for me. I scheduled a meeting with the cartoons early tomorrow morning. Paul called me and-"

"Damn! I knew if Gilbrech heard you were coming to see my fight, he'd tap you for something else. Strobert does the same thing to us. Lynn told him this time if he tried it, she'd cut one of his balls out while he was sleeping. She vowed to do it with such razor-sharp expertise, he'd wake with an itch later in the night, scratch it, and come away with a wet hand."

I listened to Nick contemplating Lynn's threat with much humor. "Oh... oh God... I bet Strobert took that to heart."

"He did indeed. Is this thing Gilbrech wants done anything we can help you with?"

"Not this time, DL, mostly due to plausible deniability. Are you training in the Bay until the day before the fight?"

"Yep. I did something I wasn't supposed to in LA. Lynn and Tommy told me if I had so much leftover energy, we'll be going out on the boat every morning until I leave for the Vegas pre-fight festivities. I deserve it."

Nick chuckled. "You fought again blindfolded?"

"Blind Fury 2 on YouTube."

"I imagine you're in the doghouse at home, huh?"

"I handled it with first-class Recon Marine proficiency, maggot!"

"Don't start that shit with me, DL. I'll join you tomorrow afternoon. We'll drive in the Ford. It would be easier if you could give me and the cartoons a ride into Vegas in the Gulfstream. I'll copilot going and Cala can copilot back to the Bay. We're taking some special items and equipment. I'll get a limo to my house."

"About that, Nick... we needed to use your house for a special side job. I'll explain it to you tomorrow."

"Mi casa, es su casa, brother."

"Thanks. Count on the lift into Vegas. You're right about this stream of events beginning to tighten perceptions. All time will slow for me in the water tomorrow morning. Count on that."

"Just you, Cruella Deville, and Rocky the poke pole – oh my, the thought makes me nauseous. I think I'll go get a Beam and contemplate your morning on the balcony while watching the fog drift in."

Nick disconnected. "Prick!"

Screw it, I'm going to get a couple of Beams on ice until Al goes to sleep, and then complete my unfinished business with Lora. I entered the entertainment room with firm convictions. Lora handed me a Beam brother on ice. Al had 'Soldier' with Kurt Russell cued up to play.

"Join us, Dark Lord." Lora pulled me toward the couch.

"This is because I have entertainment pleasure heading toward the Bay, right?"

Lora smiled. "Al just confirmed Nick and Joan at the Marriott tomorrow night from her sources."

Nighttime for Lora stretched into the early morning hours.

* * *

Florence Brown hugged Nick and Joan at their respective places near the piano. She then strode to the microphone. "Hello, Oakland. I'm Flo Brown."

Loud applause from the over seven hundred attendees grew into an audio avalanche. Flo motioned for quiet. "We will start every gathering with the 'Pledge of Allegiance' and the 'National Anthem'. If those offend you... get out now. If there are any kneelers, sitters, or fist wavers in the ballroom, we have people here to bodily throw your useless, anti-American, disrespectful butts out on the sidewalk. That goes double for any leftwing media wonks covering my events."

Wild appreciation for the warning died to silence as Joan's violin played the first strains of the Star Spangled Banner. Nick's voice rang out in splendid form with his hand over heart, facing our huge flag. People leaped to their feet with hands over hearts. No one knelt, raised a fist, or tried to sit it out. All of the Monsters, Snow Whites, Unholies, and select gang members the Oaktown Cartel absorbed were in MIB black outfits with security badges throughout the Marriott's Grand Ballroom. When Nick and Joan finished, Flo led everyone in the 'Pledge of Allegiance'.

Flo's voice carried. She epitomized confidence without being strident. "I am here tonight to gather support for my mayoral campaign. I'm also here to detail what a mayor can and can't do. The mayor of Oakland marshals support from the public to make the city council members representing them do what's best for the city. I present an annual budget, which from now on will contain no entitlements. I appoint a City Administrator. I will appoint one who will help me do only what improves the city and enforces the laws. We will back the Blue and they will be on the job to serve and protect the citizens of this city. I'm putting gangbangers, homeless, and illegal aliens on notice."

"We will not be a sanctuary city any longer," Flo continued. "Our police will detain illegal aliens for ICE to deport. Homeless will seek shelter and treatment or be put on city work crews and forcibly sheltered and treated. No longer will vagrants badgering our citizens and fouling our streets be permitted to stay here. Parole violators will be immediately sent back to prison. The city will not look the other way when any crime is committed. It will be our police department's job to enforce all laws and I will back them. Any threat of riot or illegal protest will be broken up and all rioters and protesters fined the maximum for civil disobedience. That's it folks. I want to clean our city and make it safe for our citizens to walk down the streets at any hour, without fear. It will not be easy, but if I'm elected, it will be done. Enjoy the entertainment and please be generous in your contributions. Tables are set there at the side for pledges, donations, and to accept volunteers to work for my campaign. Thank you!"

Flo was a hit. People who wanted her to be mayor came tonight. It would be her campaign's duty to make sure the media and special interest groups understood she would be defended. Nick and Joan took over the entertainment portion of the evening while Flo mingled with Jess and Dev at her side. The rest of us danced. We paid to have the fundraiser catered. Tomorrow, signage would be all over the city, including billboards. Flo understood she would be asked questions and badgered by the media and freeloaders in the city.

The present mayor made an appearance. She was a white liberal sycophant, plagued with guilt for everything. Tibby Quafe made the police stand down at illegal assemblies, which turned into riots and property damage. Vagrants and homeless were permitted to roam the streets without being stopped, while she gave lip service to give them homes. Tibby had no clue how to run a city except into the ground. Lynn and I joined Jess and Dev, because Tibby had four guys with her. After the introductions ended, the snide accusations started.

"What if I had been here and either knelt, sat, or put a fist in the air, Flo?"

"I would have had you thrown out on your ass, and I have the lady here next to me who could do it. You weren't invited anyway."

Tibby gasped. I could tell she thought Flo was going to make nice while Tibby insulted her. "This will always be a sanctuary city, by the way."

"Not if I'm elected. If you try to bus in illegals from all over to vote in this city's election, I will call in ICE agents to stop them. You won't be stealing any more elections."

"Undocumented workers are permitted to vote here in Oakland. They have rights."

"I'm FBI Special Agent Lynn Montoya Dostiene." Lynn was our team's spokesperson. "We will stop you from busing in illegal voters. I not only have a team of agents living in this area on Florence Brown's campaign, we also have a contingent of US

Marshals, who will be helping us on days leading to the election and election day. The only way you can win this election will be if you are elected by the citizens of this city."

"This is an outrage! I know this Harding character standing next to you runs an intimidation force and breaks the law, fighting street fights. From now on, I'll enforce the law, making sure he's arrested."

"Alexi Fiialkov owns the building where legal mixed martial arts matches, inside a revamped sporting arena, take place. He has his city licenses and pays his taxes," Lynn explained calmly. "Mr. Fiialkov hires Oakland police officers to make sure his arena is safe before and after an event. FBI Agent Harding is the UFC Heavyweight Champion. He fights there legally."

"I've had enough of this! You will not undo my hard work in this city!"

Flo smiled. "Sure. I will."

Tibby stormed off with her contingent. I couldn't help but think November would be a long time coming in this campaign war. It did make me forget my morning in the water, where Lynn and Rocky poked me into perdition.

* * *

I helped the Unholies unload their equipment at the airport, where a limousine awaited their arrival. Nick copiloted to give Laredo some time off. Cala would copilot back to the Bay. She sat with Johnny during the flight into Vegas. The flight gave Nick and I an opportunity to talk over his mission. I didn't like the fact he was taking out another sitting Senator, but at this juncture in time, we didn't have a trustworthy Department of Justice to prosecute anyone lately. They had been weaponized by liberals during the last administration.

"You closed the loop on the reason Khaled organized the Isla Magdalena meeting. I wish there were another way to get Cooker, Nick," I told him as we shook hands on the tarmac.

Nick grinned. "I hate that guy, Cooker, so I'll make the best of it. Thanks for the lift and for bringing our dependents to Vegas in a few days with your crew."

"Flying here gave me a reprieve from Lynn and Rocky poking the crap out of me this morning. You and Joan were incredible last night. Thank you for doing the fundraiser."

"I had a great time. Uh… I do have some bad news for you. Tommy told me he's putting you in the water when you get home from here."

When my mouth dropped open, Nick walked away laughing. "That wasn't funny, you prick! If somehow Tommy gets a thought spike to do it for real, I'll burn my Muerto t-shirt."

* * *

After Cooker retired to his suite at the MGM Grand, Nick and Johnny visited his head of security, a former member of Mabahith, the Saudi Arabian secret police. Ibrahim al-Saleha was assigned by The Muslim Brotherhood to accompany Cooker in Las Vegas until the meeting in Searchlight took place. Johnny knocked on al-Saleha's door.

"Who are you?" The voice spoke in heavily accented English. He did not open the door.

"I am Ebi Zarin. I have Amin Jutoh with me. We have journeyed far," Johnny said in Arabic. "Gamar Kostler hired us on his boat to go after John Harding and his crew. It was an ambush. Their boat was akin to a warship. Only Amin and I escaped in a life raft. We have Gamar's laptop to give you for Senator Cooker."

The door opened. The security head looked them over. Johnny showed him the laptop. "How do I know you are who you say? I have heard Ebi Zarin was dead."

Nick and Johnny looked cautiously down the hallway in both directions before producing their Saudi passports. Ibrahim inspected them. He then motioned them inside. When al-Saleha closed the door, Nick stuck him with a syringe to render al-Saleha unconscious. They caught him as al-Saleha's legs gave out.

"I hope I didn't use too much," Nick said as he and Johnny carried al-Saleha. "I had to guess at his weight."

"Better too much than not enough." Johnny called Gus. "Bring the wheelchair, Payaso."

"On the way."

Fifteen minutes later, the three pushed al-Saleha to Nick's Cadillac Escalade. After loading al-Saleha, Jian drove them to Nick's Las Vegas house. They prepared their prisoner for interrogation. Nick brought al-Saleha out of his drugged state with another syringe. When al-Saleha realized he was strapped tightly into a chair, naked from the waist down and gagged, he began making pleading noises. Nick shushed him.

"I have a couple questions for you. We gathered your laptop and cell-phone, so we know when the meeting is tomorrow morning from your phone's notepad. I only needed your index finger to get into the phone. I have it recognizing mine now. I want you to give me your laptop PIN number so I can unlock it. Here's what will happen if you don't give me the number."

Nick used his stun-gun nightstick on al-Saleha's groin. When he removed the gag a few minutes later, al-Saleha blurted out the access PIN. Johnny unlocked the laptop and changed the PIN.

"Thanks." Nick gagged him again.

"All the files are unlocked," Johnny said. "I did not think we would ever do the Ebi and Amin show again. It nearly blew up in our faces last time."

"Johnny's right," Gus agreed. "You're a writer. Use your imagination to think of a better plan."

"I agree round-eye," Jian piled on. "I believe you are slipping. I think the Unholies need a new Muerto. I would be an excellent Muerto. My first order would be to reduce round-eye to mascot."

"Don't make me shoot you again, Dragon Breath."

"Mascots are forbidden to carry weapons. They exist only to carry equipment. I am El Muerto and I approve this message."

"That's it! I'm getting my M107. I'll give you a five-hundred-yard head-start, poser," Nick ran to get his sniper rifle.

Jian stopped laughing when he saw the grim faces of his companions. "He… he did not mean that, right?"

"Don't ask us. He never ran for his sniper rifle after issuing us a head-start warning," Gus replied. "If I were you, I'd head for the Strip."

"Nick's already shot you once," Johnny added. "I am sure it will be easier this time. Maybe he will only shoot to wound again."

* * *

Nick put his range finders down. "Perfect. They have a crawl space under the house. I thought I saw it was raised from the satellite photos. They picked a place on a dried out dead end too, with nothing around except the hills on one side. I'll stuff my Saudi Secret Police buddy under the house's center. I added enough C4 to his vest, that he will blow the house to smithereens, along with everyone inside. It's good they like their privacy."

"I wish you'd let us help you position him," Gus said.

"I got this, Payaso. You had your workout for tonight running after Jian."

"It was no big deal, I called out to him a couple times and he stopped."

Jian turned from the driver's seat. "Oh... so funny... not!"

"Calm down Dragon," Johnny said.

"I'll carry al-Saleha to the rear, pry a few of the crosshatched boards off, and drag him into position. No muss, no fuss. Their meeting's at 7 am, so we won't have long to wait. I made both a detonator switch for his hand, and of course his cell-phone into a detonator we can use. No moon tonight either. It's pitch-black. Keep the lights off and drive me in front, Dragon."

Jian drove in front of the meeting house from their dead-end position. "Maybe I leave round-eye to walk back to his house."

Gus's Glock pinned against Jian's head in an instant. "Mission enabled, Dragon. No one leaves Muerto anywhere."

"Just kidding... sorry." Jian put the Cadillac in park with Nick chuckling.

"Be right back, guys." Nick retrieved the breathing al-Saleha from the back and with a fireman's carry, he walked around the house with al-Saleha over his shoulder and a prybar.

"Oh man, this looks like a fine entry, my friend." Nick put the Saudi Secret Police agent on the ground.

Nick needed to pry only a few of the half-rotted boards away to gain entry into the crawl space. Once underneath the house, Nick dragged his drugged prisoner to a position near the center of the house. He made sure all wiring and detonators were in place, including the one to be held by al-Saleha.

"Remember not to push the button, buddy." Nick gave him a double dose of his knockout concoction before crawling out from under the house.

Nick entered the Escalade. "Drive down to the corner and backtrack a couple hundred yards, Dragon. We'll still be able to see the house and the arrivals. Then we wait. After it's over, I'll buy you guys breakfast. Since we don't have Jean with us, I'm thinking an Irish or three before the eats."

"Oh yeah," Gus said.

"You guys doze off. I'll wake you when the targets begin arriving," Nick directed. "I need to get another thousand words in the new novel done."

"Did you write me in as a character like you promised?"

"I sure did, Dragon. You're going to be Jed's gay neighbor, who watches his house and waters his flowers while he's away. The next book signing should be interesting."

Jian cursed Nick in Chinese for three full minutes. Nick answered each curse with his own in Chinese. Humorously appreciative, Gus and Johnny listened intently to their companions' sing/song bantering back and forth, watching as Nick and Jian's facial expressions matched each volley with inflections of rage.

* * *

Nick put down his range finders. "Cooker's in there and the arrivals ended half an hour ago. We can't wait any longer."

Nick detonated al-Saleha. The explosion vaporized the house, sending particles all the way to the Escalade, with the ground rumbling and rocking the Cadillac violently. Nick continued watching with the rangefinders. He smiled as some of the smoke and debris settled, making the property blurry, but visible.

"That's a wrap, Dragon. If anything is alive in that place, he ain't happy. Let's get out of here. Drive straight to my house. We'll get cleaned up and leave the Escalade. I think we should get a limousine for the ride to breakfast, compadres."

* * *

The weigh-in surpassed any of our expectations. The MGM Grand Arena rocked. My crew and Nick's arrived in MIB regalia, even our dependents. It was hilarious. Jean, Sonny, and Al strode around us in perfect synch. I saw Rock Costigan and Tat-face Northman in the front row. I would need to deal with those two in the future. The Unholies loved being part of my MIB crew. The news media plastered everything about a terrorist attack in Searchlight, killing Senator Rory Cooker and eighteen others, all over the news wire. The coverage disappeared as Cooker's terrorist entanglements appeared shortly after his demise. Another Muerto miracle of adjustment for traitors and terrorists happened flawlessly. He even scheduled another book signing after the fight.

Ian Wolf and I went through the weigh-in and posed for all the hype photos. Ian seemed more than slightly outraged while doing it. He made as if to bitch-slap me during the photo shoot of us after the weigh-in. Fat chance. I caught his wrist in an unbreakable grip, with the crowd appreciative of the added entertainment, and Wolf's crew playing the 'hold me back' card. My guys waited for me.

"What the hell do you think you're doing, Ian?"

Security surrounded us in an instant, pulling, tugging, and shouting for us to disengage. I let Ian go when sure his handlers had him. If I dropped him now, we could forget about sales.

"I want you so much, bitch, I can taste it!"

"We have a cage meeting ahead, punk. Why jeopardize that at a weigh-in, dummy."

Suddenly, Ian Wolf relaxed. "I've seen your wife, Harding. Lora's her name, isn't it? I bet I could console Lora after your loss… or death."

Well… okay Wolfy… you have my attention. My cage crew groaned immediately on cue. "I will see you in the cage, pussy. When I finish with you, my wife will be the last thing on your mind, if you have a mind left."

It was so on then. The rumble at the raised podium reached a point where even extra guards rushed in for safety couldn't contain it. I stayed away from the mayhem. I had my guys. They knew if Ian Wolf reached me, I would snatch his heart. Dev backed away and sang out the rain spell in strident melodious Latin with fists pumping. It stopped everything. He finished and good God Almighty, the sprinkler system turned on. We all stood there in stunned amusement as someone hit the shutoff. Every security employee rushed in from the MGM Grand to quell a riot. We all separated with riotous applause and hoots as the monitors replayed the scene.

I grabbed Dev with Jess, Jafar and Tommy around us. "All I can say is… damn."

"Man… you got to get that shit under control, brother," Jess said in reverential tones. "We need to teach DL some counter-spells."

When I could speak, I just said simply, "that was the best of all time, Dev. Don't do the rain spell before the fight, brother."

"I need a drink," was all Dev could say.

We all did.

* * *

Gloriously, the fight night extravaganza nearly equaled Dev's indoor rain spell. When finally called on to approach the cage, Sonny, Jean, and Al, all in MIB black with Ray-Bans led us. The Marine's Hymn blared in blood pumping symphony with my mood. The killer inside, awakened to the call, enjoyed the hype to the fullest. I knew by the uneasiness amongst my crew, they were figuring to weep and moan over Ian Wolf's demise. We reached the cage. The entertainment began again with 'Montego Bay' playing.

I led at center. Tommy, Dev, Jess, and Jafar surrounded me in a moving circle. We performed, driving the crowd to a standing be-bop to our music until the music ended. Yeah, we hit the big-time on that ploy. Ian Wolf approached with his retinue. Comically, he picked the theme song from the 'Rocky' movie. I liked it. I scrapped my idea of doing the robot.

They played the National Anthem and Ian Wolf's group knelt.

I sighed as I heard 'Recon' shouted out from my Pap. I turned and saluted my mentor. Strap in, Wolf, this would be a bumpy ride.

Tommy grabbed my chin. "Spit it out, John! What the hell are you going to do. We need to know."

"Calm down, T. I'm going to get me some."

"Leave him be." Dev yanked Tommy back.

Ian Wolf featured the attitude I loved to face. He hopped around, pretending to be the most intimidating prick alive. His features writhed with anticipation, fists pounding together in rhythm with his dancing bullshit, while intermittently popping a fist in my direction. The dance off was over. We met at center cage. The referee stated all he needed to say, indicating we should touch gloves. Wolf backed toward his crew. I turned and did the robot in Dark Lord fashion to my crew. On every monitor in the place, my Dark Lord robot retreat played to the 'Exorcist' theme song. Then Dev took over as I had contracted with the Arena. The 'Exorcist' theme kept playing, but Dev did his exorcism incantations in 'High Mass' form. His companions stood with bowed heads, all in line with me in the middle. It was so good, the fight seemed like a secondary deviance. Oh my, did Dev ever seize the moment. I half expected the sprinkler system to kick on.

The referee signaled us once he received our nods of readiness. I did what I never do. I rushed Ian with a side-foot strike to the chest that sent him flying into the cage. I didn't follow. I did the 'Sugar Pie, Honey Bunch' chorus of the song with all the dance steps, body swaying, hands going in tick-tock form, and feet gliding in rhythm. The crowd enjoyed the hell out of my dance form. Ian charged me. I met him with a forearm smash, nearly jarring his head loose. The introductions ended. Ian took me down. I slipped into a locked-legs around his waist countermove, as he tried to pound me into oblivion. I made him squeak as the power of my legs caused him to shift from attack to defense. He twisted off and I let him. We reached our feet at the same time, but I whipped a behind the knee beauty that sent him back to the mat, scrambling to the cage for support.

I didn't follow, I did the Four Tops 'Sugar Pie, Honey Bunch' until Wolf regained his feet. The crowd literally turned the arena into a wall of sound, either hoping Wolf would smash me into atomic dust or I would keep playing. Wolf was no dummy. I just aced his best ground and pound full mount. No one can calculate the effect of daily training, avoiding Rocky the pole poke while swimming full bore. When I get my legs locked around you, you're in trouble. Wolf came at me in defensive form feinting and flicking jabs at me. I smashed a right cross into his temple, sending him crashing into the cage and collapsed on his side. I did 'Sugar Pie, Honey Bunch' to screaming approval. The MGM Arena people caught it and played the song for me. It was the greatest. Wolf lurched around with the confused referee watching his eyes. By the time Wolf embraced comprehension, the round ended, and I had music to do a sideways 'Sugar Pie, Honey Bunch' dance to my crew.

"You damn fool!" Tommy was not happy, but Jess, Dev, and Jafar were laughing their asses off. "We could be doing that damn dance together in the bar with Nick entertaining. What the hell's gotten into you?"

I glanced up at Tommy with grim faced certainty. "I don't like anyone mentioning Lora to my face, brother. I plan to entertain Ian for a while."

"Oh God… don't kill him, DL," Jess pleaded. "We'll all be spending our damn Las Vegas time in 'sack cloth and ashes'. Lora will be fine if you simply hammer fist his face flat."

"Maybe… maybe not." I had the Wolf promise he would console my Lora, after he maimed or beat me to death, playing in my head. It hadn't faded yet.

"Do something, Dev!"

Dev sighed, glanced at his pleading brother-in-arms, studied my face, and turned toward Wolf across from us. He gave him 'Last Rites' in full Latin excellence. I stood as the crowd again hushed in reverence for Dev's Latin weapon of destruction. I hugged the prick.

"Thanks, brother."

"Thank Jess. I doubt I could care less. Don't drop your guard, brother."

"I won't."

The referee signaled us to get it on. I went at him in sparring form. Wolf was good, but I owned him. I shot jabs in to smash him between the eyes until he raised his hands. I smashed a right hook to his rib cage that almost ended the fight. He stumbled away, hurting and gasping for breath. I moved toward him and ripped at his head with both hands. I heard the crowd roaring for a final accounting. I didn't give it to him. The Monster was loose inside. The round ended with me pummeling him enough to appease the fight Gods. Ian still made attempts to defend so as not to get the referee involved. I retreated to my crew doing 'Sugar Pie, Honey Bunch' to the now very attuned guy in charge of the sound booth.

"Good Lord, DL," Tommy exclaimed as the other guys sponged me off. "This isn't like you."

I stood, even though I had more time. "Yeah, it is."

Jafar's job, other than mouthpiece rinsing, was to watch our opponent's side. "Uh oh. Wolf got an upgrade just now, John."

I smiled at the new and improved Ian Wolf. His eyes nearly glowed red with anticipation. "Good call, little brother. I'll go say hello."

Wolf met me at center cage, shooting left jabs with combination kicks in impressive form. We mixed it up center stage until he dropped nicely for a takedown, maneuvering for a full naked choke immediately. While I fought it off, he kept whispering Lora in my ear. I spun to the side, grabbed him at the legs and neck, dead lifted him from the mat, and threw him against the cage. Oh boy… did the crowd noise wake me from my delirium. I waved and did the 'Sugar Pie, Honey Bunch' back and forth while my audio fan in the booth accompanied me. Wolf made it to his feet by the time the round ended.

Tommy stuck to business, only muttering, "this punk couldn't beat you on the best day of his life. What the hell got him the flying smash into the cage, John?"

"He started chanting 'Lora' in my ear while we were grappling in ground and pound. All I remember is him hitting the cage."

"Are you done yet?"

"Yeah, T, I'm done. Last round, unless he rattles my cage."

"He got another upgrade," Jafar noticed. "It didn't do any good last round, but I'm surprised the referee's not picking up on it. I'll bet he's afraid to stop the fight for fear the crowd would riot."

"It's a small thing, little brother."

I met the raging Wolf with a straight left jab I could launch now at lightning fast speed. It smashed his nose into blood shooting devastation. To his credit, he backed away on defense. I assaulted his ribs with both hands against the cage. I backed away the second his elbows dropped to protect his ribs. My left hook nearly decapitated him. Wolf hit the mat, snoring in a crumpled Raggedy Anne Doll form. The referee took one look and stepped between us, waving his arms. There was no need for that. I hadn't planned to follow him down and hammer fist him into bloody froth. Oh… wait… yeah, I did.

The ring celebration proceeded with solemn happiness. I embarrassed this punk. I hoped it had been entertaining enough for the crowd. They seemed to think so, greeting me with a standing ovation as the referee raised my hand in victory. The victory march back to the locker room was a dancing frolic of celebration. We didn't pretend it was anything more than how it ended. It was just business.

Tommy hugged me. "You are indeed meaner than a junk yard dog."

"I admit it. I didn't kill him though. That gets me points, right?"

"Not in this dimension, Dark Lord."

* * *

Later, I came to sit next to Nick as he finished another tune. I was hammered in my own hollow legged way. "Would you mind… doing a tune with me?"

"Name it, Dark Lord."

"Sixteen Tons."

"Oh yeah! Here we go, DL. Follow my lead." Nick jazzed into 'Sixteen Tons' in a way I could not describe, both lilting and country. We sang that sucker together with my bass voice able to harmonize with his tenor.

He elbowed me when we finished to wild applause. "One more, DL… 'Proud To Be An American'."

"Yeah… and hell yeah!"

He and I sang that sucker, my arm around his shoulders, and tears in my eyes.

America lives yet another day. I vowed I would perish before she did.

The End

If you enjoyed **Hard Case Book X: No Mercy**, please take a moment to review the novel on Amazon. We appreciate your consideration in taking the time to review **No Mercy**.

Thank you for your support.

Bernard Lee DeLeo

Amazon: http://bit.ly/BERNARD-DELEO-BOOKS

Made in the USA
Columbia, SC
07 May 2018